AND THE
STARS

WERE
BURNING
BRIGHTLY

AND THE
STARS
WERE
BURNING
BRIGHTLY

DANIELLE JAWANDO

SIMON & SCHUSTER

First published in Great Britain in 2020 by Simon & Schuster UK Ltd
A CBS COMPANY

1 3 5 7 9 10 8 6 4 2

Simon & Schuster UK Ltd
1st Floor, 222 Gray's Inn Road
London WC1X 8HB

www.simonandschuster.co.uk
www.simonandschuster.com.au
www.simonandschuster.co.in

Simon & Schuster Australia, Sydney
Simon & Schuster India, New Delhi

A CIP catalogue record for this book
is available from the British Library.

PB ISBN 978-1-4711-7877-1
eBook ISBN 978-1-4711-7878-8

Typeset in the UK by M Rules
Printed and bound by CPI Group (UK) Ltd, Croydon, CR0 4YY

MIX
Paper from
responsible sources
FSC
www.fsc.org   FSC® C020471

For my dad, Stan Jawando.
Thank you for everything

AL

prologue

When a star reaches the end of its lifetime, it explodes in this violent supernova. Sometimes the outer layer of the star blows off, leaving behind a small, dense core that continues to collapse. Gravity presses down on the core material so tightly that the protons and electrons combine to make neutrons, and they combine to make a neutron star. Something born from a death that ripples out from thirty-three light years away. The core of the star speeds up, and it spins faster and faster, up to 43,000 times per minute, so that eventually the universe just becomes this blur – a blur of time and space – where nothing can hurt you because you don't really exist. Not properly. You're just a floating cluster of subatomic particles, trapped in this perfect world.

Last summer, me and Nate went to the fair. We climbed on

to the Spin Master, one of those rides with the metal cages that catapult you forward, and Nate's face was all stretched out and weird. He kept shouting and yelling because he loved it so much. And, as the wind hit me in the face, I could feel the corners of my mouth lift and then I closed my eyes and thought, This is the closest I'll ever get to being a neutron star. *Me and Nate, together in this whirl of colour . . . this rush of light and sound. Pulsating. Rotating. Orbiting. Lifting off the ground.*

I held on to the metal safety gate and thought of the patterns that were all around. I thought of the Fibonacci sequence and how everything in life is made up of numbers. I thought about how you can time travel in your mind with your memories. You do it, without even realizing. It's called chronesthesia. I thought about Van Gogh leaving out the bars on the windows of his room in his Starry Night *painting. I thought about how it can take ten million years for a star to form, but it can only happen once there's been the perfect gravitational collapse.*

And I thought of me and Nate on the boxing-gym roof. Me and my little bro up on that roof, and my chance to tell him everything, but not being able to find the right words.

Then I sat back and prayed that the ride wouldn't stop. Because I knew that when it did I wouldn't be a neutron star any more. I'd just be Al.

Al who was nothing.

Al who wanted to disappear.

Al who wanted to be up there instead . . . where nothing can touch you and all you know is helium and nitrogen and dust.

NATHAN

chapter one

One day, little bro, you'll see. It will happen and you won't even realize it. You'll look up at the sky, stare at all those stars burning hundreds and thousands of miles away, and you'll think: I get it now. I get all that stuff that Al was banging on about – I really do.

'It is not in the stars to hold our destiny, but in ourselves.' That's what Al said.

It was the last thing he told me before he disappeared. He said it was from some play he'd been studying in English, and then he ripped it out his school book and tossed it to me. He'd scrawled all these drawings down the sides of the words, cramming his pictures into the margins. All these people with no faces. I hated reading more than I hated school, so I screwed it up and flushed it down the bog. Then I told Al exactly where he could shove his poetry. I didn't care that he thought it was a good one.

At least I didn't *then* anyway. Cause Al was always coming out with crap like that. Talking to me about some book, or a fact he'd remembered, or going into one of his weird moods when he couldn't get a drawing right. He'd get all stressed out and start running a hand through his thick Afro, pulling at the tufts of hair. Then he'd screw the whole drawing up and toss it in the bin. His room was full of half-finished faces and half-finished things, all split in two and scattered round the place. He had proper sketches, but he'd never let me see them. He kept them hidden, locked inside one of his desk drawers.

Al was full of secrets, but that didn't stop our mum from loving him the most. Al would be the one to get out of Wythenshawe. Al would be the one to do something with his life. To end up in one of those posh university halls and make her proud. Al, Al, fucking Al. Mum loves my little sister, Phoebe, probably cause she's the only girl. She loves Saul, probably cause he's the oldest. But, with me, it's like she didn't have enough love left to give. Maybe she doesn't love me so much cause I look most like our dad.

I turn over in the dark and I wait for it to stop hurting. Not the kinda hurt when someone gives you a dead arm in school and you laugh your head off, pretending it doesn't sting, even tho it kills. This is a different hurt. One that seems to come from inside and pull down on me. Like all these different parts

4

of me are slipping away, and I can't do nothin to stop it. It's this hurt that takes over. That splits me right down the middle. That reminds me every minute that Al ain't here, and there's nothing I can do to change it.

I hear the muffled sound of the telly coming from downstairs, forcing its way through the cracks in the floorboards. Mum's probably fallen asleep in front of it again. Since it happened, she hardly ever goes upstairs. She doesn't even sleep in her room any more. She spends more time praying, tho, heading down to this crappy church round the corner from our house or bringing these old fogeys to ours. People who've never bothered with us before, who hold her hand, and bring her stuff, and tell her that '*Al is in heaven now*'. That '*at least he's with God*'. That '*he's in the best place*'.

Mum nods like heaven is better than our house, or Civic Town Centre, or the pop-up funfair. That Al's better off dead than necking as much alcohol as he can, or getting on the Spin Master or the Miami Wave. And all I want to do is tell her there's no point in praying to some idiot in the sky. That God is just a taker, like one of those idiots in your year, who nicks a new pair of trainers even before you've managed to break them in. God *took* Al. And, if anyone asks, that's all I'd say he is – a taker of brothers and trainers and really important shit. I never believed in God much anyway, but I believe in him even less now.

The floorboards outside my room creak. I watch as my bedroom door begins to open and the light from the landing floods in, making me cover my eyes. And, for a moment, he's there. Al. Standing in the doorway, his Afro blocking out most of the light, his body leaning to one side, his dark shadow stretched. He shakes his head slowly, like he can't believe wot a fool I've been, and I think I hear him say, *'Got you!'* Like this is all a joke. One of the stupid tricks that he'd play when he was messin around.

'Al?' I whisper, and my throat tightens. 'Al . . . ?' But all I can see is a shadow.

'It's just me,' a small voice says. Phoebe.

The door opens wider and I suddenly feel stupid. Phoebe moves towards me, a bright yellow dressing gown wrapped round her, the end of her long plait slowly unravelling. She's clutching this old teddy. The thing looks like a rabid cat shoved into a small doll's dress. Al bought it for her one Christmas ages ago. I hadn't seen it for years, but the night it happened she came into my room with it. She didn't speak, she just lay there. Curled up on her side, with this teddy pressed to her chest.

'I can't sleep,' she says. 'I can hear Mum crying again.'

I move over and peel the covers back. I don't mind Phoebe coming into my room cause at least then I'm doing summat for her. At least then there's summat I can try to fix.

Phoebe climbs in next to me. 'It smells funny in here,' she says.

'Well, it was fine before you came in.'

'It's not my fault that you don't wash.'

'Nah,' I say. 'D'you want me to kick you out or wot?'

Phoebe goes quiet and, even tho she doesn't say anything, I can tell that she's thinking.

'Nate,' she says. 'Where do we go when we die?'

6

I shrug. 'Heaven,' I say.

'I know *that* . . . but how do you get there? Do you just wake up and you're there? Or does an angel come and take you away? Or do you just die and then . . .'

She pauses, and I think of Al for a minute. Drifting upwards, so awkward and lanky that, if you do float up to heaven, he'd probably get caught on summat on the way up. Tangled round an electricity wire like the old socks or school shoes that people throw up there. The thought makes me smile for a minute, numbing all those bits inside me, but it soon stops.

'Do you think it hurts?' Phoebe says. 'Dying . . . Do you think it hurt Al?' She pauses. 'Was he in pain?'

I look up at the plastic glow-in-the-dark stars on my ceiling. Al got them from one of those crappy pound shops the day Dad left. He'd stuck them down, taking ages to get them in the right places. He'd said that when he didn't understand life, or if things didn't make sense, he'd just look up and, somehow, everything would just feel different. It would feel okay.

Then he started telling me that there was no point in having stars on the ceiling if they didn't look like the real thing, and he kept going on about all these names. Saying how there was some star named after this guy called Ryan, and how everything was shaped like his belt.

And, when he'd finished, he just had this one thing left. A comet that he ended up sticking in the corner, at the far side of my room. He said that he didn't know what to do with it, but that he could tell that it didn't wanna be with the rest of the stars.

7

I think of how Al looked when I'd found him. The blueish tint to his face. The green-and-black school tie knotted round his neck. His silver prefect badge glinting in the light, and the stupid faded school motto on his blazer: *In Caritate Christi Fundati*. I could hear kids playing in the street outside: someone kicking a ball against a fence; the wheels of a bike skidding round a corner; the slapping of a skipping rope on the pavement; the *thud, thud, thud* of music from a car in the distance. The chanting of, *'Who are ya? Who are ya? Who are ya? Touch me again and you're dead.'*

I think of how me and Al had had a row that morning. How he'd called me after school and I'd cut him off. Ignored his call, then turned my phone to silent. All cause I wanted him to stop bothering me and piss off. All cause I was having too much fun, drinking and smoking in the park. All cause I wanted to stay with Kyle and these two fit girls we were with.

Al had always been there for me, but, when he needed me the most, I'd cut him off.

I feel Phoebe tug at the sleeve of my T-shirt and my eyes begin to sting.

'Nate, do you think it hurts?' she asks again.

I stare up at the comet, separate from all those other stars.

'Nah,' I lie. 'I don't think it hurts at all.'

I listen to the sound of Phoebe's breathing till she falls asleep, her head resting on my arm. I close my eyes and try not to think of Al, or how I'd let him down.

Afterwards, these two police officers had come round to get

me to give a statement to explain what happened. '*Routine*,' they'd said. '*To establish that Al's death was an accident.*'

An accident.

I didn't tell them about the phone call. Or that before they'd pulled up, with their loud sirens and flashing lights, before they'd got out their car, or written down his time of death, or zipped him up in one of those white bags, I'd noticed summat.

I'd seen it on the floor when I'd found Al. It was resting beside the leg of his wooden desk chair. I didn't know if he'd left it there on purpose, or if it was a mistake, but I picked it up anyway. A drawing. Al had drawn himself sitting in the corner. The face was all scribbled out, but I knew it was him cause of the Afro, and he was wearing his favourite navy hoodie. He was hunched over, his hands pressed over his ears, and there were all these people surrounding him. Towering over him. He'd scribbled out their faces, too, but there were loads of them covering most of the page. Then, towards the bottom, beside the tip of Al's shoe, were two words. *Help me.*

I pull the covers back and get outta bed, trying my hardest not to wake Phoebe. I open the drawer of my bedside table. I move stuff around – my iPhone, a lighter, some old headphones – till my fingers brush over Al's drawing. I pull it out and make my way to the bedroom window, pushing the curtain aside to let the light from the street lamp shine in. I unfold the crumpled piece of paper.

I must've looked at it a thousand times – probably more – each time hoping to find summat different. I dunno wot.

Maybe an answer or a clue. Summat to tell me why Al did it, or how to stop it from hurting, or wot I'm supposed to do now. How I'm supposed to just carry on ... even tho Al's torn this hole right through me. And I'll never be the same.

None of us will.

I hold the drawing up against the window so the paper goes this weird off-white colour, and I stare at the picture of Al, scared and hunched over. I move my finger over the words. *Help me. Help me.* Wot if Al had been in trouble and I hadn't even known?

The screeching sound of car tyres coming down the road makes me jump. I hear the low beat of some rap music, and I watch as a dark blue Corsa pulls up outside our house. The car door opens and Saul stumbles out, the music getting louder. I see some of his mates, all crammed into the tiny car. Saul slams the door, pulling the collar of his leather jacket up. The driver presses down on the horn, beeping it in time with the song, shouting and jeering.

'Shut up, you bellend,' Saul says. 'You'll wake me mum up and that.'

There's more noise from the car, and one of his other mates sticks his head out the window, chucking a cig stub into the night.

'Oooh,' he says. 'Don't wanna wake Mummy up. When are ya moving out?'

The others laugh. I recognize most of them from our estate.

'Piss off,' Saul says. 'Your mum asked me to move in, but I ain't sure you wanna new stepdad just yet.'

There's more laughter from the car and Saul walks towards the house.

'In a bit!' one of them shouts. 'I'll come check for you tomorrow, yeah?'

Saul waves, and they rev the engine, turning the music up even louder and beeping the horn as they go. The car disappears down the other end of the road, and I see Saul shake his head. He must feel me watching cause he looks up at my bedroom window. He stares at me for a minute, scrunching up his face, and then he flicks me the V sign. I don't do it back.

Saul's key turns in the front door, and I hear the sound of his footsteps moving towards the kitchen. There's the noise of pots and pans banging, the microwave going. And I can't help but feel all this anger inside me. It's like Saul can just forget about wot happened and move on. Pretend that Al never existed. Our brother's only been dead for three days and Saul's acting like he doesn't even care. When our dad left, Saul just said, 'Shit happens,' and we needed to get used to it. Well, maybe having your dad walk out is normal, but it's not *normal* for your brother to kill himself. Is it? Not when he's seventeen . . . when he had all this stuff he wanted to do. Not when it's Al.

I fold the drawing and drop it back inside my drawer. Then I climb into bed next to Phoebe and stare up at the plastic comet. I look at it till the shape starts to blur and my eyes get heavy. I hear Al's voice inside my head: *'You wouldn't know it, but all stars, all of them, are in this constant conflict with themselves. Like, all the time. There's gravity and the mass of the star pulling it inwards, but then there's this other force pushing it back outwards against the gravity. Then, in the middle, where they meet, you get this fusion. That's where the energy comes from. The star collapses in on itself, and another one is born. Imagine that. Something in so much conflict all the time, so much pain, but it still creates something so . . . so . . . beautiful.'*

There's this tingling feeling creeping up all over my body. I'm standing at the bottom of the staircase that leads to the attic room, the darkness closing in around me. I place my hand on the wall, feeling the coldness of it spreading through my fingers. I take one step at a time till I'm outside Al's door. His bedroom light is on. I walk in, staring at the walls covered in old Blu-Tack marks. I pass this map that Al had pinned up of the places he'd wanted to visit – the Atacama Desert, Death Valley, the Empty Quarter, the Brecon Beacons. Where he could go and see the stars. He'd drawn this route across the map that led out of Manchester and went right across the world. Like he wanted to escape, like he wanted to get as far away from this place as possible.

I look at Al's paintings, his revision notes, at an exam timetable he'd highlighted. His bed hasn't been touched, and his clothes are still neatly folded at the bottom. Above his bed there's a hanging mobile of stars made outta cardboard. I walk over to his desk, looking at his open sketchbook, and I see *that* picture – Al cowering in the corner, surrounded by all those people with no faces. My throat tightens and I turn the page and the bodies are there again, but the faces get darker. I flick faster, going through page after page. It's like the drawings are coming to life, moving across the paper.

And then I see the words *Help me* again and again.

I can't stop myself from flicking through. Like I've got no control over my hand. The words get bigger:

Help me. Stop them. Help me. PLEASE.

I want to turn away, but I can't. I just keep going, and then I hear it. A sound from somewhere above me, so faint that it's almost a whisper.

'Nate,' I hear. 'Please ... please ...'

I move my eyes upwards and then I see him.

Al.

His green-and-black tie wrapped round one of the wooden roof beams. His desk chair placed just beside his feet, his skin pallid and waxy. I stare up at his body, at the way that his feet hang, at the laces of his school shoes that are undone – frayed and trailing down. His eyes are open, and he's kicking, struggling, like he's trying to move through water – or something thicker. Treacle. Quicksand. Tar.

'Help me,' Al says.

Blood pounds in my ears, and my breath echoes all around me, filling the room, pressing hard against my chest. It's like there's this balloon inside me that's being blown up and up and it's gonna burst any minute. My palms begin to sweat and I climb on to the chair, my legs trembling, reaching for Al's tie. I touch the shiny fabric, trying to undo it, but my fingers slide over the knot again and again. I can see the air slowly leaving Al's body, his face tensing. I pull and tug, trying to undo the knot.

'Hold on,' I tell him. But it's wrapped too tightly, cutting into his neck, hurting him. I shout for help, pushing my fingers against Al's neck, trying to loosen the tie, slacken it, unravel it just a little.

'Hold on,' I repeat. I can feel my chest tightening and the tears starting to come.

I shout for help again, but no one's there.

Al struggles, his face turning this weird colour, his hands raised up towards his tie.

'Hold on!' I shout at him. 'Bro, you're gonna be okay. You've just got to—'

I pull and I tug, but I can tell that it's too late. That *I'm* too late. I shout Al's name. Trying to stop him somehow, trying to keep hold of him, and then I feel it. A hand pressing down hard on my shoulder . . .

'It's all right,' a voice says. 'Nate, I've got you, yeah?'

I open my eyes. My room is so bright from the big light that's been switched on that I have to shield my eyes. I'm drenched in sweat and the bedsheets are tangled and wrapped round me. Saul is there, his fade starting to grow back, a love bite on his neck. I pull at the edge of my duvet cover, wiping away the sweat. I shuffle myself upwards, resting my head in my hands.

'I couldn't save him,' I say. 'I couldn't save Al.'

'I know,' Saul says. 'I know.'

I start to cry. I feel stupid, fucking stupid, for crying, but

I can't help it. It's like summat's broken inside me and it won't heal. Saul sits down next to me, making the mattress sag beneath his weight, his muscles showing under his thin vest. He pulls me to him, wrapping his arms round me, and I close my eyes, breathing in his cigarette and aftershave smell. Wishing it would all go back to how it used to be. Wishing I'd just answered Al's call, or left school earlier, or fucking noticed that summat was up.

Wishing that I'd been a better brother.

I dunno how long we sit there, but I suddenly feel all awkward and it's like Saul doesn't know wot to do, either. I move away, turning to look at the tangled covers and the space in my bed.

'Where's Phoebe?' I say.

Saul cracks his knuckles. 'You started screaming, so she ran to get me. I put her back in her own bed.' He pauses and opens and closes his fist, watching his muscles tense. 'It scared her, y'know. When you started screaming like that. Saying those things ... saying Al's name.' He stops. 'It's like you were possessed or summat.'

I stare at him. 'You think I started screaming for the fun of it?'

'I never said that,' he says. 'It's just ... I'm worried. It's not the first time this has happened.'

'Well, we can't all be like you, y'know. We can't all just go around pretending like none of this happened. Like Al ain't gone.'

Saul turns to me, anger in his eyes. 'You fucking think I

ain't upset?' he says. 'That I'm not hurting. Fuck, Nate. Not a minute goes by when I don't think about him. When I don't wish . . . I miss him, too. Just as much as you do.'

We sit there, in silence, staring into space.

'Why do you think he did it?' I say.

Saul stiffens and shifts over on my bed. 'I dunno,' he says. 'How am I supposed to know that? How's anyone supposed to know?' He pauses. 'It ain't like he left a note or nothin.'

I think about the drawing and my throat tightens.

'I suppose,' I say. 'But don't you wanna find out? Don't you wanna know? Wouldn't you feel better if you knew the reason?'

'Al's dead, Nate.' Saul's words come out cold. 'It ain't like we can ask him, is it? And, even then, wot will it change?'

I shake my head.

'Look,' Saul says, 'I didn't mean it like that. It's just . . . wot difference will it make? Even if we did find out, it won't bring him back. Shit happens.'

I stare up at the comet on the ceiling. It's the same words as before, so I know he's not just talking about Al. He's talking about our dad walking out, too.

'You can spend all your life tryna to work out why someone does summat. Tryna find answers and, in the end, none of it matters. That's just people.'

I shrug. 'Suppose,' I say. But I don't mean it. It all matters. *Reasons* matter.

Saul gets up and walks over to my bedroom door. 'Try and get some sleep, yeah?' he says. 'It's almost three.'

16

I nod. 'Right,' I reply.

Saul pauses. 'We'll get through,' he says. 'Same way we always do.' He stands there for a minute, like he's gonna say summat else, but he doesn't. He just gives me this weird smile, then switches off my light and closes the door. I lie back and I stare up at the dim shapes on my ceiling – the half-moon, the plastic planets, a shooting star with a curved bit at the bottom. I don't like it when I'm left alone cause then it's just me and all these thoughts. Me and all these feelings that I don't understand.

Maybe Saul's right – maybe there ain't always a reason why people do things; maybe there ain't always an answer. And, if I would've showed him Al's drawing, then he would've said that it was just a stupid picture that I was reading too much into. But I know Al. He was one of the smartest people that I know ... knew. And he wouldn't have left that drawing there unless there was a reason, unless there was summat he wanted us to find out.

And wot else do I have?

I breathe out slowly.

'Eh, bro,' I say, and I dunno if I really think Al can hear me or not, but it feels good to say it out loud anyway. 'I promise I'll find out wot happened,' I say. 'I promise I'll find out why.'

MEGAN

chapter two

The first time I met Megan, I told her that everything in life is maths. That, when you look closely, you see all these patterns, and numbers, and shapes. The same number patterns showing up in art ... or nature ... or even the number of cells in the human body. And you see it everywhere you go. Patterns and numbers repeated again, and again, and again. Bleeding into every part of your life, if you only take the time to look properly.

It's funny, but not in a *haha* way, in a weird one. A way that I don't *really* understand, like those confusing questions you get on a maths exam paper: *So and so is going to make an apple pie so they buy 578 apples. What is the percentage of filling compared to the ratio of pastry?* Or some crap like that.

Anyway, when I'd found out wot happened with Al, I thought it was some sort of joke at first, or that someone had got it wrong, cos I'd only been talking to him the day before. We'd been messaging back and forth on WhatsApp and he never said anything that made me worry. Not a single thing. I didn't get that he was upset, or that anything was even wrong. When he didn't turn up to art the next day, I thought that something must've been off cos Al never missed school. And he *never* would've missed it on a day he had art. But I just thought that maybe he was sick or something. So I messaged him:

I missed you in art, big head! Where were u?!

But I know he didn't see it cos only one of those ticks appeared. And, when I had a look at the top of our messages, it said *Last seen yesterday, at 15:42.*

It was the next day, Wednesday, that I found out Al was dead. And all I could think was that all the time I'd been messing about on Snapchat, or scrolling through Insta, looking at someone's story, all that time ... Al had been dead. And I just couldn't get my head round it. I just couldn't believe that I'd lost someone else.

I still remember the first time we spoke properly. Al was sitting in the far corner of the art class, mixing powdered paints together, and he was really taking his time. Measuring out the paint like it was *really* important for him to get the right shade, like it meant ... everything. There were all these other kids messing about, but Al was sitting on his own and you could tell that art was his thing. That he didn't just pick it cos he thought it would be easy. He actually loved it. Just like me. But I know how to have a laugh, too, and Al didn't really do that. I never saw him hanging around with anyone. Well, except his mate Lewi, but even that stopped. So I felt sort of sorry for him at first. Cos imagine having no mates at all. It's sad. Really sad.

Anyway, I'd been trying to draw my dad, using one of my favourite photos of him, but, no matter how hard I tried, I just couldn't get it right. I couldn't make it look like him and I'd used my rubber so many times that the paper was all furry, and there were these black bits everywhere. I was so annoyed, so flipping pissed that I couldn't do it, that I just threw the rubber and started swearing. Swearing the whole classroom down cos it's annoying when you're trying your hardest to make something turn out perfect, but it just doesn't work.

Then Al stopped mixing his paints and came and sat next to me, even though I never asked him to, and he said, *'You know, everything in life is maths.'* Which is a pretty weird thing to say when you think about it. He pointed at the picture of my dad that I was trying to copy from the screensaver on my phone. *'It's all about patterns and numbers. But you're trying too hard to make it perfect. No one's face is a perfect oval. Faces don't work like that. They're more of an egg shape ... with this bit that goes out towards the bottom ... this bit that expands.'* Then he looked at the photo of my dad, picked up my pencil and showed me.

And at first I was angry cos I didn't know Al and there he

was, coming over to my table, insulting my dad's face and thinking he knew everything. I was just about to tell him where he could go, but then I looked at the drawing. I almost couldn't speak. It was like Al had brought my dad back to life. He'd managed to draw my dad's stubble in and these tiny lines at the corner of his eyes, and he'd even shaded in these flecks of grey on Dad's beard.

I thought he'd say something else, but he just got up and sat back down at his table, like it was nothing. He pulled his headphones on and I couldn't stop staring at him. Not cos I fancied him or anything like that, but cos he was so ... different. He didn't have his hair shaved like most of the other boys, and he never wore a cap, and he didn't have one of those Nike bags, and he didn't even try to get away with wearing trainers instead of proper school shoes. Even when he spoke, Al didn't sound like he was from Wythenshawe. You just knew that he was gonna do something with his life. You know, when you can just tell that some people are gonna go on and do something ... amazing?

So, that day, when I got that Snap off my mate Tara – cos she'd heard from Chloe, who'd found out from Lauren, who knew cos she was going out with Al's big brother, Saul – I couldn't believe that Al had killed himself. That I'd never see him again. I didn't know wot to do, but I was certain I wanted to do *something*. Something to keep Al's memory alive somehow ... just like he'd done for me with that drawing of my dad.

Maybe it's cos I know what it's like to lose someone. How it feels when someone's in your life one minute, and everything seems proper normal, and then they're just gone, and you have to try and deal with that.

I don't know why I thought that a Facebook page would be the best way to do it. It's not like Al had loads of friends or anything, but I thought that at least everyone could see him, and remember him. So it would be like he was still here. Al was always hiding in real life, trying to stay away from people or blend into the walls of the corridors, and I didn't want him to do that any more. He deserved to be seen.

So I went through Al's profile pictures and stole one, then uploaded it to a page I set up. And then I remembered that he was *always* going on about the stars and that. He had loads of places he wanted to go, but the first place on his list was the Brecon Beacons cos although it was only in Wales he'd be able to see all the stars you can't in Wythenshawe. I spent *hours* on Google trying to find the perfect picture of the place. There were loads, like hundreds, of star pictures, and most of them looked the same cos, once you've seen one star picture, you've seen them all. But when I found it I knew. It just felt right.

It was this sky, with mountains in the distance, and a wide-set valley, and looking at it I could tell why Al wanted to go there. There was all this open space, and millions and millions of stars. So I uploaded it to the page with the photo of Al and I looked at his face shining out against the Brecon Beacons, and it made me feel sort of proud. Cos if you squinted it almost looked like Al was up there in the sky. That he was one of those stars, looking down on the valley, and I know he would've liked that. And I just sat there for a minute, staring at the page, and I wanted this moment – where it was just private, where I was the only one who knew about it – to last forever.

Like the days out I used to have with my dad, when it was just me and him.

But I took a deep breath, pressed *publish* and wrote the first comment. The first few sentences on a blank wall:

RIP, Al, the smartest guy in Wythenshawe. I know you're shining bright from way up there. xxxx

NATHAN

chapter three

My mum bought me this map when I was a kid with all these different coloured pins and two bits of string. She told me that I could use it to plan my future. Plan my life. So I spent ages pressing the pins in the places I wanted to visit, the places where you could see the stars, or the mountains, or glaciers from the Ice Age. And sometimes I'd run my hand along the string, over all the different countries, and I'd just keep adding more pins because there was so much in this world that I wanted to see.

The loud horn and shouting from the scrap-metal man outside wake me up. I turn over. If I was at school now, I'd be in third period with Kyle. Bored out my face in English, counting down the minutes to lunch. I reach over to my bedside table and pull open the drawer, taking my iPhone out. It's been switched off since Al . . .

I was sick of all the messages, notifications, missed calls, Snaps, Insta stories I'd been tagged in. There were so many and it's only been four days. Some of them were from my mates, or people off the estate, but most of them were people I didn't even know. People who suddenly felt like they had summat to say about Al. It hadn't taken long to get out, mainly cause of Saul's girlfriend, 'big gob' Lauren, who loved to spread gossip. Good or bad.

But it felt weird not having my phone on. Even tho the notifications and messages pissed me off, I felt like I was missing out. Missing out on all the stuff that Kyle and my mates had been doing. And I wanted to see Al, too. See some pictures of him alive. Happy. To replace the one that I couldn't get out my head.

I switch my phone on and type in my passcode. It *pings* straight away with a WhatsApp from Kyle. I ignore it, but then my phone vibrates with a message. Then another, then another, then another. I don't open them, but I still see what they say on the screen.

Is it tru?

Soz m8

U ok?

Wot happened?

Nate . . . u there?

Nate????

25

I go to my photos and scroll through, passing image after image, going past pictures taken in school or out in town with my mates. The memes and GIFs that I'd sent to Kyle and pictures of fit girls that I've screen-grabbed from Insta and that. I keep going till I find some photos of Al. He never really liked pictures, but I'd managed to get a few.

There's one of him messin about with me and Saul in the park two years ago.

One of him sleeping with his mouth open.

One of him wearing a T-shirt with all these planets on it, his arms folded across his chest. I zoom in on his face, making his features bigger so I can try to remember him this way, and not the way I found him. His brown skin, the gap in his teeth. His thick hair. And then, I dunno why, I find myself looking for summat else. Tryna see if he seems upset or like he's scared or in trouble. But he just looks normal. He just looks like the same old Al.

I stop on the most recent photo, one where I can actually see his face. It was taken in April. Me and my mates are always taking photos, selfies, just messin around and stuff, but Al was really funny about it. He'd never take a selfie with me or Saul, and when he did he'd cover his face with his hand, like he was hiding. And if we ever took one without him knowing, and posted it somewhere, he'd go off on one. Getting all upset and going into one of his weird moods. I never understood why he took everything so seriously.

I stare down at the photo of me, Al, Saul and Lewi. It was from sometime over Easter when we'd spent the whole day hanging round Wythenshawe Park, going on all the rides at the fair. In the photo, Al and Lewi are standing in front of one of those prize stalls – the ones where you have to get a foam hoop round one of those plastic cones – Al, with his thick Afro and headphones hanging round his neck, wearing his favourite *Geology Rocks* T-shirt, his arm draped round Lewi's shoulder and giving the thumbs up to the camera. Lewi grins, his fingers wrapped round each other and pointing upwards to make a W shape. 'W' for Wythenshawe.

Lewi's got this huge inflatable hammer in his other hand. I remember that Al had managed to win it by working out the right angle to throw the hoop. He'd said that you didn't have to be strong or good at throwing things, you just had to work out where to stand and the distance to release it at. Lewi had wanted the hammer so much that Al had ended up giving it to him. They had been best mates since primary school, always together, but, a few weeks after that day, Lewi just stopped coming round, and Al never said why.

I never thought much of it at the time, but it's actually weird. You don't just have a bust-up with your mate, unless summat's happened. Summat must have gone down between them that Al didn't tell me about.

I have to look away from my phone cause it hurts too much.

Al was all alone. He had me and Saul, yeah, but Lewi was his best mate, and he'd just gone off. Started hanging round with Eli and Cole, who were nothin like Al. Maybe, if Lewi had still been his mate , then Al wouldn't have done it. If Lewi hadn't left him, then Al would still feel like he had someone there. Someone he could turn to.

I lie back on my pillow. The more I think about Al, the more it's like I don't even know him, but all I want is to feel close to him. To tell him that I love him, even tho I never said it when he was here. I just want my big brother back.

I hear the sound of something smashing downstairs followed by the noise of glass being scraped from the floor. I climb outta bed and pull on a pair of jogging bottoms. On the landing, I pass Phoebe's room, her name painted in all these bright colours on the door. Al had done it for her and painted inside her room as well, stencilling birds and rabbits and characters from her favourite books on the walls. I pass Saul's room, his door frame splintered and cracked from the time he'd got angry and punched it in. He did it after our dad left and said that if he didn't punch the door frame then he'd end up punching someone's face. I try not to look up towards the other set of stairs, the ones that lead up to the top of the house . . . to Al's room.

I head into the kitchen and find Mum picking up bits of a broken wine bottle from the floor and dumping them in the bin. She didn't really drink till Dad left – it wasn't like she suddenly turned into one of those proper alkies that you see hanging round outside the bookie's, but we'd all noticed. Now, with Al, it's got even worse. The metal lid of the kitchen bin slams shut and she jumps when she sees me.

'Christ's sake, Nathan,' she says. 'D'you have to go sneaking up on me like that? Almost gave me a bloody heart attack.'

'Soz,' I say. 'I weren't sneaking up on you, tho.'

'Well, what else were you doing, lurking round there? I didn't even hear you come in.'

She puts the plastic dustpan and brush down on the floor, and I stare at her finger. A drop of blood is trickling down it.

'Mum,' I say. 'You're bleeding.'

She stares at me, like I've just spoken in a foreign language – maybe nothing will ever hurt as much as losing Al. But then she looks at her hand and walks over to the sink. I watch as she turns the tap on, the water thundering down into the steel bowl. She stands with her back to me, probably for longer than she needs to.

'Where's Saul?' I ask.

'He's at work,' she says. 'He took Phoebe to school this morning. I wanted to stay here, just in case we heard anything from the coroner.'

She turns the tap off and walks over to the other side of the kitchen, ripping off a piece of kitchen roll and wrapping it round her finger. I watch as the blood seeps through.

'I don't know what's taking them so long. They said they'd be releasing his body any time now. It's not enough that we have to have this *stupid* inquest! That they've been looking at my bank statements, asking about his home life, your dad walking out. Things that don't concern them. My son is *dead* and I have to *wait* to bury him! I have to wait to say goodbye properly.' She wipes her eyes and sits down at the kitchen table.

The first I'd even heard about this inquest stuff was after the police came round. They said that we could bury Al after the autopsy, but there would be this public court case where

29

they had to present the 'facts about his suicide'. They'd already asked me some questions cause I was the one who found him, but they said that they'd probably be back with more. That I'd have to go to court to give evidence, but Mum had to agree that I could. I didn't wanna go cause then I'd have to lie about the phone call. And wot if Mum found out? But also Al's death wasn't some public thing. It was private.

It was me, and Mum, and Phoebe, and Saul.

Mum looks at me. 'I know it's hard,' she says. 'But have you thought about going back to school? The routine . . . something else to focus on might help.' She pauses. 'And you've got your GCSEs coming up. Mr Ballan told me that the school will do everything they can to help with—'

I ignore her and walk over to the fridge.

'Nathan?' she says.

'What's the point?' I say, opening the door and taking out a carton of orange juice. 'Might not go back at all. It ain't like going to school is gonna fix anything.'

I push back the plastic tab and take a gulp. I can feel her watching me, but she doesn't tell me to get a glass or have a go at me for drinking out the carton like she usually does. I put the empty carton back in the fridge and I feel my mum tense.

'Why do you always have to do that?' She gets up from the table and storms over to me, pulling the carton out. 'It's empty!' She shoves it inside the metal bin. 'Is it so difficult to throw something away once you've finished with it? And there *is* a point, Nathan. You can't let what's happened to Al . . . to us . . . stop you from doing well. From passing your exams.'

I wanna laugh. She's never been bothered before about me and school, not properly anyway. There's no chance I'm gonna pass anything, but she didn't care then cause she had Al. She had one son who'd made her proud.

'You were never bothered before,' I say. 'Not when Al "the golden boy" was around. How does any of this matter now? If I get a D, or an A, it won't make no difference. All these exams . . . they mean nothing, y'know.'

My mum turns to face me, and I can see how angry she is.

'It's your future,' she says. 'You want to go through school having wasted all that time? Not even bothering to try? Life is hard enough as it is and you think, what? That you can just get a job, with no qualifications? Wake up, Nathan—'

'It won't bring Al back,' I say.

'No,' she snaps. 'But neither will giving up. You've got something that Al will *never* have again – a chance of a good future. And I'll be damned if I'll let you throw that away!'

'Can't you just get off my case?' I say.

Mum shakes her head. 'Sometimes,' she says. 'Sometimes, I just wish that you could be more—'

'More wot?' I interrupt. 'More like Al? Cause it's obvious you wish it was me that was dead and not him. If Al had come back and found *me*, would you even be bothered? Would you even care? Probably not cause at least you'd still have your favourite son aroun—'

Her slap doesn't hurt, but it makes a loud noise.

'How dare you!' she says. 'I love you, *all* of you, the same. You don't know what it's like to lose a child – and I hope to

God you never have to find out – but I'd feel this way if it was you, or Phoebe, or Saul.'

I feel bad. I didn't mean to get so angry, but I'm just being honest. She's always preferred Al to me, and sometimes I can see why.

'I'm sorry,' she says, moving her hand to her mouth. 'It's just . . . I already feel like an awful mother. Not knowing my own son . . .' She turns away from me, and I stand there, hating myself for saying all that stuff. I want to tell her that she's not a bad mum and that I'm sorry. I want to say that sometimes I can't help but fuck things up, and how I really wouldn't blame her if she did love Al more. But I can't get the words out.

She's making this sniffing crying sound like a kid of Phoebe's age. I've seen Mum cry so much these past few days that I'm surprised she hasn't run outta tears. Wiping her face, she walks over to the worktop and picks up a bottle of wine. She unscrews the lid and reaches up to the kitchen cupboard. She doesn't even bother using a wine glass, just pours the wine into a mug that says World's Best Mum on the side. I think Al bought it for her one Mother's Day. I don't say anything about her drinking at this time in the morning.

'I never thought it would be like this,' she says. 'Not when we'd been planning for all these things. Exams, university . . . And it's not as if your dad's around. He can't even be bothered to come and see us.'

It feels weird her mentioning Dad after all this time. After he fucked off, two years ago, she never really spoke about him. She doesn't like us talking about him, either. It's like he never existed. He kept in touch at first, but then he just stopped, and we got used to him not being around.

Mum doesn't look at me as she knocks back her drink. She's aged so much in the past four days that she doesn't even look like the same person any more. It was as if Al was the only thing keeping her alive. She's so thin, and her dark hair is mostly grey, and I dunno how I've not noticed that before. Plus, all these lines have appeared down the middle of her forehead and by the corners of her eyes, like she's turned into one of Al's drawings that's been scrunched up and folded loads of times.

She jabs a button on the old radio on the kitchen worktop. The house has seemed so quiet since it happened that maybe she just can't take the silence any more. Al was always going on, talking about all his facts and stuff, while Phoebe would play noisily and Saul would blast music from his room. And there'd always be some kinda argument or row between us, but not any more. Mum turns the knob, flicking through R & B songs and some country music and old people love songs, till some voices stretch out from one of those boring stations that never has any music, just posh people going on about stuff.

I listen as the voices crackle into tune and the soft fuzzing in the background stops. Then I hear some man over the static. He's droning on the way the teachers do at school when we have to sit through Mass or when we've all been playing up. I imagine him living in one of them big houses near to where all the United players are. Grey hair and loads of money, wearing a dead shit cardigan.

'Well, what we need is early intervention, Frank,' he says. 'It's because we're not talking to young people soon enough that these things happen. There's so much stress for them these days: exams, social-media pressures. You know how it is. Boys especially need to know that it's not weak to talk about their feelings. You are allowed to do it. No one's judging you.'

He laughs, all annoying and fake. I bet he only buys the dead expensive range at the supermarket, and has a proper lit car.

'Suicide,' he continues, 'is one of the biggest killers of young men, particularly between the ages of fifteen and twenty-nine. If only there was something we could do ... if only people would become aware ... learn what to look out for. That's what we need to do. We need to educate people about the warning signs. Signs that could prevent someone from—'

My mum slams the radio off, hitting the button hard.

'What does he know?' she shouts. 'With his facts and figures and studies. He doesn't know what it's like. There were no signs. Nothing.' She rests her hands on the worktop and shakes her head. 'He doesn't know how ... sudden it is. How the last thing Al said to me was something so ... normal. "See you after school."' She pauses. 'He doesn't know how one minute you can feel like you know everything about your own child and the next you realize you knew nothing.'

She breathes out slowly, closing her eyes, and tilting her head towards the ceiling, like she's trying to make sense of it all. 'We'd planned a day,' she says. 'To go down to Cambridge, look round the campus. Al had booked all the tickets. Why would he do that if ... ?'

I go over and wrap my arms round her. I can't remember the last time we hugged and I'm half expecting her to push me away, but she hugs me back. Proper tightly.

'Please, Nate,' she says, and she turns to look me. 'You have to promise to talk to me. I can't lose another child.'

I nod.

She touches the side of my face with her hand. 'You're a good lad,' she says.

My chest tightens and I feel bad for saying all those things, for even thinking them in the first place. Cause maybe she does love me just as much as Al. Maybe it was me always doing the wrong thing, or pissing about. She's always been there for all of us, working two jobs, sometimes three, so that we could go on school trips, or get new trainers. So that we wouldn't have to go without.

She straightens herself up and lets go of me.

'I'm gonna call your Aunt Maureen,' she says. 'But I do think it'll help for you to do *something*. Go back to school. Even if it's only for half a day at first.'

I nod again and Mum leaves the kitchen. I stand there alone, staring at the painted tiles and shiny surfaces. At the empty kitchen table and the metal grate that Saul fixed over our back door cause of the amount of times that we'd been broken in to. Even tho everything looks the same, without Al it *feels* so different. Empty.

I think back to two weeks ago, standing in this spot while Al was looking in the fridge, holding open the door. I can almost hear him say: '*Do you know that it's safe to eat mould? They've done all these studies and it never did anyone any harm. That's what medicine's made out of anyway. So it's all in your mind. All of it. You can eat it, but you just can't* think *about eating it. You've got to trick yourself, that's all.'*

For a moment, it's like none of this has happened. I ain't someone who's trying to keep hold of all these thoughts and feelings that don't make sense. I'm just Nate and my brother's there.

Alive.

Breathing.

Happy.

MEGAN

chapter four

When things got tough, I used to think about vanishing. Disappearing. How it would feel . . . how maybe it would solve everything. I'd go and sit on this bench in the middle of Civic, between Iceland and Costa, and I'd stay there for hours, watching all these people go by, and think about Atlantis. How a whole city could be swallowed up without a trace. Because, if an entire city can just disappear, then surely someone from Benchill could, too.

The memorial page had only been up for a couple of days, but it already had 657 *likes* which was a lot. The comments started to come through straight away. At first, I just sat there, hunched over on my bedroom floor, with my back pressed against the radiator, watching all these posts appear. It made me feel good, seeing all these people writing nice things about Al. I spent the first few hours just *liking* everything, or pressing the *love* reaction, or replying to comments. Then I started inviting more people to *like* the page. Everyone I could think of from school or around Wythenshawe.

Maybe that was a stupid thing to do, but I just wanted Al to be remembered, and the more *likes* the better. I guess I wanted to make sure that he wouldn't disappear, or fade ... That's the saddest thing. People die, then eventually they're just forgotten about.

But today it's all got a bit too much. Every time I look at my phone, there's *another* notification and I can feel myself starting to get pissed off. Not cos of the notifications, but cos there's no need for Al to be dead. For him to think that life was one of those things you could just take for granted and decide to throw away. I'm upset, yeah, but I'm also proper fucking angry.

My dad never got a chance to decide. He was driving home and went into the back of a lorry. That was that. They said he died instantly, but what does that matter? I know that if there was some way I could speak to him he'd tell me that he never wanted to die. That he wished he could be back with me and Mum. He didn't have a choice, but Al did and all the feelings about my dad dying that I thought were gone are coming back cos of Al.

I force myself to stop looking at my phone and make my way downstairs. The lean-to is the only place in the house that

38

feels like my dad even lived here cos all his junk is still piled up in there. Mum tried to clear it out a year after he died, but I kicked off and wouldn't let her touch anything. I just kept screaming and shouting. I know this makes me sound proper weird, but there are only two places in the world where I feel safe. Where I don't have to think about anyone else or anything. Where I don't have to act a certain way, or pretend to like things that I really couldn't give a toss about.

One of them is my dad's lean-to and the other is the art classroom. Well, it was. Without Al, it's just an empty room. So it turns out he was the reason I felt safe there. He just took me for who I was – sad, or miserable, or pissed off – and never expected anything more from me, y'know? And it was like I was a different person with him. I could talk about all the things I'm too scared to talk about in front of Tara and my other mates. Like the things I love, or what I want to do in the future, or the fact I secretly fucking hate house music even though everyone else seems to love it.

Al never made me feel stupid or weird. He never made me feel like I had to hide all these other parts of myself. He wanted to be my friend. Even though I let him down.

You see, after that day in art when we first talked, I bumped into Al at the museum. I'd gone there to do some sketching for my art portfolio and I saw him standing near these paper cranes. He looked . . . sad. Lonely even. So I went over to him and blurted out some stupid joke. Not just cos I felt sorry for him, but because I liked him. We started hanging around with each other more and more. I don't remember how it happened, but we'd meet up after school, or sit together in art, or spend hours sending each other voice notes.

But it was only when no one else was around. It's bad, but a part of me was embarrassed. Too embarrassed to let anyone know that Al was my mate. It's not like we ever had that conversation or anything. It was just this unspoken thing between us. I was worried about what Tara and my other mates might say. Bothered about what people would think. How messed up is that? How pathetic is that?

Maybe, if I'd been braver, if I would've just not given a fuck about other people, if I'd been a better friend, then Al would still be here. It hurts so much.

I pull open the door to the lean-to and walk over to one of my dad's old deckchairs. I sit down and put my feet up, bringing my knees close to my chest. It's raining outside, and I turn to look out of the window, even though it's proper dark outside so I can't really see anything. I just sit there and listen to the sound of the rain hitting the roof. And I keep getting flashes. Flashes of me and Al. Flashes of my dad. It's funny cos sometimes you think you're over the worst of something, y'know? And I felt proud cos I thought I'd moved on like my dad would've wanted. I mean, I miss him, of course I do, but I've got to a stage where I can enjoy stuff. My dad's gone, but it doesn't rip through me the way it used to.

But now, with Al, it's like losing my dad all over again. Another person I'll never see again and having all these things I want to say. All these feelings that I don't know what to do with. I feel the tears coming and I press my head against my knees. I hope Al knows that I never meant to hurt him. How sorry I am for not being more like him. I cry till I can't any more. Till my eyes are puffy and my leggings are drenched in tears and snot.

I lift my head up, and think about this painting that Al was doing in art. He smudged these green and blue pastels with his fingers and told me all about this city that managed to just disappear underwater. And I remember how I'd thought things can't just vanish. Cos even if you can't see them they're still there. They always will be. Like losing my dad. And now Al.

I pull my phone out of my jacket pocket, and I go on to Al's Insta. There are loads of videos and photos on there. Stuff that I'd only glanced at when he'd been alive. There's this one video he'd taken at night, in the centre of Civic. It was this concrete square in the middle of all these shops, with just a few benches, near the big Asda. Al had filmed the sky and all these fireworks going off. It hadn't been Bonfire Night or anything – maybe someone in the flats round the back had just been having a party. Al had filmed all the colours exploding, then bleeding into the night. He'd managed to make something so *ordinary* look so ... *special*. It was just like his art. Where he drew things in a way that you'd never seen or thought about before, as if you were wearing special glasses.

I scroll through more of his pictures. Photos of paintings he'd done of Wythenshawe, and other random photos he'd taken around town or the estate, and they are all proper good. Like he was able to see through all the crap and find something beautiful. People are always saying how much of a dump Wythenshawe is. That it's *chavvy* or *proper rough* and how you can't even go to the shops for milk without getting stabbed. Which is a load of rubbish! Al would always say that, if anything, he felt lucky to be from one of the '*biggest council estates in Europe*' cos it also had so much history. Looking at his Insta makes me think that maybe I'd taken it for granted. Cos Al was able to look closely and find all this good stuff and capture it. People only ever talk about the bad things that happen around here. No one ever talks about how green it is, or how people look out for each other, how everyone on our estate helped us pay for Dad's funeral. How our house had been full of flowers and food.

I move further down in my chair and I can't help but smile a little bit. Cos Al might be gone, but his paintings aren't and neither is his way of looking at the world. And, whether he knew it or not, he can't just vanish. He was too special. He was too ... *Al*.

NATHAN

chapter five

I still remember the first time I saw the paper cranes in the Manchester Museum. I'd gone there to sketch one of the mummies, and I'd stumbled across the cabinet by mistake. It was full of all these tiny paper birds that looked like they were about to take off. I'd never seen anything like it before. And for some reason, just standing there among all those tiny birds, made me forget. Just being in that museum made me feel free.

I close my bedroom door and pick up my phone. There's another message from Kyle:

Yo, wen u bk at skl?

I ignore it and open Facebook instead.

Mum was right. I do need to do summat useful ... I don't care about school, tho. I wanna figure out wot was going through Al's head. Find out wot he was doing ... where he was ... wot he was thinking ... before he died. Saul's wrong – there had to be a reason. Someone or summat that pushed Al over the edge. I can't just sit around doing nothing. Not when our whole family's been torn apart.

Fuck that.

I go to my profile, then watch as my news feed updates. I've not been on Facebook since it happened.

Fifteen friend requests.

Seventy-five notifications.

Twenty-five messages.

I ignore them all, and type Al's name in the search bar. His face comes up straight away. His huge Afro takes up most of the picture and he looks nuff awkward, like he doesn't know how to smile properly. My chest goes all tight, knowing that I'll never see him for real again, that he'll only ever be this person in a photo.

Al's been tagged in all these status updates – loads of people saying how sorry they are, or writing other stuff on his wall. I recognize some of the names and faces from school, but I don't look at them. I know it will only make me sad or proper angry. Angry that people he didn't even know are posting about him. Pissed that people who weren't even friends with Al are going on about how upset they are, or how they wish he was still alive.

I click on through to his *check-ins* and, when it loads up, a map appears. It makes me think of the one in Al's room of where he wanted to go, but the red marks on this one are places he actually visited – McDonald's, the art gallery, the Portico Library, the Whitworth, Wythenshawe Park, the University of Manchester. Three things come up when I click on *Recent Places*: the Whitworth, Manchester Art Gallery and the museum. I stare at the list. Al had been at the museum on September 12th. Two days before he died.

My phone makes a popping noise and a message comes up, some girl in my year tryna talk to me.

Hope ur ok?

The grey bubble goes up and down with the dots where she's writing something else, but I close Facebook before she's finished.

I click on Insta instead and, ignoring even more notifications, I go to Al's page. The last picture he posted is of all these paper cranes in a glass cabinet. There's loads of them, on bits of string, hanging down inside the cabinet. It was posted on September 12th, so I guess it's from the museum. But it's the caption I can't stop staring at. Al had written:

Some birds are not meant to be free.

I don't even know wot he means. Was he talking about himself? Was it Al's way of saying there was no other way out for him? Did summat happen at the museum? Did he know then wot he was gonna do?

I'm probably reading too much into it, but I wanna try to understand. Not just why Al did it, but everything about him. Why he liked that stupid museum so much. Or why he couldn't stop going on about paintings. I just wanna feel closer to him again.

I pull out a hoodie from my wardrobe, tugging it on over my T-shirt. I pick my school bag up off the floor and stuff some money inside, along with my phone. I grab Al's drawing from my bedside-table drawer and put that on top of everything. It's not folded properly, so the edges of the paper gape open and the tip of Al's shoe on the picture peeks out. I pull at the zips on either side of my rucksack, watching as the material closes and Al's picture disappears inside the bag.

As I walk to the bus stop, I notice that our estate's pretty quiet for once. Everyone's either at work or school. I get my phone out to check the time – 15:10. I need to hurry, otherwise the bus will be full of people from school. It's proper cold out, so I pull my hood up to cover my neck and some of my face and walk past the rows of houses. The houses are so close together that you can hear people arguing or playing music. Most of them look the same, all red brick with white window frames and rusty metal gates. The gardens are proper massive, tho. I pass this house on the corner with a manky old settee outside and another one with a broken bike leaning against the wall. I kick a half-finished can of Coke on the pavement towards one of the drains, watching as the contents spill out on to the road. In the distance, I hear someone's dog barking and the couple from around the back of the estate who are always fighting.

The wind gets harsher as I turn on to the main road, so I shove my hands into the pockets of my hoodie and put my head down. I imagine Al walking beside me, in that weird way he had, his arms hanging down by his sides, like they were too long for his body.

When I reach the bus stop, there's a group of people huddled underneath the shelter. I stand away from them, leaning against the railing. I search through the pockets of my hoodie, trying to find my headphones, but they're not there. I must've left them at home and I can't be bothered to go back for them. A 43 bus turns the corner and this old woman with one of them old people trolleys sticks her hand out to make it stop.

She gets on in front of me, pushing her trolley towards the front of the bus and sitting down next to a woman with a screaming baby on her lap. I throw some money down for a day saver, and then make my way to the back. The bus is pretty full, but I don't wanna go upstairs in case I bump into someone from school, so I slump into one of the empty seats just as the bus lurches forward. More people get on, someone rings the bell, someone gets off, another kid starts crying. But it all fades into the background as I stare out the window, thinking about Al.

The bus pulls into another stop, just before the petrol station, and a group of girls get on. They're all laughing and joking, talking dead loudly. A few of them make their way up to the top deck, scrolling through their phones, without looking up. One of them is taking a picture or filming or something. The last one stops when she sees me. I recognize her from school. She's in Al's year and I think I remember seeing him talking to her. I can't remember her name, but I'm sure he'd mentioned her. I think they had art together or summat.

I suppose she's fit. I mean, I obviously ain't blind. But, if she was mates with Al, there's no way she'd ever bother with me. Not when I'm in the year below. Not when I'm Al's stupid kid brother. So I'm surprised when she walks towards me.

One of her mates leans down over this plastic bit of the stairs. 'Eh, Megs!' she shouts. 'You comin' up or what?'

'Be there in a minute,' she says. Her friend pulls a face and stomps up the stairs, and I wish I'd remembered my headphones so I could put them in and ignore her. She sits down next to me, moving her hair over her shoulder. It's this dark blonde colour and there's a bit of it clipped away from her face. I try not to look too hard, but up close I can see all these freckles across her nose. She licks her lip and I feel myself staring at her mouth. But I don't want her to think I'm a perv or nothin, so I look away, and shove my hands into my pockets.

'Hi. You're Nathan, right?'

I nod. 'Yeah.'

'I'm Megan,' she says. 'I'm in ... I was in Al's year. We were in the same art class and that. We used to sit next to each other.' She takes a deep breath, and pulls on the sleeve of her jacket. 'I'm *really* sorry. I mean, I proper couldn't believe it when I heard.'

48

My throat tightens. I can see some people moving in their seats. An old man on the opposite side of the bus turns round and I'm worried that they're all listening, that maybe somehow they know as well. That they've all heard about Al and know wot she's talking about.

'It's all right,' I say, even tho we both know it ain't.

She pauses, and starts to pick some of the varnish off her nails. 'He was so clever,' she says. 'He always knew the answers to, like, everything. Every question anyone would ask, or anything the teachers would say, Al would know.' She pauses. 'He was going to do so much … I mean, he'd gone a bit quiet and stuff these past few weeks, but I didn't think anything was wrong, y'know? I just didn't see it.'

I turn in my seat, shifting away from her so that I'm closer to the window. I know wot Megan means, tho, cause I didn't see it coming, either, but I don't wanna talk about it. Not with some random that I don't even know. Not on a bus with loads of people listening.

'Anyway,' she says, sighing and leaning back in her seat, 'I wanted to do something to remember Al by. I've set up a memorial page on Facebook,' she blurts out. 'I just thought people could post stuff. It might help.'

I stare at her and she smiles. I feel like shouting down the whole bus, telling her to just jog on, and asking how it's supposed to help. How a bunch of people going on about how much they miss Al will make things better?

'I don't need some stupid page,' I say. 'He's my brother. I'll always remember him.'

Megan blushes. 'I know that,' she says. 'It's just ... I was trying to do something nice.' She pauses. 'Well, you can at least have a look. See how many people have posted things already.' I don't say anything, and she looks like she's getting a bit annoyed. 'Or not,' she shrugs.

I dunno if she expects me to say thank you, or wot, but I don't. She must be able to tell that I want her to clear off cause she stands up. I just keep staring out the window as she walks off to join her mates upstairs. The bus carries on. Outside, it's starting to rain. Like, properly. Loads of it, just lashing down. Al was always going on about how crap the weather was – another reason he couldn't wait to get outta Manchester.

I'm so busy staring out the window that I almost miss my stop. I press down on the bell just as I see the large uni building. I jump up, tripping as the bus throws me forward. As I step out on to the pavement, the rain pummels into me so I pull my hood up over my head and hold on to the straps of my rucksack.

I glance up as the bus drives off. Megan and her mates stare out from the top deck. Megan holds her hand up towards the window, like she's about to wave. I know that she ain't done nothing, not really, but I don't feel like pretending to be nice, so I just turn away and head towards the museum.

MEGAN

chapter six

Sometimes me and Megan would sit in the art room for hours. Talking about space, or Van Gogh, or all the things we wanted to do once we'd both left school. The exhibitions we'd go and see, or maybe the galleries our work would be on display at. And I never wanted our time in that art room to end. Because I knew that, as soon as we both walked out of that door, things would change. Things between us would shift. I'd go back to being alone, and Megan would just walk right past me in the corridor.

I stand there, holding my hand up towards Nathan from the other side of the grubby bus window and I feel like a right *idiot*. I don't even know why I'm bothering to wave, not when he was so rude, but I do it anyway. At first, I think he's going to wave back cos that's what normal people do, but he just scrunches up his face and pulls up the hood of his tracksuit.

Then he's gone. A grey blur disappearing into the rain and the traffic. Part of me is pissed off at how he acted, but the other part can't really blame him.

When my dad died, I was angry at everyone for such a long time. Maybe cos it was easier that way. When you're angry, it takes you away from the pain somehow. Stops it from tearing into you. There was one time when I even lost it with this old woman in the pound shop. She wasn't doing anything really, just taking her time, counting out her change at the till. I started shouting and kicking off. Then I threw down the drink or whatever it was I was buying and stormed off. Tara was with me and found it hilarious, but I just felt proper bad afterwards. It wasn't this old woman's fault that my dad was dead. It wasn't anyone's.

It was actually a bit weird seeing Nathan. I've seen his picture loads of times. He's all over Al's Facebook and tagged in some of his Insta posts, and I've seen him around school, too, but I never really thought much about him. But when I walked on that bus it was almost like I was looking at Al. That I'd gone back in time or something. And it wasn't just cos they looked alike. It was in . . . everything. The way he was sitting, the way he kept looking around, even the way he frowned.

And I liked it. That sense of the familiar.

I lean back against the bus seat and Tara looks up at me from her phone. She's been so busy scrolling through Eli's

52

Instagram page that she hasn't said a word since. Eli's in our year at school. Him and Tara have kind of been on and off for, like, two years. But recently they've started to get even closer. I spent most of the summer hanging around with Tara, Eli and his mates in the park. Eli and his mates are mostly idiots, apart from Lewi who was always all right.

Tara runs her fingers through her ponytail. She dyes her hair this bright red colour and I notice that the dark roots are starting to show.

'No way! Did he just blank you, Megs?' she says. 'Proper rude that. He could at least let on. Especially after everything you've done.'

'It's fine,' I say. 'I've not *really* done anything.'

'Erm, you set up that page for his brother. Look how many *likes* it's got as well. He should be kissing your feet for that. Trust me, it's more than most people would've done.'

I nod, but I feel like telling her that Al would've done it for me. He would've done more than just set up a page. He would've found another way for me to be remembered. I want to tell Tara how much I care ... cared about Al. How even though we passed each other in the corridor at school and barely said 'hi', it was only cos I didn't want people knowing he was really important to me.

Something inside me would light up whenever I'd walk into art and see Al. He'd smile and stop sketching in his notebook. '*Megs,*' he'd say. '*Look at this! Come and see what I've found ...*' and he'd bring up a Van Gogh painting on his phone, or some YouTube video of a meteor shower, and I'd do

53

the same. I'd show him a photo of an exhibition at the museum. Or a video of a star being born, of it exploding in on itself, then burning brightly through this outer layer of gas, and into the night.

I breathe out slowly. I don't want to be on this bus any more. I feel Tara staring at me. She must be able to tell that something's wrong cos she gets up, and sits down next to me. I don't want her to see how upset I am. She won't understand. How can she? When I kept the fact that me and Al were such good friends hidden. Hidden from her, hidden from everyone really.

'Hey,' Tara says. 'You all right?' She rests her head on my shoulder, but carries on scrolling through her phone. I nod, although part of me feels numb. Tara's my best mate. She always has been. We only live a few streets away from each other and we went to the same primary school and everything. Sometimes we stay at each other's houses for three or four days, and we talk almost every night. But recently . . . I dunno, things just feels different. Like there's something missing between us. I could be imagining it cos nothing's really changed. I still go round Tara's after school, or hang out in town with her and the others. But there's small moments when it's almost like I'm not part of them any more. When I'm on the outside, just looking in, and I don't know what to say. I don't know what version of myself is the right one. The one who used to share paint jokes with Al, or the Megan I've always been. But it's only for a split second. Then it goes and everything feels normal again. I'm probably just being stupid.

Tara lifts her head and pokes me in the ribs. 'Megs,' she says. 'You sure you're all right?'

No, I'm not. How can I be?

'Yeah,' I say. 'I'm fine.'

Tara pauses. 'Is this about that Al?' she says. 'I know you knew him a bit from art and that, but I dunno.' She wraps her arm round me. 'Maybe some people aren't as strong as others.'

I don't even know what she means by that.

She pulls me in closer to her and I can smell her shampoo and hairspray. She doesn't say anything for a minute. She just sits there, holding on to me, like she did the day my dad died. She breathes out slowly and a part of me thinks that she knows. That she can tell that this Al stuff has brought up all these feelings about my dad.

I bite down hard on the inside of my cheek cos I don't want to start crying.

'I know you ain't fine,' she says, lowering her voice. 'But, if there's one thing I've learned about life, it's that there ain't nothing a Zinger burger and a McFlurry can't fix.' I shake my head, but I can't help but laugh.

'Am I right?' she says.

'You're right,' I say.

Tara squeezes my hand and, even though I still miss Al, I feel better. Cos it makes me think that maybe I am being stupid. Al might be gone, but everything else around me is still the same.

NATHAN

chapter seven

I used to send Nate message after message, trying to get him to come to the museum with me. I'd send pictures over WhatsApp, or try and tell him about something I'd seen there, but he'd just shrug it off and say, 'That boring shit ain't for me.' He didn't get it, but I just wanted something to make us feel close again. Something we could talk about. So that maybe he could understand why I liked the museum so much. And maybe it would help him to understand me.

I head along the pavement, stepping round all these puddles so that my trainers don't get too wet. I look up at the uni building. It's massive, stretching along most of Oxford Road. It's one of those really old places, made up of long windows and grey stone.

Pillars and roofs that spike at the top. There's a million different archways as well, all leading to a different part of the uni.

The rain starts to get heavier, so I run towards the archway that leads into the museum. Al was so smart that he could've gone here if he'd wanted to, but he was always going on about moving away from Manchester. I didn't think to ask him why cause I didn't really care and, if I'm honest, part of me just thought he was saying it to show off. To prove how clever he was, how much better he was than the rest of us. But now I think that maybe he wanted to get out cause he was running away from summat, not running towards it.

I walk inside the main entrance of the museum, passing a big group of tourists. There's an old couple and a few people with cameras round their necks. I feel them all stare at me as I walk past. The old woman moves her handbag closer to her chest, pressing her hand over the top like I'm about to rob her or summat. I'm used to that, but it still pisses me off. That people just look at me, then make their mind up – *council-estate chav, dangerous, bad* – before they've even given me a chance. They're probably wondering wot I'm even doing here cause someone who looks like me doesn't belong. Al could always go to places like this and fit in. No one would look at him all strange. It was like they could tell he was clever and that one day he'd do summat proper good with his life. It hurts to think that. Knowing that someone like Al, who could put his mind to anything, who had all these dreams, won't ever get to do any of them.

I want to find that glass cabinet, with those paper cranes

in, that Al put up on his Insta. I came here with him once before, so I kinda know where I'm going. My trainers make a squeaking sound on the polished floor as I walk, but I try to ignore it. As I make my way up the stairs, I imagine wot Al was thinking the last time he was here. Was it just like the other times he'd come, just thinking about drawing summat in one of those cabinets? Or did he know? Maybe he knew that this was gonna be his last visit.

I reach the top of the stairs, looking around me, but I can't see that cabinet with the birds in. Then summat outta the corner of my eye catches my attention. And I'm suddenly sure that I see Al standing there. He's wearing his long navy coat, his Afro sticking up at the side. I catch a glimpse of his face, his thick jawline, the shape of his nose. I know it can't be him cause I'd seen the ambulance people zip him up into one of those body bags and wheel him away, but it looks so much like Al that, when the figure walks off, I follow anyway. I walk as quickly as I can, pushing past people, barging them out the way.

'Al!' I shout. 'Al!'

I slam straight into someone, and I hear them tut, but I don't care. I start running, passing glass cases of weapons – spears, revolvers, arrows – looking around, tryna see where he went. There's crowds of people taking pictures, some kids laughing and crying. I start to feel all hot and sweaty, but I keep running. My heart is thumping, slamming hard against my chest, and there's sweat gathering at the bottom of my back, making my T-shirt and hoodie stick to me, but I *need* to find Al . . . I can't stop till I do.

I wipe away some of the sweat on my forehead, trying to stop myself from feeling dizzy. I look around at all the people, who blur into the background, merge into one, and then I turn and see him. He's standing beside one of the display cabinets, near this glass case that's got these two mummies in it, two brothers that I remember Al telling me about. I walk towards him, my throat drying out. He just stands there, slowly moving his hand across a large sketchbook, tugging at the curls at the nape of his neck.

'Al?' I say. The words come out hoarse, croaky, and seem to echo all around me. He stops drawing and I grab the sleeve of his coat.

'Al?' I repeat. He pulls his arm away as he turns round, and I expect to see Al's light brown eyes, his dark skin, the gap in his teeth . . .

But the guy standing there looks nothin like Al. He stares at me and I move backwards, shaking my head.

'Soz, yeah?' I say. 'I thought you were someone else.'

The guy looks at me like I'm some sort of weirdo, then closes his sketchbook and walks off. I lean back against one of the glass cabinets and press my hands over my face. The museum lights suddenly seem too bright and it's like there's hardly any air in here. A few people are staring at me and I can feel the sweat pouring from my forehead. They look away when I make eye contact, and I pull my rucksack tighter on to my shoulders, and move away from the cabinet.

One of the security guards in the far corner eyes me up, then takes out his radio and begins to talk into it slowly. I still wanna find those birds, tho. I walk off, in the opposite direction, my rucksack making this slapping noise as I move. I turn round another corner and pass more cabinets with stuffed animals in. I keep going, staring down aisle after aisle. I head into another room and the museum seems to open up. It feels bigger, lighter here and there's less people about.

Then I see it. That same cabinet that was on Al's Insta. I walk towards it, staring at all the tiny bits of paper that have been folded into small birds. The bits of string make them look like they're flying. Not just in the case, tho. There's more of them on the outside of the cabinet, hanging down from the ceiling and making their way across the museum. Al didn't get all that in his photo.

I lean my head against the wall behind me, staring at the birds. I start to understand why Al liked it here so much. Why he was always disappearing off to the museum. It's quiet and there's so much stuff to look at, it kinda makes you think. It doesn't even feel like you're in Manchester. It doesn't feel like you're anywhere. It's somewhere to escape everything.

I stare at one of the paper birds and I feel bad that I never tried to understand why Al liked this stuff before. I just hated him for it cause it made me feel thick. I never even questioned or thought that he might be doing all this stuff to get away. Maybe that's wot the caption was about: *Some birds are not meant to be free.* Wot if Al felt trapped? Wot if someone, or something, made him feel like there was no other way out? I need to find wotever pushed Al to do this. *Whoever* pushed him to do this.

*

I turn my key in the front door, closing it firmly behind me. It's quiet and the house is all dark. I push open the kitchen door and see Saul standing beside the microwave, heating some food up. It *pings* and he pulls the plate out, carrying it to the kitchen table with the sleeve of his hoodie covering his hand. I notice another empty wine bottle beside the recycling pile.

'Where's Mum?' I ask.

Saul bends over his plate, shovelling some food into his mouth. 'Gone Carol's,' he says. 'You hungry?'

I shrug. 'Could eat,' I say.

Saul pushes his chair back. 'Can't you always,' he says, ruffling my hair as he passes me. 'Got a stomach like a pit, you.'

'Well, at least I don't look like I fell down one.'

'Funny!' he says. 'You should be at the Apollo, not in Benchill.'

I shake my head and sit down as he puts another plate of food in the microwave for me. I see an open letter next to Saul's plate. I can't read wot it says properly, but the words FINAL NOTICE are scrawled across it in red letters. The microwave *pings* and Saul puts a plate down in front of me. He picks up the letter and shoves it in his pocket.

'I'm handling it,' he says. 'Y'know Mum hates asking for money. Rather let these pile up than ask for help.'

I pick up my fork. 'Yeah,' I say.

To be honest, I don't know wot we would've done all this time if it hadn't been for Saul. He stepped up when Dad left. He dropped outta college and started working on a building

61

site, so that he could bring in some extra money to give to Mum. So that she wouldn't have to do it all on her own.

I eat some of my tea, tho it doesn't really taste of anything. Most things stopped tasting the same after Al. Saul picks at some meat that's caught between his teeth with his knife.

'Where've you been?' he says.

I shrug. 'Just out,' I reply. 'Went to go and see Kyle and that.'

Saul watches me carefully, and I hope he won't push me any more than that cause I don't wanna explain that I've been wandering round some stupid museum, tryna get into Al's head.

Saul pushes his plate away. The love bite on his neck has turned a different colour and looks more like some sort of bruise now.

'Nate,' he says. 'I've been looking some stuff up, online and that. These nightmares . . .' Saul pauses. 'I think you should talk to someone.'

I stop eating. 'I've spoken to you.'

'I know,' he says. 'But I ain't enough. You need to talk to a doctor or someone who can help you. Who's better at that stuff than me. I can't do nothin. You've been through a lot.' Saul pauses again. 'Coming home to Al and . . .'

I stand up and try not to think of Al's face when I found him.

'I'm all right,' I say. 'I've been out. I'm seeing me mates . . . I'm *fine.*'

I make my way to the other side of the kitchen. Would Saul still care this much if he knew about the phone call? That things might be different if I hadn't ignored Al? Would he and Mum blame me for not helping Al?

62

'Nate,' Saul says. 'You ain't listening. You can't keep ignoring stuff. Don't run away from this . . . don't be like Dad.'

I pick my rucksack up off the floor. 'I ain't nothin like him!' I snap.

I leave the kitchen before Saul has the chance to say anything else.

In my room, I peel off my hoodie and unzip my rucksack. I'm mad at Saul for saying I'm like Dad just cause I don't wanna talk about shit. Wot good would it do? Nah, I need to find whoever's to blame for making Al kill himself. That's how I make things better.

I take out Al's drawing and place my thumb next to the Al on the paper. I look again at all the people surrounding him. Even tho their faces aren't there, I now see that Al's still managed to get the details of their bodies in. Some of them are broad and muscular, and one of them is long and skinny. Wot if this ain't just a drawing? Wot if it actually happened? If someone – or more than one person – had given Al a hard time? But he never said nothin. And wouldn't I have seen summat in school?

Frustrated, I throw the drawing down and climb on to my bed. I close my eyes for a minute, and, for some reason, I think about that Megan. I can hear her voice in my head, loud and clear, all high-pitched and a bit shaky: *'I wanted to do something to remember Al by. I've set up a memorial page on Facebook. I just thought people could post stuff. It might help.'*

I sit up, pull my phone out of my rucksack and open Facebook. I've got even more notifications now, but I ignore them again and type *Al Bryant* into the search bar. I wait and I watch as the grey wheel appears and the page starts to load. Al's profile comes up, then beneath it I see the memorial page. The picture is one that's been taken from his profile. I click into the page. There's also a picture of some stars uploaded as the cover photo and the caption underneath Al's picture says:

RIP, Al, the brightest star in the sky. This is for anyone who knew him, friends and family. 2003–2020.

It's actually kinda nice and I feel a bit bad for being so rude to Megan on the bus. I scroll down the page. Megan only set it up a few days ago, and it's already got 700 *likes*. The first person to comment was Megan and I stare down at her picture, filtered and posing for the camera, the brightness adjusted so that the blue in her eyes stands out. I look down the wall, past posts and YouTube clips, sad faces, song lyrics:

RIP

Gone but not forgotten

I'll miss u m8

Rest in Peace

Dnt kno wot 2 say

It won't b the same wivout u

There's a few comments from people that I know – there's one from big-gob Lauren:

RIP. I'll miss u. xxx 💔 😢

One from Kyle:

RIP m8. So sad . . . hope ur resting easy 🙏 ✒️

I scroll through comment after comment, past pictures and posts, all of them tagging Al. People have reacted with a *like* or *love* or *wow*. As if there's summat to *like* or *love* about Al being dead. Other people have commented underneath some of the posts, not even bothering to write their own. There are all these stories of Al being so smart and clever and talented. I keep scrolling till my eyes get sore and my head is crammed with comment after comment.

I take my thumb off the screen of my phone and then I stop. I'm right at the start of a thread towards the bottom. The first post is from Lewi. I stare down at it. He hasn't bothered to call round to see us. Or sent a message like everyone else has. Al's been dead for four days and Lewi, who had known Al for so long, has just stayed silent. I stare down at Lewi's post. He's written:

RIP m8, I'm so sorry.

I can't stop looking at the words. *I'm so sorry.* Wot did Lewi have to be sorry for? Cause he knows summat? Or cause he left Al when he would've needed a mate the most.

I take a screenshot on my phone, and then I click on to Lewi's Facebook profile. I don't really know wot I'm looking for, but maybe there's summat that will tell me why they fell out. And, when I think about it now, that's when Al started to change. He started spending more time in his room ... or wanting to walk to school on his own.

I scroll through Lewi's page. We've got fifteen friends in common, most of them from school, or from around Benchill and that, but Al ain't one of them. They must've unfriended each other after they stopped talking. I go to Lewi's profile pictures. There's one of him in his bedroom with a bandana pulled up over his face, one of him with his top off standing in front of the mirror at the gym. In another he's holding his dog, and there's one where he's sticking his finger up at the camera, holding a spliff and wearing a T-shirt that says: *Smoke Weed Every Day*. I click through them all till I'm right at the beginning of the album, in 2014, at Lewi's first profile picture. It's a picture of Lewi and Al in Civic Town Centre. The caption underneath it says: *Me and mi best m8. Bros 4 lyf.*

I click off Lewi's profile pics, then go to his tagged photos. There's loads of him taken with Eli and Cole. Pictures of them standing outside McDonald's in town, one of them all lined up in the gym, their muscles flexed in the mirror, even tho it's only Eli who seems to have any. There's a tattoo down Eli's forearm that says '*Defender*'. Which is Eli's stupid nickname. A photo taken about seven months ago catches my eye. It's of Lewi, Eli and Cole, standing round the back of the sports block, their arms draped over each other's shoulders. I dunno wot it is, but there's summat about Lewi in the photo that feels off. He's standing between Eli and Cole. Eli is sticking a finger up at the camera, his hoodie pulled up, so that it's covering most of his face, and it looks like he's wearing a balaclava. There's some writing . . . or drawing or summat . . . that's been scribbled on Eli's hand. Cole is laughing his head off, but Lewi looks scared. Frightened.

I didn't even realize that Lewi was hanging round with Eli and Cole. Eli's bad news – everyone knows it. And one time I saw Eli and Cole hassling Al. It was nothin major, but why would Lewi ditch his best mate to hang around with people like that? I put my phone back on my bedside table. Lewi let Al down. Wot if Al had killed himself cause he felt alone? Wot could have happened between them to make them fall out so hard?

I ain't gonna find out wot happened by looking at a few pictures, tho. I need to talk to Lewi.

I switch off my bedroom lamp and turn over in the dark. I'd planned to stay off school for as long as possible, at least then I wouldn't have to sit any of my GCSEs. But school was where I'd find Lewi, so I needed to go back on Monday. Maybe then I could figure out wot Al had been tryna tell me when he called.

MEGAN

chapter eight

There's this painting that Picasso did, of a boy leading a horse down a dirt track. The first time you look at it, you think that the boy is holding on to some reins because his fist is clenched and his arm is out at an angle. But, when you look carefully, you can see that the reins were never there. You've just imagined them. And, once you see it, once you notice that gap ... that space ... you'll never look at that painting the same way again. No matter how hard you try.

It had all been fine when we'd first got to town, going round all the shops, trying to find the right pair of jeans for Tara, or looking at tops we'd never be able to afford. And, for a bit, it all felt normal. No pain. No crying. No going over the last conversation I'd had with Al, again and again, in my head. Tara pulled me to one side as we left H&M, pushing through all the crowds on Market Street. She linked her arm through mine and stopped for a minute, so that the others could walk on ahead.

'You know you can talk to me about anything?' she said. 'I mean, I am your best mate ... right?'

I nodded and Tara looked away for a minute, like she was embarrassed that she'd even asked. We could talk to each other about almost everything. The boys we fancied, or the stuff that kicked off on our estate. The latest Beyoncé album, or this new series we'd both been bingeing on on Netflix. I could even talk to her about my dad. For ages, it was like we both kept each other's secrets. When I started going to see this counsellor after my dad died, Tara never told anyone. And, when we'd all gone drinking in the park and I threw up all over myself, Tara never took the piss. She let me stay at hers cos she knew I'd get into trouble, and she stayed up with me. The whole night. While I cried and was sick. Cried and was sick. When Tara first slept with Eli, I was the only one who knew.

And, when her mum cleared off to London for three weeks, Tara came and stayed with me. We both had each other. But I dunno, I didn't feel like I could talk to her the way that I could talk to Al. I couldn't tell Tara how much I loved art, or the fact that I secretly liked school. Or that maybe I wanted to go to uni, too. Being around Al made me realize how much more there was to life.

But Tara was still part of that. She always would be, so I just laughed. 'Don't be daft,' I said. 'You'll always be my best mate. Couldn't get rid of me if you tried.'

Tara smiled. Then we cut through TK Maxx so that we could catch up with the others, and get inside the Arndale much quicker. Then Tara started picking things up, or shoving past people, so that she could go through one of the clothes rails.

'Eh, Megs,' she said. 'D'you remember when we used to do this? Try on the ugliest thing you can find . . .'

And she started pulling on a grey jacket, and grabbing an old person's hat. We hadn't played it since we were kids. It was daft really, and it shouldn't have made us laugh as much as it actually did, but we'd always end up in stitches. I just stood there for a minute cos I didn't want to look like an idiot, even though it was only me and Tara.

'Oh, come on,' Tara said. 'You really gonna leave me hanging? I swear, you're the one who came up with this stupid thing in the first place . . .'

She ran over towards another rail, pulling on a fluorescent orange coat with all these feathers stuck to it. And I thought, *Fuck it!* So I started rummaging through all the different rails, pulling out old fleeces, or shiny PVC jackets. Tara kept shouting, 'Megs, look at this one!' I didn't even care that the others would be wondering what was taking us so long, or that the shop assistants kept giving us dirty looks. It just felt good mucking about with Tara, like we used to.

Tara had put on this coat that was covered in green and

yellow patches and was staring at it in the mirror. 'What the fuck is this?' she said. 'Looks like someone went on a bender and threw up on it.' She smelled the arm. 'Urgh, smells like someone has, too!' She turned and started fixing her hair and then her phone went. Tara stared down at the screen for a minute, then she pulled the coat off, and dumped it on top of the clothes rail.

I knew from her face, from the way everything about her seemed to change, that it was Eli. I pulled off this cape thing I had on round my shoulders. Eli and his mates were hanging about inside the food court and, of course, Tara wanted to go. She started walking towards the exit we were heading to, the one that takes you into the Arndale, but I didn't move. Part of me couldn't. I hated being around Eli. I hated the way he made me feel. But, most of all, I hated the way that Tara acted when she was with him.

Everyone in school fancies Eli, especially Tara. But personally I think they all need their heads testing. I try not to make it too obvious, but, whenever he's there, I feel myself starting to shake. I get really nervous and stressed, and sometimes, my chest goes proper tight. It's like I'm always waiting for him to say something. Take the piss or make a comment. And, I just shut down.

So I tried to think of an excuse. I told Tara I wasn't feeling well, and she said, 'What, all of a sudden? You were fine a minute ago.' Then she linked her arm back through mine. 'Come on, Megs,' she said. 'Don't be a killjoy. Thought you wanted to get some food ... and anyway we were supposed to be hanging out together.' Tara paused. 'Is this still about that Snap?'

'No,' I said.

Even though it was.

You see, Eli took this picture of me earlier this summer, before we started back at school, and I'll never forgive him for it. Tara and Eli had only kissed a few times at parties and stuff, but it wasn't till the summer that they'd started going out properly. We'd all meet up in the park and then the two of them would go off somewhere, leaving me just sitting with Eli's mates. Anyway, that day I was wearing this strappy top and didn't have a jacket on cos it was obviously too hot, and Eli took a picture of me on his phone. I didn't even know that he'd taken it till I got home and Tara called me asking if I'd seen his Snap.

She was laughing, which was what hurt the most. When I looked, I saw he'd posted the picture of me with '*when girls are flat as fuck, r u even a girl, bruv?*' written on it and a massive red arrow pointing to my chest. And Tara thought it was funny. Of course everyone in school saw it, and were laughing about it for ages. I was proper mad at first cos it's *my* fucking body. *Mine.* He had no right taking a picture and posting it to make me into some sort of joke. But it was as if none of that mattered to anyone else, like he could do what he wanted. Then a few more people shared it on their story, too, cos they thought it was so funny. There was nothing I could do, either. I just had to sit there while this picture of me went round and round. While people I didn't even know were posting things about my body – saying I should get surgery, or that I should at least have a better arse to make up for the fact I've got no tits.

I kept looking at all the stories again and again. Even though I knew the picture would still be there. Even though I knew it wouldn't make me feel any better. I just kept scrolling. It was like I wanted to punish myself for not looking the way I was supposed to. I spent ages going through Tara's Insta and all these other girls from school, or models and famous people and stuff, and I cried and cried. Not just cos of the picture, but cos I'd never look like them. I threw the strappy top in the bin and just wanted to disappear.

I thought about deleting every photo I'd ever posted, too. Cos I felt ugly. And, when I looked through my pictures, all I could see was what was wrong with me. What needed fixing. What I would never be. I just couldn't understand why Eli would do that to me. Why he thought it was okay to make me feel like shit. I'd tried to talk to Tara about it, but she just said I was being stupid and too sensitive, cos it was only a Snap. Then she laughed it off again and that hurt even more, cos Tara's supposed to be my mate and she was taking his side, saying my feelings were wrong.

Things shifted a bit after that. That's when I started to feel those moments. Those moments where I don't belong. It started with Eli's Snap. But it's only sometimes, then things go back to normal. I stood there, in the middle of TK Maxx, and I really wanted to go home. But sometimes it's like I don't have any control over my own life. I want to say no, but I don't know how to. And I don't want to let Tara down.

So I just nodded and said, 'All right, I'll come.' Even though the thought of seeing Eli made me feel sick.

Tara started to jump up and down and she threw her arms round me. Sometimes it's like she only wants me there so she can make herself feel better by putting me down. Comments about how I look, or the fact I haven't even had sex yet, or making fun of Al, the '*weirdo*' I'd hang around with in art. But then I think that maybe I'm being too sensitive. We've always been in each other's lives. And she was there for me when my dad died. When I couldn't bring myself to get out of bed, she'd lie next to me for most of the day, so that I didn't feel alone. She brought me ice cream. Phoned me every night. Tara helped me to piece my life back together.

And, even if now she did say stupid things when Eli was around, it doesn't mean that she's a bad person. It doesn't mean that I can forget everything we've been through, or how things used to be.

NATHAN

chapter nine

Do you know that there's this artist, Yayoi Kusama, who is famous for the way she uses patterns? When she notices one thing somewhere, she begins to see it everywhere, and it's like it overwhelms her. It frightens her. Her art often starts off as one thing. One symbol. One dot. Someone else might look at her work, and just think that she's painted some stupid pattern. But it's more than that: she uses her obsession with certain shapes as a way to escape. As a way to paint out the pain. So she can immerse you in her world and share her endless experience of dots and nets and mirrored space. And I think that maybe her art was a way for her to not be so scared of the world around her, you know?

Most of the weekend seems to go past in this blur, and I'm looking at Megan's Facebook page again. It's like I can't help being some weird stalker. She's changed her profile picture since Friday, to one of her and Al. It looks like it was taken in a classroom or summat, and it has to be about a year old cause Al's fro is still quite small. Megan's smiling at the camera, but Al's doing that thing he always does, where he tries to hide. I click through the rest of her pictures, even tho I've seen most of them already.

Megan's fit. *Proper fit.*

I go back further this time. There's pictures of her and the girl she was with on the bus. There's the pink *One Love Manchester* picture, from three years ago, and another one of the bee. I go back to four years ago and I stop on this one of Megan looking proper young and a guy who I guess must be her dad cause they really look like each other. I read the caption underneath:

RIP, Dad. I still can't believe that ur gone xxxx

I didn't know that Megan's dad had died. I feel bad for being so rude on the bus now. She *does* know wot it's like to lose someone. I put my phone in my pocket and pull on an old T-shirt before heading downstairs. Phoebe's already sitting at the kitchen table, eating some cereal, and wearing this frilly dress. Mum sits beside her, holding a mug of coffee. The empty wine bottle from two days ago is gone. Mum rubs at her temples, then moves a hand across her forehead, like she's trying to smooth out some of the lines.

Phoebe kicks the leg of the chair with the muddy trainers she's wearing. She picks her bowl up and drinks the milk from it, but Mum doesn't say anything like she usually does. She doesn't even notice.

I shake my head. 'Phoebes,' I say, pointing at her feet, 'wot's going on with them?'

Phoebe pulls a face. She glances at Mum for a minute, like she might get in trouble, and I sit down next to her.

'Don't see why I've gotta wear this dress,' she whines. 'Just cause we're going to church. I look *stupid*.' She looks down, folding her arms across her chest.

'Eh,' I say, lifting her chin up. 'You could never look stupid. D'you know how special you are? How perfect you are?' The corners of Phoebe's mouth move. 'But I'm telling ya,' I say, 'you need to change them trainers cos they do not go.'

Phoebe pulls a face again. I look back at Mum, but she's still staring into space. I notice that she hasn't even touched her coffee.

'Mum,' I say. 'Where's Saul?'

She snaps out of her trance, then walks over to the sink with her mug. She pours her coffee away.

'He's gone to see Lauren,' she says. 'We're going to church. I want to talk to the vicar so we can at least start thinking about the funeral.'

I shove my hands in the pockets of my tracksuit bottoms. I can't imagine wot it'll be like seeing Al in that coffin. Knowing how final it will be.

Phoebe stares at us both. 'Will I get sick, too?' she says. 'Will I get sick like Al?'

My mum's face crumples and she pulls Phoebe in for a hug.

'Sweetheart, no,' she says. 'Al had been . . . poorly for a long time. You won't get sick. I promise.'

I stare at my mum as she says this. I'm sure she can feel me looking, but she tries to ignore me. I don't like all the lies, but Mum thinks Phoebe won't understand. How do you explain something like suicide to an eight-year-old? How do you explain it to anyone really, when you think about it? I don't understand it, either. Maybe Phoebe's too young, but part of me thinks she deserves to know the truth.

Mum looks down at Phoebe's feet. 'Phoebe,' she says. 'Go and change your shoes *now*.'

I watch as Phoebe gets up and walks out the kitchen. I can tell she's not happy, but she ain't brave enough to answer back. Which is wise, if you ask me. I turn back to Mum.

'And don't you start,' she says.

'Wot?' I say. 'I didn't even say nothin!'

'I saw the look you gave me.' She pauses. 'I'll tell her when she's old enough. It will just confuse her now, upset her more.'

She picks her coat up from the back of the kitchen chair and turns to face me.

'Are you going to be okay by yourself?' she asks. 'You could always come with us to church?'

'Nah, I'm all right,' I say. 'I'm going round Kyle's anyway.'

My mum looks disappointed. I dunno why, tho, cause we've had this conversation a million times before. Stormzy could be giving the sermon, and you still wouldn't catch me there. Maybe that's how Mum deals with it all, by turning to God, but not me . . .

'Right,' she says, and, even tho I can tell she's a bit pissed, she kisses the side of my head. 'Be good. Any problems you call me, all right?'

'All right.'

She disappears into the hallway. Phoebe doesn't say anything cause she's probably still sulking about her shoes. I hear the jingling sound of keys in the door and then the slam of it closing. The house is so quiet without anyone around. I hate it when it's like this cause I just replay every single thing with Al. Not just the phone call, but how we'd drifted apart in the last year or so.

I send a WhatsApp to Kyle:

Wot u up 2? Can I cum over?

Nuffin. Cum rnd.

Then he sends me a GIF of some guy, with shades covering his face, holding a spliff in one hand, and his thumb up with the other.

B there soon

I pull one of my headphones out my ear as I knock on Kyle's door, my rucksack pulled tightly to my back. There's no answer at first, so I make my way to the front window and I bang on the glass. Kyle's dog barks from inside and I hear his sister shout, 'Door. Door! Someone's at the door!'

The front door opens and Kyle's mum stands there in her dressing gown. Her face goes a funny colour at first, a bit like Megan's did when she first saw me on the bus.

'Nathan,' she says. 'Come in, love. It's so good to see you.'

'Thanks, Caroline,' I say, walking inside. The sound of barking gets louder, and I can hear the TV blaring. There's rows of shoes shoved underneath the radiator and toys and clothes all over the floor. Kyle's is always messy and loud; nothin like mine right now. His sister, Chelsea, is in the living room, sprawled out on the carpet, watching some reality show with her friend. She looks up when I come in, then turns back to the TV.

'Kyle's been trying to get in touch with you,' Caroline says. 'I told him you probably wanted some time to yourself . . . what with everything that's happened. How's your mum? I did send some flowers.'

I stop, my foot on the edge of the stairs. I like Kyle's mum, I always have, but, if there's one thing I can't be doing with, it's the way that everyone looks at me now. Like they have to feel sorry for me just cause my brother's dead.

'She's all right,' I say. 'She got the flowers and that. I know she thought it was proper nice. It's just been a bit mad, y'know?'

Kyle's mum smiles and I almost think that she's gonna start crying on me.

'Yeah,' she says. 'I can imagine. I was in the bed next to your mum when she was pregnant with Al. I was in there with our Jamie. And I just remember how much hair Al had!' She pauses and I can tell that it's gonna come. That word, that word everyone's been saying to me. 'I'm sorry,' she says. 'I really am. He was such a lovely lad. You will let us know when the funeral is, won't you? Or if there's anything we can do?'

'Yeah,' I say and I feel a bit awkward.

That's the thing about round here, tho. Whenever anything happens, people always come together. They do wot they can to help, even if they don't have much.

Kyle appears at the top of the stairs. '*Mu-uuum*, man!' he shouts. 'Will you leave Nate alone, and stop bugging him?'

'I'm not bugging him,' she snaps back. 'And what have I told you about calling me "man"? I'm not one of your little friends, Kyle—'

'Just leave it,' Kyle says. 'He don't want you asking all them questions.'

Kyle's mum shakes her head. 'Don't be coming with your attitude while you're still under *my* roof, Kyle!' She turns to me. 'I'll see you in a bit, Nate,' she says and walks off into the kitchen. There's no way I'd wanna get on the wrong side of Kyle's mum, that's for sure.

I glance over towards the living room, and notice that Chelsea and her mate have turned the volume right down on the TV. She's staring at me with her mouth open, then she looks away, and turns the volume up again.

'You coming up or wot?' Kyle says.

Kyle's room has been the same for as long as I can remember, all these United posters stuck to his walls and a picture of Bob Marley that belonged to his brother. His room is always full of food: packets of sweets and giant Lucozade bottles and one of those big boxes of crisps that you only get from the corner shop.

He climbs across his bed, and pulls a packet of crisps out the box, chucking it over to me. I catch it and sit down on the bed next to him. FIFA is on pause on the TV in the corner.

'Been tryna get hold of you for ages,' he says. 'Thought I'd done summat wrong at first ... but me mum was saying that I should just give you time and that. She said you might not wanna talk to anyone.'

I shove a handful of crisps in my mouth. 'Yeah,' I say. 'I just ... I couldn't be doing with everyone asking me wot happened, y'know?'

Kyle shrugs. 'I get you,' he says. 'But I ain't everyone, I'm your best mate. Anyway, it's been dead boring without you. I've had to sit next to Jeremiah in science and oh my days, he don't half stink. No wonder people call him death breath. Nearly knocked me out.'

I laugh. I've missed Kyle.

He pauses. 'Is it true wot everyone's been saying? That you're the one who found him?'

I scrunch up the crisp packet in my hand. 'Yeah,' I say. 'That same day, y'know, after we'd been to the park ...'

Kyle shakes his head. 'Nate, man. I'm proper sorry.' I pick a football card up off the floor and turn it over in my hand. The edges are torn and ripped.

'If there's anything I can do,' Kyle says, 'just let me know, right?'

I wanna tell him about the phone call. How Al had tried to ring me that day when we'd been out, but I'd just cut him off. Cut him off cause I thought that wotever it was could wait. Wotever it was wasn't as important as having fun. And then I found him. But I'm scared that Kyle might say that I'm right to think it's my fault. That if I would've answered then Al would still be here.

I put the football card down, and turn to face Kyle. His face is all scrunched up, and I can see that he's got some new lines shaved into his eyebrow.

'Nate,' he says, 'I don't mean to ask and that, and you can just tell me to shut up if I'm being too nosy. But d'you know why he did it?'

I shake my head. 'Nah. Not really. But, I dunno ...' I pick up my rucksack and put it on top of his bed, then I unzip it and pull out Al's drawing. 'I found this. It's one of Al's ... I think he was in some sort of trouble, that he wanted me to find this.'

I hand the drawing over to Kyle and he unfolds it, staring down at the picture. Kyle screws his face up again, then turns it over, like he's expecting to find summat on the back.

'It's a bit weird,' he says. 'I mean, with all those faces and stuff, but it's just a drawing, innit? Al was always drawing stuff.'

'Wot about the words, tho?' I say. '*Help me*? Summat had to be wrong for him to write that ... Wot did he need help for? He didn't write a note or nothin, but he left this.'

'I mean, I write "*help me*" all over my worksheet in maths

cause I just want it to end. Doesn't mean I'm in trouble,' Kyle says. He runs his hand over the paper, across all the different figures and faces. Wotever he says, I can tell that he thinks it is a bit weird. Not just cause of the way that the faces have been scribbled out, but how the pen has torn through the paper. Like Al had been proper frantic and desperate, like all his pain had been coming out in this drawing.

'It's more than that, tho,' I say. 'I know it is. And I need to find out what happened to him. Someone must know summat. Lewi left this weird comment on Al's memorial page – saying he's sorry. Wot's he got to be sorry about?'

Kyle shrugs. 'I mean, I ain't being funny,' he says, 'but you sure you ain't reading too much into all of this? It ain't like Lewi was confessing anything in that post.'

'I know, but I just think there's summat to it. And I've been thinking about why Lewi sacked off Al for Eli and Cole. Everyone knows that Eli's a knob, so why would Lewi wanna hang around with him? And I saw him and Cole hassling Al once ...'

'Mate,' Kyle says, 'Eli hassles everyone. You should've seen him the other day with Lewi. Had him pinned up against the vending machine. Lewi was proper shitting himself. Not surprised if I'm honest ...'

'Wot? Why would Eli do that if they're supposed to be mates? It don't make no sense ...'

'I dunno,' Kyle says. 'Cause he's Eli. They probably just got into some shit or summat. I heard Eli telling him not to make it bait. Maybe they robbed someone, I dunno.'

My mind is spinning. I know that summat ain't right. Why would Eli turn on Lewi like that? Especially if they were supposed to be such good mates now. Wot if their fight had been about the comment Lewi put on Al's page? Like it was him admitting summat he shouldn't?

It weren't like Lewi was saying sorry to me or Mum or anyone cause we'd lost someone. He was saying it to Al.

I turn to look at Kyle, as he holds the drawing up underneath his bedroom light, squinting. He brings it closer, then holds it back up again, rubbing his finger over the page.

'Wot's that?' he says.

'Wot?'

He walks over to me, and sits back down on the bed.

'That thing here,' he says. 'Can't you see it?'

I take the drawing from Kyle, but it still looks exactly the same.

'I can't see nothing.'

Kyle shakes his head. 'Put your finger over that bit,' he says. 'That bit near the top . . .'

I do and I feel the texture of the paper change, like there's an indent or summat. I stare down at the drawing and see a faint outline near the top, like when you press down too hard on a sheet of paper and it goes through to the page underneath. I run my thumb along the paper and there's another one, and another one. Al must've drawn something else before he'd ripped the sheet out of his pad.

'Hold on,' Kyle says. He gets up and walks over to his school bag, emptying it out on the floor. One of those gold maths tins falls out – the ones with a compass, and a protractor, and that inside. Kyle opens it and pulls out a small pencil. He takes the drawing off me, then scribbles over the bits of white on the paper. It turns a light grey colour, then beneath it a shape shows up ... almost like a swirl, with these triangles inside it. Kyle keeps going and more of the same shape appears across the page, maybe about four or five of them. 'Should be in MI5, me,' Kyle says. 'Wot's he drawn? Is it a mountain or summat?'

I stare down at the shape. 'Looks like a symbol,' I say.

'Of wot?'

I shrug. 'Dunno, but Al's drawn it a lot. It must've been all over that other sheet of paper.'

I look at the faint shape – it looks proper familiar. Maybe Al had put it on one of his other drawings, or maybe I'd seen him doodling it at home?

Kyle picks up the PlayStation controller, and unpauses the game, moving one of his players across the pitch.

'Look, Nate,' he says, 'I know things are messed up right now. But, if Al was in trouble and stuff, you'd have known. He would've said summat ... about Lewi or wotever. Or you would've found out. He was your brother.'

Kyle presses the controller, holding his fingers down on two buttons at the same time.

Guilt weighs down on me. Kyle's right. I should've known if summat was up with Al. And maybe he would've told me if I'd have picked up the phone. Or maybe I'd have worked it out if I'd talked to him more before, instead of going off with my own mates all the time. But I didn't wanna hang around with

Al cause I thought all his museum and art shit was boring. That he was weird.

Kyle scores and I hear the sound of a fake crowd cheering from the game. The player runs about, throwing his arms up into the air.

'I mean, I know you're tryna find a reason,' Kyle says to me, still looking at the TV. 'I get it. You want it to make sense. But wot if there ain't one? Wot if he just did it?'

I shrug. He sounds like Saul, but I don't believe it. Al wouldn't have just given up on everything. Not when he had so many plans. And Al only drew things that mattered to him. That he cared about. Which meant the shapes were important.

Kyle throws the other controller towards me. 'You playing?' he says. 'Or you just gonna sit there, looking all miserable?'

I pick up the controller. 'Course I'm playing,' I say. 'And don't think I ain't gonna wipe the floor with you, either.'

'Ha,' Kyle says. 'Your head's still as big as ever then.' He clicks back towards the home screen.

I've missed this. Just doing *normal* stuff. I need it right now.

But, wotever Kyle or Saul think, tomorrow, when I go back to school, I've gotta find out wot Al couldn't tell me. I'm gonna find Lewi and talk to him. And maybe there's more to this Eli stuff. I know we'll have the inquest, but all that will do is tell me wot I already know. How Al died and the fact that he meant to take his own life.

The inquest won't get to the bottom of why Al did it, but maybe I can.

MEGAN

chapter ten

You know, one of the most interesting things about stars is that it might look like all of them are out there on their own, but lots come in pairs. They're called binary stars. Where two stars orbit one common centre of gravity. One thing pulling these two separate entities together.

It'd been two days since that shopping trip with Tara and the others in town. Meeting up with Eli and his mates had been exactly how I thought it would be. At first, Tara started up about girls who walked past, about one of them looking like a dog, or being a slag, just so that she could make Eli and everyone laugh. But then she'd moved on to me. Stupid things about how boring I was, or the fact I'd never tried drugs, or even had a proper boyfriend, and everyone else was pissing themselves about it.

Tara kept leaning over and saying, *'I'm joking, Megs – it's just banter. I love you really.'* But it hurt a lot. Eli kept smirking and staring at me. And all I kept thinking that whole time was why I'd gone in the first place and put myself in that situation. And why I didn't just get up and leave ... But it's like I was stuck.

And it made me miss Al even more.

We stayed in the food court till it was pretty late. Then Eli said that everyone could go back to his brother's flat cos it was empty and there was loads of alcohol there and Cole had a bag of weed on him. Tara begged me to go, but I'd really had enough. 'All right, be a boring cow,' she said. 'I'll call you later, all right? Message me when you get home, so I know you're back safe.'

I sent her a WhatsApp when I got in, but, even though she read it, she never replied and she didn't phone me, either.

In fact, I've not heard from her all weekend and it feels like all I've done is keep checking my phone for anything from her. So, when my mum asked me to go and get something for tea earlier cos she was having one of her migraines, I didn't moan, like I usually would. I was quite glad, to be honest, cos it gave me something else to think about. Something else to do.

I walk through the metal gates that lead on to Civic. It's usually packed on a Sunday cos everyone's rushing to get to Asda, but there's hardly anyone about today. Maybe it's cos it's almost four and everything will be closed soon. I walk past Poundland and Shoe Tree, shoving my hands in my pockets cos it's proper cold.

And that's when I see Nathan.

He's sitting on a bench wearing a grey tracksuit, with his hood pulled up. He's just sort of *staring*. Not at anything exactly, but into space. It's weird cos he's sitting on mine and Al's bench. We used to sit there for hours and I liked it cos we just talked and talked and no one bothered us. I never would've told Al this, but the other reason I liked it was cos no one else would see us. Most people from school went to the Trafford Centre or town, and Tara hardly ever hung around Civic. It hurts to think about it now. How much I could share with Al, but that I was embarrassed to be seen with him, too.

When I was with Al, I felt like I could be more myself than with anyone else. I could be the Megan who didn't give a fuck about *likes* or what people thought about me or if I fitted in or if I was pretty enough. He'd helped me think about uni and a future away from here.

And all I gave him for that was a secret friendship on a grubby bench.

I stop, right in the middle of the walkway, cos Nathan looks so much like Al that for a minute it's like I've gone back in time. I can see the memories, one after the other: me and Al sharing a bag of those fizzy sweets you get from the pound shop, Al showing me the drawings he was working on in his sketchbook, me telling him a rubbish joke and Al cracking up.

I feel this pain tear right through me. I'm never going to sit on that bench sharing shit jokes with Al again. And I'm suddenly exhausted. Sick and tired of having to hide who I really am. Making out that I'm having fun with Tara and that lot when, deep down, all I really feel is alone.

Pushed out.

Different.

Deep down, I knew that Al felt like that, too, but I ignored it. Only thinking about how it would look if people knew how close we were. But I should have paid more attention, been a better friend and not worried all the time about what people might say if they saw us together.

The last conversation I'd had with Al on that bench – the last conversation we *ever* had – comes back to me. It was a few days before Al died and he'd been *proper* upset. Going on about the old town hall building in the park being set on fire. Which was weird cos that was old news and they started fixing it up ages ago. But he kept talking about people destroying things and I just thought he was being typical Al, getting upset about stuff most people never really think about. I was only half listening, not in a horrible way, but my mind was busy with all these other things – like school and exams and the fact that people were still going around calling me *pancake tits* after Eli's Snap.

I can't even remember what I'd said or how we'd said goodbye. But maybe Al was disappointed in me for not listening properly. Maybe he was waiting for me to say something to let him know how much he mattered . . . How much the world needed him.

And I let him down. I should've done more. I should have noticed that Al, who always seemed so strong, so brave, so bright, was crumbling right in front of me.

I walk up to Nathan and he doesn't seem to notice me at all at first. He was rude the last time I saw him so I'm not expecting much, but I know that if I walk off and pretend that I haven't seen him then I'll regret it. Just like I do with Al. I try to act all normal, but then I start to feel embarrassed and nervous. And I wish that I'd done my hair properly, or at least bothered to put some make-up on. When he finally looks up, Nathan gives me a funny look, and I feel even worse cos he probably just thinks I'm a right weirdo.

'Hi!'

In my head, it was supposed to come out friendly and cool, but it just comes out all croaky and strained. Like I've been possessed. *For fuck's sake, Megan*, I think. But Nathan sort of smiles.

'You all right?' he says, pulling his hood down.

It's funny cos him and Al look so similar that they could almost be twins, apart from the eyes. Nathan's are dark green, with flecks of yellow in them. Although I can see that the white bits are red, like he's either been crying or smoking.

I sit down next to him on the bench. He looks down at the ground, staring at this flower. Part of it has been trodden into the ground, and some of its petals are missing. But it's still sort of pretty. These bright white petals surrounded by all this muck and chewing gum.

Al taught me that. To try and find the beauty in stuff. In whatever was around you.

'I know Al used to come here,' Nathan says. 'To do some of his drawings and that. He'd just sit here for hours.' He shrugs. 'I mean, I don't really get why. It's just Civic, innit?'

I smile. 'I didn't get it at first, either. But Al could make anything look . . .' I trail off.

Nathan nods. 'I keep thinking he's gonna turn up,' he says. 'That any minute Al's just gonna come strolling down there, with his lanky self and massive fro. And all of this will just be some messed-up dream. I just wish I'd paid more attention, y'know?' He shoves his hands deeper into his pockets, but he still doesn't look at me.

I lean back against the metal bench. I keep thinking about my dad and how I felt when he died. You think that once you've been through something like that nothing will ever hurt as much again. But I suppose that's not the way it works.

'It was like that with my dad,' I say. 'He used to go on about all this stuff and I'd just think, *Yeah, yeah, whatever.* But I wish I would've listened. Or I at least had a day when I could go back into it all and properly pay attention to the small stuff . . . All the things he did that I didn't think anything of. When really he was showing me how much he cared. How much he loved me. I know it sounds dumb, but I just want to see those moments again. Live them again.'

Nathan stares at me for a minute, and I'm suddenly properly embarrassed. I can feel myself going red, but he just nods a few times.

'Maybe that's why I keep doing all this dumb shit. Sitting on this bench ... going to the museum.' He shrugs again. 'I just wanna understand. I just wanna feel close to him. Again.'

We sit in silence for a bit. I expect it to feel awkward, but it doesn't.

'What happened to your dad?' he asks after a while.

'Car accident,' I say. I suddenly notice how cold it is, and I pull the zip of my coat up, to cover my neck.

'He just lost control of the wheel. Even though he'd been driving for most of his life. One minute he was here, then the next ... It still doesn't make sense.'

Nathan looks at me. 'Been tryna work it out myself.' He pauses. 'Thanks, yeah, for setting up the page. I didn't mean to go on like a knob when we met.'

I shrug. 'At least you can admit when you've been a knob – that's more than most people.'

He laughs, and I notice that our knees are touching. He must realize, too, cos he gets a bit funny, then moves over.

'Only someone who really knew Al would've put those stars as the cover photo.'

I smile, but part of me feels numb. Cos if I *really* knew Al then I should've been able to tell that he was upset, shouldn't I? My eyes start to sting. But I don't want Nathan to see me cry, so I pretend to look around.

'Took me ages to find the right stars,' I say. 'I wanted to get it right cos it was Al's dream, y'know? And maybe it's just a cover photo, but I wanted it to be how Al imagined it.'

'He would've been chuffed,' Nathan says. Then he

94

pauses for a minute. 'Did Al ever talk to you about some symbol?' he asks.

It's so random that it catches me off guard. 'What you on about?'

'I dunno. I'm just tryna remember if he said summat about a symbol . . . or maybe it's that stupid maths thing. Like how you get numbers in a pattern and that.'

I burst out laughing and Nathan gives me a funny look. I know *exactly* what he's talking about. Al was always, always going on about lots of things, but he was *really* into this pattern. He told me about it after he showed me this artist who was obsessed with dots. He loved it when things made sense, or when one fact would lead him on to something else.

'The Fibonacci pattern?' I ask.

'I dunno. I just remember Al saying that there was this one pattern that you could find everywhere.'

'Yeah, that's it,' I say. 'You work out what the next number is in the pattern by adding the two numbers before it. Al told me that it's everywhere . . . in art, plants, space and in certain shapes as well. Swirls and spirals. Al used to do it in his art all the t—' I stop cos Nathan is looking at me in this really weird way. 'What?' I say.

He shakes his head. Then he leans forward, staring at the ground. 'Nothing. It's just . . . you're a bit like him, y'know?' he says. 'Like the way your face lit up when you were talking about all those numbers and shit.' He laughs. 'I can see why you were mates. You're both geeky saddos.' He laughs and nudges me.

'Oh, shut up,' I say, nudging him back. 'You're the one who brought it up in the first place.'

Nathan smiles, and, even though we're both here cos of Al, I can't help but smile, too.

He reaches down and picks the flower up off the ground, staring at the petals. He looks at me like he's about to say something else, but my phone vibrates in my pocket. I pull it out, even though I already know it's going to be my mum wanting to know why I'm not back. If she knows that I've not even been to Asda yet, she'll have a proper fit. I don't answer the phone, but I stand up, even though a part of me just wants to stay there with Nathan.

'I'd better go,' I say.

Nathan holds the flower out to me.

'Here,' he says. 'I'm sorry about your dad, yeah? I know I didn't know him or nothing, but I reckon that if he was still around then he'd be proper proud of you.' He looks at the ground again. 'Only someone dead clever and kind could be friends with Al and get him the way you did.'

I stare at the flower, and, even though I know that it's a trampled-down thing that some poor idiot dropped, I can't help but feel sort of touched by it. I take it, and he pulls his hood back up over his head.

'I'll see you around, yeah?' I say.

'Yeah, see you around,' he says, then he shoves his headphones into his ears.

I walk off towards the shops and it starts to rain. Before I get to the double doors that lead into Asda, I turn and take a final look back at Nathan. He's still on the bench, sitting there in the rain, hunched over, just a grey tracksuit blurring into the distance, not bothered by the rain lashing down on him.

NATHAN

chapter eleven

I told Lewi about the Fibonacci sequence once. We were sitting in my room, after his mum's boyfriend had given him a black eye, and I told him how special it was because the shapes of spiral galaxies and hurricanes follow it. Everything in nature and art follows it and once you add up the numbers you'll start to see it everywhere. Lewi just shook his head, but he put his arm round me. 'This is why we're best mates,' he said. 'You're dead clever and you know all this cool stuff. We're so different . . . but that's why it works. I can't ever imagine not being mates with you.' And, even though he was probably still in pain from his eye, he leaned back on my bed and kept repeating, 'Fibonacci, Fibonacci, Fibonacci,' like he was trying not to forget.

I turn on the shower and let the water hammer down on me. I dunno wot time I got in last night, but I sat on that bench for a while after Megan left, listening to music and waiting for the rain to stop. My mind wouldn't stop thinking about that symbol and wot it meant to Al.

I turn the shower off, then reach for my towel and make my way back to my room. I get dressed for school quickly. I stare at my reflection in the mirror. There's these dark circles under my eyes, and my skin has gone a weird colour. I flatten the top of my hair. I could really do with going to the barber's, and getting it trimmed and that. It never grows into a thick Afro, like Al's or Saul's, just goes all weird and sticks out everywhere when I don't get a trim. I pick up my school tie and try and do it up, but my hands start to shake and my palms are suddenly all sweaty. I see Al hanging, the green and black stripes knotted round his neck. My chest tightens and it's almost like I can feel my own tie squeezing my windpipe, tryna cut off those last bits of air. I pull it off and throw it to the floor. They send us home if we don't have the right uniform, but I don't care. I don't think I'll ever wear a tie again.

I pick up my school bag and shove Al's drawing inside. I couldn't sleep last night so I just lay there, working out wot I need to do today, who to talk to, how to get through being around everyone at school again. Lewi first, to find out wot him and Al fell out about and why he put 'sorry' on that post. Then Eli and Cole. When you think about it, how likely is it that the time I saw them hassling Al was the only time?

My phone *pings*. Kyle's sent me a picture of a girl in her underwear that he's taken from Insta. He's written *Proper fit!!!* with three fire emojis. *She goes 2 MEA dwn the road. Look at this 1!* He sends another picture, this time of her standing in front of a mirror in a tight dress. She's used one of them Snapchat filters, so there's all these pink hearts floating round her head. Kyle's always sending me screenshots of girls he thinks are fit and it gets on my nerves sometimes cause my phone ends up full of pictures of girls I don't even know. And today it's more annoying than usual cause it's like he's forgotten about wot I said yesterday ... that I have more important stuff to deal with. I don't type anything back, just delete the picture and make my way downstairs.

Mum and Phoebe are sitting at the kitchen table and Saul's standing beside the cooker, frying some bacon in a pan. The love bite on his neck is just a faint mark now, and his muscles bulge through the vest he's wearing. My phone *pings* in my pocket again, but it's just gonna be Kyle sending me a picture of another girl, and I can't be bothered to look.

'Nate!' Phoebe says.

'All right, trouble,' I say, wrapping my arms round her.

Phoebe nods, and my chest tightens. I *never* want anything to happen to her. Maybe I couldn't look out for Al, but I have to make sure that she's okay. Be the same kind of big brother Saul has been for me and look after her. I need to make sure that she always knows how much I love her. That she can tell me anything.

'You don't smell any more,' Phoebe says. 'Maybe God does answer prayers!'

'Don't be cheeky!' I say and tickle her. She starts laughing, wriggling about in her chair.

'You're going back to school?' Mum says, clocking my uniform.

I shrug. 'Yeah, I can't take too long off. Like you said, I've got exams coming up and that.'

She smiles and I feel bad for lying, but it ain't like I can tell her that I only wanna go back to school so I can find out who's to blame for Al. I don't give a toss about my exams. I never have. The only thing I care about is the truth. I owe it to Al.

The bacon crackles in the pan, and Saul turns it over with a spatula. I haven't seen him properly since the other night, since he said that I should try to talk to someone.

He turns to face me. 'You sure you ready for this?'

Nah. I ain't. I can't be doing with the questions and the looks, I think.

'Of course he's ready,' Mum snaps. 'You know how important his GCSEs are. Besides, getting back into a routine might help.' She pauses. 'But if it does get too much, Nate, please, just let someone know . . .' She trails off and glances at Al's empty chair that no one has sat in since it happened.

Phoebe picks at some loose skin by the nail of her thumb. And, for a second, I see something flash across Saul's face. He looks broken, upset. He turns back to the frying pan and it's gone so quickly that I wonder if I'd imagined it. It's like we can all feel it – Al's absence – stretching out between us.

101

And we know, all of us, that we'll never go back to being the same. How can we?

'All right,' Saul says, and he slides some bacon on to a plate. He holds it out to me. 'Nate? You want some?'

Normally, I would've shovelled it down, but I don't really feel like eating anything. I shake my head. 'Nah, I'm good.'

It's still early, but I don't wanna wait around. I grab my hoodie off the back of one of the kitchen chairs. Mum smiles at me like I've actually done summat right for once. I can't remember the last time she looked at me like that.

'Take it easy,' Saul says as I walk out. 'Any problems, you let me know, all right? I'll keep my phone on me at work.'

I pick up my rucksack. 'I'll be fine,' I say. 'I'll see you in a bit, yeah?'

Saul nods and Phoebe shouts bye, with her mouth full of food, as I head out the kitchen.

I shove my headphones in my ears and turn my music all the way up. I head down my road, the sound of Stormzy drowning out the traffic and the other noises around me. Maybe if I did try at school then I'd be all right. If I bothered to do the homework, or pay attention in lessons, but I hate it all. It's not like I was good at anything anyway, so wot was the point?

I turn the corner, the lyrics filling my head, and walk past all these other kids making their way to school. I'd usually jump the tram with Kyle, but I can't be doing with seeing everyone on there, asking me all these questions, tryna talk to me about wot happened.

I keep walking till I can see my school in the distance, all these brown bricks, with a few painted green, or yellow, or red, to make it look better. More exciting, I guess. They'd tried their hardest not to make it look like a dump, but it hadn't really worked.

I pass a group of kids and my palms begin to sweat. Some of them are laughing and joking, but most of them are staring at me, or whispering and that. I pull my hood up and turn the volume down on my phone so I can hear wot they're saying.

'His brother . . .'

'D'you know he killed himself?'

'That guy in Year Twelve . . . the one with the fro.'

'The tall one.'

'The dopey one.'

'Dead.'

'I heard he found him.'

'I heard he slit his wrists.'

'Nah, he did it with his tie . . .'

'Did you write on his wall?'

'Who kills themself, though?'

'I'd kill myself if I was that ugly, too.'

'Don't be tight.'

My heart starts to pound harder in my chest. I don't wanna listen any more, so I turn the volume right up again. It feels like my eardrums are about to burst with the beat, but it's better than hearing any more whispering about Al.

As I walk towards the main entrance, someone grabs my arm from behind and I turn round quickly, getting ready to go off, but then I see it's Megan. She's outta breath, and her face is all red, like she's been running.

'I was shouting you from all the way down there. You walk like a maniac!' She pauses to fan her face. 'I didn't know you were coming back today. You should have said something yesterday.'

I slow down and she falls into step beside me. Megan moves her hair away from her face – she is *definitely* pretty. She smiles and I feel a bit awkward. When she told me about her dad yesterday, I felt proper bad for her. She looked all cut up and that, but I didn't know wot to say or nothing, so I just gave her that stupid flower. She probably thinks I'm a right idiot, picking shit up off the ground. It had been so easy to chat to her and part of me was proper gutted when she had to go. Megan moves her hair again and I feel myself getting all hot.

'Yeah,' I say. 'I couldn't stay off any longer. It was doing me head in.'

Megan nods. 'I've been going to the art room at lunch . . . no one else bothers to come up. If it gets a bit noisy today, you can always come find me. It's nice because you're on your own, you know?' She pauses. 'Guess that's what happens when you're a geeky saddo.'

I laugh. 'You ain't ever gonna let me forget that, are ya?'

'Nope.'

'Wot if I take it back?'

'Too late – the damage has been done.'

Megan smiles and I pull my hood down, flattening the top

104

of my hair. I dunno if she really wants me to go up there later, or if she's just saying it cause she feels sorry for me. I feel like I'm supposed to say summat else, but I dunno wot. I stuff my hands in my pockets and we head towards the glass door that leads into the main school entrance. I start to feel nervous and I just think: *Ask her anything, you idiot. Just say summat.* But then I hear a voice behind us.

'Nathan Bryant. You stop there right now.'

I turn round and see Ms Weir who works on the reception desk. I shake my head. The last thing I wanted was all the teachers sticking their noses in or making a fuss. Megan points towards the door, looking back at me, then at Ms Weir.

'Good luck. She can chat for England, her,' she says. 'I'll catch you later?'

I kick the edge of my shoe against the ground. 'Yeah, catch ya later.'

Megan walks through the glass door and heads along the corridor. Ms Weir comes over to me and places both her hands on my shoulders. I hate it when teachers touch you like that. She leans forward, like she's about to give me a hug or summat, but then she stops herself.

'I didn't know you were coming back, Nathan,' she says. 'No one said anything.'

'Just decided.' I shrug. 'Didn't think it was a big deal.'

She sighs slowly, then points towards the green sofas, the ones that parents and visitors usually sit on.

'Take a seat there,' she says. 'I know that Mr Ballan will want to speak to you.'

I have to grit my teeth so I don't say summat I regret. Mr Ballan hates me. Why would I wanna see him? The headteacher who was so close to kicking me out? I'd lost count of the amount of times I'd been in his office. It was always for the same things: smoking, or having fights, backchatting the teachers and getting kicked outta lessons. All the usual crap.

I turn to Ms Weir. 'Wot for?' I say. 'Am already gonna be late.'

'Don't worry,' she says. 'You're not in trouble. Mr Ballan will just want to make sure that you're ... *okay*. I'll call him now, and tell him to come and collect you. But do me a favour? Take your hoodie off. You know you're not supposed to be wearing it indoors.'

I kiss my teeth and pull my hoodie off, then sit down on one of the chairs. I can't be doing with Mr Ballan pretending to be all nice to me. Not when I could be getting on with things. Not when I could be tracking down Lewi.

Ms Weir picks up the phone, talking in a low voice, and I watch as more kids rush past me, worried that they're gonna be late. I look round at the display boards – they haven't changed in forever. There's all these crosses that have been painted or coloured in, along with all these different coloured faces. *Equality and faith. Working together to learn together* it says at the bottom. Which is a load of crap cause hardly anyone in this school works together. I look at the two television screens above the door, which always have this film constantly on repeat. There's two closed hands, one with *faith* written on it, and the other with *love*. They open and close, showing more words inside the outstretched palms: *Loving to learn and learning to love. Forgiving and loving those around us.*

I screw up my face and watch the video a few times. There's a few kids here who believe in God, but most don't. It's supposed to be one of the best schools in Wythenshawe, tho, so people go to church for a few weeks so they can pretend to be religious and send their kids here. Our dad used to say he believed in God. But fucking off and abandoning your kids ain't very godly if you ask me.

The first bell rings and I stare at the glass pane that overlooks the corridor. I see a few people heading to form, rushing past and pulling their hoods down or taking their caps off. Then I see Lewi. He's walking with Eli and Cole. Eli is scrolling through his phone, laughing and showing summat to Cole. Lewi ain't laughing or even looking.

I stand up, rushing over towards the glass pane so that I'm directly in front of Lewi. He stops and I look him straight in the eye. Summat flashes across his face. Like he's just seen a ghost. Eli and Cole stare at me, too. Then Eli nods his head and mouths, '*Safe*,' then he places his arm round Lewi and moves him on. He's almost pushing Lewi along the corridor.

Lewi hadn't looked sad when he saw me, or even sympathetic. Nah. He'd looked scared . . . like he had summat to hide.

I turn to go after them, but then I hear the heavy footsteps of Mr Ballan behind me. He reaches me before I have time to go through the glass door.

'Nathan,' he says, putting his hand on my shoulder and blocking the way. 'Come with me, son.'

I wanna tell him that I *ain't* his son. And I definitely don't want him to touch me. But I don't say nothing. The sooner this is over, the better. I pull my rucksack further up my shoulders and follow Mr Ballan to his office.

MEGAN

chapter twelve

I'd try to tell Megan all the time that unless you had something to say, or some pain to share, then there wasn't any point. Because that's what you were supposed to do with art: you were supposed to make someone look at the world differently. And, even though I didn't talk about it, everything I felt when Dad walked out ... everything that happened after ... I tried to sketch and draw and use art to express my feelings. Because that's the whole point of art: to show things from your point of view, to make people see the world through different eyes ...

The first bell goes and I make my way into school. I turn back to glance at Nathan, but he isn't even looking in my direction. He's too busy screwing up his face at something Ms Weir is going on about. Which doesn't surprise me cos that woman loves to chat like there's no tomorrow, next week or next year. The corridor is pretty packed and I push past people to get to form.

I would never admit this to anyone, but you should've seen the way I carried home that flower Nathan gave me. I was just glad that it was dark otherwise I would've looked like I needed locking up. Walking home with an Asda bag full of food and holding this shit, crumpled flower like it was the most important thing anyone had ever given me. I did think about chucking it in the bin. I mean, it had been on the floor in the middle of Civic, which meant that it was probably covered in piss or goz or something disgusting like that. And it did look pretty pathetic, all trampled down on one side with a few of its petals missing, but it felt like more than a flower . . . I can't explain it, but, in a way, it made me feel a bit closer to Al. Maybe it was cos Al was always picking shit up off the ground so he could draw it. Or maybe it was what Nathan said about me being just like Al. Or my dad being proud of me. It just felt like there was more to it. And I guess it made me feel close to Nathan, too, which I quite liked.

I'm not even sure why I told Nathan about the art room, but he'd looked a bit lost and it always makes me feel better being alone in the classroom. It's the one place in school where I can hide, where I can escape, and I know that Al felt the same. So I thought Nathan might like it, too.

I lean back against the wall outside my form room. There's already a few people there, waiting for the second bell to ring.

The corridor is proper noisy and I just watch as everyone carries on. Scrolling through their phones, taking selfies, watching videos, shoving into each other. Laughing. It's only been seven days and it's like Al never existed.

Al's life is over and no one here even cares.

A group of kids in the year below pass me. I hear one of them, this boy with an Afro comb stuck in his hair, say something about Al. I don't hear what he says, but they all start laughing. Hard and loud. The one with the Afro is doubled over, laughing so much that he has to cover his face with his hands. One of his mates is leaning against a display board, proper cracking up. I hear him say: 'Nah, that's deep. That's deep.' And then they walk off.

I feel an arm link through mine and turn to find Tara standing next to me.

She rests her head on my shoulder. 'Eh, Megs,' she says. 'Missed you this weekend. You should've come to Eli's brother's. We all got proper smashed! That Cole made a right fool of himself. I swear, you should've seen it . . .'

I try to force a smile, even though I feel a bit hurt. It's not like I didn't message her; she just didn't get back to me. And now it's as if it's all my fault for not going with them to Eli's brother's place.

'Have you seen Jeremiah's Snap?' she says, pulling her phone out of her pocket. 'It's tight, but it's proper funny.' She laughs and scrolls through her phone, then brings up Jeremiah's Snapchat story. Some photos appear, one of him taking a selfie in the mirror, another one of him smoking before school, a video of him running out of a shop after stealing a chocolate bar, one of him pulling a prank on this old woman at a bus stop. I'm bored already. Jeremiah's always been an idiot, so it's not like Tara's showing me anything new. I look at her and she can probably tell that I'm getting impatient cos she brings her phone closer.

'Just wait,' she says.

And then I see it flash up. A picture of Al, the same one I'd put on the Facebook memorial page. But a filter's been put on his face and his features have been stretched out so much that it doesn't really look like him any more. His lips have been made bigger and his face wider. Jeremiah's put the caption:

> When ur so ugly, even God's pissed that he'll have
> 2 look at u

with the screaming emoji, skeleton face and laughing-crying face.

Tara laughs. I feel sick. That's what those boys must've been laughing at. Al's dead and people are making a *fucking* joke about it. I move away from Tara. Al isn't some stupid meme. He was a person.

Tara nudges me. 'What's wrong?' she says. 'I mean, I know it's a bit tight, but you've gotta admit it. Jeremiah *is* pretty funny.'

I stare at her. Even though I hid how much Al and I hung out, Tara still always made snide comments about Al. Saying that I secretly fancied him, or that he smelled, or that he

112

looked like he had something wrong with him. All those times I just used to stand there and smile. Not say anything back cos I didn't want to piss her off. I didn't want to cause an argument, or give Tara a reason to push me away even further, to like me less.

'Megs?' Tara says.

The second bell rings and I see our form tutor reach our classroom down the corridor and unlock the door. People start to go in, but I don't want to be around Tara. I don't want to be around any of them.

'You think it's funny?' I say.

Tara stares at me. 'Wha—'

'Al's dead and you think it's a joke?'

Tara pulls a face. 'I didn't upload it.'

'No,' I say. I can feel my voice shaking, but I don't care. 'You're sharing it, though. You're laughing about it. You're showing me . . . Why would you do that?'

'Oh, come off it,' Tara says. 'It ain't like you two were dead close or nothing. And anyway everyone gets shit said about them online. It's just banter.'

I freeze.

Banter.

My throat tightens. 'Al killing himself is not "banter". You think his family are going to sit around and laugh? This is someone's life,' I say. 'And actually he *was* my friend. We were "dead close". But, even if we weren't, Al was someone's son, someone's brother, and you—' I stop cos part of me wonders what the point is. Why I'm even standing here, having this conversation with Tara, in the first place. 'Sometimes I don't know why I bother with you,' I say. Tara looks hurt, but I don't care. I turn and walk off. Our form tutor comes out of the classroom and I hear her shouting after me, but I don't turn round.

I feel weirdly free as I head up the first set of stairs. I'm glad that I've finally told the truth about me and Al. No one in this school knew just how close we were cos I kept that hidden. I'm never going to do that again. Hide what I like, who I like, for the sake of fitting in. I used to think that having no one to hang around with would be the worst thing ever. But hanging around with people who make you feel bad, who constantly say snide things about you, or push you out, that's even worse.

I open the art-room door and sit down at an empty table, breathing in the smell of the wet paint and charcoal, and it reminds me so much of Al that I have to hold back the tears that spring to my eyes. I've realized too late that I shouldn't have cared about what people thought of our friendship. I just wish that I could go back and do things differently. Hang around with him in public and not care about being seen. Stand up for him when I should have. I wish I'd listened more and let him know that he could've come to me about anything.

I put my head in my hands, the words of Jeremiah's Snap spiralling in my mind:

When ur so ugly, even God's pissed that he'll have
2 look at u

Al was smart, kind, talented, but no one cares about that.

I'm really crying now and I don't know what else to do, so I go and pick up my sketchbook from the side, open it up and start to draw. And even though I miss Al like mad, even though Jeremiah's Snap is still going around, even though I've had a fight with Tara ... sitting here, in our place, sketching, makes me feel so much better.

NATHAN

chapter thirteen

Do you know that if two pieces of the same metal touch when they're in space then they will bond permanently? It's called cold welding and it happens because the two pieces have no way of knowing that they're separate. It doesn't happen on earth because air and water are always between the pieces. But in space there's nothing to keep them apart and by just touching each other they become bonded forever.

Mr Ballan closes his office door behind me, and points to one of the seats. I've been in here so many times that I already know where everything is. Which seat ain't broken, or doesn't sag in the middle. Where I can sit without Ballan spitting all over me. There's a cross nailed to the wall behind him, with the same words that are in reception: *Loving to learn and learning to love.*

I drop my rucksack on the floor beside my feet, and Mr Ballan sits down in the chair opposite me.

'Nathan, it's good to have you back,' he says, smiling.

I look away. The amount of times I've been in trouble, I know that he's lying, but I just wanna get outta here as quickly as possible.

'Your mum didn't mention that you were coming back yet,' he says. 'It's a good job Ms Weir spotted you. Anyway, never mind that. You're here now and I just wanted to let you know that we're all here to help in whatever way we can. We can sort out extra revision classes and I've already written to the exam board on your behalf to let them know that there's been ... extenuating circumstances.' He leans closer. 'And Nathan, if you want to talk to me about anything, anything at all, my door is always open.'

I stare at him, hardly able to believe that this is the same Mr Ballan who told me that I was close to getting kicked outta school a few months ago and that I'd leave without any GCSEs, amount to nothing, if I didn't sort my attitude out.

'Thanks, yeah,' I say. 'But I'm good. I don't need to talk to anyone.'

'I understand,' he says with another fake smile. 'But maybe, if you don't want to talk to a member of staff, then you could go and talk to God? The chapel is always open if you ever want to go in and pray. It's times like this, Nathan, times when the world seems cruel and dark, that we need our faith the most. That we realize just how important it is.'

I stare at him. I wish I could tell him to do one. To shove his stupid school and his stupid crosses and all that crap about *loving to learn* cause it never helped anyone. Al was probably the one who believed in God the most, but it didn't help him. I pick up my rucksack. I can't be doing with all this, with Mr Ballan pretending that he cares.

'Yeah, sir,' I say, standing up. 'Can I go to my lesson now?'

He nods. 'Nathan,' he says. 'You will get through this, you know.'

I shrug and head back towards the reception area. I'll 'get through this' like it's some exam I haven't bothered to revise for. Or a shit PE lesson. How do you ever 'get through' losing someone? Wot a load of crap.

First lesson has already started, but I don't wanna go to English, I just need to find Lewi and then get the hell outta here. I make my way up the stairs that lead to the sixth-form block. I dunno which classroom Lewi will be in, but he has to be here somewhere. I walk along the corridor, looking in each of the windows at the top, pushing my face against the glass so that I can see who's inside. Some of the kids see me looking in, and some of the teachers do, too, but I don't care. I just keep going. I head to the last classroom along the corridor and then I stop. In the corner, sitting by himself on one of the back tables, is Lewi. Cole is sitting just in front of him, leaning back in his chair and listening to music through his headphones. Eli's not there. Lewi looks shit, like he ain't slept in weeks. Some girl throws a screwed-up piece of paper at the back of his head and he doesn't even flinch, doesn't even turn round. He just sits there, staring into space, like he doesn't really know where he is.

I rest my hand on the door handle. I wanna go in and confront Lewi, ask him about Al, but I haven't thought this through. Not properly. He's not gonna say anything now. Not in front of the whole class. And if I just barge in the teacher will probably send me packing and all. No, I need to get Lewi on his own.

I turn to go, but, just as I move, I slam straight into Eli. He stares at me, then back at the classroom door.

'You fancy him or summat?' he says. 'Cause you were staring at him before, and now you're following him about like some sort of bitch.' Eli smirks, and I can feel my hands start to shake.

'I just wanna ask him summat.'

'I wouldn't bother if I were you,' he says. 'He ain't into boys ...' He eyes me up, then laughs, opening the door and releasing a flood of noise from the classroom into the corridor. I watch as he heads over to a table at the back, sitting down next to Cole. He leans towards him and says summat. They both look over at me and I wonder wot they're saying. Lewi hasn't moved at all, even to acknowledge Eli. I know there's no point in me hanging around, looking like some sort of idiot, so I head off, in the direction of my first lesson. Lewi will have to wait. I need to find a way to talk to him alone.

Kyle's already in English by the time I get there. Some of the other kids are sleeping with their heads on the desks and only a few of them are bothering to do their work. We've got some supply teacher who doesn't even seem arsed that I'm late. Kyle's face lights up when he sees me and I sit down next to him.

'Weren't sure if you were coming in,' he says. 'Didn't see you on the tram this morning. You could've given me a shout.'

I dump my rucksack on the table. 'I couldn't be doing with everyone asking me about it and that. I've already had Ballan banging on with his God talk. Calling me "son".'

Kyle smirks. 'You know it's serious when Ballan starts going on, like he's your dad. Just hope he didn't spray you with his spit.'

'Nah,' I say. 'You sit in the broken chair and it don't reach you.'

I look round the classroom. There's a few people staring at me and nudging each other. I pull my pen out and try to ignore them. I dunno if I should say anything to Kyle about Lewi cause I know he thinks I'm reading too much into all of this, but I can't keep it to myself and maybe Kyle can help.

'I went to find Lewi,' I blurt out. 'I saw him come in this morning and he was acting all weird. So I went to his class, yeah? And you should've seen him. He looked proper messed up.' I pause. 'He knows summat about Al. I'm telling you, *he does*.'

Kyle stares at me. 'Nate, man, not this again,' he says. He leans back in his chair so that the front two legs are off the floor. 'His best mate's dead. I know that him and Al stopped talking or wotever, but they'd known each other for ages. Course Lewi's gonna be acting all weird. He's upset!

That's why he's going round looking like that, not cause of anything else.'

'But wot about that fight you said he had with Eli?' I say. 'Eli telling him not to "make it bait".' I pause. 'And, when I think about it, you should've seen the way Eli was acting as well. It's like he's tryna keep me away from Lewi. He moved Lewi on in the corridor when I first saw them and then, when I went to Lewi's classroom, he more or less told me to do one.'

Kyle puts his head in his hands. 'Jesus, you're worse than me mum with her conspiracy theories,' he says. 'So wot, now you think Eli knows summat as well?' Kyle picks up his pen and puts it in his mouth, chewing on the lid.

'Yeah,' I say. 'I do. Maybe Eli's protecting Lewi or summat. Why else would he stop me from talking to him? Maybe Lewi said summat to upset Al? Wot if they all did, him and Eli? Or wot if Al tried to turn to Lewi when he was upset, and Lewi sacked him off? Al could've killed himself cause he felt like he didn't have anyone.' My gut twists at that last bit. Even if Al did try and speak to Lewi, it wouldn't have just been his best mate that let him down when he needed someone ...

Kyle spits his pen lid out. 'D'you know how mad you sound?' he says. 'I just don't get why you're so desperate to pin this on someone? It's shit wot happened to Al, but it ain't no one else's fault.'

I go quiet. I don't expect Kyle to understand, but I know that there's more to Al's death.

There has to be.

I want there to be.

121

Al wouldn't have just given up on his dreams for no reason. He wouldn't have just left me. Left all of us.

I shrug and stare down at my English worksheet on the table.

Kyle sighs. 'You can't go confronting Eli, Nate, not unless you want your face broken. Y'know I've always got your back, but I ain't getting involved in that mess. I heard he got kicked out of that PRU down the road for putting some kid in hospital.'

'I know,' I say. 'That's why I need to get Lewi on his own. He ain't gonna tell me nothing if Eli's there. Especially if Eli had a part to play in it, too.'

Kyle stares at me for a minute, but doesn't say anything else, probably cause he knows that there's no point in wasting his breath. I put my head down on the desk and breathe in the weird chemical smell of bleach or polish. I close my eyes and I don't care if people are staring at me, or think I'm weird. I just stay like that, waiting for the lesson to end.

I head into the corridor with Kyle as the bell for dinner goes. I see Jeremiah at the other end of it, making a fool of himself and taking a picture with some girl in the year below. I look around, but I can't see Lewi or Eli. The hallway's proper busy and there's all these people shoving and shouting. There's a few girls taking selfies beside the vending machines.

I look at the green-and-black school ties and suddenly the image of Al with one wrapped round his neck flashes in my head. I stop in the middle of the corridor, my palms go all sweaty and my legs start to shake. There's too much noise and too many people . . . Kyle's banging on about some girl he fancies and all I wanna do is get outta here.

I remember Megan talking about the art room being quiet and I turn, heading towards the staff staircase. We're not supposed to use it, but I know that no one else will be going that way. Kyle yells after me, but I just keep going, taking the stairs as fast as I can, leaving all the noise behind me. I reach the top floor and wipe away some sweat from my forehead with the sleeve of my hoodie, feeling calmer now I'm away from the crowd.

There's two art classrooms on the top floor and I head towards the first one. I push the door open and see the side of Megan's face. It's weird, but just being in the same room as her makes me feel better. She's bent forward over one of the wooden tables, sketching summat on this big sheet of paper. I walk closer, and she looks up, chucking some bits left behind from a rubber on the floor. Megan smiles, but I can see her eyes look a bit red, like she's been crying.

'You came. I told you it's all right in here,' she says. 'It's quiet at least.'

I walk round the room, looking at all the paintings and drawings on the tables and walls. There's this thin piece of wire running across the wall at the top, with paintings pegged to it, waiting to dry. My chest goes all tight. Everything about this place reminds me of him. The smell, the paintings. It's like being in Al's room. There's some drawings of the old town hall, Civic, the Jimmy Egan boxing gym, some of the museum and the art gallery, the Manchester bee. I look over all the paintings till I see one of his ... I can tell that it's Al's from a mile away. The paint on the face has been blended, so that it looks like real skin, and he's managed to get the exact shade – just between his and Saul's – and he's got the thick curls that stick out in the middle right, too. It feels like a punch in the guts.

'That's me?' I say to Megan. 'Al had been drawing me?'

It's like looking in a mirror. I reach up and pull the picture down from its peg.

Megan nods, and I sit down next to her.

'Yeah,' she says. 'He'd been doing it as part of his portfolio for his exam ... He wanted to get it right. You wouldn't believe how many times he started over.'

I stare down at the flash of colour in the background, the blur of lights, the outline of the ride ... the way my face is scrunched up, like the painting could come to life any minute. It's from that time me and Al had gone to the fair, over Easter. It's me on the Spin Master ride. I dunno why that day meant so much to him. Maybe cause it was the last time me, him, Saul and Lewi had all been together. Or cause me and Al had spent the whole day laughing and laughing. Not ripping into each other or arguing for once.

Suddenly I remember us walking home and Al turning to me and saying: *'I've had the best day, Nate. I never want it to end.'* Five months later, he was dead ... How can that be right? He seemed so happy, like he had so much to live for. And then ... gone. I swallow hard, not wanting to cry in front of Megan, but I feel sad cause Al is never gonna finish his painting. Maybe that's why he wouldn't let me see any of his proper drawings. Not cause he was hiding stuff or full of secrets, but cause he wanted to keep this one as a surprise?

I put the painting down on the table. I can't look at Megan cause I don't want her to see how hard I'm finding it all. How painful it is. Sometimes it's like there's all these emotions and all these feelings, and I don't know wot to do with them. I don't know how to react. That's when I lash out and get angry instead.

'Have you eaten?' Megan asks me. I turn round and see her pull a sandwich out her bag, all wrapped in crumpled foil.

'Nah,' I say. 'I ain't really hungry.'

She pushes it towards me. 'Take half,' she says. 'It's a bit squashed and that, but it's all right.'

I sit next to her and take half the sandwich, eating it in no time. I didn't realize how hungry I was, but Megan doesn't seem to notice. She takes a packet of crisps out her bag and tears the packet down the middle. We don't say much really, just sit in silence, staring at the painting and eating crisps. It's nice to be quiet with someone for a change and Megan doesn't push me to talk about my feelings, like everyone else.

Megan clears her throat. 'I know it's hard to imagine it now, but it does get better y'know,' she says. 'Like it gets to a point where it stops hurting so much. Sort of like a cut . . .'

I shrug cause I can't imagine it ever being like that. My phone vibrates in my pocket, but I ignore it. I just wanna sit here, talking to Megan. I flatten the sides of my hair and suddenly wish that I'd gone to the barber's to sort it out before I'd decided to go back to school.

I look at Megan. 'Did Al ever talk about Lewi or Eli to you? Did he ever mention anything about them?'

Megan looks surprised. 'Not really,' she says. 'Me and Al first started talking two years ago, and he and Lewi used to hang around then. But they had some kind of fall-out and then the next minute Lewi was with Eli and Cole.' She pauses. 'I did ask Al once what happened. But he just said something about people letting you down. Disappointing you.' Megan stares down at the painting. 'Why are you interested?'

I shrug. I don't wanna tell her my suspicions about Lewi. I know it sounds stupid, but it's like I need to do this on my own to make it up to Al or summat.

'Did Al say anything else?' I ask.

Megan shakes her head. 'Not that I can remember.' She moves her hand so that it's resting on the table. And I dunno if she's done it on purpose, but our hands are now slightly touching. I try really hard not to move. I don't wanna break contact with her. But then she stands up and goes to the other side of the classroom. I stare at her, then look away cause I don't want her to think I'm checking her out . . . Well, even if I am, I don't want her to *see* me doing it.

There's a ledge beside this rusty sink that's cluttered with paintbrushes and upturned palettes, and a stack of sketchbooks in plastic folders sits just to the side. Megan searches through them, then pulls one out and walks back towards me, putting it down on the table in front of me.

'Wot's that?' I say

'Al's sketchbook,' she says. 'For his portfolio. Al's drawings were his way of figuring out the world.' She shrugs. 'It might help you understand him a bit better? And anyway it just seems weird keeping it here.'

I pick up the plastic folder just as the school bell rings, but neither of us moves. I hear the sound of kids making their way in from the playground outside. Part of me just wants to stay here, but I still need to chat to Lewi so I put my rucksack back on my shoulder and pull my hood up over my head, stuffing my headphones in my ears. I feel my eyes go to Megan's legs, even tho I don't mean to.

'Thanks, yeah,' I say, before I head out the art classroom and disappear into the corridor.

MEGAN

chapter fourteen

I never told Megan this, but the reason I wanted to see my work up in a gallery is because no one would expect it from someone like me. Because of who I am and where I'm from. And why should I let that stop me? Why should all that mean that I can't dream big, too?

I stand there for a minute, looking at the art-room door after Nathan leaves. Then everyone comes in, scrambling to the back of the class to chuck their bags down.

I sit back down at the table just as Ms Baker, our art teacher, comes in, and stare down at my sketch, trying to ignore the noise around me. I try to start drawing again, hearing Al's voice in my head as I do. He'd said that to make things look more real I needed to remember that nothing is ever a blunt, neat line. Everything blends into something else, just like life. But I can't concentrate.

I look at the empty seat opposite me. No one's sat there since Al, which I'm fine with. I know it's just a chair, but, each time I look at it, it reminds me of a different moment with him. Me and Al sitting there, laughing about the daft voice notes we'd sent each other. The time I'd made him listen to Beyoncé, trying to convert him. Playing that stupid 'Heads Up' game on my phone and how bad Al had been at guessing the things I was acting out. Al turning to me and saying: *'You're really special, Megs. Y'know that, don't you? I'm really glad you threw a strop over your drawing that day. I'm glad that we're friends.'*

I throw my pencil down and feel myself shaking. I'm working on a picture for my portfolio that's supposed to be a local building. I'd chosen the Jimmy Egan boxing gym, in the middle of Benchill. Al had told me that the roof there was the best place at night cos, if you climbed on to it and looked closely, you could see some of the planes taking off from Manchester Airport, or sometimes the sky would be so clear that you could see all these stars. He'd told me that sitting on that roof made him feel like he was somewhere else, that among all the noise of the dogs barking, and the police sirens, and the house parties, all that stuff that made it Wythenshawe, the roof was just like this *other world*. A place within a place, and I thought that it just sounded perfect so I wanted to capture that in my drawing. But, looking at it now,

129

I know that my work will never be as good as Al's. It feels pointless to even try.

I remember Al sitting here, his drawings spread across the table. '*One day, Megs,*' he'd said, '*I'm gonna do it. I'm gonna have my paintings in a gallery, you'll see. That's all I want. That's all I've ever wanted . . .*'

I look at Ms Baker as she walks round the classroom, stopping to help other people out with their work. She gets to me, and then she crouches down beside the corner of the table, touching the top of my shoulder.

'Megan,' she says, and she doesn't say it loudly, even though the classroom is proper noisy. 'Are you okay?'

I want to tell her I'm not. I don't want Al's dreams to die with him. The memorial page just isn't enough. Not any more. Maybe it will help people to remember him, but it's soulless. It isn't who Al *really* was. I want people to understand just how talented and bright and special he was. I turn to Ms Baker as I realize what it is that I can do.

'I'm all right,' I say. 'But can I talk to you about something after class? Something we could maybe do for Al?'

She smiles. 'Of course.'

She walks off to the other side of the classroom to help someone else and I hear a *ping* as a girl takes her phone out and starts smirking. Part of me wonders if it's still Jeremiah's Snap going round, and my stomach sinks.

I thought of telling Nathan about it earlier, but I knew that it probably would've just upset him, or made him angry and it's not worth it. When Eli had sent round that picture of me,

I'd wished that I hadn't seen it or that Tara hadn't bothered to show me. Every time someone walked past me and laughed, or stared down at their phone, it made me paranoid. So I didn't want Nathan to think that about the one of Al. I'm not sure if that makes me a bad person, but I'm only trying to protect him.

I pull my phone out of my pocket to check the time. It's been on silent all day and this is the first time I've looked at it since before lunch. I've got loads of WhatsApp messages from Tara.

> R u being serious?!
> U actually being funny about this?
> Megan, it's only a story, FFS it'll be gone soon!

Normally, I'd rush to reply, to fix the argument, but this time I just put my phone away and pull my drawing back towards me. And, for the first time ever, I leave Tara on *Read*.

NATHAN

chapter fifteen

There was this bee once, crawling across the desk in my room. It was trying to climb over one of my dried-out paintbrushes, the sort that I use when I want to paint a really thin outline. The bee was moving really slowly and its wings were folded in on themselves, like they'd been stuck together. The tips had gone this strange white colour, almost see-through, and it was making a faint buzzing noise. I'd read about this thing bees get called deformed wing virus and figured that's what was wrong with it and it was trying to find a safe place to die. So I picked it up and sat with it inside my palm. I don't know if it made much difference, but I thought at least it meant that it wouldn't be alone.

The rest of school goes by proper quickly. As soon as the last bell goes, I head off. I don't wait for Kyle. I don't mean nothing bad by it, I just wanna be on my own. I head out the main school gates and walk along the pavement. There are groups of kids starting to make their way home and in the distance I see Lewi walking with Eli and Cole. There's a girl with them, too. The one who was with Megan on the bus. They're all laughing and joking about summat. All of them except Lewi.

I turn on to my road, passing the same upturned sofa that's been there forever, and then I stop. There's a police car parked outside my house. A group of kids stand next to it, lighting a spliff with the car in shot and taking pictures on their phones. Someone throws a half-empty Coke can at the window and then they laugh and leg it off. I walk towards my house, my legs trembling. Wot if something bad has happened to my mum, or Saul, or Phoebe? Or maybe it's about Al ... Wot if they've discovered summat while they've been doing their inquest? Wot if they know about the phone call to me? Maybe they've looked at Al's phone records?

I pull my key out my coat pocket, my hand shaking, and unlock the door. As I walk inside, I throw my rucksack along with Al's art folder on to the floor.

'Mum!' I shout. 'You all right?'

I look in the living room, but there's no one there. I push open the kitchen door and pause, my heart pounding. Mum's sitting at the kitchen table with these two police officers. They're the same ones who came round with the ambulance people when it happened. It feels like we've gone back in time . . . to the day that everything changed. There's a plate of biscuits in the middle of the table that no one's touched and I can tell that my mum's been crying.

This police officer with a bun turns to face me. 'Hello, Nathan,' she says.

I stare at her, then back at my mum. And, for a minute, it's like I'm there again. Back in Al's room. Watching as the paramedics cut him down. Unable to move. Not just cause he's gone, but cause he might still be here if I would've picked up the phone.

The male police officer taps the edge of his cup with his finger, and looks round the kitchen, eyeing the dirty dishes on the worktops. He doesn't say it, but I know wot he's thinking: *council-estate scum.* He clears his throat. When they were first here, they'd told me their names, but I can't even remember them now.

'Wot's this about?' I say. My voice comes out more shaky than I mean it to. 'Why are you here?'

Mum pulls at the gold cross around her neck. 'Nathan,' she says. 'They've just come to ask me some questions for the inquest. I spoke to the coroner today. They've released Al's body. Can you give us a minute, love?'

I stare at her. 'I'm staying,' I say. 'If it's about Al, then I wanna know, too.'

The female police officer smiles. 'We won't be long, Nathan,' she says. 'Then you can talk to your mum afterwards. It's important that we speak to her alone first, just to ask a few things.'

'Fine,' I say, and then I head out the kitchen. But I don't close the door properly and then climb halfway up the stairs, making as much noise as possible so they think I'm out the way, before sneaking back down the stairs to listen. I wanna know wot's going on, not wot my mum decides to tell me later.

I strain to hear them talking, trying not to breathe too loudly and give myself away. I did the same thing when Dad walked out, listening to my mum tell Saul and Al in the kitchen that he wasn't coming back. I'm always the one shut out and I'm sick of it. I sit on the stairs and hear my mum talking proper slowly.

'Al *really* wasn't that type of boy ...'

'We just want to rule out all options,' the male officer says. 'Get a sense of what might have been going on with Al beforehand. What his state of mind was like. The pressures he might have been under.' He pauses. 'It's not uncommon. Boys get involved in stuff. They get in over their heads. Owe people money—'

'My son was *not* selling drugs,' Mum says, her voice cracking. 'I know what you think. What kind of mother am I, if I couldn't even tell that my own son was about to ... ?' She pauses. 'I've always done my best. I've always done what I can. And just because we're from around here doesn't mean that Al was involved in drugs.'

'Mrs Bryant,' the policewoman says, 'I assure you we're really not here to judge. We're just trying to get a sense of Al's home life. And there's been a few cases around here of drugs being sold to kids. We just thought that if you'd seen anyone ... or heard anything, then it might help us establish the facts when we present them in court.'

'The facts?' my mum says. 'The facts are that Al was a good boy. He didn't have many friends. He didn't have people knocking on or anything like that. He always found it hard ...'

Mum starts crying and the policewoman says summat in a softer voice. I head back upstairs, not wanting to hear any more. I don't even bother to be quiet. My mum didn't say it, but I know wot she was getting at. It wasn't just cause we live on an estate, it was also cause Al was black, well, mixed-race. That's why we get followed in shops whenever we go to town or searched by the police for no reason. And Saul's forever getting pulled over in his van. Al always said that some people don't think you'll do certain things cause of where you come from. That they have this ... expectation of you cause of wot they read and see, but most of the time it ain't true.

That's why he wanted to make summat of himself. Prove everyone wrong. Show that you could still be from a council estate and do wotever you wanted. That being from Wythenshawe was summat to be proud of. So wot changed?

Phoebe's bedroom door is open and I can see through the gap that she's made a den out of bedsheets and towels. Al used to help her do that all the time. I go into her room, crouching down near a gap in the sheets, which must be the entrance.

'Phoebes?'

'You ain't coming in without the password,' a voice says back.

I shrug. 'I dunno ... is it Phoebe?'

A hand moves one of the towels to the side.

'That ain't it, but I'll let you in anyway.'

I climb into the den on my knees, careful not to pull on anything and bring it all crashing down. Phoebe's piled some pillows in there and there's the teddy that Al gave her and lots of his drawings. She's stuck them to the sheets with bits of Sellotape, and one hangs down above our heads. It's a drawing of all these stars that have been painted different colours, bleeding out on to the page. I put my arm round my sister and close my eyes for a minute. Being inside with her sort of feels safe. Like we can just shut the rest of the world out.

'It's nice in here,' I say. 'Y'know Saul wouldn't fit in, tho, with his massive meat head.' I nudge her, but she doesn't say anything, just buries her face in my chest. I pull Phoebe closer.

'I miss him, Nate,' she says. 'I really miss Al.'

I kiss the top of her head. 'I know,' I say. 'I really miss him, too.'

I feel my phone vibrate in my pocket, but I ignore it. I just want Phoebe to be okay.

'It's not fair,' she says. 'Why did he have to get ill and die?'

I wrap my other arm round her. I wish that I could take away her pain. She shouldn't have to go through this, not at eight. I want Phoebe to know that it won't be like this forever and I know exactly wot Al would say.

I breathe out slowly, then I say: 'Y'know Al used to tell me about wot happens when stars die. He said they explode in this violent supernova thing. Then sometimes the outer layer of the star blows off, leaving behind this small, dense core that gets pressed down by gravity so tight that the stuff inside – all the protons and electrons and that – combines to make neutrons and then they come together to form a star. So stars never really die cause they create summat new. Summat beautiful.'

Back in my room, I unclip the plastic handle on Al's art folder, popping the teeth out of the small holes. My phone vibrates again. I look and see I've got loads of WhatsApps from Kyle. There's also a Facebook friend request from Megan. She's changed her profile picture to this one where her head's tilted towards the camera, and her face is lightened with one of those filters so you can see one dimple in the left corner of her cheek. I don't care if I look too keen, I click *confirm*, then click through more of her pictures. She looks proper nice in them, but she's even fitter in real life. It's not just that, tho. I actually like hanging around with her, and not just cause we talk about Al. I can't explain it, but Megan makes me see this different side to life or summat.

I go to her *about me* section cause she's probably got a boyfriend, but, when I click on it, there's nothing there. I go back to her posts. Most of them are about art and drawing and stuff. Even if she wasn't with anyone, it's not like she'd fancy me anyway. I *like* a few of her pics and I think about writing a comment, but I don't wanna make a fool of myself.

I turn back to Al's folder and slide his sketchbook out. It smells just like him ... I turn over a page, but it's hard to look at. Al's gone and all I have left are these drawings. I'm suddenly angry cause maybe me and Al weren't as close as we used to be, but he still could've spoken to me. He could've told me that he was finding things hard. Or talked to Mum or Saul. Al could've fixed all this if he would've just opened his fucking mouth.

The first drawing is of this bee, with its wings all twisted and folded, curled up inside a palm. It looks sad, like it's about to die. I turn over another page. There's a drawing of the mummies in the museum, the two brothers. Another sketch is of the boxing gym round the corner from our house, and then one of the benches in the middle of Civic and another of the old town hall in the park before someone set it on fire. Al's shaded in the different textures of the dark wood that crosses over the white panels. He's even managed to get the tiles on the roof right, making them slant up towards the pointed steeple at the top. And he's drawn in the faint diamond patterns on the windows.

Each of the drawings is so careful, so delicate that I almost forget I'm angry as I get sucked into them. Al was really good. I keep flicking through. There's a whole load of drawings of parts of a face ... page after page of them ... and then some blank pages before I see one with an outline of Al's body, exactly the same as the one on the drawing he'd left behind.

He's scribbled over his face in this one, too. I keep going and see more just like it, and it feels a bit like one of those books you'd get when you were a kid, where you could make the character get up and move by flicking the pages faster and faster. The drawing of Al seems to get up, slowly, and walk up and down the page before he lifts his hands up to cover his ears, and then he stops. I dunno if Al had done it on purpose, or if it's a fluke. But it's kinda scary, like the sketch version of Al was in trouble, too, and trying to escape the pages of the book.

On the last page I see the symbol that Kyle found in the drawing I'd shown him. Al's drawn it over and over again next to a drawing of a girl. Her features haven't been filled in and her hair hangs loosely round one shoulder. A name's been scribbled out, but not fully, like Al couldn't bring himself to get rid of it completely.

Sophie.

I dunno who she is, or how this even links to everything else, but it's given me summat else to look into. I've got to find this Sophie girl cause maybe there's summat she can tell me. I can't give up till I've found out how it all connects together.

MEGAN

chapter sixteen

One of the most fascinating things about art is how something you've created can live on long after you've turned to stardust. Long after you've gone . . .

I look through my phone while I wait outside the art room for Ms Baker to finish talking to another student. I've got loads and *loads* of Facebook notifications. I haven't been on the memorial page in a few days, so they're probably to do with that. I think about reading the comments, but then I notice that Nathan's accepted my friend request. I didn't think he would do it *that* quickly, and I had to really talk myself into adding him. Like, you know, tell myself that we'd spoken more than once now, and it wasn't weird or anything like that. I'm not going to lie, I'd already looked him up a few times. More than a few, to be fair. I just wanted to find out a bit more about him. See what he liked, who he was friends with, if he was going out with anyone . . .

The fact that he's accepted nearly straight away must mean that he likes me a little bit at least. Suddenly I feel nervous cos Nathan's probably been looking through my pictures and what if they're not okay? What if he thinks that I look better in the photos than I do in real life? That the real me is actually ugly? I look at the last picture I'd posted. It's got sixty-five *likes* and all these comments, but that doesn't mean it's a nice picture. If I'm honest, I never think that any of my photos are. I make sure that I only post my best ones and do things like cropping my arm out if it doesn't look that toned or make sure that the angle's right so my chest doesn't look too flat, or my nose too weird. And, even then, it doesn't feel like it's enough. I never feel like *I'm* enough.

All I can see is what's wrong with me. How much I hate the way I look. A few months ago, I posted a selfie on Insta and a girl that I didn't even know commented with '*Ugly*' and the throwing-up face. Eight people *liked* her comment, including Tara. When I asked Tara about it, she just tried to brush it off, and said that she must've *liked* the comment by mistake. I got really upset and deleted the photo cos all I kept thinking was how disgusting I looked. And maybe that's what Tara really thought of me, too? Sometimes, when she tags me in photos that aren't nice, I feel really sick. I only want my best photos online cos, if you don't get enough *likes*, then everyone knows that you're not good enough. That there's something wrong with you.

I'm worried that Nathan's scrolling through all my pictures now, laughing with his mates.

The other student heads out of the art classroom, and Ms Baker holds the door open for me. She smiles, but I can see the dark circles under her eyes.

'Come on in, Megan,' she says. 'Thanks so much for waiting.' She points at the table closest to the door, and we both sit down.

'What did you want to talk to me about?' she asks.

I suddenly feel a bit awkward – what if she thinks my idea's stupid? I breathe out slowly. It's hard to talk about Al without feeling this rush of emotions. Ms Baker puts her hand on top of mine, but it only makes me want to cry even more.

'Look, Megan,' she says, 'what happened is just terrible. I can't even begin to imagine how you must be feeling. I know how close you both were and if there's anything I can do . . .'

'I want to put on a mini exhibition,' I blurt out. 'In honour of Al. He was always talking about having his paintings on display, and I want to make that happen for him.'

I look down. I want to say that I don't want Al to be forgotten. That part of me wants him to live on forever in his drawings or the things he's left behind, but I can't seem to speak. I feel really sad all of a sudden cos I don't even have the words to explain how special it was knowing Al. What a difference he'd made to my life.

Ms Baker squeezes my hand, and I can see that she's got

tears in her eyes. 'Oh, Megan,' she says. 'That's a wonderful idea. Al would've really loved that. I can talk to Mr Ballan. I'm sure he'll let you use the assembly hall.'

'Will you help me?' I ask. 'I've never done anything like this before.'

Ms Baker nods. 'Of course I will.' She pauses and looks at Al's seat for a minute and I see something flash across her face. It's more than sadness, though – it's like she can't believe that Al isn't here. 'Al was such a little star,' she says. 'You are, too. You're just as talented as he was, Megan. You could really go far.'

I smile. 'Thanks, miss,' I say, then I head out of the classroom.

I keep smiling as I walk along the corridor. Especially with Ms Baker saying I'm as good as Al. When I draw, it almost feels like nothing else matters. Everything kind of just stops. Al used to say that drawing helped him escape, and it makes me feel the same way, too, so I'm made up that Ms Baker thinks I'm good.

I told Tara once that I was thinking about doing art at uni, but she laughed and said that you didn't have to be very clever for that, and it would never help me to get a job anyway. That I should do something more realistic, like work in a bar, or maybe a shop, where I'd get a good discount and come home with a load of money. But, when I'd told Al, he'd said, *'Why is it unrealistic to do what you love?'* Like it was that simple. And, even though there's all the stuff with money and the rest of it, I suppose, in a way, he was right.

And now I can help to make Al's dream come true – for people to see his work, see what he loved to do. I feel good about that cos, if he's looking down on me from heaven (even though I'm sure that, out of all the places in the world, you're not going to be looking at Wythenshawe), he'll be smiling. One of his Al smiles, where you can see the gap in his front teeth. I can hear him saying something like: '*Megan, that's neat. That's really neat.*' And maybe with this exhibition, in a way, I can make up for some of the things I didn't do for him when he was still alive.

I head out of the school gates and open up Snapchat as I walk. Tara has uploaded a new story. A video of her in McDonald's mucking about with Eli and Cole. She's used a filter so that their faces have been swapped and merged and they're all laughing at the camera. Tara's arm is round Eli's neck. I'm not really surprised that she didn't tell me she was leaving, especially after the row we had, but even so it hurts to see her having fun without me. Like she's not even bothered any more. I put my phone away and keep walking towards the tram stop.

When I get there, I go to the middle of the platform and sit down on one of the benches. There's a group of kids hanging about near the other bench, and I see Lewi staring at me from the far end of the platform. He's leaning against the ticket machine, smoking, in an army print hoodie. He walks over to me, flicking his spliff on to the tracks as he does.

I shake my head. 'You know you're going to end up with no brain cells left if you keep on with that stuff?' I say.

Lewi smiles and sits down next to me. It's not that cold out, but he's proper shaking. I've only seen him a few times in school since Al died. He must be really cut up, too. He stuffs his hands in his pockets and nudges me with his elbow. It's weird cos, even though he's smiling, he still looks so bad. Like every part of him is trying to hold it all together.

'I don't have many brain cells anyway,' he says. 'So I reckon I'll be all right.'

NATHAN

chapter seventeen

Jackson Pollock hid his signature in one of his paintings once. A historian's wife found it, but she could only make out three letters at first: S O N. Then she realized that JACKSON ran across the entire top and below that was POLLOCK. Sometimes paintings have hidden meanings. And sometimes artists want to say something, but can't, so they hide it behind patterns, or swirls, or dark patches. But it's there if you look hard enough.

   Hiding in plain sight.

Whoever this Sophie was, Al must have been friends with her, so Facebook seems like a good place to start looking for her. I go to his friends list, then click on the search box, typing the name *Sophie*, but no one comes up. I scroll through his pictures, looking at all the *likes* and comments, trying to see if Sophie had written something, or *liked* one of his photos, but there's nothin.

I go to the memorial page. There's even more comments than before and 1,200 *likes* now. Plus, loads of posts about how sad it is, or how Al was such a great guy. I don't wanna look, but I can't help it. I scroll through, reading all the posts that have been put up.

I'm so sorry

RIP

Such a shame

Then I see one that says:

Selfish ppl. Killing themselves 4 attention. U cnt luv ur family that much if u'd do that.

It's been *liked* three times, and has two laughing faces and one *love*. Someone else has commented:

I'd kill myself 2 if I had lips like that. lol.

Three *likes* for that one. Then:

U shouldn't make fun of ppl who've killed themselves that's sick.

No, killing urself for attention is sick.

Why u commenting on this page if u don't know him?

It's just selfish.

Call urself a Christian wen u take ur own life.

He cnt have loved his family that much, if he went and killed himself.

Selfish

He must have been so messed up.

He must have had a screw loose.

People do anything 4 attention.

Shut up.

Why don't u fuck off and kill urself 2? Lol. It's not like any1 will miss u . . . I'll gladly send u the rope . . .

How can people who don't even know Al say stuff like that about him?

Further down the wall someone's posted a screenshot of Al with the words:

When ur so ugly, even God's pissed that he'll have 2 look at u

Al's features have been stretched out and changed, even tho you can still tell it's him. The picture has got over 900 *likes*, laughing faces and wows. I look more closely at the screenshot. Someone's tagged Jeremiah in the comments with:

Lol. Jeremiah, man, ur savage!!

I want to punch through the screen to tear down all the *likes* and posts. Tell them that Al wasn't selfish – he didn't do none of this for attention and he *wasn't* messed up. He was my brother, my big brother, not some sort of stupid joke. He'd killed himself and now this page – *his* page – was turning into somewhere that people could take the piss. I click on Messenger and type in Megan's name. This is her fault. If she hadn't bothered to stick her nose in and set up the page, then people wouldn't be saying all this stuff about my brother. I type:

U happy now? Have u seen wot ur fucking page has gone and done?

I turn my phone off.

I'd always thought it was funny looking at the comments that other people had put, rating girls on their Insta and that, stealing their pictures and sending them to Kyle, or watching videos of kids fighting, and laughing about it all. Everyone does it. But I guess it's funny when it's someone else. When it ain't your brother.

I hear a key turn in the front door, and then the sound of Saul's footsteps downstairs. I grab Al's drawing out my rucksack and shove it in my hoodie pocket before heading downstairs. I walk into the kitchen just as Saul is unwrapping soggy packages of white chip paper on to some plates. Phoebe's there, too.

'Nate,' Phoebe says, 'we've got chips for tea!'

The police ain't there. I didn't even hear them leave. The place where my mum was sitting is empty, too. Saul grabs some juice out the fridge.

'How was school?' he asks me, pouring Phoebe a glass.

I shrug. 'Fine,' I say. 'Same as it always is.'

He nods. 'I'll go and get Mum,' he says, and then he disappears towards the living room.

Phoebe must be feeling better cause she puts some chips inside a buttered piece of bread, then folds it in half and tries to shove the entire thing in her mouth.

'Calm down,' I say. 'Your tea ain't going nowhere.'

'It is,' she says, chewing loudly. 'It's going in my stomach!'

I sit down and try to eat some chips. Like everything is normal. Like I never read any of those comments or heard the police tryna make out that Al was a drug dealer or summat.

'She said she ain't hungry,' Saul says as he comes back into the kitchen. He sits down and reaches for a pot of gravy, pouring it over his food. 'We'll save her some, just in case she changes her mind.'

I nod. I'm still angry, but I don't wanna tell him why. Not in front of Phoebe.

'Saul,' Phoebe says. 'I've made a den. Nate says you won't fit in it, though, cos you've got a big meat head.' She laughs.

151

'Am I lying, tho?' I say.

'Like you can talk,' Saul replies. 'Your head's bigger than mine, mate, and you've got the weird ears to go with it.'

'E-yar, yo!' I say, but I notice that Phoebe has suddenly gone quiet.

She pauses and stares down at her plate. 'It's got some of Al's drawings in there,' she says. 'It makes me feel like he's still here.'

Saul swallows hard. 'He is,' he tells her. 'Al'll always be with us in some way.' He moves closer to Phoebe. 'Just cause he ain't around don't mean you can't talk to him.' He looks at me. 'He'd wanna know we're all okay.'

Phoebe nods and carries on eating, but I can't move. I can't even speak cause we're *not* okay. *We never will be.* Phoebe starts going on about some school play that she's in, but I can't concentrate. All I can do is go over wot Al's drawing meant and how Lewi had hurt him, and who Sophie is. The same questions running over and over in my head. Finally, Phoebe finishes her chips and Saul clears her plate away.

'Go and get ready for bed,' he says. 'I'll be up in a minute.'

Phoebe nods and leaves the kitchen and I turn to Saul. 'Police were here earlier,' I say.

He pauses, then dumps the plates in the sink. 'What?' he says. 'What did they want?'

'They wanted to talk to Mum about Al. I heard them tryna say that he'd been selling. Asking her if he was involved in stuff and that's why he . . .'

'They're fucking unbelievable,' Saul says. He sits back

down and the vein at the side of his head starts to throb. 'There's always gotta be something. Drugs, gangs. He can't just be a normal lad who got a stupid idea in his head.'

He leans back in his chair. Saul always gets mad about stuff to do with the police cause they're always on his case. Trying to accuse him of summat or other. He's got a few dodgy mates, but he stays outta trouble and I know it's cause he wouldn't be able to look after us if he was inside.

'Wish I'd been here,' Saul says. 'Inquest or no inquest, I'd have told 'em where to go.'

I pull the drawing out my pocket. I dunno why I'm doing this now, why I'm showing Saul. Maybe it's cause part of me feels like I'm going round in circles with it and thinks he might be able to help. And I dunno wot else to do.

'I've been looking into some stuff,' I tell him. 'I found this picture and Lewi wrote this weird comment on Facebook. Then there's some girl called Sophie that I think Al might have been hanging around with. Did he ever mention—'

'Stop!' Saul shouts. It's so loud that it makes me jump. 'Will you just *stop* all this! What you even going on about?'

I hand him Al's drawing. He takes it and stares down at it.

'It's just a drawing, Nate,' he says. 'Why do you think this even means anything?'

I can't tell him that I want it to mean summat. That I'm desperate for it to mean summat . . .

'It was in Al's room,' I say. 'That day. I found it on the floor. It says *help me*. Wot if he was tryna tell us summat? That he was in some sort of trouble?'

Saul tosses the drawing down on the kitchen table. 'What's wrong with you?' he says. 'You're looking for stuff that ain't there. People kill themselves all the time and there ain't always a reason. This is just a picture. Al's room was full of drawings like this – it don't mean anything.'

'No,' I say. 'It don't make sense! Al was going to uni. He was going to have everything he wanted. Why would he just decide to do it? To leave us—'

'Enough!' Saul says. He puts his head in his hands. 'D'you not think it's hard enough without you going on all the time?' He pauses. 'Mum's started drinking again, I'm only just getting Phoebe to sleep in her own bed and you wanna go on about some picture.' He shakes his head. 'I know that it's hard to believe cause it's Al. But you don't always know everything about a person, Nate.' He pauses. 'You gotta stop,' he says, his voice softer now. 'There ain't *one* reason that makes people decide they've had enough. Sometimes there's loads. Loads of things that pile up and then something tiny can just push you. You're gonna drive yourself mad trying to figure this out. You're looking for something that ain't there.'

'Well, wot am I supposed to do?' I snap. 'Walk around not giving a toss? Carry on like you, pretending everything's fine?'

Saul slams his fist down on the table and stands up.

'Stop acting like a little kid,' he says and I can see how angry he is. 'You think there's only one way to show that you're grieving? Have you not thought that keeping it all together, trying to look after everyone, is the only thing that's making me feel normal? It don't mean that I don't feel it, too.'

154

Saul steps away from me. 'This ain't some detective story, or one of them murder-mystery shows. Life ain't like that. People don't go leaving clues in a drawing. If Al wanted to tell us something, why didn't he just leave a note? Just stop, Nate, yeah? Al's gone and you're not gonna bring him back with all this crap.'

He shakes his head and walks out the kitchen. I swallow hard. Al didn't leave a note, but he did try to call me. He did *try* to tell me summat. I don't care wot Saul says, I know that stuff happened, that there's more going on . . . Al would always tell me how important his drawings were. How they helped him speak when he couldn't find words. Al had secrets and his picture was gonna help me find out wot he was hiding.

I close my bedroom door and look round at the wallpaper peeling near the top, the clothes shoved on top of my chest of drawers, all the trainers covering the floor. I look up at the stars on my ceiling and hear Al's voice in my head: *'Nate, come on. It's going to be okay.'*

I pick up his sketchbook and it makes me proper angry cause I can't believe he'd do this without trying harder to talk to me . . . How was I supposed to know wot would happen if I didn't pick up the phone? I tear at the drawings in the pad, pulling them out one by one and ripping them down the middle. Why couldn't he just speak to me? I carry on tearing up his drawings till the paper piles up on the floor. Maybe all them comments were right. Al *was* selfish, or he wasn't right in the head.

I've reached the cardboard part of the sketchbook now, the bit that holds it all together with a thin black spine. I throw it down on the floor and notice a drawing that I must have missed when I'd been flicking through the pages before. It's Al sitting on a hill with his arm round some girl, looking up at the sky. The girl has a long plait, which reaches the bottom of her back, and, even tho it's much smaller, every last detail is exactly the same. It's Sophie. But this time Al's scribbled: *Al and Star Girl*.

Wot if I couldn't find Sophie cause she was under a different name?

MEGAN

chapter eighteen

I showed Lewi this picture of the Elqui Valley once, and told him how I wanted to go there. I'd spent ages online, trying to find the best photo to show him. Then I found one – with this gold bit of light near the bottom. I told Lewi that it was the best place on earth to see the stars because the whole of the region experiences 360 clear nights a year. And that the strongest telescopes in the world are there. Lewi put his arm round me and said, 'Maybe I'll go with you. Just to see what all the fuss is about. And anyway I'd miss you too much ... I don't know what I'd do without my best mate.'

I lean back against the metal seat at the tram stop and Lewi pulls at this bit on his shoe that's starting to come away. I feel a bit awkward at first cos I don't *really* know Lewi that well. I'd hung out with him a few times over the summer, but that was only cos Tara had started seeing Eli again, so we'd all meet up in the park. Tara and Eli would go off, and Cole would normally disappear to smoke, so then it would just be me and Lewi.

He seemed nice, even though he hung around with Eli and Cole. And it was weird watching him with Eli cos it was like he'd just try really hard to say stuff to make everyone laugh, or take the piss out of people, or phone up girls he was seeing and put them on loudspeaker. Eli and Cole would say things to put him down. About how poor he was, or that he was too skinny. Tara would laugh her head off, but you could see that it upset Lewi. More than he ever let on. It was just like me and Tara and how quickly she'd change when other people were around, the comments that she'd make. That was one of the reasons why I started talking to Lewi in the first place.

Usually, we'd ignore each other pretty much and just look at our phones and that, but then one day we started talking. Part of me could never understand how you could go from being friends with Al to hanging around with Eli and Cole. So I asked him what had gone on with Al. Why they'd stopped talking. Lewi looked dead sad, but he just shrugged and said: 'Sometimes people grow apart, innit?' He didn't say anything else, and then Al told me that thing about people disappointing you, so I guessed it had to be something important, but neither of them wanted to deal with it. So I left it, too.

Now Lewi leans forward and turns to face me. 'Saw that you set up Al's memorial page,' he says. 'Y'know that cover photo? Al showed it me once . . . He had it on this list of places he wanted to visit.' Lewi pauses. 'I remember it cos of that gold bit at the bottom. Summat to do with the fucking light.'

I smile. 'Yeah, it's the Elqui Valley.'

Lewi doesn't say anything.

'Why aren't you out with Eli and the others?' I ask.

He rubs underneath his eye. He looks like he hasn't slept for ages. 'I'm off to me dad's in Altrincham. Going there for a few days. It's just like . . .' He pauses. 'I dunno. All I wanna do is get away. From everyone and everything. I can't be round here too much no more.'

I stare at him and part of me wonders if the 'everyone' is Eli. I know what he means. Everywhere you go there's memories of Al. They were mates forever so it must be worse for him. Lewi pulls another spliff out of his pocket even though I think he's pretty stoned already. I always knew he smoked, but he seems more out of it than usual. He lights it, then takes a drag, turning away so that he doesn't breathe the smoke towards me.

'I wanted to write something proper,' he says. 'On the memorial page. Say all this stuff about how top Al was. You know, he always knew *all* the answers to that Chase quiz show. I swear, I used to sit with him and think – how do you even fit all that knowledge in your head?' Lewi's face lights up. 'I used to say to him, you need to work at NASA, or walk on the moon or summat.' He pauses. 'He was so much better than me. At words and talking and that. I can't even say what I want to on his fucking wall.' He breathes out.

'I'm sure he knew what you thought of him,' I say and Lewi looks sad again.

There's the noise of the tram approaching and I stand up as I see it coming towards us.

'This is mine,' I say as it pulls to a stop. 'See you around?'

Lewi nods. I press the button to open the tram doors and step on. The group of kids that were at the other end of the platform pile on, too, shouting and running to the back of the tram. Lewi doesn't move. He doesn't even look at the electric screen to see how long he'll have to wait. He just sits there, smoking.

I feel sorry for him cos he looks so lost. Like he doesn't know what to do with himself. It's obvious how much he misses Al. I could see it in his face. The hurt and regret. Maybe that's why he's getting stoned. To try and block out the pain. I put my hand up to wave, but Lewi doesn't even notice. The tram starts up and I pull my phone out of my pocket. I've got a Facebook message from Nathan. I suddenly feel nervous. Although a small part of me is excited as I open up Messenger:

> U happy now? Have u seen wot ur fucking page has gone and done?

I have to read it a couple of times to make sense of it. I dunno what I thought he'd send me, but there's no way that I expected *that*. How do I respond? I type:

> What are you talking about???

160

But I delete it straight away.

I hadn't checked Al's memorial page in a few days. I'd done it for a bit at first, but then it all just got too much. My phone kept *pinging* all the time with new comments and posts. And, on top of that, there was Snapchat and Insta and WhatsApp and my own Facebook. Plus, all this new stuff I'd been thinking about with my dad, and my mum going on about her *migraines*, then the arguments with Tara. And I still had to do my art coursework and revise for both of my English exams ... It was all just really stressful.

I wanted to be left alone. I know it sounds like I'm moaning and that, but it's hard to concentrate with the amount of things going on sometimes.

I go into Facebook. A picture of Tara comes up in my newsfeed straight away. I can see she's still at the McDonald's in Civic cos she's *checked in* there and the photo shows her sitting on Eli's lap, their heads touching. It's already got 300 *likes*. She looks proper happy. It makes me feel a bit sad cos I wonder if things between us would've stayed the same if Tara hadn't started seeing Eli.

I go to Al's memorial page and scroll down to the comments. I feel sick. There's so many bad ones. People saying that Al's selfish, calling him ugly, or stupid, or that he'd killed himself for attention.

Well, who really cares anyway??? It's not like he had any friends.

No1 even liked him

He fort he was 2 gd 2 be frm rnd ere

Wot a shame, looks lyk there's no uni 4 him now LOL!!!

Someone's taken a picture of Jeremiah's Snap and posted it on the page, too. It's got 900 *likes* and a few laughing faces. I see that Tara has *liked* it.

I keep reading the comments and I feel like the air is being pushed out of me, as if something hard is pressing down on my chest, and I can't breathe. This wasn't what I set this *fucking* page up for. These aren't the things I wanted people to say about Al.

I go through them all, trying my hardest not to cry, then I delete them one by one. There's so many that I don't even bother to press *report*. There's no point. I just delete, delete, delete.

Tara's *liked* more than just Jeremiah's Snap – she's also *liked* the comment about Al being ugly, about him doing it for attention, about him not being able to go to uni. How can someone say those things or even *like* them? I keep deleting all the comments till only the nice ones are left. Then I WhatsApp Tara. Normally, I'd just ignore the things that she says. Even if they upset me, I'd pretend that I wasn't bothered, but I'm so angry, that I don't even care any more.

> It's not just a fucking Snap. Al was my friend. How can u like all those comments? I dnt know wot's happened 2 u!

I don't even think about it, I just press *send*.

162

NATHAN

chapter nineteen

Sometimes I'd see Saul with his girlfriend, or the way that Nathan could go up to any girl if we were out, and I'd wish that it was that easy. I'd wonder if it was me. I'm not as cool as Nathan or Saul, so why would any girl like me? But there's around 66,959,016 people in the UK so probability meant that I should find someone. It's just maths when you look at the numbers, and maths is always right. And then I met Sophie ...

Everyone's already in the kitchen having breakfast when I get up the next day, but I don't go in there cause I can't face talking to my mum or Saul. I just wanna leave and get to school. I'd already sent Kyle a message and told him I'd meet him at the corner shop beforehand. I'm about to head out, but my mum comes rushing out the kitchen.

'Nate,' she says. 'You leaving already?'

'Yeah,' I say. 'Gonna go meet Kyle.'

'Oh.' My mum stops. 'Well, at least have something to eat. I can put you some toast in, or—'

I push the door open. 'I'm all right. Just don't fuss, yeah?'

I can tell that she wants to say summat else, but she doesn't. She just sighs and heads back to the kitchen. I put my headphones in and leave the house.

Outside, I turn the volume up even louder. I pass a few mums taking their kids to school as I walk towards the row of shops. I couldn't really sleep again last night cause of those comments and everything else. I can't stop thinking about the funeral, either. If they are gonna release Al's body, then that means we'd finally be able to bury him. That means all our family would come down.

Including Dad.

Mum called him as soon as Al died, but he didn't bother to come and see us. He just spoke to us on the phone, which was awkward cause he hadn't done that in so long. I don't know why I was surprised – he's not interested any more, not now he has this other family. He only really speaks to Mum if he has to or shoves some money at us every so often. Why would Al being gone change that?

I cross the road and see Kyle waiting outside the news-agent's, tipping his head back and pouring this packet of lemon sherbet down his gob. He nods when he sees me, wiping his mouth on his sleeve. He's got a thin plastic bag hanging from his wrist and as I get closer he opens it up.

'Spent all me tram money on these,' he says. 'Take your pick. Not the KitKat Chunky, tho.'

I pull out a Snickers bar, peeling off the wrapper, and shove it in my mouth.

'Wot's up?' Kyle says, sticking his straw in a carton of Ribena.

'They're releasing Al's body,' I say as we head towards school.

Kyle pauses. 'Nate, I'm sorry, man. But that's good, ain't it? It means you can sort out the funeral. That you get a chance to say goodbye.'

I shrug. 'I thought it would be. But it's weird. Al's body ... makes it seem more real. And, on top of that, there were all these comments on that Facebook memorial page.'

'Wot kinda comments?' he asks, finishing his carton and dashing it into someone's garden. I shake my head and put my wrapper in my coat pocket. Al was always banging on about how dropping litter *ruins the planet* so I didn't think it was worth the hassle.

'Just some crap,' I say. 'About Al killing himself for attention and shit.'

Kyle stops and turns to me. We're at the corner of the road that leads to our school. A few kids walk past us and Kyle lowers his voice.

'You know that ain't true,' he says. 'People don't do stuff like that for attention. That's a load of bullshit. Al loved ya.'

'Yeah,' I say. 'I know.'

But part of me doesn't believe it. I don't know wot to think any more. We carry on walking towards the school gates.

'Just don't go running off again,' he says. 'I had to eat dinner on my jack, y'know. Only cause I can't stand sitting next to that Ryan. All he goes on about is his flipping girlfriend.'

'Soz,' I say. 'I just couldn't be doing with all the noise and that. It's bad enough with people staring at me.'

Kyle nods. 'I get you,' he says. 'I'm used to it, tho. Can't help it if I'm God's gift to Wythenshawe.'

I shake my head as we walk through the school gates and across the playground.

I avoided going that way yesterday cause I didn't want anyone speaking to me, or running up to ask me wot had happened. Saul's girlfriend, Lauren, is standing in the far corner with her mates. They all stare at us as we walk into the main building. Kyle's going on about the maths homework, which I ain't even done, but I'm not really listening. I scan all the blazers and faces, all the Year Twelves that pass me, but this time I'm not looking for Lewi or Eli, I'm tryna find Megan. I feel bad for sending her that message. I know that she's seen it, but she hasn't replied. I'm still pissed about the page and all the comments. I'm still pissed about those *likes*. But I guess it's not really Megan's fault. All she wanted to do was a good thing. I was just angry.

And then I see him. Lewi. He's pulling off his large hoodie and shoving it into his locker, but he still looks proper bad. Out of it. I head straight towards him, leaving Kyle behind.

Lewi closes his locker and bends down to pick up his school bag, straightening up just as I approach him.

'Yo, Lewi,' I say.

He doesn't look me in the eye, scanning the crowd around us instead, but his face does that weird thing again, where it goes all ashy and pale.

'All right, Nate?' he says and then he turns to go.

I stand in his way. The other kids in the corridor can obviously tell summat's going on cause I can feel them looking, gathering round, taking out their phones, waiting to see if there's gonna be a fight. I keep staring at Lewi. He's well nervous. His legs won't stop shaking and his eye keeps doing this weird twitching thing.

'"All right, Nate?"' I echo. 'Is that all you gotta say? You didn't even bother to come and see us, or nothin. All the years you've been mates with Al? You know summat. About why he did it. I know you do.'

Lewi looks down at the ground.

'I dunno wot you're on about,' he says. 'I think you've g—'

'Yeah, you do!' I shout, moving closer to him. 'Yesterday you looked proper scared of me. More or less hiding behind Eli. Why don't you wanna speak to me?'

Lewi tries to get past me again. His school tie is loose and I look at it, unravelling from around his neck. Flashes of another tie come into my head. Of not getting to Al on time. I start to sweat.

'Look, Nate,' he says, 'I dunno nothing ... I'm telling ya. I just—'

167

I stare into Lewi's eyes, which are raw and bloodshot. I'm starting to feel even hotter and my heart pounds in my chest, but I don't move. I can't leave it.

'I'm sorry, yeah?' he says. 'I *am*,' and I believe that bit at least. 'I'm sad about Al, but I dunno nothing. Why would I? Me and him ... we stopped chilling ages ago, you know that. I didn't even talk to him no more.'

He turns to leave again, but I grab him, holding on to his collar.

'You're a fucking liar,' I say. 'Wot about that comment you left on his memorial page?'

Lewi's eyes widen. 'Wot comment?'

'That you were *sorry*. Wot d'you have to be sorry about if you don't know nothin? Or was it the fact you left him? Abandoned your best mate when he needed you? Wot kind of shit friend does that?' I say.

I push Lewi hard against the lockers, grabbing on tighter to the front of his shirt. I hear a ripping noise. There's a bigger crowd now, watching and waiting.

'Leave it, Nate!' I hear Kyle say next to me.

But I can't. I know that Lewi's covering summat up.

'Why'd you even fall out in the first place?' I ask him. 'Wot went on between you two? Wot did you say to him?'

Lewi's face starts to sweat, and he looks around, shaking. 'Nothing ... It was ... Just get off!' he says. 'All I meant was that I was sorry that he did it. That's what you say, innit? When people are dead? That you're sorry they're gone?'

'You're a liar!' I shout.

Lewi tries to prise my hand off his shirt, but I grip on to it harder.

'Maybe if you'd have still been around then Al wouldn't have done it. If he'd have had someone else to talk to, then he'd still be here.'

Lewi's face goes even paler.

'I just wanna know wot happened to my brother!' I'm shouting now, but I can't help it. Lewi looks scared, genuinely scared. 'You should've been there for him when he needed you!'

I'm starting to feel light-headed. My chest is all tight and my hands are sweating. All of these emotions are rushing through me, knowing that I'll never see Al again, that he'll only ever be this name on a Facebook page, or a laughing face, or someone's comment. Inside, I feel like I'm on the Spin Master at the fair or something, being thrown around like mad. It's all too much, and I let go of Lewi, and press my hands over my eyes.

'I just wanna find out wot happened,' I say. 'Please ... If you know anything, just tell me.' My voice cracks. I don't even sound like me any more. I look round at the crowd in the corridor and spot Megan. She looks worried and I feel a bit stupid making a big scene in front of her. But I can't be thinking about that now. Not if it means I can get to the truth about Al. I don't care that Kyle's staring at me, or that people have their phones out, recording everything, or that some of them are whispering and laughing.

'You'd come to ours all the time,' I say. 'Even Christmas you'd come round. You were best mates.'

Lewi shakes his head and rubs his face. 'I know,' he says.

'I know ...' I see suddenly how much he misses Al, too. Probably how much he missed him long before Al died even. I lean back against the locker, the anger gone. I suddenly feel a bit sorry for him.

Lewi still can't look at me. He's still all jittery, like he's taken summat, and he's chewing at the inside of his cheeks.

'I miss him,' he tells me. 'I wish it weren't like this. I didn't mean for it to be ... for it to get ...' He pauses. 'I'd give anything to have him back, Nate.' Then his tears start to come and he stares down at the space where my tie should be. He opens his mouth, like he's about to say summat else, and then I hear a voice say:

'Yo, Lewi, everything all right?'

The colour drains from Lewi's face and he looks scared. I already know who it is before I turn round.

Eli walks past me and puts his hand on Lewi's shoulder. Eli smiles. He's wearing his cap indoors and he's had two diagonal lines shaved through his left eyebrow since yesterday. Cole comes and stands behind him, his hood pulled up.

'I said,' Eli repeats, staring me out, 'everything all right, Lewi?'

'It's fine, yeah?' Lewi says, looking down at the floor. 'It's nothin.'

I know that Eli could easily beat me up, but I still don't move. He rubs at the stubble on his chin.

'I'm asking Lewi wot he knows about Al,' I say.

Eli and Cole share a glance, but then Eli raises his eyebrow and shrugs.

'Look, yeah,' he says. 'I'm sorry bout what happened and that, but what would Lewi know? He didn't even speak to the guy no more.' He points to Lewi. 'I know you already wanna piece of him, but it's getting serious now. You're getting on my nerves. And I don't think he swings that way.'

Eli pauses and I can hear a few people laugh, but I can't take my eyes off Lewi. I'm sure there was summat else he was gonna tell me, right before Eli came over.

'I'll tell you what,' Eli says. 'I'll let you off this time cause of what's happened. But you keep doing this, it's gonna cause problems. You keep following my mate around and I'll have to do summat about it, yeah?' He comes closer. 'And you'd better be careful,' he whispers, 'or people will start thinking you're not all there in the head. Just like your weirdo brother.'

He thumps me on the shoulder and walks off. Cole sniggers and follows him, but Lewi seems to have disappeared into the crowd.

Everyone's still staring at me, like Eli was right, like there is summat wrong with me. I look at Kyle, who shakes his head and looks down at the floor, then I see Megan creasing her brow. I see the look on her face. Pity. The bell rings and everyone pushes past to go to their form rooms. I start walking back to the entrance. Kyle shouts my name, but I don't turn round. This was all a waste of time – coming back to school, speaking to Lewi. And now Megan thinks I'm some sort of idiot.

I hear the sound of footsteps running across the varnished floor.

'Nate!' Kyle shouts. 'Eh, Nate ... wait up ...'

But I keep walking. I just wanna get away from this school. Away from everyone.

'Nathan!' Kyle shouts again. 'Will you just stop, man?'

I do, beside this picture of St Paul in a frame. One of his fingers is raised to the sky, and there's a book and a sword pressed to his chest.

'You're off your head,' Kyle says. 'Eli could've wiped the floor with you. And now look. Did you find anything out?' He pauses. 'You need to drop this,' he says. 'I ain't gonna tell ya again.'

He's wrong, tho. I did find out summat. Lewi was about to tell me summat if Eli hadn't got involved. And why is Eli so bothered about keeping me away from Lewi? He was the same yesterday. I know they're mates, but Eli doesn't give a shit about anyone but himself usually.

'We're gonna be late for form,' Kyle says.

'I ain't going,' I say and I walk off.

'You're lucky you're me best mate,' Kyle says. 'Cause you're acting like a right weirdo.' I hear him kick a locker and then his footsteps as he stomps off back down the hall, but I don't turn round. I head out the side door and back across the playground.

I don't really know where to go, so I just sit at a bus stop. If I go straight home, my mum will probably give me a lecture for walking out or start fussing, and I can't be doing with it.

I pull my phone out and go to Al's friend list on Facebook

and type: *Star Girl*. Nothing comes up so I go to Al's photos and click on the *likes*. I look through them and see that someone called SG has *liked* every photo. I hadn't even noticed her on Al's profile before. I click on her page and as soon as I see the picture I know it's Sophie. She looks exactly like Al's drawing. Her long blonde hair is plaited over one shoulder, her eyes are a pale grey. She's well fit.

Most of her profile pictures are public. In some of them she's smiling at the camera, and there's a few of her with her mates, but in the rest of them she's all pouty and that. There's one taken in her bathroom pointing her phone at the mirror, one of her in a tiny dress, some of her in the gym, and one of her lying down on her bed. There's some pictures of stars and planets, and she's got loads of comments. Loads from guys, saying:

fit

sexy

marry me

DM me

Wot's ur Snapchat???

Msg me

Msg me!!!!!

I would!!

Some girls have written:

so jealous

so pretty

you make me want 2 kill myself

Wish I cud be as pretty as u

Perfect

I'm going to kill myself right now

bitch

slag

ur ugly anyway

I see that Al's put a heart emoji and a star on every picture. On one he's put:

I'm so lucky.

I'm so lucky. Wot does that mean?

Was Al going out with her? I'd never even known him to have a girlfriend before. He didn't speak about girls much, but if he was seeing this Sophie, and she was this fit, then I don't know why he never mentioned her. And she must know that Al is dead – she would've seen it on his profile and all those status updates and pictures he'd been tagged in. The memorial page. It was all over the estate ... and school. Why hadn't she been in touch? Why hadn't she posted anything anywhere? I send her a friend request and then shove my phone back in my pocket. Something ain't right.

MEGAN

chapter twenty

Did you know that symbols can take on a different meaning once someone gives it to them? There was this girl in Japan, Sadako Sasaki, who survived the Hiroshima bomb, but was diagnosed with leukaemia and she became 'the girl who folded 1,000 cranes'.

She said she made a wish with each fold, and used it to let out her suffering and pain. Each crane meant something to Sadako, and, when she died, the crane became a symbol of peace and healing because of her.

I walk through the glass doors and push my way along the crowded corridor. I hadn't stopped thinking about Nate's message or the comments on Al's page all night. I'd typed out a response so many times, but I just really didn't know what to say. Part of me was a bit annoyed that he'd got arsey with me, especially when all I'd wanted to do was make something nice for Al.

I turn to go up the stairs that lead to form and there's this massive crowd in the way. A boy rushes past me, pulling his mate by the arm. People have their phones out and there's a big group laughing, or sniggering, or shouting. I catch someone saying Nathan's name, and then bits of what people are saying:

'Is he gonna knock him out?'

'I ain't hanging around here if there ain't gonna be no fight.'

'Have you got it on Snap?'

'Do you think it's about his brother, you know, the one that killed himself? What's his name?'

'Al . . .'

'Eh, get it up on Snapchat.'

'Nah, mate, you need to Facebook Live that . . .'

'I hope he kills him . . .'

I head through the crowd. I knock into elbows and bags, trying my hardest to get to the front. I think I hear Nathan shouting, but I can't work out what he's saying over the noise in the corridor. Finally, I manage to squeeze my way through and I see him. He's holding Lewi up against one of the lockers and shouting in his face. I haven't known him long, but Nathan being this aggressive doesn't seem like him. What's gone on? He lets go of Lewi and leans against one of the lockers, and for a minute he looks like he's going to cry. There's people laughing all around me, but I can't take my eyes off Nathan. How hurt he looks. How desperate he seems.

Jeremiah shoves someone out of the way so that he's really close to get a better view on his phone. He's filming the whole thing. He turns the camera to face him and does this boxing commentator impression:

'Bruv, what kinda fight is this? Maybe if they threw some punches instead of hugging each other then it would be worth watching . . .'

People start to laugh. Nathan begins shouting again and Lewi looks dead scared. He scans the crowd to see if someone's going to help him. Then Eli and Cole come over. I feel the excitement start bubbling around me again. Like everyone wants a fight. As if people want to see someone get hurt. And suddenly I'm back to three months ago. I'd been walking to class with Tara and seen Al with Eli and Cole. Eli was really close up to Al and kept saying, *'What's wrong with you? You fucking special or what? Eh? Eh?'*

Kids around us had laughed, including Tara, but Al looked really frightened. You could see how much he wanted to be left alone. He'd tried to say something, but Eli had started taking the piss out of the way he spoke and then kicked his bag across the floor. I remember Al picking it up and looking over at me. But I hadn't said a thing. I didn't tell Eli that he was wrong or Tara and the others to shut up. I didn't go over and help. It was like I was glued to the spot and too scared to say anything cos I didn't want Eli to turn on me. And I guess I thought it was okay cos he'd only ever done something to Al that once . . .

Now I look at Nathan as Eli says something before walking off with Cole. Most people are moving on cos they realize there isn't going to be a fight, then Nathan catches my eye. He looks embarrassed. I want to go up to him, to see if he's all right. But he just turns and walks off.

The bell goes and I head up the stairs. I think about sending Nathan a message or something, but I still don't know what I'd say. I push open the classroom door and see that Tara's already in there. She's not got as much fake tan on as she normally wears and she looks different – the way she used to when we were kids. She'd tried to call me a bunch of times last night, but I'd kept my phone on silent. She moves over in her seat and smiles.

'Megs.' She waves and points to the chair next to her. Part of me wants to sit at a table on my own. Especially after all the stuff yesterday and the fact she *liked* all those comments on Al's page. But then the other part thinks that she's still Tara. She's still the same person I've known for most of my life. So I sit down next to her. Up close, her face is blotchy and I realize that something's wrong.

'I'm sorry, yeah?' she says. 'Maybe I shouldn't have *liked* those comments, but I didn't think it mattered. They're just *like*s. I didn't know you were even that close to Al. I just thought that you talked to him in class a bit.'

I don't say anything. I feel guilty. All the time I spent with Al and no one even knew.

'I didn't mean to upset you,' Tara says. 'You're me best mate. I hate it when we fall out.' She leans closer. 'Can we just

179

forget it? *Please*.' She nudges my arm and it feels so much like the way it used to that my anger fades. I don't want to fall out with her, either. She is my best mate after all.

I nod. 'Yeah, all right,' I say.

Tara throws her arms round me and I hug her back.

'I don't think Eli wants to go out with me any more,' she says, picking at the nail varnish on her fingers. 'He keeps blowing hot and cold and, if I ain't got a boyfriend, what else do I have?'

'You don't need him,' I say.

Tara looks down at the table. 'It's okay for you, though,' she says, and she looks embarrassed. 'You've got a plan for what you wanna do with your life.' She shrugs. 'I don't have none of that.'

'You'll figure it out,' I say. 'Whatever it is you're meant to do, you'll find it. And you've got loads going for you.' I lean back in my chair. 'Fucking hell, boys can come and go, but we'll always have each other.'

Tara nods and she rests her head on my shoulder. 'You're right,' she says. 'Sorry, I've just been a bit shit lately.'

I think of Al, and how I walked off and left him in the corridor. I wonder if he ever forgave me for being a shitty friend as well.

'It's all right,' I say.

Tara pulls her phone out of her pocket. 'Eli's been messaging all these things to me. About me not looking right. Maybe he's got a point. Maybe that's why he's gone off me . . .'

I stiffen. I want to tell her that Eli's a waste of space, that

180

he needs to just get in the bin, but if I go off about him now Tara will use it against me later if they end up working it out. So I don't say anything. Tara opens Insta and goes to her profile. She's following over 5,000 people. Most of them are celebrities or influencers, make-up artists or models. Mine's the same, apart from a few artists and museums. She shows me a picture of a girl in a bikini. 'I don't look like her, though,' she says. 'And Eli *liked* that picture.' She brings up another photo. 'I don't have an arse like her.' Then another. 'I don't have hair like her. I don't have *fucking lips* like her. I don't have a stomach like her.' She goes back to her home page and carries on scrolling through pictures of celebrities or models. People with diet shakes or in the gym.

I shake my head. 'They don't even look like them,' I say. 'It's all Photoshop. Or most of those celebrities or whatever, they've got trainers, surgeons, stylists. They can spend all day in the gym. None of it's real.'

I glance back at her phone. Even though I know what I'm saying is right, that it's all fake, I can't help but be jealous of these girls, too. I feel the same way as Tara. That we'll never be good enough, no matter how much we try or what we do.

Tara sighs, then clicks off her phone. 'Suppose,' she says, then she wipes her eyes. 'What you doing after school? You wanna come mine? We can go and grab a McDonald's and binge on some Netflix.'

'I told Ms Baker that I'd stay behind after school and pick out some paintings. We're doing this exhibition thing for Al.'

Tara's face goes funny. 'All right,' she says.

'I can meet you after, though?' I say, not wanting us to argue again. 'Shouldn't be more than an hour.'

A smile spreads across Tara's face, and she brings me in for a hug. 'It's a date, Megs,' she says. 'But I ain't letting you pick the series this time.'

The rest of school goes by pretty quickly and I make my way to the art room. I'd given Nathan Al's sketchbook, but I'm sure that there's enough of Al's drawings around the classroom for the exhibition and I've got a few at home that I can bring in, too. I look at my phone as I walk. Jeremiah's video of Lewi and Nathan is all over Insta and Snapchat, but I don't watch it and I don't look at the comments, either. Instead, I go to Nathan's Facebook profile, just to see. But he hasn't posted anything since his status about missing Al last week.

I'm so busy on my phone that I walk straight into Lewi. As in I practically trample all over him cos he's sitting on the stairs. He lets out this yell, which makes me jump, and then he moves a few centimetres away from where he was sitting, rubbing his leg.

'Ow, man!' he says.

He's wearing this dark blue Nike hoodie, and he stretches his legs back out, so he takes up three of the steps.

'Sorry,' I say. 'But what are you doing sitting there anyway?'

Lewi shrugs. 'Nothing,' he says.

He looks up at me and his eyes look like he's been smoking again. He's pulled the sleeves of his hoodie all the way down, so that they cover his hands, the way that little kids do.

182

I can hear everyone in the playground outside and I don't know why Lewi hasn't gone out with Eli and the rest of them. His leg is shaking *really* badly, and the plastic JD bag that he's got across his back makes this scrunching sound, as he leans back against the steps.

'I'm waiting for everyone to clear off. There's nowhere to hide in this stupid school,' he says. 'Not like you can hide anyway. People can tell when you've read stuff, when you've seen stuff ... been online and that. Where you've been and who with.'

He puts his head in his hands. I don't really understand what he's talking about. He looks awful, though. Like *really* ill. He straightens himself up, and I can see how big his pupils are. Then he points at the picture of the cross on the wall.

'You reckon all this is true?' he says. 'All this ... God stuff. Heaven and hell, being forgiven. All that crap about being a good person.'

He starts to rock a bit and I feel kinda creeped out. I've never seen him like this. He just used to act stupid, like the class clown or something. But this is proper ... weird. I sit on the step below him.

'Yeah,' I say. I turn to the picture. 'It has to be.' I'm dying to ask him what happened with Nathan earlier, but I don't want to make him more upset.

He clasps his hands to stop them shaking. His shoes are all battered and scuffed, and his trousers are way too short for him.

'Why do you think it has to be?' he says to me.

183

I shrug. 'Well,' I say, 'you can't just have bad things happen in the world all the time, without any good. I mean, there has to be some sort of balance. There has to be somewhere you can go afterwards. It's pretty sad if there isn't. If you just die and that's it. You're gone. Forever.'

Lewi is silent for a moment.

'Al used to say that, when you die, you become stardust,' he says with a smile, suddenly looking happy. 'That every atom in your body came from a star that exploded and when you die it just goes back to how it started.' He stops and takes a breath. 'Al was so different. Sometimes too different ...'

'I know,' I say.

Lewi puts his head in his hands. 'It's really messed me up. All of this. I can't think about nothing else, except that he's gone.'

'We're doing this art exhibition,' I say. 'For Al. To remember him. Ms Baker said that she'd ask Mr Ballan if we can use the assembly hall. Set it up properly. Pick some of his paintings to display and stuff. I'm going to sort it out now.'

Lewi lifts his head up and he smiles, showing his chipped tooth. He shakes his head. 'Al would've been buzzing over that. All he used to go on about was having his work in some exhibition.'

His phone vibrates and his face darkens. He stares down at it. The screen's cracked, probably from all the times he's dropped it. He moves it from one hand to the other.

'Al was a proper mate,' Lewi says. 'The best mate I ever had ...' He pauses. 'No one will ever come close to him. It's like he was too good, too good for all of us. And I messed that up.'

I don't say anything cos I feel like that, too.

'I just wish we'd never stopped speaking,' Lewi says. 'That things were different. That I hadn't . . .' He stops and shakes his head, and, standing up, he pulls some Rizla papers out of his pocket. He turns to walk down the staircase and then he stops.

'Megan,' he says, 'there's a few of Al's paintings I know he really liked. There's this one on the roof of the boxing gym near his house. Y'know the Jimmy Egan one? And he just got everything right, like the stars and the estate and that shit park. And there was this other one he drew of all these paper birds and that. He said they were a symbol of hope.' He pauses. 'I know they were Al's favourites.'

I nod. 'Thanks,' I say. 'I'll find them.'

'You're proper like him, you know,' he says. 'A bit weird and that, but in a good way . . . an Al way.'

I smile.

'I'll see you around, yeah?' he says.

I nod. 'Bye.'

Lewi walks down the staircase, and I stand up and head towards the art room. I smile cos Lewi's right, Al would be buzzing if he knew we were going to show his paintings. I know *just* how much all this would've meant to him. Having people look at his paintings, his artwork taking up the whole of the assembly hall, his heart would've just . . . exploded with pure happiness. And, even though it won't bring him back, maybe Al will look down on it from up there. Among all those stars. Al will be there, burning brightly. And he'll see his paintings, his work, all on show, and in that moment – just for a little bit – everything will be fine.

NATHAN

chapter twenty-one

This one time Lewi had stolen some weed from his brother and we were out in the park, near to the abandoned town hall. I told him about how powerful symbols can be. How they can be used to fuel hope or fear. Then I kept pointing up at the sky and showing him where all the different stars were and it just felt really peaceful and nice. Lewi was smoking more and more, and he kept shaking his head and saying, 'You're dead weird you ... dead weird.' And then he leaned in and kissed me. When I pulled away, he said, 'I ain't gay, I ain't gay.' But I didn't care if he was. He was my best mate, and I would've been there for him no matter what. I'd never have told anyone what had happened between us. Never.

It's almost dark by the time I get home. It's not late, but I spent a bit of time just walking around after school. I must've checked my phone about a hundred times to see if Sophie had accepted my friend request, but nothing yet. I open the front door and hear the sound of the television coming from the living room. Some kinda lame quiz show is on. The lights are on, but the door is tightly shut. I walk in and Saul and Lauren are sitting on the sofa. He's got his hand down the front of her top and she jumps, pulling at it to make sure she's not showing anything.

'Get a room,' I say.

'Jesus,' she says, then turns to Saul. 'Thought you said you had a free house?'

'I thought he was out,' Saul says.

'Don't worry,' I say. 'I ain't gonna stick around while you two get off with each other.'

Saul smooths down his hair, and looks pissed that I'd interrupted them, but how was I supposed to know?

'Go on then,' he says. 'Clear off.'

'Where's Mum?'

Saul sighs. 'She's gone round Carol's,' he says. 'She's taken Phoebe with her. They're tryna sort out funeral stuff. You know, hymns and that.'

'Al wouldn't have wanted hymns,' I say. 'He'd want one of them shit indie songs he was always playing.'

'It's what Mum wants,' Saul snaps. 'She thinks there should at least be some religious stuff.'

I kick against the edge of the door with my foot, and see Saul mouth a *sorry* to Lauren out the corner of my eye. She

188

tosses her head back, to shake her thick curls, and wraps her fingers round Saul's hand. Her nails are painted this bright orange colour, and she rests her head on his shoulder.

'Why didn't you go with her?' I ask Saul.

'I've got my own life,' he replies.

Lauren sighs loudly and stands up, reaching for her jacket. 'I'd better go anyway,' she says to Saul. 'My mum will go *proper* spare if I'm not home soon. She likes us all to have tea together. You walking me?'

Saul nods. 'Yeah, course,' he says. 'What sort of boyfriend d'you think I am?'

'One who lies about having a free house,' she says. Saul can't stop staring at her, probably cause he knows how lucky he is.

'Nathan,' she says. 'What was all that about with Eli this morning? You know everyone's been talking about it. Everyone's been saying that you looked like you were *proper* gonna lose your rag. You don't wanna be starting nothing with Eli.'

'What's she on about?' Saul asks.

'Nothing,' I say.

He looks at me and then at Lauren. Out of all the girls he could've gone out with in Wythenshawe, it had to be her. Yeah, she's fit, but she can't keep anything to herself.

'I just wanted to speak to Lewi, all right? I wanted to find out wot he knows . . .'

'Not this again,' Saul says. 'I thought you were gonna stop all this rubbish?'

'It ain't rubbish. You didn't see him today. He was proper shady. I know he's hiding summat more than ever now.'

Saul picks up his leather jacket. 'Nate,' he says. 'Honestly, I ain't gonna tell you again ... '

He turns the collar up and I see a smirk flash across Lauren's face, like she's happy that she caused an argument or summat. I shake my head and she reaches into her handbag and takes out her lipgloss.

'Anyway,' she says, 'I'm not saying people don't feel sorry for you, but you can't go around acting all weird. Eli was saying that you were being a bit of a ... you know.'

I stare at her. 'No, I don't know.'

'A psycho,' she says.

I feel my face getting all hot. Maybe that's wot Megan thinks, too. That I'm losing the plot. Maybe that's why everyone's been staring at me, not cause they feel sorry for me, but cause they think I'm cracking up.

'And I tell you what,' Lauren continues, 'you don't wanna make an enemy out of Eli. He don't even need an excuse to start something.'

'He wouldn't dare touch him,' Saul says quickly. 'Over my dead body would he lay a finger on Nate.'

Lauren shakes her head. 'Anyway,' she says, 'I know it must be hard. You're the one who ... found Al and that. But, if you go round doing stuff like that, it's not gonna help anyone.'

Wot else am I supposed to do? That's wot I wanna say, but they don't get it. They don't know wot it was like for me to find Al. For me to look up at him hanging there and know that, if I would've come home sooner, I would've been able to stop him. That if I would've picked up the phone he'd still be here. I can't just shut it all out and not want to find out wot happened.

'All right, yeah,' I say. 'I'll drop it. Everyone thinks I've got a screw loose. I get it.' I don't mean it – I won't drop it till I find out wot happened – but I don't need Saul on my back.

'I won't be long,' he says as Lauren loops her arm through his. 'Call me if you need anything, yeah?'

'Yeah.'

Lauren moves her hand across Saul's bicep, running her fingers along his muscles. They're always all over each other – it's a bit too much if you ask me. The charm bracelet that Saul got for her birthday glints in the light. She thinks it's from one of those really posh jewellery shops in town, but Saul got it off this guy on our estate who nicks things, then sells them on for a cheaper price. As I stare at the bracelet, something else catches my eye.

'Wot's that?' I say, pointing.

She jiggles the charm bracelet. 'Saul got it me,' she says. 'You've seen it loads of—'

'Not that,' I say. I walk closer, and point to the top of her hand that's exposed. '*That.*'

Lauren unlinks her arm from Saul's, then looks at her hand.

'Oh ...' she says. 'Yeah, I just did it in one of my mock exams. I'm always forgetting what those symbols mean ... you know, in chemistry? Gases and all that. My dad said if I got a B he'd give me a hundred quid. And my teacher's so blind that I could scribble the answers on my flipping forehead and he wouldn't notice.'

I look at the scribble on her hand. It's just one of those equation things, with a bubble around it. Lauren nudges Saul, and my throat goes all dry. Maybe it's cause of the position of the scribble on Lauren's hand, but it suddenly comes back to me. Where I'd seen the symbol in Al's sketchbook before ...

I run up the stairs to my room and close the door. I empty my rucksack out on to my bed, picking up my phone from the rest of the crap. I open up Facebook and go to Lewi's profile. I scroll through his photos till I find wot I'm looking for.

The photo that was taken around the back of the sports hall with Lewi, Eli and Cole. I zoom in on the screen, focusing on Lewi's hand. I hadn't taken much notice before – I'd just thought it was some stupid mark – but now I can see it clearly. It's the same symbol from Al's drawing ... the mountains, or triangles, all inside this swirl. I look at the three of them in the photo: Eli's dark skin, Cole's finger sticking up towards the camera. I dunno wot this symbol is, or wot it even means, but Eli and Cole and Lewi all have it. I take a screenshot of the photo on my phone.

I type *SG* in the search bar. Sophie's profile comes up again, but she's still not accepted my friend request. If Al was going out with her, then she might know wot the symbol means. Maybe Al told her things that he couldn't tell me or Saul. I click on Messenger and then I type:

I'm Al's brother ... he's dead. I need 2 talk 2 u.

Why had Al drawn this symbol so many times? And why was Eli protecting Lewi? And who exactly is Sophie? I stare up at the plastic comet on my ceiling, and try to come up with reasons, but nothing makes sense. I get up and head out my bedroom door towards the second set of stairs that lead up to Al's room. I haven't been up there since it happened. But I need to figure this out and his room might have more clues.

I walk up the stairs slowly. My palms are all sweaty and my legs feel weird. Like I've just taken some stuff or downed a massive bottle of vodka. I force myself to keep going, one stair at a time, till I'm standing outside Al's door.

His name is carved into the middle panel and he's painted all these stars and planets around it on the wood. I touch the edge of the drawing with my finger and I feel sweat, or maybe it's tears, on my face. I breathe out and push open his bedroom door.

MEGAN

chapter twenty-two

When you're in love, it's as if your whole world feels different. It's like everything before, like the way you used to look at life, has somehow changed. All of a sudden, there's all this colour and there's teal where you hadn't noticed it before and purples bleeding into every part of your life. Everything around you seems so bright and you just want to stay there, you know? Among all that colour, and all that brightness, and all that life. That's why I tried to paint it, so that I could make it last for as long as possible.

I lay Al's paintings out on one of the art-room tables. They cover every centimetre of it with different shades and colours and textures. Ms Baker told me that we could definitely use the assembly hall and I want this exhibition to be as big as possible. I want everyone in school to be there, and I want to invite Al's family. I know they'd want to see Al's work on display, just as much as he did.

The more I think about it, the more I know I'm doing this to try and make it up to Al for not noticing that something had been wrong with him. And for not being a good enough friend to stand up for him when he needed me. I'm not just talking about the time in the corridor with Eli, either. There were all those times when Tara asked me why I even spoke to Al, what was so special about him. And I'd just shrug it off and say nothing. I never once told her that it was cos he was funny and kind and different. I'd never even set foot in a gallery or a museum till I started hanging out with Al. I'd never even thought about uni till I met him. Cos he made me realize how bored I was. Bored of just going round town and drinking in the park and caring what people thought of me.

I walk round the table and run my hand along the different canvases. There's loads of them: some are just rough outlines and sketches, but others are like explosions of colour. Al's painted the sky purple or gold. He's managed to bring the estate to life – make it beautiful somehow.

I'd found one of the paintings that Lewi had told me about straight away. All these tiny paper birds hanging down from the ceiling – he'd drawn loads of them, but each one seemed unique, different.

I start to go through others in a pile Ms Baker left me. I flick past one of the centre of Civic, another of the crowded bus station near Piccadilly Gardens, one of his sister and his mum. I keep going till I see the other one that Lewi had talked about: Al and Nathan sitting on the boxing-gym roof, their legs hanging over the edge as they both look up at the sky. I can see why it was one of Al's favourites. He's used teal and purple, and everything around them looks so bright. The estate in the background has been charcoaled in. Out of all of Al's paintings this is the best one. I've never seen anything like it. I move the painting to the middle of the table and I feel this sadness tearing through me again. Al was only just getting started – he was only just at the beginning.

I lift another painting up and something drops out. I bend down and pick it up off the floor.

At first, I think it's just a bit of scrap paper. But, when I look closely, I see that there's a wing and a tail and a beak. It's all flattened, but the shape is still there – a paper crane. Carefully, I hold it out in my hand, like it's a real living thing. Then I put it down on the table and gently pull at the sides so that it isn't squashed. I move the wings and the tail so that it's back to the shape that it should be. I remember Al telling me about how powerful symbols can be, and that these paper cranes had come from something so horrific. He'd said that the crane symbolized peace. Peace and healing.

I look round the empty art room. Whatever happened with Al, whatever he was going through, he'd been in so much pain – too much to handle.

NATHAN

chapter twenty-three

Sometimes I think maybe it would've been simpler if I'd just told someone. If I'd gone into Nathan's room, or mentioned it to Saul, or written it down. I tried to. I did. There were times when I was so close ... when I wanted someone to just figure it out. Because sometimes it's hard to find the words when you don't have them. When it's like they don't exist. And maybe that's why I paint and draw routes on a map to places to escape to. Maybe that's why I make paper cranes. Because they can express a little bit of what I could never say out loud.

I sit on Al's bed and look around me. Everything still seems the same, but it's hard to be in here. I keep getting flashes of wot's real and wot's not. My nightmares and the way the room is now. They all blend into one: the tie wrapped round Al's neck. Al begging me to 'save him' in my dream. The paramedics cutting him down. My mum screaming, '*No, not my boy. No!*'

My hands won't stop shaking. I stare at the map and tickets Blu-Tacked to the walls, his clothes folded at the end of his bed – one of his school blazers is hanging on the outside of his wardrobe. There's an old sheet of newspaper on the windowsill with paintbrushes spread out along it. It even still smells like Al. More than anywhere else in the house. Like he's just gone out and he'll be back in a minute.

I look at his desk chair, still in the same place as that day, and something twists in the pit of my stomach. I feel sick, like I might throw up. I know it sounds dumb, but I can't look up, even tho I know he won't be there.

I pick up a hoodie with *To Boldly Go!* written on it that's on the bed next to me. I hold it up to my nose and try to breathe him in. I can almost smell that chemical stuff he used to clean his brushes with . . . now it doesn't just make me think of Al, but of Megan, too.

I press the hoodie against me. I never really bothered with any of that hugging shit when Al was around, but, if he was here now, it would be different. I'd hold on to him so he knew just how much I loved him. My chest feels tight and I suddenly can't breathe as all the hurt comes rushing back through my body. Being alone here in his room, I can't escape it – the hole he's left, and I'm not sure I can take it.

I look at the exam timetable that he's stuck above his desk, all the dates highlighted. The last exam has got this bubble drawn round it. Al was so busy planning for his future ...

I put down the hoodie and walk over to the desk, reaching down to pull on the handle of the drawer. It's locked, just like I knew it would be. I try to pull harder and force it open, but it won't budge. Al always kept that drawer locked, so if he'd been hiding something that would be a good place to look first.

I pull open one of the smaller side drawers. There's a pack of charcoal crayons, some dried acrylic paints, bus tickets, folded bits of paper, all these crisps and sweet wrappers, but nothing else.

I try his wardrobe next, pulling down on all his clothes so that the plastic hangers break and his hoodies and jeans fall to the floor. I go through his pockets, turning them inside out, trying to find something. There's more crumpled bus tickets, a stale bit of chewing gum, old pencil sharpenings ... I keep going, pulling and tugging through the clothes, and then I move over to the other side of his room, emptying things out, tipping them upside down. I look through the maple-syrup tin he kept his art brushes in, his school bag, his wastepaper bin. Pens and school books and files scatter across the floorboards. I don't even know wot I'm looking for, but I don't wanna stop. I can't stop.

And now the anger's back.

I tear up Al's books, kick some of his stuff. I wanna find something, *anything*, that shows me wot I'm missing. Wot was really going on with him. But, at the same time, I wanna hurt him. Hurt him for being a *know-it-all* prick, for being selfish, for taking his life and not even bothering to explain why. I wanna hurt him for leaving me cause I miss him more than anything.

I kick and I tear and I smash. I throw his desk lamp on to the floor and crush the bulb into loads of little pieces. I keep going, and it feels good to get it all out. But then I stop, tryna catch my breath. Al's room is trashed ... More than trashed, his stuff is all ruined. I look at the mess around me and sit down on the floor, I can't move cause I feel broken. Wot kind of brother does this make me? Destroying the only things we have left?

I glance at the wardrobe. The door is ajar, and I see a pile of old shoeboxes neatly stacked at the bottom that I hadn't noticed before. I get up and pull them out. I take off the lid of the first one. It's empty apart from some scrunched-up tissue paper in the corner. I kick it and it skids across the floor. The next one has some old trainers in it, the laces frayed, and I shove the lid back on. It feels like one of those weird fairground games where you have to try and choose the right box that has a prize inside it. I open the last one and at first all I can see is more scrunched-up tissue paper. But I move it aside and at the bottom, hidden in the corner, is an old Samsung phone.

Downstairs, the front door slams. It's probably Saul or my mum, and I don't want them to find me in here. I don't want them to go on at me for trashing Al's room. So I shove the phone in my pocket and walk over the mess, back down to my room.

*

200

Why would Al have another phone? And why did he hide it inside some shoebox? I know that Kyle's brother had two phones and he'd been sent down for armed robbery. People only had two phones if they were hiding something. I sit on my bed and press the *on* button. *Insert SIM* flashes across the screen, which means Al must've got rid of the SIM card for some reason. I go straight to the messages. None of them are saved with any names, and there's just the beginning of the phone numbers. There's a few telling him that his credit is running low, and loads from this number ending in 03.

I click on the first message:

I cnt wait 2 meet u. Sxx

I scroll down to the next one, and the next.

No one understands me like u do.

Me and u, we're special. xx

Come on WhatsApp. Sxx

Did u see that comment last night? It reminded me of u. Sxx

Did u get the picture? xx

I've sent u a picture xx

Did u get it? xx

I've never felt like this about any1 b4. Sxx

I read through all the messages from S, which must be Sophie. There's loads of her going on about her day, saying how much she missed him, how clever he was, how she couldn't wait to meet him. There's pictures of heart emojis, a face blowing a kiss, a face with hearts for eyes. They go back at least six months. I stare at one sent a week before Al killed himself:

> Come online xxx there's something I want to show u. xxxx

That's the last message that she sent him, and the last one in the phone. I reach for my phone and copy Sophie's number into it. Then I look through my messages, the ones that Al had sent to me:

> Yo, bro, I've not got my key, will you let Mum know?

> K

> Was that u, who just went upstairs?

> Yea

> U all right???

> Yea

> Yo, where u at? Mum's been tryna call u.

> Out

> Where??

> Museum

> Will u stop sending me those star videos, man?!

> K

> U all right?

> Yea

It was like Al could talk to Sophie way more than he could talk to me. All I got was one-word answers. I throw the phone across the room.

'Why couldn't you talk to me?' I shout. 'Why couldn't you just tell me?' I put my head in my hands and start to cry.

MEGAN

chapter twenty-four

No matter where you are on earth, Orion will always rise above the eastern horizon in the early evening. I'd tell Megan to look out for it, to try and spot the three stars of his belt. Once you can make them out, it becomes a map for you to see other constellations. But the thing about Orion is that he reaches his highest elevation around the middle of the night. In the hours before dawn, the giant figure is seen over your western horizon. And, in a way, it's almost like he's always there. Watching over you.

It's *proper* cold and depressing by the time that I leave school, even though it's only just before five. I button up my coat to keep out the cold and cut through Civic, passing the row of cash machines and a few of the shops with their shutters halfway down. I make my way to the Poundstretcher near the big Asda. I'd messaged Tara to tell her to meet me there, but she's *always* late so I'm not surprised I'm there first. I shove my hands in my pockets. There's a group of boys hanging around outside Asda. A few of them whistle and one of them shouts something, but I just ignore them.

I can't stop thinking about Al's crane. I'd put it in my bag, making sure I was dead careful with it, so that it wouldn't end up squashed again. I just felt like I wanted to take care of it.

Tara comes rushing towards me. She's changed into some jeans and a white top since school, and she pulls her thin jacket round her, trying to keep warm. She seems in a much better mood since this morning and I can't help but think that it's got something to do with Eli.

'Sorry, Megs,' she says as she flings her arms round me. 'Mum started going with herself, didn't she? Why couldn't you tell me you'd invited people round? The house is a tip – *blah-blah-blah*. I told her it was only you. I wouldn't mind, but when has our house ever not been in a state?'

I laugh. 'Yeah, it's true. Sorry, but it is.'

Tara links her arm through mine. '*I know!* Anyway, she's fine now. Think she's going out. So we'll have the big TV in the living room.'

'Sounds good,' I say.

We head towards this brick walkway so that we can get to the McDonald's quicker, and we pass the group of boys standing outside Asda. One of them whistles again, and another one says: 'Nah, she's fit, man!'

But Tara pulls a face. 'Mate,' she says, 'give it up! It ain't *never* gonna happen.' His friends all fall about laughing and as we carry on walking one of them shouts after us, calling Tara a bitch, but she doesn't seem to care. I wish that I could be more like her, that I could just say whatever I wanted, and not worry about it.

'Did you sort out that art thing?' Tara asks as we cut through the car park. I don't think she's saying it to take the piss. It seems genuine.

'Some of it,' I say. 'But I've still got loads to do. I want to get it right, pick Al's best paintings. Cos I thought that I could invite his family and stuff, and mayb—'

I feel Tara stiffen and I stop talking.

But then she just shrugs. 'It's all right,' she says. 'You can talk about it.' But there's something in her tone that's a bit off. 'I mean, I know I don't get all that art stuff, and you probably think that I'm just your stupid mate . . .'

I pull her closer. 'As if,' I say. 'Daft? *Yes.* But stupid? *No.*' We approach McDonald's and I can't help but laugh. 'D'you remember the time we watched that horror film and your mum's boyfriend was more scared than us?'

Tara sniggers. 'Yeah, then we put that hat on top of the broom and held it up in front of the kitchen window. He actually shat himself. Ran out screaming.' She laughs. 'I always thought that one was all right, to be fair.'

'Yeah,' I say. 'Me too.'

We cut across this bit of balding grass and get to the main entrance of McDonald's. It's pretty full, and through the glass windows I can see groups of kids sitting at the tables inside.

'I'm glad we're hanging out,' Tara says as she turns to pull open the door.

I smile cos I've missed this. I've missed the way we used to be. And, right now, everything feels normal.

Then someone shouts Tara's name. She lets go of the door and my stomach sinks as I turn round to see Eli and Cole across the road.

They leg it through the traffic and something in Tara changes. Shifts.

'Are you two all right now?' I say under my breath.

'Yeah,' Tara says. 'I sent him something on Snapchat. That got him talking to me again. Y'know what boys are like.'

But I didn't cos I'd never really had a boyfriend. Not properly. I'd kissed a few people, but I hadn't been out with anyone.

Eli puts his arm round Tara. 'Look who it is,' he says. He leans in and kisses Tara and I swear I want to be sick. Eli pulls away and I just want him and Cole to go. Why did they have to be here as well?

'So you're not ghosting me no more?' Tara says.

Eli pulls her in closer. 'Nah. Not after you sent me that photo anyway – how could I?'

Tara smiles and I see Eli and Cole share a smirk. Tara doesn't seem to notice. Eli must've shown Cole the photo, too.

'What you on?' Eli asks. 'We're gonna go McDonald's, then chill in the park. Cole's got a twenty.' He wraps his other arm round Tara, then whispers something in her ear. Tara pushes him away.

'Eli!' she says, but she can't keep a straight face.

'What, man?' he says, and he kisses her neck. 'Can you blame me?'

Tara turns to me. I want her to tell Eli that we've got plans. I want her to sack him off, so that we can just go back to how it was before Eli and Cole got here. Tara looks at me, then back at Eli.

'Tara,' I say, and the words come out hoarse. 'We're meant to be going to yours.'

Tara's face crumples for a minute.

'It's all right, pancake tits,' Eli says. 'You can come, too.'

He smiles and Cole and Tara snigger. There it is again. It makes me so angry that she just laughs along. That she changes whenever they're both around. I want to tell Eli that I'm not fucking called pancake tits. But I can't get the words out.

As always.

I look at Tara. Inside, I'm pleading with her, begging her to just say no.

'Come on, Megs,' she says. 'We can watch Netflix any time. Let's just go, yeah?'

Normally, I would do. Like I had done this whole summer.

'*Please, Megs*,' Tara says, and part of her seems desperate. Desperate for me to be there. But not cos she wants to hang out with me, probably just so she can make herself look better around the boys. 'It'll be a right laugh.'

I shake my head. 'Nah,' I say. 'Sorry, I'm going home.'

Tara stares at me and she looks upset for a minute. '*Fine,*' she snaps. 'What, just cos I'm not that fucking weirdo Al, you think you're too good for me now?'

Eli and Cole both laugh.

'What?' I say, but Tara's words sting.

'You sure you didn't fancy him? That there wasn't something going on between you two? I mean, why else would you be doing all this stuff? That page ... some stupid exhibition.'

'We were just mates,' I say.

'Come off it!' Tara says. 'You two spending time together. The way you've been going on about Jeremiah's Snap. You even had a photo of you and Al up as your profile picture.' Tara pauses. 'Anyway, it's not like you can do any better. That fucking weirdo is all you're ever gonna get!'

'Oh, savage!' Eli says.

Eli and Cole laugh harder, and I stand there, stunned. *Say something, Megan. Say something*, I tell myself. But I can't. For a minute, Tara smiles to herself. Like this is all a game and she's won. But then she looks hurt. Almost sorry for what she's just said.

'Megan,' Tara starts, 'I didn't mean—'

I turn and walk off, my legs shaking. I feel so stupid for thinking that one afternoon of hanging out and Netflix was going to change anything. Tara turns into someone else when she's around Eli and Cole – someone I don't even recognize – and her words sting. I'm suddenly angry at myself cos I wish I'd said something back. But, like always, I just stood there and let Tara say whatever she wanted to.

I turn on to my street and everything's really quiet. It's so silent that I can't even hear any music, aeroplanes, or passing cars.

I turn round and look up at the sky. There are all these tiny little stars, and then two really bright ones in the corner. Glowing. Shining. Burning brightly. I squint my eyes, and I try to work out if I can see any of the constellations that Al used to tell me about.

I find the three stars in a row that he always told me to look for and then I pull out my phone and take a few pictures and upload them to Insta. I don't use a filter or anything cos they don't need one. Then I type *Thinking of you, Al xx* and tag him in the post, even though he'll never see it. Then I video the sky and upload it to my story. It's so beautiful that I just want to share it.

I don't know what made me look, but deep down I hope it was Al.

I go inside my house and head straight to my room, chucking my art folder down on my desk next to the cup that still has Nathan's flower in it, although the petals are properly dried up now. I stare round my room. It's covered in all these sketches I've been trying to do and some of Al's paintings, too. A few of them are rough drafts that Al had wanted to throw away, but I'd taken them out of the scrap-paper tray when Al hadn't been looking. Or drawings that he'd given me.

I can't stop thinking about Tara's words. I would always hide my painting stuff whenever she came round. But really I was hiding a piece of myself. I didn't want her to think that I was weird or boring. But I'm not going to hide any of this any more.

I look at my phone. I've got two Insta notifications. One says that Nathan's followed me, and the other is cos he's sent me a message. It's a bit weird that he's followed me, especially after the Facebook message.

I go to my DMs and I see that he's responded to my story of the sky.

> It's not in the stars to hold our destiny ... Soz 4 being a tool in that FB message. I know it wasn't your fault xx

NATHAN

chapter twenty-five

There was this photo of me, up on one of the display boards in the school corridor, with the words Meet Your School Prefects *printed at the top. I'd been so proud to be a prefect because my art teacher had put me forward for it and said, 'You're such a great role model, Al, you're going to go so far . . .' And I remember how happy her words made me feel. Then, one day, I noticed that someone had ripped my face out of the picture. Torn it straight out. And I remember asking myself – why would someone do that? All I could think about for ages was that hole in my photo. And I stopped drawing my own face after that because maybe I didn't deserve to be seen.*

I wake up before the alarm on my phone goes off, not that I really slept much anyway. I click on Megan's Insta story again and watch as it loads and the video of the sky comes up. I'd looked at Megan's Insta a few times just cause I wanted to see more of her pictures and that. Then I saw the story and it reminded me of a quote Al was always banging on about, so I decided to stop being a fool and send her a message. I know she was only tryna be nice and it ain't like the comments were her fault anyway.

I get out of bed and throw my uniform on, shoving Al's Samsung inside my rucksack.

I hear Mum and Saul talking in hushed voices through the kitchen door when I get downstairs and they go silent when I walk into the room, sharing a look that means they must have been talking about me. It feels proper strained and I make my way over to the fridge and pull out a carton of juice.

'You all right, mate?' Saul says, then he turns to Mum. 'I'll leave you two alone, yeah?'

Mum nods, then Saul disappears out the kitchen. I don't know wot this is about, but Mum points to an empty chair.

'Sit down, love,' she says. Her voice sounds hoarse, strained. I take the carton with me and sit down. She doesn't say anything at first, but she reaches forward and places a hand on top of mine.

'Nate,' she says. 'I went to find a suit, for Al to be buried in. I saw his room.'

I look down, embarrassed. I didn't clean it up. I didn't even try to hide the mess. I expect her to go on at me, but she doesn't, she just holds my hand tighter.

213

'It's okay,' she says. 'I'm not annoyed with you – it's just stuff.' She pauses. 'But I'm worried about how you're coping. Maybe it's my fault for pushing you into going back to school too soon. But I think you should talk to someone. A professional.'

I stiffen and move my hand away. 'Nah,' I say. 'I'm *fine*. Wot's talking gonna fix?'

'Everything,' she says. 'And you're *not* okay. Trashing Al's room, the nightmares ... And Saul told me that you're obsessed with a drawing that Al did? I know you're looking for an answer, we all are, but there isn't one, Nathan. It's not right and you're worrying me. You're worrying *us*.'

I pick up my rucksack. I don't wanna listen to this. I don't wanna talk to a complete stranger about Al cause how will that help? Proper men don't talk about their feelings. People would just take the piss if they found out. And anyway I know that once I find out the truth, once I figure out wot had been going on with Al, then I'll feel better. I have to. Talking ain't the answer, action is.

'I ain't gonna talk to some stranger about Al. That won't work for me.'

'How d'you know?' Mum says.

I don't wanna hear any more. I stand up and walk towards the door. 'I'll see you after school.'

'Nathan!' she shouts, but I don't turn round. 'I don't wanna lose another son. *Please*, you need to let someone in.'

I stop in my tracks. The words hit me hard. 'Maybe if Al had spoken to someone,' she continues, 'then he wouldn't have done what he did.'

If Al had spoken to someone ... Wot would she do if she knew I didn't pick up the phone when Al needed me most? She's right: if I had done, then things would be different.

Mum sits back down at the table and puts her head in her hands. How am I supposed to tell her that I'm scared? That a small part of me is worried that I might not be able to handle this on my own. But that I can't tell anyone the truth about that day.

'I'm fine,' I say. 'You don't have to worry.'

I head out the kitchen just as Saul comes back down the stairs. I'm pissed that he's told her about the nightmares, that he's mentioned Al's drawing. That they both think they know wot's best for me.

'Thanks, yeah?' I say. 'How many times have I gotta tell you that I'm all right? That I don't need you sticking your nose in.'

'You're not, tho!' Saul snaps back. 'It's obvious, Nate. And you can't just keep ignoring it.'

I shake my head. 'You dunno nothing,' I say. 'Trust me, I ain't ignoring this.' Then I slam the front door.

I walk along the pavement. There's a thin layer of frost on the ground. I pull my hood up and blow into my hands, rubbing them together to try and keep warm . I feel weak from not sleeping. The nightmares haven't been as bad, but I still have that same dream. The one where I try to save Al, but I can't.

I head down the main road and check Facebook on my phone, but Sophie still hasn't replied to my message or accepted my friend request. I scroll through her profile,

215

looking at all the places she's *checked in* – town, the art gallery, the museum – they are all the *exact* same places as Al, but they haven't *checked in* anywhere together and they haven't *checked in* on the same dates. Did that mean that Al never actually met up with her?

I go to my phone settings and change my number to *private*. I call Sophie's number, but it just goes straight to voicemail. I try again and again, but it's always the same. I think about leaving a message, but I don't. No one even listens to voicemails anyway. I hang up and put my phone back in my pocket.

I reach the school gates, but it's so early that the playground is deserted. I head to the main building and push open one of the heavy glass doors, but I ain't sure where to go. My form room will be locked, and I don't wanna go and sit in the library. I walk towards the main staircase at the end of this long corridor, but I can't concentrate. I feel all these emotions rushing through me, but I don't know how to contain them or wot to do. All I can hear are my mum's words again and again: *'Maybe if Al had spoken to someone, then he wouldn't have done what he did.'*

I turn round and I punch the wall, right above this Year Seven display. How was I supposed to know that he was gonna go home and do that? I punch the wall again and again. It hurts like hell, but at the same time it feels good cause I hate myself for wot I did. I hate myself for not being the kind of brother that Al needed me to be. I keep going till summat cracks and this sharp pain shoots up my wrist. I yell out in agony.

Then I stop. There's a picture of Al on the wall next [to a] Year Seven display. *Meet Your School Prefects* it says at the top and Al's picture is there with a few other kids in his year. Well, half of his photo is there anyway. Part of it has been ripped out ... there's a hole in the middle and most of his face is missing. Just like those blacked-out holes that Al had scribbled on his drawings. But Al wouldn't have done this, would he? So why would someone tear his face out?

My knuckles start to sting and I look down at my hand to see that it's bleeding. I walk up the stairs and keep going till I reach the top floor. It's so early that I don't even know if she'll be there. But I do know that Megan's the only one who'll make me feel better.

I mean, yeah, I fancy her, but it ain't just that. And it ain't just cause she gets how I feel without Al, that I don't have to pretend to be okay. I like spending time with her. I don't have to try when I'm with her. It just feels ... easy.

I push open the art-room door and feel relief when I see her sitting there. All these other feelings come rushing through me. But not bad ones this time.

'Nathan?' she says.

MEGAN

chapter twenty-six

The fascinating thing about space is that it's completely quiet because sound waves need a medium to travel through, and up there there's no atmosphere. So space will always be eerily silent. You won't even hear anyone breathe or walk or fall or yell. Sometimes I imagine how great it would be to just float in this void of quiet. No phones, no noise, no people . . . just silence.

I'd decided to go in early so I could keep going with Al's exhibition. I hadn't slept much last night cos I was still upset over the argument I'd had with Tara. She hadn't even bothered to send me a message.

I pull a sheet of paper out of my bag. I'd done a rough plan of how I wanted Al's exhibition to look, but I wanted to check with Ms Baker to make sure that it was okay.

I *still* hadn't replied to Nathan's Insta DM, either, but I must've looked at it a million times. It made me smile and I kept thinking about the kisses he'd put at the end . . . They *must* mean something. Unless he goes around putting kisses at the end of *all* his messages? The art-room door flies open and it makes me jump cos I *really* don't expect anyone else to be in school at this time. Then Nathan walks in. He's got the hood of his jacket pulled up, and he just stands there for a minute, opening and closing his fist.

'Nathan?'

He turns to look at me, and he smiles, but his face is sweating a bit. And then I look down at his hand. The skin on his knuckles is all cracked and bruised, and the bottom part of his hand is covered in blood.

'Oh my God, what did you do?' I say.

He sits down on one of the stools next to me.

'I dunno,' he says with a shrug. 'I just got angry . . .' Nathan pauses, then he turns to look at me. 'How did you do it? When your dad died, how did you just carry on?'

'I went to talk to someone,' I say, and I suddenly feel proper embarrassed. 'I thought it would be weird talking to a stranger, but it helped me make sense of stuff. Sometimes I felt like I had all these feelings inside me, and I didn't know what to do with them, y'know?'

Nathan nods. 'I feel the same,' he says.

He pulls his hood down and runs a hand through his hair. I

find myself staring at him, thinking about how fit he is, and I have to look away. Nathan moves closer to me.

'Did Al ever mention some girl called Sophie or Star Girl?'

'No, I don't think so,' I say. 'What's going on, Nathan?'

Nathan looks down at his hand, and I don't know why, but I just get this feeling that he's hiding something. That there's something he's holding back.

He shrugs and stands up. 'I really don't know any more, but I'm trying to fix it all.'

I don't ask him what he means by 'fix it'. I'm not sure he even knows anyway. I watch as he walks round the big table, staring at all the sketches and watercolours, running his hand over them, just like I did.

He turns to me. 'These are Al's,' he says. 'He used to think that I wasn't interested, but I could always tell it was his work from a mile off. You just know it's him, don't you?'

'Yeah,' I say. 'I'm doing this exhibition for him. It's going to be in the hall, so that people can see Al's stuff. I wanted there to be something else to remember him by. And at least one of his dreams will sort of happen, you know?'

Nathan smiles. It seems to take up most of his face and he walks round the table again, shaking his head.

'Al would've loved that,' he says. 'He would've been buzzing off this for weeks. Months. I would've made out like I thought it was really shit, but, deep down, I'd've been proper proud.' He pauses. 'I always was. Even though he wound me up sometimes.'

I laugh. 'If Al could hear you now,' I say.

'I know, yeah.' He pauses again. 'Al was lucky,' he says. 'To have a friend like you.'

I feel myself go red. 'Oh, I dunno,' I say, and I look down at the floor. 'I reckon I was the lucky one.'

Nathan goes silent for a minute. 'Me too,' he says. 'And I ain't just saying it cos he's my brother. I'm glad that he was even in my life.' He points towards the painting of the bus station, with all the figures. 'That one's good,' he says. He looks round the art room. 'It's so quiet at home without him. Not that he was proper loud or nothing, but he'd always be going on about summat.' He shrugs. 'I ain't used to it. The silence.'

I nod. 'That's what it feels like in here, too.'

He walks back over to me and then he's standing so close that my heart starts to pound. It's beating proper loudly. He must be able to hear it, too. I'm sure he can. Nathan looks down at my mouth and I think he's going to kiss me ... I *want* him to. But then the first bell goes and I hear some kids shouting outside the art-room door. Nathan moves away and he suddenly looks really awkward.

'Will you let me know when Al's exhibition is and that?' he says.

'Course,' I reply, trying to hide my disappointment.

He smiles. 'I'll see you in a bit,' he says. Then he walks out.

NATHAN

chapter twenty-seven

I remember the day that our dad walked out was the first time that you could see Mercury, Venus, Mars, Jupiter and Saturn just by looking at the sky – you didn't need a telescope or anything. I remember how upset Nate had been and I hadn't known what to say, so I'd taken him up on to the roof of the boxing gym so we could see the sky properly. The rest of the street was quiet and we just stared up at those five tiny planets. I wanted to tell Nathan that it would be okay, that we still had each other, and Mum and Phoebe and Saul. That nothing would break us because we were a family. Us five. But I couldn't find the right words – it's like the bigger feelings are, the harder it is to let them out. So the next day I went out and bought glow-in-the-dark stars to put up on his ceiling. I

thought that if I couldn't tell Nate that it would be okay, that
we would all be okay, then I could at least show him.

l push my way through the crowds of people as I head to form.
I should've just kissed Megan. I kept wondering wot it would
be like. How her lips would feel and that, but I chickened out of
doing anything about it cause wot if she doesn't fancy me back? I
couldn't believe it when Megan said she was doing that exhibition
for Al, tho. It made me smile and forget just how much everything
hurt. I push open my form-room door. My hand's proper killing,
but I try to ignore the pain as I make my way to the back of the
class. Kyle's already sitting there. He's got his coat on and is
leaning back in his chair, listening to some music. He pulls an
earphone out when he sees me.

'Fucking hell,' he says, pointing to my hand. 'Wot
happened?'

I sit next to him and look down at my hand. It's even worse
than before. My fingers are all twisted and my knuckles have
gone this weird colour. I can feel the blood throbbing all the
way along my fingers and up my arm.

'Did Eli get to you or summat?' Kyle asks.

'Nah,' I say, scrunching my face up. 'I did it to myself.' I
put my head down on the desk cause my hand's *proper* hurting
now, and I feel Kyle stiffen.

'Wot?' he says. 'Why would you do that to yourself?'

But I don't say anything.

Kyle sighs. 'Nate, man,' he says. Then I hear him shout, 'Yo,
Ms Davis! Ms Davis! Nate's fucked up his hand.'

'Kyle!' she says. 'Language.'

I feel Kyle slump back in his chair. 'Sorry, miss,' he says. 'But he has, come look!'

I lift my head up off the desk as Ms Davis makes her way over to me. I didn't want anyone to make a fuss about my hand, but I'm in too much pain. Ms Davis crouches down next to me. She looks genuinely worried.

'Nathan,' she says. 'What on earth have you done?'

I shrug. 'Fell,' I say.

'Okay, well, you can't go walking around like that. Get yourself to reception and see who's on First Aid.'

I stand up. 'All right,' I say.

Kyle stands up, too. 'Miss, can I go with him?' he says. 'His hand could drop off or anything. I saw this programme on Netflix, yeah? Where this woman tried to hide this cut, and she got an infection, and then the next minute she had to have her whole hand chopped—'

'All right,' Ms Davis interrupts. 'There's no need to be so dramatic, Kyle! But yes, you can go with him. Take your coat off, though. You know you're not allowed it on indoors.'

Kyle pulls his coat off, and Ms Davis turns to me. 'If you need to go home, Nate, you can do. All right?'

'All right,' I say.

She smiles, but she looks sad. And I know that it's cause of Al. Ms Davis walks back to the front of the classroom and I feel everyone staring as me and Kyle head out. We walk along the corridor in silence.

'I wish you'd tell me wot's going on,' Kyle says. 'And I don't mean all that Lewi stuff . . . I mean, wot's really going on. Why would you mess up your hand like that?'

I look at the floor as we walk. Wot am I supposed to say? That I did this to myself cause I thought I deserved it?

'Look, Nate,' Kyle says, 'wotever it is, you can talk to me about anything. I'm always here for ya.'

Part of me wants to tell him. Cause it's so hard keeping all of this to myself. But, as we pass the canteen, I see Eli and Lewi. They're standing by the row of vending machines in the corner. I stop and I feel Kyle stiffen. The rest of the canteen is empty and all the tables have been stacked to one side. Eli's got Lewi pressed against the drinks machine and he's standing really close to him. I can't hear wot they're saying, but Lewi's got both hands out in front of him and is shaking his head. He looks scared, panicked. Like he's talking really fast.

Eli punches the drinks machine near Lewi's head and Lewi goes still. He stops talking. I turn to Kyle, but he just shakes his head.

'Thought they were supposed to be good mates,' I say, and I can't take my eyes off Eli. Eli moves away from Lewi, then he clocks me. He stares at me for a minute and he sort of changes. Lewi is cowering like he wants to disappear, but suddenly Eli puts his arm round Lewi as if they're good friends. Like everything's all right.

'Come on,' Kyle says, and he carries on walking.

'Yo!' Eli shouts, his voice echoing round the hall. 'Is there summat I can help ya with?'

I don't say nothing. Instead, I turn to catch up with Kyle. I hear Eli laughing as I walk off. Wot was that even about? Wot was the issue between them and why would Eli pretend like it was fine when he saw me?

I drop my rucksack on the floor, and hear voices coming from the kitchen. 'You know, he ain't even spoken about what happened, not properly,' Saul says. 'I'm worried—'

I walk into the kitchen, stopping him mid-sentence.

My mum looks down at her mug on the table. 'Hi, love,' she says. 'We didn't hear you come in.'

'You need to stop talking about me when I ain't here.'

I turn and look at the kitchen door. Al's suit is hanging from one of the hooks at the back.

'I'm taking it to the dry cleaner's,' she says.

Al wouldn't have wanted to be buried in that. He hated wearing suits. She should've picked a T-shirt, or one of his hoodies. There's photographs spread out on the table along with some of Al's certificates from primary school and an old shoebox with more photos in. Mum's picked a few out already. Her holding Al when he was a baby, one from his first day of school, his Year Seven school photo.

I feel sick looking at them. Al's life all laid out in front of me that starts when he was baby, then stops at seventeen. Seventeen.

'I'm picking out photos for the order of service,' she says. She stares down at a photo of all of us. Me, Mum, Saul, Al, Phoebe and Dad. It was taken at Christmas four years ago. 'It's strange how quickly life can change,' Mum says. 'One minute

226

you have everything. Then the next . . .' She looks away from the photograph, like it's too painful for her to remember how happy we used to be. We might not have had loads of money, but we had each other. And now . . .

I see that look flash across Saul's face again. Pain. Hurt. I don't move cause all I can think is, *Did I do this? Did I do this by not picking up the phone?*

Mum snaps out of it and glances down at my hand. 'Jesus, Nate,' she says. 'What on earth have you done?' My hand's been cleaned up since this morning, but there's still some bits of dried blood on my knuckles. She gets up to have a closer look, but I still don't move. I can't stop staring at the photos of Al. He'll never eat chips again, or cry, or paint, or draw. He'll never have another birthday. Or know wot it's like to be eighteen.

'Have you been fighting?' Mum asks. 'Do you want some painkillers? Let me have a look – you might need to get it checked out.'

I feel numb.

Why didn't I just pick up the phone?

'Nathan?' my mum says.

'Stop it,' I snap. '*I'm fine, yeah?*'

The words come out harsher than I mean them to. I move my fingers, but they're even more swollen than earlier and it hurts like hell, but I don't want her to know that. Or that I did this to myself.

'Oi! You don't have to be so rude,' Saul says. 'Mum's only tryna help.'

227

But that only makes me feel worse. 'Why you starting?' I say.

'All right,' Mum interrupts. 'D'you not think we've been through enough without you two tearing into each other?'

I look down at the floor. She doesn't just mean Al – she means Dad, too.

'Whatever this is, whatever's going on, it needs to stop, you hear? We're supposed to be a family.' She pauses. 'We need to help each other through this. We have to.' My mum turns to me. 'I called Mr Ballan after you left this morning. And I've spoken to your form teacher, too—'

'Wot?'

'I know you said that you don't want to. But everyone thinks it's a good idea for you to talk to someone. They don't mind you missing a few hours of school if it'll help.'

Saul nods. 'She's right, mate,' he says.

I should've known they'd be on the same side. It was always like that. Mum and Saul. Or Mum and Al. I shake my head. They've all been talking about me, like any of them know wot's best.

'I ain't going,' I say. 'You think that you all know wot's best? Fuck that! It's *my* life and I ain't gonna talk to some stranger about Al.'

My mum shakes her head.

'What you so afraid of?' Saul asks, but I don't reply.

'I'm going Kyle's,' I say.

'Remember it's a school night,' Mum says, but doesn't try and stop me. Saul doesn't say anything, either. I turn to go, but Phoebe comes rushing in. She's holding a piece of paper in her hand.

'Nate! Nate!' she says, but I'm not in the mood.

'Not now, Phoebes,' I say. I just wanna get out of there, be away from them all. Maybe there is summat wrong with me, but it ain't for them to decide.

'Nathan,' Phoebe says. 'Look what I've—'

'*Not now!*' I snap. Phoebe's face crumples and I feel proper bad. 'Phoebes,' I say. 'I'm sorry . . .'

But she slumps off to the other side of the kitchen, her lip trembling. Saul wraps his arms round her. He crouches down and takes hold of the piece of paper in her hands.

'Phoebes,' I try again.

'I think you've done enough, don't you?' Saul says and shakes his head.

Phoebe stares down at the floor and I turn to Mum. She looks disappointed, like I've let them all down again. She moves her hand towards one of the photos of baby Al. I can't help but think that she's wishing he was here now and not me . . . And she's probably right. If it was me, then everyone wouldn't be so upset. Al was the better brother. The clever one. The good one.

I slam the front door behind me as I leave.

Saul's words ring in my ears as I walk down my road towards Kyle's: '*I think you've done enough, don't you? I think you've done enough, don't you?*' There's the noise of cars and horns and sirens, but even all that won't drown out Saul's words.

Maybe Al had the right idea. Just disappearing.

I turn on to Kyle's street and knock on his door. I hear his dog go mad, barking and that.

'Nate,' Kyle says, opening the door and holding his Alsatian back. The dog barks louder and tries to run out into the garden. 'Hunter, man,' Kyle says. 'Wot you going on like that for? You know Nate.' He opens the door a bit wider, trying to hold Hunter back. 'You coming in?' he says. 'Or you just gonna stand in the garden like some creepy gnome?'

'I'm coming in,' I say, and squeeze myself through the small gap.

Kyle lets go of Hunter and he runs around, barking and jumping up at me. I reach down to pet him, moving my messed-up hand out the way.

'How does that look even worse?' Kyle says as he points to my hand. 'Come on, we'll go upstairs. Everyone's out.' I follow him up as Hunter rushes off to the kitchen.

Kyle shuts his bedroom door and I sit down on his bed, but I can't look at him. I feel too embarrassed. Too ashamed. I hear Saul's words again: *'I think you've done enough, don't you?'*

'Nate,' Kyle says. 'You all right?'

I shake my head. 'Nah,' I say. 'Kyle . . . it's all my fault. Al being dead . . . He phoned me just before . . . He called when me and you were at the park and I ignored him. If I would've just picked up, then he'd still be here. I *fucking hate* myself,' I say. 'I'm a shit brother.' I put my head in my hands. 'I can't tell my family – they ain't never gonna forgive me. How can they?'

I start to cry and I feel so stupid. I'm scared of wot Kyle will think, that he'll blame me, too. But weirdly I also feel a bit relieved to have finally said it out loud. To get it off my chest. Even if it means Kyle will hate me now.

'Is that wot all this stuff has been about?' he says. 'Nate, it *ain't* your fault. How could you have known? It's not like you can tell from a phone call. Al could've called you by mistake, or he might not have even told ya if you had picked up. You didn't do this. You can't put this on yourself.' He moves closer and puts his arm round me.

I sniff. 'Maybe,' I say.

Kyle pauses. I don't tell him that I *need* to find someone to blame. That maybe I have to, so I know that it wasn't just me. He doesn't go on about me telling my mum or Saul. He just sits there with me. And even tho it hurts, even tho I'll *never* forgive myself, Kyle rubs my shoulder and I feel a bit better and a bit less alone.

MEGAN

chapter twenty-eight

You know, the most spectacular thing about a comet is the yellow dust tail that you can see from billions of miles away. It's the part that looks like a white light stretching out across the sky. But, if you were to look at it under a microscope, you'd see that it's made up of all these small, solid particles. And that they're the same size as the ones you find in cigarette smoke. All the dust and gases have formed because of the heat from the sun . . . and, when you think about it, with all the particles in the human body, the stem cells and molecules, the oxygen and hydrogen . . . then maybe one day we'll all become comets, too.

I'd managed to pick twelve of Al's paintings that I really liked, and Ms Baker had picked a few of her own, too. There were still loads more that I needed to go through and choose, though. Ms Baker had said that we could use as much of the assembly hall as we wanted, and that she'd get flyers printed, and letters sent home, so that we could let everyone know. I wanted the exhibition to be just how Al had imagined it. Just how he'd dreamed ...

I'd gone back to the art room after school so that I could look through more of Al's paintings. It's weird cos, even though I was concentrating on getting this right, all I kept thinking about, the whole day, was Nathan. How nice it was to see his face light up when I told him about the exhibition. How we'd almost kissed ... The more time I spent with him, the more I fancied him. Which meant that I just wanted to be around him, I guess.

I pull my phone out of my pocket and open Insta to see if Nathan's posted anything since I've last been on, but he hasn't. And I *suppose* that seeing as he was the one who sent me that message first then I should be the one to reply. Tara would've told me to wait a bit longer and not look too keen. Or that I should post a selfie where I looked *really* good instead, then wait for him to send me another message. But I wasn't sure that any of the stuff that Tara told me was good for me any more. And I didn't feel like I had to do any of that with Nathan. It felt different.

I hear someone coming into the room and I turn round, expecting it to be Ms Baker, even though part of me is hoping that it's Nathan. But, when I look up, I'm surprised to see Lewi. I don't even know how he knew I was here.

He seems even worse than yesterday. He's sweating loads,

and his face is so sunken in on itself that he looks like he's wearing one of those Halloween skeleton masks. He stinks of stale smoke and weed.

'Megan,' he says, 'I've been looking all over for ya . . . then I bumped into that Tara. She said you'd probably be here.' He rubs his forehead with his hand and keeps doing this weird pacing thing, like he just can't keep still.

'Yeah,' I say. 'I've been trying to get this sorted.' I pause. 'I found those paintings you were telling me about. Of the paper cranes and the boxing gym. They're *proper* amazing.'

Lewi moves towards Al's paintings that have been laid out on the table. I see his sadness. How much he misses Al. 'Sometimes I'll be sitting on the tram, or at home, and it's like he's still 'ere, y'know? Like I'll just think of summat mad to tell him or I'll wanna ring him up, just to hear him talk some crap. Then I remember that I ain't never gonna hear his voice again.' He looks down and pulls at the sleeves of his hoodie. 'I just wish I could talk to him.'

I nod. 'I know.'

He reaches down and touches a painting of him and Al at the fair. Al must've done it from a photo taken a while ago cos they look very young. They've both got their arms wrapped round each other and there's an outline of all these different rides in the background. Lewi's head in the drawing is bent towards Al's. Both of them are laughing. You can see how close they were. How happy they were. And it makes me wonder again why things changed between them.

Lewi runs his hand over the painting and, for a moment,

he just stands there with his head bent in the same way as the drawing, like he's trying to go back to that day.

'I'm sorry,' I say. 'I thought it would be all right.'

Lewi sits down next to me and puts his head in his hands.

'It is,' he says, and his voice cracks at the end.

Lewi snorts, then he scrunches up his face, as if he's trying not to cry. I feel a bit weird, and I don't know if I should hug him or something, but I don't *really* know him well enough. So I just sit there.

'D'you know how hard it is?' Lewi says. 'Pretending to be something you ain't. How messed up it is? Like, I go on Insta and that, yeah, and that person in my posts . . . it ain't me and I'm fucking sick of it. I'm sick of all of it.'

'Trust me,' I say. 'I definitely know what *that's* like.'

I pick at this loose bit of skin on my finger and I think, *I always do it myself.* Follow people I don't care about. Try to get all these *likes*, or look prettier, or make out like everything is fine and that's not life. People don't post selfies where they look shit or videos of them crying cos they're sad. And they don't mention how their best friend who's just *liked* five of their posts isn't like that with them in real life.

I was sick of it, too.

Lewi pulls his phone out. He scrolls through and shows me a picture on his Insta feed.

'See this?' he says. 'This ain't me.'

I peer down, through the cracked screen, and I see a woman bending over in her underwear. The caption underneath says *wifey* with three of the fire emojis. I pull a face.

'I know,' he says. Then he goes to the three dots at the top and presses *delete*. He scrolls to another picture. It's a girl with a finger in her mouth and a mouse Snapchat filter covering part of her face. Her arms are folded across her chest, so that she's pushing herself up towards the camera, and he's written: *WHO iz she??? I need 2 find her.* Lewi shakes his head and clicks *delete* again.

He carries on going through, deleting all these pictures on his profile, most of them of girls in their underwear. Some of them are selfies he's taken in the gym, lifting weights with his top off, or standing in front of a mirror with Eli and Cole. One of them all in the park together, drinking and smoking. He keeps pressing *delete*, *delete*, *delete* till there's only one picture left on his Instagram feed. This old one of him and Al. They look really young, maybe about eleven.

'Al never cared,' he says. 'About being something that he wasn't – he just did him.' He pauses. 'Sometimes I think it scares people when someone's different. It's like they don't know what to do.' He shoves his phone in his pocket.

'I know what you mean,' I say. 'I've decided that I'm going to live my life more like Al did from now on.'

Lewi nods. 'I like that,' he says, but he still looks so broken.

'I just wish he was still here, so he could see how much he really meant to people,' I say.

Lewi snorts hard again, then he puts his hand inside his pocket. He pulls out this silver rock and flicks off some of the dirt that's stuck to it.

'What's that?' I say.

'It's why I wanted to come find you,' Lewi replies. 'Did Al ever tell you that there's all these bits in comets? The same size as the ones you find in smoke?'

I smile. 'The dust tails.'

Lewi nods. 'Well, he got me this, yeah? From the museum or some shit. I thought he just brought me back a rock at first, but then he told me it was part of a shooting star. He said it showed how something you think is just proper ordinary is actually dead special.' Lewi pauses, and hands the rock over to me. 'You should have this, y'know. Not me.'

'I can't take that,' I say.

'Yeah, you can,' Lewi says. 'Al would've wanted you to have it. You were mates with him when I fucked off. When I abandoned him. When I . . .' He trails off and then gestures to the paintings. 'Look wot you're doing for him,' he says. 'It's like you're bringing a part of him back to life. That's pretty fucking special,' he says. 'Take it, *please.*'

I nod. 'Oh, all right then. Thanks.'

Lewi hands me the rock, then he gets up and heads over to the door, his JD bag making a crunching noise as he walks.

'If there's anything I can do, just let me know, yeah?' he says.

'Yeah,' I reply.

'Catch you later,' he says.

After he's gone, I just sit there for a minute, holding on to the bit of comet. I stare at all of Al's drawings on the table. Lewi was right: Al didn't care. He wasn't trying to be anyone but himself. I think about what it would be like for a minute, to go off to university or to have an exhibition of my own. Have some of my paintings hanging somewhere . . .

I open up Insta on my phone and go through and unfollow people who make me feel shit. Who make me feel worse about just being me. I don't want to see all these diet teas or filtered pictures any more. I don't want to see photos that make me feel as if I need to be perfect. Like I'm *not* perfect as I am. I keep going till my feed is just paintings and people I know. Finally, I reply to Nathan's message:

> It's not in the stars to hold our destiny ... Soz 4 being a tool in that FB message. I know it wasn't your fault xx

> ... but in ourselves xx

NATHAN

chapter twenty-nine

When Dad walked out, Nate was devastated. Mum would hardly say anything and, even though Phoebe was upset, I guess she was too young to feel it properly. Saul was the one who held us all together. But sometimes, when I'd be making my way up to my room at night, I'd hear Saul crying in the bathroom, and running the tap to drown out the sound of his tears.

I think everyone must be asleep by the time I get home. I stayed at Kyle's till pretty late cause I didn't wanna come back and face everyone. But, when I go into my room, Saul's sitting there, hunched over at the end of my bed.

'Is there no privacy in this house?' I say.

'Mum's gone bed,' he says. 'I told her I'd wait up till you got back.'

I shrug. 'Well, I'm back. You can go now.'

Saul shakes his head, but he doesn't move. 'You're so angry all the time,' he says. 'That's wot I used to be like.' He pauses. 'You need to do summat with that hand. At least let me clean it up. Or you could wait for it to get infected.' He shrugs. 'Choice is yours. Ain't my hand.'

I sit down on the bed. I'm too tired to argue back and he's right – it does look a right mess.

'Fine,' I say.

Saul gets up and leaves the room. I hear the sound of the bathroom cupboard opening, then he comes back with a first-aid kit. It's gotta be about a hundred years old, and I'm surprised there's anything still in it. He pulls out an antiseptic wipe and I try not to wince too much in pain as he cleans up some of the blood.

'Ow, man,' I say. My hand feels like it's on fire. 'You ain't even checked that they're in date.'

'It ain't gonna kill ya,' he says. He dashes the wipe at my bin, but it hits the side and lands on the floor. 'You gonna tell me wot happened?' he asks, wrapping my hand up in a bit of bandage.

I shrug. 'Punched a wall,' I say.

'Fuck's sake, Nate,' he says. 'Punching shit doesn't solve anything. Trust me, I've done it enough times to know.'

He ties the bandage near my thumb and I feel bad for wot I said earlier. And for the way that I spoke to Phoebe and Mum.

'Thanks, yeah?' I say.

Saul shrugs. 'You can be a right tool sometimes, but you're still my brother. I love you and I'm gonna look out for you, no matter what.' He moves over on my bed, and stares up at the ceiling. 'I know you think I don't care about Al cause of how I've been acting. But just cause I've tried to carry on it doesn't mean that I don't miss him, too.' Saul pauses. 'It's the hardest thing I've ever been through. Knowing that my little brother is gone and that I couldn't even look after him . . .' Saul turns to me. 'There's more than one way to grieve for someone, Nate. We're all missing Al in our own way.'

'I'm sorry,' I say. 'I shouldn't have gone off at you earlier.'

'When Dad left us, I had to be the one to pick up the pieces. The one to make sure the electric didn't get cut off. That Mum had enough money to put food in the fridge.' He shrugs. 'So since then that's how I've always tried to be. Stable and brave, but trust me I've cried myself to sleep about Al a load of times.'

I don't know why it shocks me. Maybe cause Saul's always been the one to hold us all together.

'You have?' I say.

Saul gives me a weird look. 'I am human, Nate. D'you think I'm just some walking lump with no feelings?'

'Well . . .' I say. 'Walking *muscle* with no feelings maybe.'

Saul laughs and puts his arm round me. 'Flipping cheek,' he says.

We sit there for a minute, and maybe I shouldn't say anything, but I haven't been able to stop thinking about Sophie.

'You know, Al had a girlfriend and that?' I say.

241

Saul looks surprised. 'He never said . . .'

'I sent her a message on Facebook cause wot if she ain't heard?'

Saul breathes out slowly. 'Nate,' he says, 'I really think we should all try and move on. Just get through this the best we can. You can't keep going over the past. Trust me, it doesn't help.' He stands up. 'You should at least think about what Mum said. Talking to someone. There ain't nothing wrong with it.'

'All right,' I say. 'I'll think about it.'

But it's a lie. I don't wanna go over wot happened with Al . . . I don't see how talking about feelings will help anything.

'Try and get some sleep.' Saul pauses. 'Love ya, mate,' he says.

It seems weird cause we don't say it a lot, but I don't want Saul to think I don't care. And he's already said it twice. And maybe if I would've told Al that I loved him more then he'd have opened up to me . . .

'Love ya, you meat head,' I say.

Saul laughs. 'We really getting into this again? Cause y'know you don't want me to start on them ears . . . Night,' he says, then he closes my bedroom door.

I put on some old jogging bottoms and a T-shirt and climb into bed. I feel like I'm a little kid again. Nothing makes sense any more and I feel scared . . . scared of everything. Scared of wot it's like to die. Scared that I might never find out wot happened to Al. Scared that none of this will ever stop hurting. I know everyone else thinks I should let it go, but I can't move on, not till I've figured out why.

I look on Facebook on my phone again to see if Sophie's accepted my friend request, but still nothing. I open up Messenger to check there, but her profile picture is grey. There's just an outline and the words *Facebook User*. I stare down at where Sophie's picture should be – her face smiling at the camera, and her hair twisted into a loose plait. She's deactivated her account. But why?

MEGAN

chapter thirty

Do you know what the trick is to drawing still-life art? Some
people think that it's about the way you arrange the objects . . .
that it's about finding the best set-up, or conceiving the most
striking composition. But actually it's about drawing the life
of something. Seeing it for what it really is, right there, in that
moment. So, if you were drawing a flower, you'd find all the
details that give it its own uniqueness. Its own likeness. Just
like you would when trying to draw a person.

I turn over in the dark. I just can't sleep, so I get out of bed
and put my light on. I go over to my desk and try to carry on
with the sketch I'd started earlier of the flower that Nathan had
given me. The way it looks now is beyond tragic. More or less

all the petals have fallen off, but I was trying to get the bits of shading right. Filling in the parts that were meant to be a different texture, but I just couldn't do it.

Normally, when I got stuck, I'd message Al and he'd say something dead clever that would help. And I just wish I could see him, speak to him, hear his voice again.

Suddenly I don't feel in the mood for drawing, so instead I reach for my phone to see if Nathan's messaged me back. But he's not even read my reply.

A few selfies of Tara come up, and I see that she's updated her story. We've not spoken since our argument, but I click on it anyway. A few photos appear, then a video of Tara in bed. She's moving her head around, and mouthing the lyrics to some song with the puppy Snapchat filter on. She's added a quote. Something about it being less important to have a load of friends and more important to have real ones. She's written *100%* over the top of it. I can't help but think that she's talking about me. A few more photos flash up: Tara and Eli posing together, Tara with some other mates in town. Why am I even looking at this stuff? I go to click off Tara's profile, but then another video flashes up. The camera shakes, and I hear Tara's voice and the pounding of footsteps. Eli and Cole come on screen running down the road. They're both holding something in their hands, but I can't tell what and they're laughing and shouting. Eli holds his finger up towards the camera and I hear Tara laugh as she turns the phone round to show her face. '*He's proper mad that one,*' she says, then she moves the camera back to show Lewi running towards them.

I hear Eli say: '*Yo, gimme the lighter, man!*' There's something bright in Lewi's hand, like a luminous orange. I stare down at the light burning in the darkness and up at his hand and I realize that it's a firework. That must be what Eli and Cole are carrying, too. I can see now that they're on the pavement beside the tram tracks. A tram comes towards them, and Eli says: '*Do it now, yeah!*' And they all hurl their fireworks into the road. All these different colours start to explode, and bounce off the side windows of the tram. It screeches to a halt, and a girl at the tram stop screams.

They all run off, laughing. But Lewi seems to be making the most noise. '*It's just a few fireworks!*' he shouts to the girl and then Eli starts to laugh just as Tara's video stops.

I've never known Tara to be that stupid, not when someone could get hurt. And Lewi seemed so different, too. Not like the way he'd been when I saw him earlier.

I search for his profile on Insta. All of those same posts are still gone, but he's got rid of that picture of him and Al now and uploaded a picture of him, Eli, Tara and Cole instead. He's not captioned it and, though the rest of them are grinning, Lewi looks like he doesn't *really* want to be there at all.

I suddenly feel terribly alone. I don't have anyone. I don't have Tara, I don't have my dad, I don't have Al ... Was this how he felt before he did it? Alone? With no one he could talk to? I scroll through all the messages that me and Al had sent each other on WhatsApp, jokes and pictures, screenshots, links to facts about artists or space. Loads of messages, but nothing from Al about how he was feeling.

Maybe it was my fault for not asking enough. I stare down at my phone and, even though I know Al will never see it, I type:

I'm so sorry if I let you down xxx

NATHAN

chapter thirty-one

Sometimes Nate would get so angry that it scared me. It was like anger was the only way he knew how to cope. And I wanted him to see that life wasn't just about the shitty things that happen to you. It was full of wonder and beauty and hope. So I'd try to calm him down, by telling him all these facts. One time, not too long after Dad, Nathan was kicking off at home. Smashing things, tearing stuff up. I started telling him about the Northern Lights – how, even though the temperature of them can reach thousands of degrees Fahrenheit, if you were to reach out and touch them, they would just feel cold, because the temperature in the air is so low. Nate looked at me, and even though the anger was still there, even though I could see it inside him, he stopped smashing things up.

It's freezing outside and I stuff my hands into the pockets of my hoodie. It's still pretty early, but I got out the house as quickly as possible. I wanted to leave before Mum started banging on about me going to see someone again. A thin layer of frost covers the pavement and bits of it glint in the light, like pieces of broken glass that have been crushed into the ground. I try Sophie's number again, but it still just goes straight to voicemail.

I've got an Insta message from Megan:

... but in ourselves xx

At first I'm confused, and then it hits me. It's the final bit of that quote I sent her.

Ha! U and AI are just as bad as each other with this poetry shit...U in the art room l8r?

Typing . . . comes up straight away, then Megan sends me a laughing emoji and a screen grab of the message that I'd sent her first with another message:

Ur the one who started sending me this 'poetry shit'. Yeah, I'll be in there at dinner. U coming up? xx

U can blame AI for that one. I'll be there ... c u l8r xx

I wasn't sure about the two kisses at first, but Megan had put them in her message and I didn't want her to think that I wasn't interested. I'm not even sure when I started fancying her, but the more I spend time with her, the more I really like her. Like, proper like her. I shove my phone back in my pocket just as I reach school. I head through the metal gates and look round the playground. I see Eli standing in the corner, chatting to that mate of Megan's that I saw him with before. Cole's there with him, but no Lewi. Eli stares at me and I can tell that he's saying summat about me to Cole and this other girl cause they all start laughing. I turn away and head towards the main school building. A few of the other kids stare as I walk past them, but it's like most of them have forgotten. It's like Al being dead is old news.

I head down into the science block and try calling Sophie again, but it still goes straight to voicemail. I try again and again ... voicemail, voicemail, voicemail. Then, for the first time, there's ringing on the end of the line. I lean back against the wall, hardly able to believe it. The school bell goes and there's loads of noise around me as people shove their way down the corridor, but all I can really hear is the ringing of the phone. She has to answer ... I'm about to give up when someone picks up. They don't say anything, but I hear the sound of breathing and footsteps. I put my free hand over my ear, so that I can try and hear better.

'Hello,' I say. 'Hello? Sophie?'

She doesn't speak, but it's wot I can hear in the background that makes my heart pound: the echoing sound of shrieking in a corridor, the bustling of bodies and swearing, and then the noise of the second bell. It's *exactly* the same as wot's happening around me. Whoever Sophie is, she has to be here ...

in this school. I hear the muffled sound of footsteps, and then a scraping sound over the receiver.

'Sophie?' I say again, but the phone goes dead.

I head towards the door of my form room. Ms Davis is already doing the register as I walk in. I pull my rucksack off my shoulder and slump into the seat next to Kyle. He's got his English book out and I suddenly remember that we've got a mock. I've been so distracted by everything else that I've forgotten.

'Sorry I'm late, yeah,' I say to Ms Davis.

A few of the people in my form look up, including Jeremiah. He leans back in his chair, staring at me, then he says summat to the girl who's on his table. I pull my hoodie off, and dump it on the desk in front of me, and then I turn to Kyle. 'It's a bit late for that, ain't it?' I say.

Kyle shrugs. 'Nah. Gets in your brain quicker that way,' he says. 'As if you can remember stuff from months ago. I wouldn't bother, but me mum told me last night that she'd get me a new pair of trainers if I did all right in this. The amount of trainers I've had passed down from me brother.' Kyle pauses. 'You all right?' he asks.

I know he's talking about wot I told him at his house.

'Yeah,' I say. 'Thanks for yesterday and that.' I look round the classroom. 'Do you know a girl who goes to this school called Sophie?' I ask.

Kyle stares at me. 'You off your head? There's about fifty million Sophies in this school ... Who ain't called Sophie in Wythenshawe?'

'This one has got blonde hair, freckles and that ... proper pretty.'

Kyle shrugs. 'I dunno. Why? You like her or summat?'

I open my mouth to respond, but I can see Ms Davis staring at me. 'Nathan,' she says.

'Wot, man?' I say.

'You're not wearing your proper uniform,' she says. 'And how many times have I told you it's yes, miss, not what, man?'

I slump back in my chair. It didn't take long for her to switch on me since yesterday. She's looking at where my school tie should be. Surely she's not that stupid? She should know the reason why I can't wear it.

Jeremiah moves his chair back again and he turns his head round so that he's facing me. He pulls on his tie, holding it upwards behind Ms Davis's back, pretending to choke, then die. Then he looks around and laughs.

I feel my hands beginning to shake.

'He ain't wearing it, miss,' he says, 'in case the same thing happens to him as his brother.' He pulls at his tie again, like it's wrapped round something ... A few people on his table laugh, but most of my form just look really shocked, and I see Ms Davis go pale.

'That's enough, Jeremiah,' she says.

But I'm already on my feet. I'm proper angry and that. I don't even know how Jeremiah found out that Al used his tie – it must have been Lauren.

'You got summat to say?' I shout.

252

I walk over to his table, my blood pumping hard through me. I dunno why he thinks it's all right to make fun of Al like that. Why he thinks it's funny that he's dead. How he can make this out to be one big joke? A girl in the back of the class whispers summat about Jeremiah taking it too far and Jeremiah turns to face me. For a minute, he looks like he's sorry, but everyone in the classroom is staring at us, watching, almost like they're waiting for things to kick off. He steps up.

'Nathan, Jeremiah, sit down now. Otherwise you'll both end up going to see Mr Ballan,' I hear Ms Davis say.

But I don't care. 'Wot the fuck is wrong with you?' I ask Jeremiah.

Some of his mates on his table are pulling their phones out and Jeremiah smiles at me, like we're friends or summat and we're both just messin about.

'Chill out,' he says. 'It's just bants. I'm only joking with ya.' He pauses. 'And anyway I ain't surprised your brother killed himself.' Jeremiah looks round at everyone. 'Did you see how ugly he was? I'd kill myself, too, if I looked like that. He did us all a fa—'

I feel my fist connect with his jaw before I know wot I'm doing. It's the hand that's all swollen, and it hurts like hell, but I keep going. All my anger about the comments on the memorial page, Jeremiah's Snap, the laughing emojis, people *loving* and *liking* all of those comments, all of it boils over. Jeremiah falls backwards, knocking over a chair, and I push one of the tables aside so I can get to him.

Ms Davis shouts for someone to go and get Mr Ballan and

Jeremiah hits me back, but I'm so angry that I keep punching, over and over. Around us people are shouting or cheering. Jeremiah is yelling at me to get off, but I don't. I keep punching him. He tries to hit me back, but I'm too strong and too angry. I hear a noise, like the sound that something makes when it breaks.

'Nathan!' Ms Davis shouts, but I still don't stop.

And then Mr Ballan is there, pulling me away. Jeremiah's on the floor and I look around. Everyone's standing up and lots of people are filming it on their phones.

'Nathan, you're coming with me. Get your stuff,' Mr Ballan tells me.

Kyle comes over and passes me my rucksack and my hoodie, and I can see that he's the only one who looks bothered.

'He deserved that,' Kyle says to me as I take my stuff.

'All of you better put those phones away now,' Mr Ballan says. 'You shouldn't even have them on you in school, and if I so much as get a whiff that there's any footage online, you'll all be suspended and I'll be bringing your parents in.' He turns to Jeremiah. 'Go to First Aid,' he says.

Ms Davis helps Jeremiah up, and I follow Mr Ballan out. I walk with him along the corridor, and back towards his office, shoving my hoodie into my rucksack as we go. He doesn't say anything, but I listen to the sound of his keys clinking in his pocket. I look down at my fist. It's still bandaged up from where Saul fixed it last night, but now there's fresh blood seeping through it. I try to forget about the pain. We get to the reception area.

'Sit,' he says, and I do as I'm told. 'First things first. I suppose I'd better get your mum in.' He shakes his head. 'I know you're not having the easiest of times, Nathan, but violence is never the answer. Especially not in *this* school – haven't we taught you anything? Those aren't our ethics. You can't just go around having fights.'

'Jeremiah started it. He was saying all these things about Al. Making fun of him for killing himself. Wot am I supposed to do, just stand there and let him diss my brother?'

'You turn the other cheek,' Mr Ballan says. 'Be the bigger person by not rising to it. Like it says in the Bible.'

I kiss my teeth hard, and I dunno if Mr Ballan hears me, or if he pretends that he doesn't.

'I know it can't be easy,' he says. 'But they're just words, Nathan. You rise above it, and then you come and tell us. You know we have a strong Be Kind policy.'

Mr Ballan heads off towards his office and I wanna walk out, or throw something. I wouldn't be surprised if he kicks me out now. It's probably one fight too far. I don't get how I'm supposed to do all this 'Be Kind' rubbish in the real world. Not when someone's laughing about your dead brother. I know that if someone was talking about Mr Ballan's son or brother like that then he wouldn't turn the other cheek.

I lean back in the chair and look down at my blazer. It's ripped. I dunno when it got so bad that I couldn't stop my anger. It just takes over. It's bad now cause of Al and that, but it happened before, too. Maybe after Dad walked out. Even tho he only left us, it still felt like a death. One minute

255

someone's in your life all the time, and the next they're just gone.

Back then Al would always help to calm me down, or talk to me, whenever I got too mad and that. Now I need to do that myself. And it's hard, it really is ...

MEGAN

chapter thirty-two

Did you know that before the eighteenth century most paintings didn't have titles? Even now, if you go to a gallery or exhibition, you'll see lots of art that just says: Untitled. Which has a sort of power to it, you know? Because we always expect paintings to have names. And, when our eyes search for one, only to find that it isn't there, we tend to look at that painting differently. We allow it to speak for itself. To show us whatever it is we want to see ...

Nathan's messages made me smile like a *complete* idiot for most of the morning. Like, if anyone had actually seen me, then they definitely would've thought I'd been smoking something before I'd gone to school. Either that or I'd downed a bottle of vodka.

I felt all giddy and I just kept reading and rereading his messages. I was supposed to have form then enrichment class, but Ms Baker had managed to get me time out of both of them, so that I could work on Al's exhibition. I was secretly glad that I didn't have to go to form, though, cos it meant that I wouldn't see Tara.

I look at the two big tables in the art room. Both of them are covered in Al's paintings. Ms Baker comes into the classroom. 'Sorry, Megan,' she says, 'I got caught—' and then she stops as she stares round at the paintings I've picked. For a moment, I see it on her face. Sadness. Loss.

'Oh, Megan,' she says. 'These are perfect. You've done such a brilliant job!'

I point to the painting of Nathan and Al. 'I think this one should go in the middle,' I say. I wanted that painting to be the one that everyone talked about. The one that everyone kept going back to look at. There was just something about it. The outline of the estate, the two of them together on that roof, the sky and all the bits of light . . . It was like Al had managed to get the right balance, y'know? The right balance of being somewhere else, somewhere completely different, yet still on the estate. Still in Wythenshawe.

Ms Baker nods. 'I completely agree,' she says. 'That one's really something.' She pauses. 'If you let me know the date you want the exhibition to be on, then I can get some flyers printed off.'

'Maybe a week?' I say. 'It'll give me time to get the labels sorted. Most of his paintings have got titles on, but the rest . . .'

I pause. Al was always saying that he didn't want all of his paintings to be named. That there were some he wanted to keep as 'untitled', so that he could let his art speak for itself. I feel a sudden rush of sadness and Ms Baker sits down next to me.

'I know it's hard to think about the future right now,' she says, 'but I wanted to ask you if you've thought about university? Maybe an art course even? I meant what I said about you being really talented.'

I pause. I know that there's all the debt. And that Tara took the piss out of me when I told her that I was thinking about doing art at uni. And part of me is scared cos no one in my family has ever even gone to university. And I've always thought that maybe people like me – people who live on council estates – don't belong there. That's how we're made to feel anyway. But Al wouldn't have let any of that hold him back. And why should he?

Why should I?

I want to make the most of the life I have. Do the things that make me happy. The things that make sense.

I look at Ms Baker. 'Yeah,' I say. 'I'd really like to go.'

NATHAN

chapter thirty-three

There's supposed to be a part of Gaudi's cathedral in Barcelona where, if you stand underneath a certain area and shout, your voice sounds different. It's to do with the building ... and the roof ... and the way that it all carries sound. When me and Nathan were kids, sometimes we'd go and stand right inside this tunnel that ran underneath the motorway. It was dark and smelled really funny, but we'd walk right into the middle and stand there with the sound of the traffic above us. It was almost like we were in our own space, our own Gaudi's cathedral. We'd cup our hands over our mouths and shout as loudly as we could, then we'd stand back and listen to the sound of our voices, sharp and loud, stretching out to the other side of the tunnel and echoing all around us.

I sit in the reception area while I wait for my mum to arrive. It doesn't take long for her to come rushing through the visitor doors. She turns to look at Ms Weir, but then she sees me and she is proper mad. I can feel a throbbing in the side of my jaw, which must be from where Jeremiah lamped me.

'Christ's sake, Nathan,' Mum says, walking up to me. 'Look at the state of you. I really thought we were past all this fighting. I thought you'd *finally* decided to grow up.'

She storms over to Ms Weir, so she can let Mr Ballan know that she's here, and I sink down lower in my chair. There's nothing scarier than my mum when she's pissed.

I know that I've probably gone too far, and I'm pretty sure I'm gonna get suspended for fighting … which means I won't see Megan for a few days, so I pull my phone out and click on Insta.

Wer R U? xx

Art room, why? xx

I don't respond, but I click off my phone and make my way to the art room. My mum will go mad when she sees I've disappeared, but I don't care right now and I don't need another lecture from Mr Ballan about all this Be Kind stuff, either.

I push open the art-room door. Megan's sitting at one of the tables near the back. She's got her earphones in, so she doesn't even notice that I'm here, and she's surrounded by all these paintings. They must be for Al's exhibition.

I can't look away from her. She's so pretty.

I move forward, but she still doesn't realize that I'm here. Something about the darkness of the art room today reminds me of being inside this tunnel with Al when we were younger. We used to go down under the road and yell up into the tunnel, waiting for our weird echo to come back. I cup my hands round my mouth, just like me and Al used to do when we were kids. I think about shouting summat to make Megan jump, but, for some reason, I can't. Normally, I don't really care about looking like an idiot in front of anyone, but I didn't want Megan to think I was stupid.

I walk towards her and Megan looks up. She smiles and pulls her earphones out, and I feel even more nervous. I can't believe that I'd never noticed her properly around school before or when she was hanging out with Al. That I'd never tried to talk to her.

'You all right?' I say, but it comes out a bit weird and I feel myself go proper red.

Megan laughs and I wish that I had summat smart to say.

She looks down at my shirt.

'What the—'

'I had a fight with Jeremiah,' I say. I don't want her to think that I lamped him for no reason, so I add, 'He was taking the piss out of Al.'

She shakes her head. 'I know what Jeremiah can be like,' she says. 'It was only a matter of time before someone whacked him one. I'm surprised it hasn't happened sooner, to be honest.'

I smile at that and stare down at one of Al's paintings. Suddenly I don't wanna be kicked outta school any more. Not

262

just cause Megan's here, but cause part of me wants a future, too. Mum was right. Al won't ever get his life back, but I've got mine. And maybe I should at least try . . .

'These are all the ones I've chosen for his exhibition,' Megan says.

I still can't believe she's doing this for Al.

'This is gonna be summat else when it's up,' I say. I swallow hard and, even tho I feel broken cause Al will never get to see it, I can't help but smile. I can just imagine how proud Mum and Saul and Phoebe will be.

'I hope so,' Megan replies. 'I'm going to create a Facebook event for it tonight.' She stands up and grabs hold of my arm. 'Come on,' she says. 'There's something I want to show you . . .'

MEGAN

chapter thirty-four

Most people don't know this, but Van Gogh checked himself into the Saint-Paul-de-Mausole asylum because he had a breakdown. It's where he painted The Starry Night. *He had iron bars on his window, but he just imagined that they weren't there and painted everything around them. So when you looked at his most famous painting, with its dark sky and swirls of light, you didn't know that, deep down, he was secretly trapped.*

I lead Nathan to this other table that's covered with more of Al's paintings. I try my *hardest* to keep cool, but I can feel myself starting to sweat with nerves. It's not bad nervous. More the kind of nerves you feel when you're about to go on one of those proper fast rides at the fair. It's weird, but the more I see Nathan, the more I stop thinking of him in terms of Al. I've started to see him as just Nathan now, not Al's brother. I don't have to say which painting it is cos he spots it straight away.

For a minute, he looks like he might cry. Then he moves closer to the table, before leaning over and touching the edge of the painting. He runs his finger across the tail of the comet in the corner. Then he turns to face me, but it's like he can't look at me properly.

'I remember that night,' he says. 'Me and Al were just sitting there. It was after our dad walked out and I was proper upset. Angry. Al took me up there, and he told me it would get better. That I should look at all those stars burning brightly, at how beautiful they were. Then some bellend went and called the police, said we were tryna break in and that. That we were tryna steal stuff from the boxing gym.' Nathan shakes his head. 'And, when Al said we were just looking at the stars, you know wot they said?'

I shrug. 'What?'

'That they didn't believe us cos people around here don't look at stars, they burn down buildings. They mug people, they beat them up. But no one from our estate ever climbs on the roof of some building cos they wanna look at the sky.'

I pull a face. 'Can't believe they said that.'

Nathan shrugs. 'I can,' he says. 'Al was proper upset by it at first. He said that people never gave us a chance cos of where we come from. That they probably wouldn't expect us to go on and do anything. But that he was gonna prove them all wrong . . .' He looks down at the floor again. 'I'm probably gonna get suspended over that fight with Jeremiah. But I just wanted to see you first . . .'

I feel myself go red again, but then my heart sinks. If Nathan wasn't going to be here, it meant that I wouldn't see him for ages and he'd started to be the only good thing about school.

'You'll be at Al's exhibition, though, won't you?' I ask. 'I'll let you know when it is.'

Nathan nods. 'I wouldn't miss it,' he says. 'This'll be you soon, with your own exhibition. Someone putting all your paintings up and that.'

I laugh even though I desperately want that to be true.

'Just don't go forgetting us when you're famous and that,' he says.

'As if,' I say. 'D'you not know me at all by now?'

Nathan moves closer to me and I can see the tops of his ears have gone a bit red.

'Megs,' he says, 'I know I probably won't be in school for a bit and that, and I know that you can't talk to me about all that clever stuff, like you used to with Al. But . . .'

I look at him and try not to think ahead. But – what? But – what? He looks around again, and I can see that he's starting to go even redder.

'I just wondered—' His phone vibrates in his pocket. Nathan pulls it out and stares down at the screen. 'Shit,' he says. 'I'm gonna have to go. My mum's gonna go spare at me for running off. She's already on one . . .'

I try not to laugh. 'I'll see you later,' I say.

'In a bit,' he says, and he rushes off towards the other end of the art room, his trainers making this sharp, scuffing sound on the floor. But he turns round, just before he's about to leave, and he says: 'I'll message you on Insta later. Don't keep me hanging, Megs. Make sure you message back.'

'I won't,' I say back.

Nathan smiles and heads out of the door. But his words are still there, echoing round my head, long after he's left: *'Don't keep me hanging, Megs.'*

NATHAN

chapter thirty-five

I'd tried my hardest to talk to Lewi after that day in the park, but he just ignored me and then he started hanging around with Eli and Cole. And, when all of this started to go wrong, I suppose I could understand why he did what he did. Maybe cause he was scared that I knew the truth ... This one time in form, about a month after that kiss, I wrote down, 'It's okay. I don't hate you,' on a piece of paper. I drew a doodle at the bottom and then I dropped it on his desk. But Eli picked it up instead of Lewi and, even though they all started laughing, and calling me a weirdo, I could see it in Lewi's eyes. He was sorry. He was sorry about everything.

Trust my mum to phone me just then. I didn't wanna pick up cause I knew that she'd have a go and I didn't want Megan to hear her screaming down the phone. I was just about to ask Megan if she wanted to do summat outside of school. Maybe let me take her out or summat like that. But I bottled it.

I heave open the glass doors and turn into the reception area. Mum's gonna be really pissed. I see her standing there, her phone firmly pressed to her ear. She cuts the call when she sees me, and then shoves it into her bag.

'If it isn't enough that I've had to come in because you've been fighting, you then go running off! Well, even if you couldn't be bothered to come in and talk, Mr Ballan and I still had to sit down. He's suspended you. God help me, Nathan, I've had it just about up to here with you. Things are gonna change when we get home, do you understand?'

I think about opening my mouth to say summat, but I can see how annoyed she is, and I ain't got a death wish. She turns and stomps out the main entrance, storming ahead of me. She doesn't look at me all the way home, but just carries on walking, holding on to her handbag. She leaves this dead big space between us so that it doesn't even look like we're together.

As soon as we get home, she turns on me . . .

'How many bleedin times, Nathan?' she says. 'If I have to be dragged into that headteacher's office again, they're gonna start charging me rent.' She rubs the side of her forehead. 'Every time you get into trouble, you promise me that it won't happen again. Then lo and behold . . . You're lucky that the school have been so supportive. Anywhere else, and they would've kicked you out for good a long time ago.'

'I told you,' I say. 'Jeremiah was saying those things about Al. I ain't just gonna stand there.'

'You're fifteen, not five!' my mum shouts. 'You can't go around thumping someone every time they say something you don't like. If you're not careful, you're gonna end up in serious trouble. Locked up, or worse ... Is that what you want?'

I don't say anything, but my mum turns to face me, leaning forward to touch the side of my face.

'All I've ever wanted is the best for all of you,' she says. 'For you to have a decent future. I left school with nothin and I've spent my life scrimping and scraping. I want you to have a better life than I've had.'

'I'm sorry,' I say, and I mean it this time.

'And don't think just because you're off you can go gallivanting around. D'you hear me? You're not going to Kyle's, you're not going to Civic, you're not going to town. You'll stay in and do your revision.'

I can tell that Mum's at the end of her tether, and I know that there's no point in answering back, so I just slump off upstairs. I stay in my room for the rest of the day.

Later, I hear Saul and Phoebe come in. I still feel bad for snapping at her yesterday, so I make my way to Phoebe's room. Her door's open, and she's sitting on her bed, watching some kids' programme on Saul's laptop. The den's gone.

'Phoebes,' I say. 'Can I come in?'

Her eyes widen. 'Whoa!' she says. 'What happened to your face?'

'Got into a fight,' I say.

Phoebe moves up, and I sit down on the bed next to her. I stare down at the cartoon playing on the screen for a minute.

'I'm sorry for snapping at you yesterday,' I say, and I put my arm round her. 'I didn't mean anything.'

Phoebe hugs me. 'I forgive ya,' she says. 'But I want something from the shops to make up for it.'

I laugh. 'It's only fair,' I say. I put my free hand in my pocket and pull out this old Polo with bits of fluff stuck to it. 'You can have this ancient mint for starters.'

Phoebe pulls a face. 'Ew. No fanks. That looks like it's from the Stone Age.'

'Probably is,' I say, and I shove the mint back in my pocket. 'Wot were you gonna show me yesterday?' I ask. 'Was it summat to do with school?'

'No,' Phoebe says. 'This.' She pushes the laptop further down her bed, then reaches up to the windowsill behind her. There's loads of books stacked up along there, and a few piles of paper. Phoebe pulls down a sheet and I realize that it's one of Al's drawings. The one of the planets that she'd stuck up inside her den.

'I've seen this before, Phoebes,' I say.

But she turns it over. 'Look!' she says.

At first, I think that it's just loads of scribbles spreading out across the page. But, when I look closely, I see that Al's drawn loads of outlines of a girl. I can tell it's Sophie cause the drawings look the same as the ones I'd found in his sketchbook, but on this page he's covering every space with the same image over and over. Then along the side there are three words: *Why? Why? Why?*

Wot happened between Al and Sophie?

I close my bedroom door and pick up my phone, checking the time – *16:40*. I'd stayed in Phoebe's room for a bit, just watching cartoons on the laptop with her. It was nice not to think about anything for a few hours. To just feel normal and that.

My phone *pings* with a few Facebook notifications. When I open the app, I see that I've got an event invite from Megan, that says: *Al Bryant – Art Exhibition*. I click that I'm *attending* right away, but I don't read through the information or nothing cause I get distracted. Someone's posted a video of the fight I had with Jeremiah and tagged me. There's the comment at the top –

Wen u pick a fight wiv some1 frm Benchill!

There's the flexed-arm emoji, and all these *likes* and laughing faces. Some people have reacted with the heart button – even Kyle's *liked* it. I look at the comments:

Jeremiah, man, how culd u let him knock u out?

U should've killed him . . .

That's peak, that.

Someone else has put the laughing emoji . . .

I go to Al's memorial page. There's even more *likes* now, and loads and loads of comments. Some of the sad comments are still there, but there's some with a grey profile picture, just like Sophie's had, or ones with pictures of weird cartoon characters with big noses. I scroll through them, even though I know they'll make me mad.

So selfish

Couldn't luv his family enuf 2 stick around

He's SO ugly!

Lol, he did us all a favour.

At least there's one less queer prick in the world

Does any1 fancy some rope? Haha

I'm sick of attention-seekers like this

He obviously weren't right in the head!!!!!!

There's people arguing, more laughing faces, some GIFs and memes. There's more than the last time, even tho Megan went through and deleted them all. I think about responding to some of them, but I don't bother.

The comments just make me wanna find out wot happened even more. To prove them wrong. I grab Al's Samsung and scroll back through the messages. I stare at the last few between Al and Sophie, but there ain't nothing there that I ain't seen before.

Wot did she show him when Al went online? It still don't make no sense. I grab my phone and I dial Sophie's number again. It rings like earlier, but she doesn't pick up. I call it again and again, just listening to the sound of the ringing at the other end of the line. Her messages obviously upset Al. If I could talk to Sophie, then I could find out wot else she'd said to Al . . . or wot she'd showed him when she'd told him to go online.

I try the number one last time, and I'm just about to hang up when I hear the click of the phone connect. It's silent at first. I hear breathing, and then a voice, shaky and strained.

'I dunno who the fuck this is, but you need to stop ringing.'

The phone goes dead. My chest tightens, and I call the number straight back, but it goes to voicemail.

It wasn't Sophie that picked up. It wasn't even a girl.

But it was a voice I recognized.

It was Lewi.

MEGAN

chapter thirty-six

Do you know how black holes are formed? They appear when the corpse of a massive star collapses in on itself when the star dies and a black hole appears. It becomes so dense that it warps the fabric of space and time. It's the only thing in the universe that can trap light by its sheer gravitational force. All the light is sucked into that black hole, and any matter that crosses its horizons, or the point of no return, spirals helplessly towards an unknown fate.

I cut through Civic on my way home from school cos I can't be bothered waiting for the tram. I'd managed to write up a few of the labels for Al's paintings at lunch, and Ms Baker had even stayed in so that she could help, too. I couldn't stop thinking about Nathan and what he might have been going to say earlier, before his phone rang.

Civic is full of kids making their way home from school, or families going to the shops, and it's proper busy. I pop my headphones in and put a Beyoncé album on, to distract me from Nathan, and carry on walking. Someone shouts my name and I think I'm imagining it at first cos it's hard to hear over the noise of the music, but then it comes again. I turn in the middle of the walkway and see Lewi coming towards me. He's wearing a grey tracksuit and he's got a massive rucksack with him.

'Eh, Megan,' he says.

I pull my headphones out of my ears, pressing *pause*.

'You getting the tram?' he asks. 'I'm going me dad's again.'

'I'm walking,' I say. 'But I go past the tram stop . . . I'll head down with you.' I glance at Lewi's rucksack. 'You moving house or what?'

'I'm gonna stay there for a bit,' he says.

We carry on walking through Civic and it feels a bit awkward at first cos Lewi doesn't say anything. I think about the video of him on Tara's story. How different he'd seemed.

We cross this small road. 'Why you going to your dad's for so long anyway? Won't it take you ages to get to school?'

'Yeah,' he says. 'Fucking hour tram, two changes.'

'Why then?'

Lewi pauses. 'When I'm at home, in my room and that, it just reminds me of Al. Most places around here do. We'd been mates since primary school and I just . . .' He pauses. 'I dunno if I'll ever get over this.'

'Hanging round with Eli and Cole, though?' I don't mean to say it, but it just comes out. 'I'm not being funny, but you couldn't choose two more different people to Al if you tried.'

Lewi looks down. He rubs the side of his face.

'I know,' he says. He goes silent for a minute. 'Me and Al, we just . . . Then Eli started talking to me one day, and, I dunno, I thought that Eli was cooler, that he was a better mate.' We turn down another street and I see the tram stop in the distance. 'And, after Al died, I thought that hanging around with Eli and that, having a laugh, would make me feel better. *But it don't.* I just wish that I could disappear sometimes, too.'

We stop beside the ramp that leads up to the platform. Lewi pulls a roll-up and a lighter out of his pocket.

He still looks so broken and I can tell how much pain he's in. I can see it. What if Lewi goes home and does the same thing as Al? Al tried to talk to me and I didn't listen. I didn't even notice that anything was wrong.

I can't do that again. I can't just walk off.

'Sometimes it's worse,' I say. 'When you just pretend like it didn't happen. When you try and carry on as normal. Eventually, something tips you over the edge. It all spills out . . .' I pause. 'That's what I tried to do with my dad. Ignore it. But in the end, it catches up with you.'

Lewi shakes his head, and lights his roll-up. 'I just wish I could explain everything to Al,' he says. 'That's the worst, innit? When someone's gone and you didn't have a chance to say all the things you wanted to. Even if it's just how shit you secretly thought their taste in music was.'

I laugh, but it hurts cos of my dad. Al. They were both just *gone*, without warning. And maybe they'll never actually know how much they both meant to me.

How much they both changed my life.

'You're going to come to Al's exhibition, right? Maybe that will be a chance for everyone to celebrate his life and that. I've not just asked kids at school, but the teachers and Al's family, too.'

Lewi's face pales and I wonder what I've said.

'I'll try,' Lewi says and his voice cracks. He turns his head towards the tram stop. 'I'd better go. Got my hour and two changes to look forward to. Thanks, though, yeah? Just for listening and that.'

I nod, but it stings cos maybe I just needed to have listened to Al.

'Any time,' I say.

A tram turns the corner and Lewi shoves his roll-up in his pocket, running up the ramp to catch the tram. He manages to get on before the doors close, without buying a ticket. The tram drives off and Lewi looks out of the window, and lifts his hand up to wave. I do the same.

I unlock my phone, but this time I don't go to my music. Instead, I open up a WhatsApp conversation I'd had with Al. I flick through it till I find all the voice notes. I click down on the triangle and I carry on walking home with Al's voice filling my ears.

'Did you know that a star is in constant conflict with itself all the time?'

'Van Gogh didn't paint the bars – he left those out . . .'

'Everything in life is maths when you think about it. All life is this vacuum of numbers and patterns and shapes.'

'You do it, without even realizing. It's called chronesthesia.'

'A black hole happens when the corpse of a star collapses in on itself . . .'

'And that's how you can be sitting on a crowded 43 bus, and, at the same time, be staring up at the Empty Quarter . . .'

'You know, you can trick yourself to eat mould cos it's all in the mind, all of it . . .'

I put my key in the door and I play the last voice note:

'Someone called the police cos they thought me and Nate were trying to break in, but you've got to see the sky up there, Megs . . . And I know it's just a boxing-gym roof, but, when you see it, you'll understand. You'll look up and you'll think, I get it now. I get what Al was banging on about – I really do.'

I feel the tears fall as I make my way upstairs. I push open my bedroom door and chuck my school bag on my bed. I pull off my coat and go to hang it on the back of the door, but my phone starts to ring. It's Tara trying to FaceTime me. Maybe Eli's being funny with her again. Or she's bored and decided that she wants to hang out? I don't pick up. I just let it ring out. I'm not interested in anything she's got to say any more.

NATHAN

chapter thirty-seven

I'd tell Nathan about Van Gogh's Sunflowers *paintings all the time. How it wasn't just one painting, but a series of two, the Paris* Sunflowers *and the Arles* Sunflowers. *And that it was easy to tell them both apart cause the Arles* Sunflowers *are posed in a vase, and the Paris ones are lying on the ground. Nathan would just shrug and say: 'Why you telling me all this? I really don't care about some dumb painting.'*

I sit down at the kitchen table, shovelling cereal into my mouth. It's been two days since I got suspended over that fight, and all I've been able to think about is Lewi. And the fact he'd answered Sophie's phone. Sophie must have been cheating on Al with Lewi. How else would he answer her phone? He must have taken it off her cos of all the calls I've been making. It all makes sense now ... That's why Lewi and Al fell out. Lewi didn't just abandon his best mate, he hurt him, too. Wot if that's the reason Al decided to end it all?

Cause he felt like he had nothing left ... all cos of Lewi ...

'I got you this,' Mum says, pushing a leaflet towards me across the kitchen table. It's still early and Saul is taking Phoebe to school, so it's just me and Mum at home.

'Wot is it?' I ask.

'I know that you said you didn't want to talk to anyone, but I picked this up a while ago ... I've managed to get you an appointment for this afternoon. I think it's important that you go. Mr Ballan suggested it, too, when I met with him. I think he'll be more likely to let you go back to school sooner if he can see that you're trying to deal with things.'

I look at the leaflet, which is pink and purple like the toyboxes in Phoebe's room. *We Believe In You* is written on the front, with the outline of some guy looking gutted. *Could you be 1 in 4?* is underneath that. I open it and look through, staring down at all these quotes, all this stuff about everyone needing counselling, and the words *Trauma*, *Depression*, *PTSD*, *Disaster*, *Bereavement*, *Help*, *Stress*, *Suicidal*.

No wonder no one wanted to go with a leaflet like this. I still don't see how any of this will make it better. Everyone's gonna think that there's summat wrong with me, or that I was soft and that. I slump down further in the chair and shake my head.

'It's just an assessment first – they want to ask some questions, find out what you might need. You know, there's

281

different types of counselling and therapy, medication if you need it ...'

'Do I have a choice?' I say.

'I don't want to have this constant battle with you,' she says. 'But you've been through a lot and I think this will really help, Nate. I think it will help you to deal with everything that's happened. Not just Al ... your dad, too.'

Why would I need counselling over my dad? Wouldn't it have to be for summat serious?

'Just go in and have a chat with them.' She reaches forward and touches the top of my hand. 'There's nothing to worry about.'

I pull my hand away.

'You keep making these decisions without asking me,' I say. 'And not just this, but stuff like the funeral, too. You're just going ahead and doing things without even talking to me.'

I shove my chair back. I just wanna get outta there, but my mum lifts her hands to her head.

'Nate, please,' she says. ' I didn't ask you about the funeral because I didn't want to make you more upset. I didn't want to put that on you. You can help me pick out a song for his service. I've really got no idea what he would've wanted. I'm not trying to make decisions without you. I'm trying to look after you. Please just give today a go? For me?'

I know that this won't fix anything. How can I be okay when my brother's dead? How can I be okay when I was the one who ignored his call? But then I look at my mum and I feel bad for everything I've put her through. She deserves better

282

and I wanna try and fix it, at least for her. And Megan said this talking stuff helped her and, if it means Mr Ballan lets me back to school sooner, I'll be able to see her again, too . . .

I nod. 'All right,' I say. 'I'll give it a go.'

I climb into the back of the taxi. It smells of mould and old cigs. I wind down one of the windows, trying to get rid of the musty smell, and I sink back into the torn leather seat. My mum climbs in next to me, and the taxi drives off. I shove my earphones in and flick my music on. I sit there, staring out the window, the bass pumping through my ears, lyrics filling my head. The taxi turns, then passes the church round the corner from our house. It drives past a row of shops, and I see a group of boys hanging outside McColl's. I pull a face cause this driver doesn't even know where he's going, or that he's taken the long way round. The taxi gets closer to the group of boys, and I realize that it's Eli and Cole with a few other people.

They're smoking and laughing. I turn my music up even louder as we head down another road, following the sign for Wythenshawe Hospital. The taxi pulls up, and I get out, following my mum to this other building, at the side of the hospital. We go through these double glass doors, and into this waiting room. My mum goes over to the receptionist and I sit down. My phone vibrates, and I pull it out my pocket. It's a WhatsApp from Kyle:

Yo, have you seen the fight of u and Jeremiah going round Snapchat? Famous m8.

I go to reply, but my mum comes and sits down next to me.

'I don't go in there with you,' she says. 'It's important that you have some time alone. To talk about things without me.'

This woman comes out and calls my name. I don't wanna go. I know it sounds stupid cause it's just a room, but I feel scared to go in. I pull my rucksack further up my back.

'You can leave that here,' my mum says, but I shake my head.

I walk over towards the door. There's a woman standing beside it with short hair and glasses. She ain't old like I thought she'd be and she doesn't look that posh, either. She smiles and holds the door open.

'Come on in, Nathan,' she says. 'Just in here.'

I take one last look at my mum, and then I follow her inside. The woman walks over to the other side of the room, and sits down in one of the chairs. There's all these things in the room: some toys in the corner, a jigsaw puzzle, coloured pencils, this dying plant. She smiles, and I look down at my trainers, hating my mum for bringing me here. Hating myself for saying I'd go.

'Please,' she says, 'take a seat. I'm Jo.'

I sit down on one of the chairs, dropping my rucksack to the floor. She doesn't sound like she's from around here, and she doesn't look how I imagined her to, either. But I still don't wanna talk to her anyway.

I notice this painting on the wall behind her head. It's one that Al used to go on about all the time. All these yellow sunflowers that have been stuck in a vase. I remember Al telling me that there were two paintings like this from the same guy. But I can't remember anything else and looking at it just makes me feel bad all over again that I didn't listen to Al enough . . .

Jo smiles. 'I'm just going to ask a few questions,' she says. 'If that's all right?'

Nah. Nah, it ain't.

'I ain't mad,' I say. 'If that's wot you're gonna tell me. And I don't wanna talk about nothing, okay?'

Jo doesn't seem bothered by the fact I'm so angry. 'Firstly,' she says, 'I don't like using that word and secondly that's not what I was going to say. I won't make you do anything you don't want to, Nathan. I know that this can seem a bit daunting, scary even, but you've taken that first step. I'm here to help.'

'Help?' I say, and it comes out angrier than I mean it to. 'How are you gonna help me? Are you gonna bring me brother back? Are you gonna tell me why he did it? Cause that's the only thing that will make anything better.' I pause. 'Since when did talking about shit help?'

I feel myself starting to tremble with anger.

Jo shakes her head. 'I'm sorry,' she says. 'Nothing will bring your brother back. But sometimes talking helps you to deal with things.' She moves over in her chair. 'We often think that things don't affect us because it's not something that we can see physically. It's not a broken bone, or a cut, but that doesn't mean that everything's fine. The mind needs looking after, too, and it can be a lot harder because you can't always tell. And lots of young men – boys your age, some older, some younger – go to counselling. Talking about your feelings doesn't make you weak, Nathan.'

285

I've already heard enough. She might be a counsellor, but wot does she know? She don't know wot it's like to lose someone. The only reason I'm here is cause of my mum. I pull at the sleeve of my hoodie, and I sink further in my chair. I don't say anything for the rest of the session. I just sit there, and wait for the hour to be up.

MEGAN

chapter thirty-eight

Do you know that there's a type of jellyfish that can live forever? It's called Turritopsis dohrnii and it's the only species that's 'biologically immortal'. If the jellyfish is sick or injured, it reverts back to a younger state. Imagine that – something that's able to live … that can defy nature, and science, and time.

Al's exhibition is in a few days. Me and Ms Baker had already spent ages putting the boards up in the assembly hall. And I'd stuck most of the labels down for Al's paintings as well. There were flyers all over the school and I'd invited loads of people on Facebook, too. Not just from school, but from Al's estate and all around Wythenshawe. Nathan had clicked that

287

he was *attending* straight away, but he still hadn't sent me a message like he said he would. And, if I'm honest, I'm a bit disappointed. Even though I haven't known him for that long, I kind of miss him.

I've spent most of lunch in the art room like I usually do, and I'm heading to my locker to get my sandwiches out when I turn round a corner and see Eli. He's leaning against my locker like he's waiting for me. He crumbles some tobacco into a Rizla paper and rolls it up in his fingers. My stomach sinks. I think about walking off, but he sees me.

'Eh,' Eli says, and he comes towards me. 'You took your time, pancake tits. Been waiting here, just for you.'

My throat goes dry. Eli moves closer, licking the edge of the paper, then shoving the roll-up into his coat pocket. I don't even care about getting to my locker now. I just want to go. I try to walk past, but he blocks my way, his ear stud glistening in the light.

'Heard you and your little mate Tara ain't really speaking no more,' he says. 'D'ya wanna see some pictures I've got of her? I'd give her an eight. Cole and that reckon she deserves more, though ... Maybe I can let you be the judge of that?'

I feel sick.

Eli scrolls to the photo album on his phone. I try to walk past him again, but he moves, too, like it's some messed-up dance. Even though me and Tara have fallen out, I'm angry that Eli thinks he can treat people like this. And it brings back the anger and guilt I feel for the times I didn't stick up for Al. Who does Eli think he is?

'No,' I say, even though I can feel my voice shaking. 'I don't want to see them. You shouldn't be showing *anyone*.'

Eli shrugs. 'Well, if she didn't want anyone to see them, she shouldn't have taken them, should she? She's a bit loose your mate. Sends me all sorts, y'know? Got videos and everything.' He smiles and clicks on to something, holding the phone up near my face. I move my hand to block it. I can't even believe he'd do this to Tara.

'Piss off,' I say, even though I'm shaking like mad. Eli just laughs. 'I don't want to see them, all right? You think I won't tell Tara?'

Eli shrugs. 'D'you think I care? She told me she never liked you anyway. Always thought you were a dead weight, pulling her down.' He pauses. 'Surprised you're getting so brave, though . . .' His eyes glint. 'Almost makes you interesting.'

I suck in a breath, wanting to be anywhere but here.

'And besides,' Eli continues, 'plenty more where she came from. You're only jealous cos no one's asking for pictures of you. Not like anyone wants to see you naked . . . you ain't got nothing to show.'

I fight back the tears, but I can feel them coming. Eli must be able to tell, too. He moves closer again, still blocking my way, and starts to laugh. My whole body begins to shake with rage or embarrassment or both. I look around, but the corridor's empty. Eli rests an arm against the wall and he leans in. He pulls at the bottom of my blazer.

'Maybe I should just take a picture myself,' he says. 'That way I can compare . . .'

I push his hand away. 'Get off.'

Eli smiles. 'You might not have nothing up top, but the rest of you is all right. We could do a poll between you and Tara. See who wins.'

I hear a voice behind me say: 'Wot you doing? Leave her alone, yeah . . .'

I turn to see Lewi. Eli would probably mess him up in a fight, but Lewi doesn't seem to care. I've never seen him look this angry before.

Eli stares at Lewi.

'You think it's all a laugh to make people's lives a misery? Have you not messed things up enough?' Lewi rants. 'Fucking hit me if you want to, but I've had enough of it. Go on!' Lewi shouts. '*Go on!*'

I'm confused by what Lewi's saying. What does he mean by 'making people's lives a misery?' What has Eli messed up? Part of me is scared for Lewi cos I don't want there to be a fight. I don't want Lewi to get hurt. Lewi goes right up to Eli and I expect Eli to go for him, but he doesn't.

The bell rings and the corridor starts to fill up. A teacher turns the corner towards us. Eli shakes his head.

'You're fucking mad,' he says to Lewi. 'You need to calm down, yeah?' Then he walks off.

Lewi stares after hims. It was like he really wanted Eli to hit him . . . More kids come rushing down the corridor. There's an empty food-tech classroom opposite us. Lewi points to it.

'Can we go in there?' he says. 'There's summat I wanna show you.'

'Yeah,' I say.

I follow him inside. He closes the door, blocking out all the noise. Lewi pulls his phone out, staring at something on the cracked screen.

'Thanks for that. You all right?' I ask.

'I should be asking you that . . .' he says. 'I wanted him to hit me. To put things right. Eli thinks he can get away with ruining someone's life.' He pauses. 'Have you seen this?'

He hands me his phone and I look at the screen, peering through the shattered glass. It's a link to a news article with the headline:

Straight-A student hangs himself

The article is only a few words. Not many, just a few sentences, and it doesn't even mention Al's name, but it's him.

A seventeen-year-old boy from St Paul's Catholic School has hung himself in a tragic suicide. It is believed that he had been offered a conditional place at Cambridge University.

Lewi puts his hands over his face, sitting down on one of the plastic stools. 'He's proper gone,' he says and he shakes his head. 'I should've . . .' He breaks off because he's crying so hard.

I don't care if it's weird or not, I go over and hug him. Lewi seems surprised at first, like he doesn't expect it, and he stiffens slightly. He doesn't push me away, though. He just sits there while I hold him in the empty classroom. He stands up, then wipes away the tears and snot with the sleeve of his hoodie.

'Thanks, yeah?' he says.

I smile and hand him back his phone, but somehow accidentally click on the back arrow and another webpage loads. It's a gay chat room site. I try to click off it, but Lewi reaches over and snatches his phone from me.

'Don't worry abou—' I start.

'I was just looking at it as a joke,' Lewi interrupts. 'Don't think I'm gay or nothing cos I ain't, yeah? It was a joke.' He looks at me, like he suddenly expects me to run out of the door or something.

'Wouldn't matter to me if you were. It doesn't change anything between us . . .'

Lewi puts his hands out on the table in front of him and stares at the work surface.

'I can't imagine how hard it is,' I say. 'But d'you think Al would've been bothered, either? This whole Al thing, it's made me realize that life's too short to hide who you really are, for the sake of other people. Cos you're worried about what they might say. And why should you?'

'I'm scared, though,' Lewi says, and he still can't look at me. 'I ain't told no one. I've never even said the words out loud. I don't know how me mum will take it. Or me dad. Wot if they don't ever wanna speak to me again?' Lewi shrugs. 'I couldn't even tell Al, not properly anyway . . . but I'm sick of carrying all these things around with me. Hiding parts of myself and that. It's just *fucking exhausting.*'

I nod cos I know what that feels like. I've been doing it for *so* long. I move closer to him. 'Maybe you should think about telling your mum and that. They might be more understanding than you think.'

Lewi pauses. 'I dunno,' he says. 'Maybe. Me mum's boyfriend has got some pretty fucked-up ideas of wot men should and shouldn't be. It's like he came out the Stone Age. Then there's that idiot Eli.'

I think of Tara. Of how much we've drifted apart cos she doesn't accept me as I am.

'Then those people aren't worth your time,' I say. 'I think you should decide if you want to just carry on pretending or if you want to, I dunno, live your best Al life.'

Lewi smiles. 'I like that,' he says. 'Live your best Al life.' He turns to me. 'Maybe I'll try. I just need to figure all this out.' He hesitates and he looks a bit embarrassed. 'Thanks, yeah?'

Lewi walks over to the door, but turns round just before he gets there.

'You won't say nothing to no one, will ya? About wot I just told you and that?' he says.

I shake my head. 'Course I won't,' I say.

Lewi smiles and heads out of the classroom.

I mount the last of Al's paintings on one of the blue boards, then I turn to Ms Baker. We don't say anything for a minute. We just stand there, staring round the assembly hall. I look at the rows of Al's paintings that make their way from the entrance to the stage at the back. All of Al's work on display for everyone to see. Part of me feels like I might burst with pride. Al's exhibition looks even better than I thought it would. Even better than I'd dreamed. Ms Baker reaches over and squeezes my shoulder.

'Oh, Megan,' she says. 'This is . . .' but she can't finish the words. She moves a hand to wipe her face, and I get how she's feeling. It's sadness cos Al will never go on to make something great of his life. But it's also pride, happiness. For the things he did do in the short time he was here.

Ms Baker straightens up. 'Everyone's going to love it,' she says. 'You've honestly done an amazing job.'

I smile. 'Thanks, miss,' I say. Then Ms Baker heads off. I go to the stage at the back of the hall to pick up my coat and school bag. I pull my phone out of my pocket and check Insta – still no message from Nathan. I open Facebook, just to see if he's posted anything online, and I stare down at the notification at the top.

On this day two years ago I became friends with Al.

It's mine and Al's friendship anniversary.

There's a video underneath the notification and when I click on it a record appears with *Hey, Megan and Al* written on it. A pair of hands pull the record out of its cover and place it on this old player, then loud music starts, and the record begins to spin round. Pictures flash up of the two of us together, memories of things we'd written on each other's walls. I watch the video all the way till the end. I feel my

chest go really tight, and I click on the top memory, a picture
of a quote Al had tagged me in.

Art speaks when you're unable to.

I look at the quote. What if that was Al trying to tell me
that something was up, or trying to reach out to me, and I just
didn't notice? I just didn't look closely enough.

I go to Al's memorial page, and look at all the *RIP*s or sad
status updates. Everyone talking about Al being dead. I set up
the page, but now I think that I want him to be remembered
as something else. As *alive*. Like he's still here, living and
breathing. Just like his exhibition is doing.

I walk round the exhibition and take picture after picture
on my phone. Then I video the whole thing, making sure that
I get in all of his paintings and his drawings. So that you can
see them lined up round the hall. Then I click on Insta and go
to the *upload* button. I start to type in a hashtag, but I don't
want to put #RIP or anything like that cos I don't want Al to
be dead any more. So I hashtag them #AlBryant, #AlBryant,
#AlBryant, and then I tag Al in all of them, and press *post*,
post, *post* till there's only one photo left. I imagine how happy
Al would've been, seeing all of those hundreds of notifications
come up. All those hashtags and red marks and comments, just
for him. I stare down at the last photo, the painting of him and
Nathan on that roof, and type:

You did it, Al. You did!

I think about putting another hashtag with his name, but I look at the lightly painted stars, and the way that the dust tail of the comet has been smudged into the corner. I remember what Nathan had told me, about Al telling him to look up at the sky. The words that Al had said to him. So, this time, I just write:

#BurnBright

NATHAN

chapter thirty-nine

Do you know what the last words were that Van Gogh said to his brother, before he died? La tristesse durera toujours – *the sadness will last forever.*

My mum asks how it was on the way home, but I just shrug and tell her it was all right. I didn't talk for the whole of the session. I just sat there, staring at the clock and waiting for the hour to be up, but I'm not gonna tell my mum that.

When we get home, I go straight to my room and shut the door. I fall on to my bed and my phone *pings*. It's Kyle.

Have u seen this?

There's a Facebook link, too. I press on the link, and it takes me to a news article that's been shared on a Facebook page. It's for the local news in Wythenshawe. The headline on the page reads:

Straight-A student hangs himself

My chest goes all tight. No one had even bothered to ask us if it was okay to write about Al. I scroll down to all the comments at the bottom. It was only uploaded a few hours ago and it's already got over 5,000 *likes*. I click through them. Comments, tagging people, random emojis . . . sharing, liking . . . everyone wanting to say something about wot Al did. Even tho I know it won't do me no good, I read some of the comments:

So selfish

Man, suicide is a real killer!!!

This ain't funny

#RIP

So sad

I'll miss u everyday m8

Sick of all these selfish ppl!

Wot do u mean? Ppl like him need help.

There's summat wrong wiv u if u try 2 kill urself

I've had enough hanging around on here. Lol.

Yawn, another person we don't know killing themselves ...
where's the real news??

I look at all the profile pictures on the comments, people
pouting or with their picture greyed out, some of them kids
my age but some adults, too. A girl has tagged her friend in it.
I stare down at the comment her friend has written:

No way. They should be ashamed of themselves!!!

Wot does that mean? I don't even know if she knew Al ...
I click on her page, and I see that most of her posts are public.
She's shared the article and written:

RIP. Those of you who know should be ashamed!!!
💔 💔 💔

I click on the *about me* section and see that she goes to the
grammar school on the other side of town.

I go to Messenger and type:

 I'm Al's brother. Who shld be ashamed? Wot do u know???

She sees it straight away – the circle with her face in
appears at the bottom. The dots start to move up and down

and I listen to the tapping noise my phone makes as she types
her reply.

> The pictures. All those comments

>> I don't know wot ur talking about . . .

The *typing* bubble comes back. I wait, but then the tapping
noise stops, like she's deleted wot she was just about to put.
Summat comes up at the bottom, but it ain't even a message . . .
it's a picture. I zoom in. It's that symbol again: the circle with the
mountains inside it. It's on someone's hand being held up towards
the camera, just like it had been on that picture with Eli and Lewi
and Cole. My palms start to sweat, but I still don't understand.

She writes:

> Sorry

>> I dnt know wot that is . . . Wot's that symbol??
>> I don't understand!!!

She sees it, but she doesn't type anything at first. Then
the *typing* bubble appears again, but it's so slow, I want her
to hurry up.

> It's not a symbol.

The bubble appears then disappears again.

It's a website.

Wot website? Have u got the address? Will u send it me?
Can I phone u? Make sure u pick up!

G2g, chat l8rx

And then I see that she's no longer active.

I look at the symbol again. Two mountains inside a circle ...
two triangles inside a circle ... or a swirl? I open up Google and
I type *Two mountains inside a circle* but nothing really comes
up, nothing that's the same as the symbol anyway. There's the
flag of Nepal, something about Egypt, Adam and Eve. I type
in that Fibonacci pattern that Megan told me about, but there's
nothing useful. I type in *Mountains* and scroll through all
these pictures of Mount Fuji or Mount Everest, all these facts
and figures, but nothing to help me make sense of anything. It
all just feels pointless. I unzip my rucksack, pulling out Al's
drawing of him with his hands pressed over his ears.

Al was definitely in trouble. Maybe it's to do with some
website like the girl said? But wot kinda website would be
bad enough for people to be 'ashamed'? Unless there were
pictures of Lewi and Sophie online, and that's how Al found
out? If there was a website, then maybe Al would've known
about it ... maybe there are other clues in his room that I
missed last time.

I walk up the staircase slowly, listening to the sound of my
trainers creaking against the wooden floor. My mum's tidied
his room up from when I trashed it, so it looks even neater

than before. I breathe in the smell and run my hands along the walls. I go over to Al's desk, tugging at the main drawer that runs along the top, even tho I know it's locked. I need to find the key.

I go to Al's chest of drawers, moving his clothes and T-shirts and socks, trying to look in the places he might have hidden it, but I can't find anything. I go over to the hook on the back of his door, where his school uniform is. The police had given it back to us, after our mum had chosen the suit she'd wanted Al to be buried in. She'd washed it and ironed it, and put it back on the hanger, like this was all a mistake, and she was still expecting Al to come back and wear it. Then I see Al's school bag scrunched up in the corner. I tip it upside down, and some stuff falls out – a ruler, a few broken pastels, this metal thing that looks like a chisel. I pick it up, holding on to the plastic bit, and I head back over to the drawer. I slide the chisel down the front of it, moving it backwards and forwards, pressing all my weight into the wood, till I hear something click. I pull the drawer open, throwing the chisel on to the floor.

I put my hand in, staring down into the bottom of it. I dunno wot I'm expecting to find, but there's just a few sheets of paper and another one of those plastic glow-in-the-dark comets. Al kept this drawer locked for that? I pull the sheets of paper out, but they're all blank. Then I see summat, right in the corner, pushed to the back of the drawer. It's this dark blue notebook. I pull it out. It looks so old that the sides are all worn away and bits of the dark blue have started to turn black. I think it's supposed to be a night sky, with flecks of yellow and green from where all these stars are exploding. There's a thin strap of elastic keeping the notebook closed.

I flick the black elastic away and pull the cover open. On one side of the page, Al's written:

This notebook belongs to Al.

On the other side, there's that drawing of me and him, sitting on the boxing-gym roof. It's a mini version of the painting that Megan showed me in the hall. He's written:

Benchill 2018 – Me and Nate just sitting up on that roof. Even though it was sad, it was the best I'd felt in ages. Because the whole estate was quiet and the sky was clear and the stars were burning brightly!

I turn over the page and flick through the other drawings in the book. There's outlines of the buildings in town, and a few drawings of people at tram stops. There's a sketch of Megan drawing something in the art classroom at school. I carry on turning the pages, and then it stops being sketches and instead the book is full of Al's writing.

The first page has a date at the top, September 2019, a year before he died. I read through his writing. It's scrawled and hard to make sense of, but there are some facts about Van Gogh, or paintings, and stuff about how you can trick your mind to travel in time ... something about wanting to be a neutron star ... the dust tail of a comet.

I turn a page and see a picture of Sophie. I know it's her cause I recognize her long plait and dimples. Next to the sketch Al's written:

> I can talk to Sophie about anything. She understands me like no one else.

He's drawn another picture of the two of them together. Sophie looks just like her WhatsApp photo, but Al doesn't even look like himself. He's stretched all his features out, so that he's made himself look taller, and his lips bigger. His nose is all weird, and it's like he's used one of those Face Swap filters, but he hasn't – he's just drawn himself to look like some sort of monster.

I turn to the next page:

> Me and Sophie are finally going to meet. She always tells me how funny I am, how clever I am. I don't know why it's taken me so long to find someone like her.

On the next page:

> It's like I know her already ... like I've known her for ages. She knows about the Empty Quarter, about people being made up of stars – 90 per cent stardust – I didn't have to tell her.

I turn over another page, but the writing stops and there's loads of blank ones instead. I flick further till I spot more writing:

> Sophie said I was ugly. I don't know what I've done.
> The messages won't stop. Why won't they stop laughing
> at me? Why won't they stop?

I carry on flicking through and the drawings start up again, but now they're darker, like he's pressed down dead hard on the page.

> I don't know what to do. Help me. Help me. Help me!

I turn over and stop in shock at the drawing on the next page. I only know that it's Al cause of his large Afro, and the headphones around his neck, but it doesn't look like him at all. He's stretched out his face even more than the other picture, his eyes disappearing into the sockets, his lips taking over the page. He's made his body even taller – everything is out of place and stretched out – and it's all wrong.

I flip to the next page of the notebook and see a drawing of Al cowering in the corner. He's written beside it:

> La tristesse durera toujours. When will it stop?

I reach the last page of the notebook and when I turn it over I see my name, like he was trying to write me a letter.

> Dear Nathan, I'm so sorry

The ink is all smudged, like he'd cried on to the page, and the 'r' and the 'y' blur into one. I flick back through the pages, but there's nothing about any website and nothing that seems to be of any help at all. My eyes begin to burn as I stare down at Al's words. *I'm sorry, I'm sorry.* Maybe Sophie and Lewi had done this together. Upset Al. Made him feel alone. Maybe Lewi was the one who told Sophie to send those messages for a laugh? I still don't get why she'd do this, tho, why she'd be so cruel to Al.

I pull my phone out. That girl from Facebook still hasn't replied, but she's been online. I type out another message:

Wots the website?? I need it!!!

I can tell that she's seen it, but she doesn't type back. I click on to the Messenger call options, then ring her. The phone rings and rings, but she doesn't pick up. I type out another message:

Will u tell me the fucking website??!!!!

This time she replies, but just with:

Soz, I don't want 2 get involved.

I type another message back, but I get a notification saying that it's undelivered – she's blocked me. I shove the notebook in my pocket and head back to my room and pull on a hoodie. I couldn't get hold of Sophie, but I could go and find Lewi. Ask him wot they'd both done. Find out wot this website was, or wot these pictures were of?

I head downstairs and go into the kitchen. My mum's plating up the tea, and Phoebe's helping her set the table.

'Where does Lewi live?' I say.

My mum stares at me. 'What?'

'Lewi,' I say. 'Can you remember where he lives? I know it's the other side of the estate . . . but I can't remember where.'

'He lives off Woodhouse Lane. Near your old primary school. Why?'

'Wot number?'

'I don't know,' she says. 'What's all this about?'

I turn and head towards the front door, pulling my hood further over my head, but my mum follows me.

'Nathan,' she says. 'Where are you going? You're grounded, remember? Don't you even think about—'

'I'm sorry,' I say, 'but it's important. It's to do with Al.'

My mum widens her eyes. 'Nathan!' she shouts.

But I push open the front door and head out into the night.

I leg it to the other side of the estate. I hear the sound of fireworks going off in the distance, and some dogs barking, but I keep running. I turn down all these different side streets, and across a main road, past McColl's and the tram stop. I can hear the blood pumping through my ears, feel it rushing faster and faster, and I'm starting to sweat. I don't stop, tho. I don't stop till I get to Lewi's street. I can see the shadow of my old primary school in the dark, and I go to the first house next to it and bang on the door, but no one opens it. I go to the next one and I ring the bell, knocking on the letterbox, and lifting it up to shout Lewi's name. An old man comes to the window, but he doesn't open the door. He turns the volume of the television down, staring out the window. I go to the next house, walking up the garden path, and then I knock on the door. It opens slowly and Lewi's mum is standing there. She wraps her dressing gown tighter round her.

'Nathan,' she says. 'Hi. What are you doing here?'

'Where's Lewi?' I say. 'I need to talk to him. Is he in?'

'He's not here,' she says. 'He's gone to stay with his dad for a bit. He's . . . really been struggling. Al dying has hit him hard, y'know?'

I move my hands to my head. I don't tell her that I think this is probably his fault, that he knows summat about wot happened to Al, and that he's keeping it from me. Keeping it from everyone. My chest starts to feel tight, and I bend forward, wiping away some of the sweat from my face.

'Are you okay?' she says. 'He might be back in a few days or so. I'll tell him that you called. Do you want to come in?'

I steady myself, and then I shake my head.

'Nah,' I say. 'It's all right.'

I can feel her watching me as I walk back down the road.

The cold air cools me down, and I take a few deep breaths. I don't wanna go home just yet. I pull my phone out, and I open up Facebook, just for summat to do. I click on my notifications and stare at the last one:

You and Al Bryant have memories to look back on.

I shake my head cause, even tho he's got a memorial page, Facebook doesn't know Al's dead.

I click on the memory that comes up, me and him on the boxing-gym roof, just like that picture in the notebook. Two years ago. I read the status:

Al Bryant is feeling happy.

I carry on walking, past the turning for my street, and head towards the Jimmy Egan boxing gym. It's quiet out, and I walk up the path.

Then I hear it. Al's voice ringing out.

'*When a star reaches the end of its lifetime, it explodes in this violent supernova. Sometimes the outer layer of the star blows off, leaving behind a small, dense core that continues to collapse. Gravity presses down on the core material so tightly that the protons and electrons combine to make neutrons, and they combine to make a neutron star. Something born from a death that ripples out from thirty-three light years away. The core of the star speeds up, and it spins faster and faster, up to 43,000 times per minute, so that eventually the universe just becomes this blur . . .*'

I listen in the darkness for a minute. Was this all just some awful dream? Did Al just fake it all? How come I can hear his voice?

I start to smile, wide, and I pull myself on to the metal post near the door. I should've known that Al wouldn't do this. That he wouldn't just leave us. I reach up, then climb on to the first bit of the roof, where the sign is, and the CCTV cameras. I pull myself on to the next tier and slide on to my stomach so that my body is fully on the roof. All these emotions come rushing through me. Relief. *Happiness.*

I stand up and then I stop when I hear her swear. I see a light from a phone fall beside her feet. There's no Al – there never was. It's dark, but I can see the side of her face glowing from the light of one of the street lamps. There's an open sketchbook resting on her lap, and she shoves her hands into the pockets of this big puffa jacket she's wearing.

'Megan,' I say, and I try not to look too disappointed. 'I thought . . .' I walk to the middle of the roof and sit down next to her. My leg touches hers, and, even tho I'm still devastated that it's not Al up here after all, I feel summat. Like this current of electricity rushing through every part of me. I don't get why she's here, tho. Wot's she even doing on this roof?

'I know it's *weird*,' she says as if she's read my mind. 'But I just wanted to see what all the fuss was about. I've been trying to draw this in class . . . And then I wanted to imagine that Al was here, too.' She reaches down and presses her finger on this voice note on her phone. I stare out across the estate as Al's words echo all around us.

MEGAN

chapter forty

Did you know that lightning is an electrical force and discharge caused by the imbalances between storm clouds and the ground? Lightning is five times hotter than the sun and a typical cloud-to-ground lightning bolt begins when a step-like series of negative charges race down from the bottom of the storm cloud. They travel at 200,000 miles per hour and each segment is about forty-six metres long. Sometimes I go out into the street and watch the lightning travelling at full speed through the sky. And, when I stand there, in that moment, I feel so . . . alive.

The voice note stops, the small bar in the green rectangle reaching all the way to the end. Nathan breathes out slowly, then moves so that his elbows are resting on the tops of his knees. He pulls a lighter out of his pocket and presses down on the metal wheel, passing his hand through the flame.

'I got one of those Facebook memories and Al's status said he was happy here. That's why I came . . .' He pauses. 'Then I heard his voice and, for a minute, I thought that this was all some messed-up dream. That Al was still here.'

He turns the lighter on its side, and looks down at the shadow the flame makes on the roof.

'That sounds stupid, don't it?' he says. 'Some Facebook status making me think that, if I came here, it would make me feel normal. *Happy.*'

I shake my head. 'That's what I thought, too.' I shrug.

I stuff my hands under my armpits to try and keep warm. It wasn't just Al not being here. It was everything. Like him dying has brought it all into focus. Tara, my dad, knowing that I didn't want to stay in Wythenshawe forever, thinking about what I wanted to do . . . the future. It scared me cos it felt like I wasn't certain about anything any more.

'It's times like this,' I say, 'that I proper miss my dad. I get on all right with my mum and that, but it's just not the same. With him, it was like we could just talk about *anything*. Whenever I was upset, or I didn't know what to do, he'd just listen.' I pause. 'And I'd feel better cos I knew that he'd always be there.'

'You're lucky,' Nathan says. 'I never had that with my dad. He was around, but . . .' He shrugs. 'It weren't nothin like that. He just fucked off. Kept in contact for a bit at first, but then he didn't bother. He ain't spoken to none of us in two years. Apart from this strained phone call we had with him after Al . . .' He takes a deep breath. 'It's weird cos even tho he's still alive, sometimes it feels like he's dead. Cos he's just gone.' He looks at me. 'Does that sound stupid?'

'Nah,' I say. 'You've still lost him, even if it's cos he left.'

Nathan nods, looking back at the flame from the lighter. 'Never thought of it like that,' he says.

I watch his face as he messes about with the lighter, rolling his thumb along the metal wheel. We're sitting so close that his knee is touching mine. I feel nervous, like all fluttery in my stomach. I don't want to move away from him, and I'm *sure* he can tell how much I fancy him. My heart is going proper fast, like, beating so loudly. Making all this noise. I'm certain that he can hear it, too, just ricocheting round the empty streets of the estate.

'I don't think these things ever go,' I say. 'As much as it gets easier, it's still so hard. It's like there's always some part of you . . . a piece that's missing.' I look out towards the row of houses on the other side of the street. I turn my head and see a man walking his dog through the far end of the park. 'It stops hurting the way it used to,' I say. 'Then you know that you're going to be *okay*. That you're alive, and you've just got to take one day at a time.' I shrug. 'That's what my mum says anyway.'

Nathan smiles. 'Yeah, I wanna feel that way again. Or just have a laugh, without feeling bad about it.'

I lean forward and look up at the sky, but I can't see any stars. Even without them, I can see why Al liked it up here so

313

much. Just sitting on this roof, staring out across the whole of the estate, feeling like you're part of stuff but separate, too. Nathan leans back on his elbows.

'You can't see nothing up there,' he says, shaking his head. 'Shit Manchester sky. It's still nice, tho.'

He moves closer, so that the side of his hand is touching mine and he moves his head to gesture towards one end of the roof. His face is so close that I can see his breath misting the night. I suddenly want him to kiss me and he pauses for a minute, like he's thinking about it, too.

'If you look that way,' he says, 'you can just see the whole of our estate. All the houses and that, for miles and miles . . . and you can't even tell where it ends. It's like you're just looking out over the whole of Wythenshawe. But then if you look that way . . .' He moves his head towards the other side of the roof. 'You can see that road that runs along the edge of the motorway. All the trees, near the metal bridge and that. It's like one way is our estate and the other way is how to get outta here. How to leave . . . Al was proper proud of where he came from, but I think being able to see the escape route is why he liked it up here.'

I smile. 'I know. I think so, too.'

Nathan turns to me. 'Did Al ever say anything about a website to you?'

'No,' I say. 'Why?'

He looks down. 'This girl online told me about some website with a weird symbol that Al kept drawing. Same symbol I've seen other places, too. I dunno wot it is, but I think it was bad ...' He goes quiet for a second. 'All I want is answers, Megan. All I want is to find out why he did it,' he finishes quietly.

I think about all my posts about the art exhibition and how I didn't want it to be about Al being dead. How I want him to be remembered for how he lived. *Brave. Kind. Fearless. Burning brightly.* I want that to be how Nathan thinks about Al as well, not just focusing on the fact that he's gone. I open up Insta on my phone and type in #BurnBright. A few posts come up, the one that I'd done of the exhibition, and some from a few people at school, another one from some artist in Manchester, and then London, and then one somewhere in America.

I click on a picture of one of Al's paintings. Someone's reposted it and the caption says:

The best artist there is. #BurnBright

There are people I don't even know who have commented on the picture, too:

This guy's work is unreal!!! #BurnBright

Look at this painting! This guy is so talented! #BurnBright

This painting is sick! #BurnBright

I hold my phone out to show Nathan.

'Look at this.. It's like his paintings are going further than Wythenshawe, further than Manchester even ... They've made it to the other side of the world, just like Al used to talk about. They've made it out of his bedroom in the middle of Benchill ... to our school ... and now they're out there. And people can see how great Al was.'

I scroll to the drawing of Nathan and Al sitting right here, on this roof. It has even more *shares* and *reposts* and *likes* than the others.

'It's like part of Al is living on,' I say. 'Like his dreams are, too. You know how much you meant to him,' I say. 'How much he loved you. You can see it in this painting.'

Nathan takes my phone and stares at the screen, scrolling through all the comments and that. His eyes widen, as if he can't quite believe it. The phone lights up part of his face, and I can see how happy he looks.

'Maybe he's not gone completely,' he says.

I shake my head. 'Nah.'

He hands me my phone back and my fingers brush against his. I feel that rush again and my stomach does this weird flip. Nathan looks at me and then he moves over so we're sitting even closer in the dark. My shoulder pressed against his, our knees knocked together, the edge of my shoe touching his trainer. My heart starts to pound even faster.

'I'm so glad you came up to me on that bus. I'm glad that Al knew you. I'm glad we're here now,' Nathan says.

He looks a bit embarrassed, then he glances back towards the estate. I put my hand down, on the floor, next to his. Slowly, he inches his hand towards mine, so our little fingers touch, then he wraps his fingers through mine. Then we just sit there, holding hands, and I kind of feel this current between the two of us. I don't know if he's going to kiss me or not, but part of me doesn't even mind, I just want to stay here on this roof. Sitting like this.

I'm glad that I spoke to Nathan on that bus, too. I'm glad that Al brought us together. I rest my head on his shoulder and we sit there, listening to the sound of each other's breath and the police sirens echoing out in the background.

NATHAN

chapter forty-one

Do you know that sunflowers were Van Gogh's favourite things to paint? And he used bright yellow colours at a time when no one else would. He wanted to fill his whole house with the colour of the sun, to create twelve more paintings of them before he died. It's like these flowers became his own version of happiness and hope.

The days go past, and I try to carry on, but I can't stop thinking about being with Megan on that boxing-gym roof. Every part of me wanted to kiss her, but I didn't know if she would've wanted me to do that. I couldn't tell. And I didn't wanna ruin things. So I just sat there, holding her hand.

Megan and me had talked over Messenger a few times and

that, but I'd not seen her since and I was losing the happy feeling I'd had on the roof.

Even with moments like that, tho, where I feel normal, it's like things are getting worse. I don't mean just being angry and upset all the time – it's the pain, too. It hurts more than it did when I first found Al, even tho I don't know how that's possible. Then, on top of that, there's all these things still filling my head: not picking up Al's phone call, wot the notebook means, Sophie, Lewi, the funeral . . . the fact I'm gonna see my dad.

Kyle's here now, which is a distraction at least. Mum still wouldn't let me go round Civic or town, but she's let Kyle come over after school. She's always had a soft spot for him. We're playing FIFA in my room, but now I've started thinking about the session with Jo I can't stop.

He turns to face me and he must be able to tell that I'm distracted. That I ain't my normal self. 'Eh, Nate,' he says. 'How's it going with counselling and that?'

I shrug. I'd told Kyle cause, after how he'd been when I told him about ignoring Al's phone call, I knew he wouldn't judge me.

'I've gone a couple of times, but it ain't really doing much,' I say. 'I sit there, look round the room and that, and then I clear off home. It's not made no difference. I've got another session later, tho.'

Kyle looks at me. 'I mean,' he says, 'I ain't no rocket scientist or nothing, but have you actually tried talking to her and that? It is her job.'

'She won't get it,' I say. 'She won't understand.'

'You thought I wouldn't.' He shrugs. 'With wot you told me . . . but I do.'

Maybe Kyle's right. Maybe I should try telling her some of the stuff, just so it's not stuck in my head . . . There's even more feelings I don't understand now. And I'm sick of carrying all this Al shit around with me, but I guess I'm scared that once I open up I won't be able to stop. And wouldn't it make me weak? Besides, I don't even have the right words to explain how I really feel.

'Suppose,' I shrug, but I still dunno wot to think.

'Anyway,' he says, changing the subject, 'wot I really *don't* get is how you've been spending all this time with that Megan girl – who *is fit, mate* – and you ain't even asked her out. You waiting for the apocalypse or summat?'

I laugh, and it feels good to think about Megan again. 'I dunno,' I say, and I suddenly feel all embarrassed. 'I proper like her and that. And I ain't just talking about fancying.' I shrug. 'But I don't even know if she feels the same way.'

A grin spreads across Kyle's face. 'You're whipped, mate!' he says. Then he puts his arm round me. 'Seriously, tho,' he continues. 'You should just tell her. And if she don't fancy you back then she must be pretty blind . . .'

I shake my head, but I feel myself smiling. 'You're an idiot, y'know that?'

Kyle shrugs. 'This idiot passed his English mock, tho, didn't he?' he says, and he points down to his new trainers. 'With my sick revision technique—'

My bedroom door opens and Saul comes in. 'Nate,' he says. 'Mum's downstairs. She's ready to go.'

My stomach sinks. I really don't wanna go.

Then Kyle nudges me. 'Seriously, Nate. Wot you got to lose by actually talking this time?'

My mum sits with me while I wait to go in. I feel bad cause she's taking loads of time off work for this. I lean back in the plastic chair and she puts her arm round me.

'I'm so proud of you, Nathan,' she says, and my throat tightens cause it's not like I'm doing anything.

Jo calls for me and I go into her room. I sit down without saying nothing. I just pull my rucksack on to my knee and stare at that painting of the sunflowers.

Jo looks at me. 'How are you feeling about the funeral on Friday?' she asks.

I just shrug. That's all I'm used to doing when I'm here, but even that is starting to feel like an effort. I put my head in my hands. It's all getting too much being here.

Jo moves closer. 'Are you all right, Nathan?' she asks.

I lift my head and look at the sunflowers again.

'Do you know that painting?' she asks.

I shrug. 'Yeah,' I say. 'Al told me about it. It's that guy, innit? The one who chopped his own ear off.'

She smiles. 'Van Gogh,' she says. 'Do you know why he used all the yellow? Why the painting's covered in it?'

I shake my head.

'Apparently,' she says, 'yellow meant happiness to him. It was like his version of hope ... Something that he could look at, and see the light in. Most people don't know that, though.'

I feel like telling her that Al would of. I slide down further in my chair.

'Nathan?' she says.

I just can't do it any more. I can't sit here with everything being pushed down inside me. Everyone seems to think I need to try and talk. Mum, Saul, Kyle. I never wanted to before, but now I think it can't make me feel any worse than I already do, so why not? I can't keep all this bottled up no more.

'No, I'm not okay. How can I ever be when my brother's dead?' I tell her. 'I dunno wot I'm supposed to say.'

Jo's face softens. 'Whatever you want, Nathan,' she says. 'There's no right or wrong way to do this, but maybe start with how you feel right now?'

And even tho it's proper hard, even tho I'm scared she'll think I'm pathetic or stupid, I say: 'I don't wanna put my suit on for the funeral. Cause then it's like he's properly gone. Al's really dead, and there's all this stuff that ain't . . . finished. That I never got to say.'

It's weird, but just saying it out loud makes me feel a bit better, lighter even.

'Death can be hard to accept sometimes. Especially when someone dies so suddenly. When you don't expect it.' She pauses. 'There are often things that you wish you'd had a chance to say. That's all part of grief. You've just got to take things one step at a time. What do you mean, there's stuff that isn't finished?'

I think of Al's face, the tie, the letter, the weird drawings. The fact he could talk to Sophie and not me. I shake my head cause it's still difficult to get the words out, but Jo nods her head.

'Go on, Nathan,' she says. 'You're doing really well.'

'I found this notebook,' I say, trying not to look at her. 'Of Al's. I think he was tryna write me a letter … like a note or summat. But he never finished it … and …' I pause. 'I can't bring him back, yeah? But I wish I could tell him … how I felt.' My eyes start to sting, so I carry on staring at the floor.

'Have you thought about writing Al a letter?' Jo says. 'Maybe then you can explain how you feel? Tell him how much you love him. It might help you get all of this hurt and frustration and anger off your chest.'

I go quiet, then look up at her.

'Nah,' I say. 'I hadn't thought about that.'

I go straight to my room when we get home. I don't wanna talk to anyone for a bit cause I'm so tired after speaking to Jo. It was strange at first, uncomfortable and that. But then I felt a lot better. She didn't laugh or think I was weird or anything. It was like she actually understood.

I open up Facebook on my phone and think about wot Jo said about writing Al a letter, but it just feels dumb. It's dark outside and I can hear the sound of the rain hitting my window. I click past all these posts about wot people had for dinner, or going on a night out. A few people on my feed have clicked that they're going to some party at Megan's mate's house, the one who hangs around with Eli and Cole. The party's on Friday, the same day as Al's funeral. I scroll through the list on the event page and see that Eli's going, as well as Jeremiah and Cole.

I walk over to my window and look out. It's like everyone's just forgotten about Al. Like he wasn't a real person. Just some status update that will come up in your notifications in a few years' time. I press my forehead against the glass and watch a group of lads walking down the other end of our street. Then I see someone going past our house in a grey hoodie, a torn JD bag on his back. His hands are stuffed into his pockets and he's thin, leaning over to one side. I can't see his face, but I'm certain by the way he's walking that it's Lewi. I shove my feet into my trainers and leg it downstairs. Mum is talking loudly on the phone in the kitchen and Phoebe's stretched out on the living-room floor, doing some schoolwork. I run out the door. My mum shouts after me, but I just ignore her. The rain beats down all around me, so I pull my hood up over my head.

'Oi!' I shout, but when the guy turns round it's not Lewi.

The guy walks off, and I stare after him, looking at the houses all around me on my street. I see flashes of Al. Of us mucking about on our bikes, or winding up the neighbour's dog, then running off. Of all the times me and Al had walked down this road, laughing our heads off at summat stupid.

The rain gets heavier and it feels like it's tearing through my insides, slicing me in two. I kneel down on the pavement and press my hands over my face, the water seeping through my jogging bottoms, the coldness going into my skin. I stay there and rock in the rain, tears and snot falling down my face.

Why, Al? Why when you had so much to live for? When we loved you so much? Why? Why? Why?

I feel someone behind me and then the weight of a jacket round my shoulders. Saul leans down and helps me up. My legs are all weak and my chest is hurting. I hold on to Saul and he leads me towards the house.

'It's okay, Nate,' he tells me. 'It's gonna be *okay.*'

We get back inside, and Saul sits me down at the kitchen table. My mum rushes over to me and she wraps her arms round me. She strokes my hair and pulls me towards her. Like the way she used to do when I was a kid. Before Al, and school, and Dad, and getting into trouble. Before all of this.

'I've got you, sweetheart,' she says. 'I've got you.'

MEGAN

chapter forty-two

Sometimes I'd sit there for hours and plan everything out. The questions that I needed to revise for in my exams, or the amount of UCAS points I needed to get into uni. I'd plan out my route across America to look at the stars, or the galleries I wanted to see. And, as long as I stayed on track, then everything would work out well for me.

The days since that night on the boxing-gym roof have gone past in a complete blur. I'd spoken to Nathan a few times over Messenger, but we'd not seen each other and everything just feels completely different.

Tara's started hanging around with a new group of mates. She's said '*hi*' a couple of times when I've seen her in the corridor, but other times she's just laughed about something loudly with her new friends and ignored me. A few months ago, I would've sent message after message, asking if I'd done something wrong. And I would've stayed up all night, worrying about how I could get her to like me again. But not this time.

It was sad cos we've been mates forever and have all these memories together, but it's also pretty freeing. I still hated how much I missed Al, but there's a part of me that feels good now. *Alive.* His death changed something for me, and I haven't felt like this in such a long time.

I stare round the assembly hall at Al's exhibition. It's happening tonight and I've come in early so I can check everything one last time. Ms Baker has stuck a photo of Al to one of the boards, with these words written underneath:

In memory of Al Bryant, whose work will continue to burn bright.

I stare at Al's face in the photo. His huge Afro and light eyes, his smile ...

It's his funeral in two days and I don't want to say goodbye.

I hear someone come into the hall behind me, and then a voice say: 'So this is where you've been spending all your time? Should've known.'

I turn and Tara's standing there. She's got a bottle of Coke and a packet of crisps in her hand. She walks around, half looking at the exhibition. I'm not even sure why she's here. Unless she just came to take the piss? Tara glances at the photo of Al, and something flashes across her face. For a minute, she almost looks sad.

'Is that it?' she says. 'Isn't there supposed to be more?'

I shake my head. 'It's done,' I say. I can feel my voice shaking.

Tara shrugs. 'Right,' she says. 'I suppose that I just don't get all this art stuff then. Not like you and that *weirdo*, Al. Like anyone's even gonna be bothered about some school exhibition anyway.'

Suddenly I'm angry. 'What's your problem?' I say. 'Is it the fact that I'm doing this? Or that I was even friends with Al? You've been funny with me for ages—'

'I've been funny?' Tara snaps. 'Ever since you started hanging around with Al, you changed. It's like you think you're too good to be friends with me any more. Too good to do all the things we used to do.' She shakes her head. 'After everything I've done for you. Being there for you, over your dad.'

My throat tightens and I struggle to get the words out, but somehow I do. 'Why are you even bothered?' I ask. 'Most of the time, it's like you only want me there so you can feel better about yourself. And Eli said you'd told him that I'm just a dead weight?' I pause and I can feel the tears coming. 'I don't know what happened to us,' I say. 'We're supposed to be friends. Friends don't say shit like that about each other.'

Tara doesn't say anything. She just looks at me. And it's hard to separate the good memories I have with her from the bad. And, even though deep down I know that our friendship can't be fixed, a small part of me hopes that we can figure it out. That she'll say sorry and we'll hug and laugh and things will be different . . .

'You *are* a dead weight,' Tara says finally and any hope I had disappears. 'Crying over that fucking weirdo when you hardly knew him. You think this exhibition is something special? Well, it ain't. It's pathetic. Just like *you*.'

I want to say something back. Defend myself. Defend Al. I want to tell Tara how wrong she is about him, but I can't get the words out.

Tara shakes her head. 'See?' she says. 'Pathetic.' Then she storms out.

I try to push my fight with Tara to the back of my mind for the rest of the day. The most important thing now is Al's exhibition. I'd been worried about what Tara had said about no one being bothered about it. That no one would turn up and I'd let Al down. But, as I look round the hall now, I realize that Tara couldn't have been more wrong. It's the end of the school day and the assembly hall is proper full. Ms Baker's here and so is Mr Ballan, and every other teacher in school. Loads of kids are here, too. Some people have even brought their parents.

I stand to the side of one of the boards, watching as people look at Al's artwork. Or take pictures of it on their phones. I hear them talking about how talented Al was, and part of me feels like I might burst with joy cos I think that, wherever Al is, he'll be looking down on this and be dead happy.

He'll know that he made it.

I can almost see him standing there in the crowd, rocking

backwards and forwards on his toes. I can almost hear his voice: '*I did it, Megs. I told you I would!*' And it breaks me, but makes me so happy at the same time.

There are so many people here, but there's only one person that I really want to see. I open Messenger to see if he's sent me anything, but I don't have any new messages. I go to put my phone back in my pocket, and then I spot him.

Nathan.

He's standing with his big brother and I can see his mum and his sister walking round the exhibition. He catches sight of me and says something to his brother, then walks over, a big smile on his face.

'What d'you think?' I say.

'Megan, man,' he says, and he pulls me in for a hug. 'This is summat else.'

NATHAN

chapter forty-three

I still remember the day Dad walked out, and how I'd taken the time to stick all these glow-in-the-dark stars on Nate's ceiling. I put three stars in a row, like there is on Orion's belt, and made sure that I positioned the North Star just right. I kept telling Nathan what all the different constellations were called, but he just looked at me funny. Then Saul came in and sat at the end of Nate's bed. He watched me putting the last few stars up and he said, 'Jesus, only you would give an Einstein lecture while you're sticking bits of plastic down.' Nate sort of smiled and, when I'd finished, I got down off the chair, and went to sit with them both on the bed. Saul put his arm round me then and we all just sat there. And, even though Dad had been in our lives for a long time, it was like him walking out brought us closer together.

I dunno wot it was about last night. Maybe it's cause Al's funeral's on Friday, or it was cause I opened up to Jo. But it was like it all hit me at once. The guilt over the phone call. Al being gone. And it was dead painful, but now, even tho it still hurts, I feel lighter somehow.

Saul knew about Al's exhibition, but we'd decided not to tell Mum and Phoebe so it was a surprise. A good one for once: Mum going into school to see summat amazing that Al had done instead of being called in cause I'd been pissing about or fighting.

I look in the mirror one last time and spray on some of Saul's aftershave. I nicked it out his room cause I want to smell good when I see Megan.

I go downstairs to the kitchen. Saul, Phoebe, Kyle and Mum are there. Kyle's sitting at the table, shovelling some cereal into his mouth. Saul coughs as I walk in.

'Eh,' he says. 'You nicked my aftershave?'

Mum's busy fussing with her coat, and I see Kyle mouth, *'Some girl is gonna be there!'* to Saul.

Saul smirks. 'Is it?' he says. 'It's about time if you ask me.' He comes over and messes up my hair.

'Get off,' I snap, and I push his hand away. 'You're gonna mess up my hair.'

Saul laughs. Phoebe comes over to me and wraps her arms round my neck.

'Nate,' she says. 'Where we going?'

'It's a surprise!' I say.

Mum sighs and, even tho she forces a smile, she looks

proper tired. 'Is anyone going to tell me what this is about?' she says. 'You know, there's still loads to do ...'

'Nope,' Saul says.

'Nate?' Mum says.

'Nah,' I reply.

She turns to Kyle, but he just shakes his head. 'Me hands are tied,' he says through another mouthful of cereal.

Mum picks her bag up off the kitchen table. '*Fine*,' she sighs. 'Well, I'm ready when you are.'

We walk through the main entrance of the school and I feel Mum tense. She doesn't say anything at first, but, as we make our way through the reception area, she turns to me.

'What have you done?' she says. 'You can't have got into trouble, you haven't even been here.' Me and Saul share a look. Mum stops just before the glass doors. '*Okay*,' she says. 'I was happy to go along with this. But I can't cope with any more surprises. Will you all just tell me what's going on?'

'All right,' I say. 'It's summat for Al. Summat the school—'

'Your girlfriend,' Kyle interrupts.

'Shut up, man,' I say. 'Summat *one of Al's friends* has done for him.'

My mum's face softens and she looks like she might cry. 'Really?' she says.

A smile spreads across the whole of Phoebe's face. 'What is it? What is it?' she asks, but I don't say any more. We walk in and I can't quite believe my eyes. Phoebe's eyes widen and she grabs hold of my hand.

'Whoa,' she says. 'Are all these Al's?'

I squeeze her hand tighter. 'Yeah,' I say. 'Every last one of 'em.'

It looks fucking *amazing*. All of Al's work out on display, lined up round the hall. There's loads of people here, too: teachers, kids, other parents. I can't believe that Megan's done all this for Al.

Kyle disappears into the crowd to talk to some girl that he knows, and I turn to look at Mum. She shakes her head, wiping away tears. Saul puts his arm round her.

'He was so talented,' Mum says, and she looks so proud yet broken. 'He really was so special.' She turns to me. 'So are you,' she says. 'So are *all* of you. You can go on to do anything you want. Just like Al would've.' She cries even more, but she's smiling a bit. 'Come on,' she says to Phoebe. 'Let's go and look at your big brother's work!'

Mum and Phoebe go off, and Saul sucks in a breath. 'I'm proud of you, mate,' he says. I scan the crowd and then I see her. Standing beside one of the boards. Saul follows my gaze.

'I take it that's her?' he says.

'Yeah,' I say.

'Go on then!' He pushes me forward.

I feel proper nervous as I walk towards Megan, but also happy.

'What d'you think?' she says, and I feel that rush of emotions again.

'Megan, man,' I say and I bring her in for a hug. 'This is summat else.' I stay there for a minute, holding on to Megan.

Not thinking about Lewi, or Sophie, or the website. Or how painful it is without Al.

I'm just here with her, in this moment, and I feel . . .

Happy.

It's been two days since Al's exhibition and the happy feeling I had with Megan is gone.

Saul comes into my room, pushing the curtains back and putting a plate of toast down on my bedside table. He's already wearing his suit, and there's a red tie round his neck. Mum must've given him a haircut as well cause it looks neatly trimmed.

'Morning,' he says, and he points to the plate. 'Eat that. You're gonna have to get ready soon, you know. The car will be here in a bit.'

I stare at the toast, but I don't pick it up. Saul sits down on the edge of my bed, the mattress sagging beneath his weight, and he cracks his knuckles. He looks round my room, staring up at the ceiling.

'I still remember when Al did all that,' he says. 'Couldn't just stick the stars down, could he? Had to go on about getting them in all the right places. I remember how bored you looked.' He pauses. 'It will feel better, Nate. After today.'

I look at him. I dunno if it will.

'It's gonna be weird seeing Dad,' I say.

'I know,' he says. 'But we got through him leaving, didn't we? So we'll get through this. We're a family, Nate,' he says. 'It's what we do.'

'I wish I could change it,' I tell him.

'I know.' Saul shrugs. 'But life don't work like that. You've just gotta focus on the now, and, even tho Al ain't here any more, think about how lucky we were to have him. To know him for even a small amount of time.'

I nod. 'Yeah,' I say.

'I'm proud of ya,' he says. 'For what you've been doing and that. Going to counselling. I know it ain't easy.'

Someone knocks at the front door.

'That'll be Lauren,' he says. 'Don't be too long getting dressed.'

He leaves my room, but I don't move. My phone vibrates and when I check it's a message from Kyle:

Thinking of u m8

I open up Facebook and scroll through my feed. I've got loads more notifications and messages on Messenger from people I don't know and more people tagging Al, or sharing his photo, commenting on one of the posts. I throw my phone down on the bed, pissed off. Half of these people didn't even know Al and it's not like they'll be at the funeral.

Ignoring the toast that Saul brought me, I get outta bed and go for a shower. Tryna take everything a bit at a time like Jo said I should. After I'm washed, I put on my suit. I pull on the stiff material, doing up the buttons on my shirt. My mum's left a tie out, but I can't wear it. I go to my rucksack and I pull out

336

Al's drawing, then I fold it up so that it's even smaller, and I slide it into my trouser pocket.

When I walk into the kitchen, my mum's sitting at the table, staring into space. Phoebe's eating her breakfast. I go over to Phoebe and wrap my arms round her.

'You ready?' I ask.

She moves her arms to hug me. 'I don't wanna go, Nate,' she says.

'I know,' I reply. 'But we'll do it together, all right? Al would want you to say goodbye.' Phoebe nods and I hold my hand out. 'I won't let go, the whole day,' I tell her.

She wraps her fingers in mine and squeezes tight.

'I did my own drawing,' she says, pointing to the table. 'To give to Al.'

She's drawn us all together. Me, Al, Saul, her and Mum. My mum wipes a tear from her face.

'Al will really like that,' I say.

I make Phoebe laugh by trying to put on my coat without letting go of her hand, and Lauren stands in the hallway, clinging on to Saul. Her hair's straight and she's wearing this bright red lipstick. She pulls at her dress. She looks more like she's going on a night out than to someone's funeral, but I don't say nothing. There's a knock at the door, and Saul walks over and opens it.

'The car's here,' he says.

Phoebe holds on tighter to my hand as we all walk outside, even tho my palms are starting to sweat. Some of the neighbours are standing in the street, and a few come

337

to say sorry to Mum. Then we all climb into the back of the car. Mum didn't want to have Al's casket come to the house cause she thought it would be too hard, so we won't see it till we get to the church.

Phoebe stares out the window as the car starts to move slowly down our road, and away from our estate. My phone vibrates, but I don't wanna check cause it's probably more people sending messages or commenting on Facebook.

We turn on to a main road, and drive past more houses. It feels a bit stupid to be in a car cause the church is only round the corner. Lauren takes a selfie and then she holds the camera in front of her and Saul's face. I feel my chest go all tight. The car is hot and stuffy, and I just wanna get out and run home.

'It's a funeral,' I say, without looking up. 'It ain't some fashion show.'

'I know *that*,' Lauren says. 'You don't have to be so rude. Me and Saul have hardly got any pictures together.'

'And you really think now's the time?'

Lauren opens her mouth, but Saul interrupts. 'Just leave it,' he says.

I sink further into my seat as the car pulls up outside the church. We get out, and Mum wraps her arm round Phoebe.

'Come on, love,' she says. 'Let's go see your Aunt Maureen.'

'Lauren, will you come with us?' Phoebe asks.

Lauren smiles, then slips her phone into her handbag. 'Only cos it's you,' she says. A grin spreads across Phoebe's face, then they all disappear into the crowd. There's loads of people waiting. Most of our family is there. I see Kyle arriving with his sister and his mum. Mr Ballan and Ms Davis are there, too. I look around for Megan, but I can't see her yet. Then I turn and he's there. My dad. Standing with the woman he walked out on us all for. He looks the same as I remember, just older. His dark skin has got more lines in it. His eyes catch mine, and then he says summat to the woman he's with. When he first walked out, I wanted him to come back, but now, seeing him here, it's like he's a stranger.

I feel Saul tense beside me. 'You okay?' he asks.

'Yeah,' I say.

Dad comes over to us and I feel this mix of emotions: hurt, disappointment, sadness. I thought I'd feel all this anger, too. But somehow it's gone.

'You all right?' he says. 'Saul? Nate?'

'Good,' Saul replies. But I can tell he's only saying it to keep the peace.

I shake my head. Saul was right. You can never fully understand the reasons why people do things. And you can't change them, either. Sometimes shit happens.

'You didn't even know him,' I say. 'I feel sorry for you cause you never even got a chance to know someone as amazing as Al. Not properly.'

My dad looks broken, but it's too late for him to feel bad now. Saul puts his hand on my shoulder. Saul and Al had been the ones to help me when Dad walked out. Saul had brought the money in so we didn't go without. Al got me glow-in-the-dark stars and took me on to that boxing-gym roof to try and make me feel better. To protect me. They were my family. Saul, Al, Phoebe and Mum. And there was no point in going over the past with my dad.

'You all right, mate?' Saul asks again.

And I nod. 'I'm fine,' I say. 'We're here for Al.'

This time, we're the ones that walk away from Dad. Me and Saul leave him behind to say goodbye to our brother.

MEGAN

chapter forty-four

I read once about ice caves filled with colour. If you ever went down there, all you would see were these sheets of blue and white reflected around you. And it's because the ice has been there for hundreds ... thousands ... of years. And it's so cold that there's almost no air bubbles. But the ice absorbs the light from everywhere else, anything around it. Then it all changes. And that's how something so ordinary becomes so ... special.

I feel a bit out of place when I first get to the church cos I can't see Nathan. There's loads of people waiting outside, and I lean against this brick wall. I haven't been to a funeral since my dad's and that's all I can think about. How I didn't want to get out of the car cos it meant that I could go on pretending that he might come back. I scroll through Facebook to try and distract myself. A few people have *liked* my new profile picture. I'd used one of those layouts to put together all these pictures I had of me and Al. Nathan had *liked* it straight away.

I see that a few people from school have put that they're going to some party tonight. Everyone knew that Al's funeral was today cos word had just got round school. I can't believe someone would have a party on the same day. I click on the event information and see that Tara's the one who created it. My stomach flips with anger. How could she do that? Didn't she even consider Al? I see people starting to go inside, so I shove my phone in my coat pocket and follow everyone else into the church.

A man hands me an order of service and I sit down in one of the pews. There's a framed photo of Al at the front, smiling so widely that you can see the gap in his teeth. His Afro is proper wild and sticking out everywhere, and he's wearing this red T-shirt that says *Geology Rocks*. The slogan makes me smile cos it's just so Al. I stare at the photo, and then it hits me hard in the chest. All those times we spent together, I never once thought that Al would do this.

The church goes quiet and I turn to the back and see some of the undertakers carrying the coffin. Nathan and his brother are helping to carry it, too. Al's name is spelled out in sunflowers on the top.

I hear a few people crying as the coffin is carried down the aisle. That's when the music kicks in. Drums first and then an electric guitar starts. The drums get louder and then lyrics fill the church. I can't help but smile cos I *know* this song. It was Al's favourite. I'd heard it again and again coming out of his headphones in the art room. I hum along in my head and, even though Al's not here, and it's still *really* sad, the music makes me want to move and dance and just . . . *live*. I can't stop smiling and crying, smiling and crying.

The music carries on and they put Al's coffin down at the front. The vicar stands waiting at the side and Nathan and his brother sit with their mum and sister. Nathan looks round the church, scanning all the different rows. He sees me and my stomach flips, just like it did that night on the roof. He lifts his hand and mouths, '*Hey*.' I do the same as Al's song plays out between us in the church. Then the music stops.

The vicar starts reciting a passage from the Bible and suddenly Nathan stands up. A few people stare at him and I try to work out what's going on as he storms off towards a person standing in the church door. There's the flash of a dark grey hoodie and a torn JD bag and I know who it is right away.

NATHAN

chapter forty-five

I still remember the first time that I'd spoken to Sophie. We talked about the Elqui Valley and the dust particles in the tails of comets. We talked about how you turn to stardust after you die and why Van Gogh liked to paint sunflowers. I'd felt so different for so long, and all of a sudden I was so happy. Because I'd finally found that one person who got me ...

People are staring at me, but I don't care. I run towards the door, my shoes scuffing the floor, the blood pumping loudly in my ears. My breath squeezing its way through my lungs. I pull open the church door and look around, but Lewi's gone. He isn't by the entrance, or near the main street. I turn to my left where there's this long stretch of grass that runs down

344

the side of the church, next to the car park. There's these two benches and this huge wooden cross that's been stuck into the ground, but Lewi ain't there, either.

I walk down the concrete steps and then I see him leaning against one of the side walls of the church. He's bent forward, his head in his hands. He looks like he might be sick. I walk over and he looks up, putting his hands out in front of him.

'Nathan,' he says. 'I—'

But I don't listen. I just grab hold of him, gripping the side of his hood and pushing him up against the wall. Close up, I can see that his jaw is covered in all these spots and the circles under his eyes are proper dark. He doesn't even really try to push me off, but just stays there, trembling and crying.

'Wot are you doing here?' I say. 'Why did you even come?'

'I just ... I wanted to ...' Lewi says. 'I wanted to say goodbye.'

I grip him tighter. 'After everything you've done?' I say. 'Cheating on Al with this Sophie.'

Lewi looks confused for a moment and I can feel him shaking. He looks around him, like he's waiting for someone. Then his face crumples and he cries even harder.

'Nathan, please,' he says. 'If you're gonna do summat, just do it, yeah? I won't fight back or nothing. It ain't like I don't deserve it.'

I stare at Lewi, and I remember all the times he was round at ours. Him and Al laughing. Best mates. Tears roll harder down his face. He just looks scared, frightened. I let go and he slides to the floor.

'Just tell me wot happened!' I shout. 'I know there's summat you're hiding. Wot's this website and that weird symbol? Wot did you and Sophie do?'

'I'm sorry,' he says. 'Nate, I am. I cared about Al, too, y'know. I never would've done it if I'd have known. I never meant for it to turn out like this.'

'Done wot?' I say. 'Never would've done wot?'

Lewi looks at me.

'*I'm* Sophie,' he says. 'I wanted to know what it would be like if Al . . . if he felt the same way as me. I wanted him to like me the same way that I liked him. So I set up a fake profile. It was easier for me to tell him how I felt when I was Sophie.' Lewi pauses. 'Then I started hanging around with Eli and they found the messages in my phone. I was embarrassed. I didn't want them to know that I was doing it cause I fancied Al. So I lied.'

He stops and catches his breath in between tears. 'I told them I was doing it for a joke. That I was catfishing Al and that. Eli and Cole said that Al always thought he was better than everyone, like he was summat special and that. That he never even acted like he was from around here. They said we should carry on taking the piss outta him.'

I stare at Lewi. He fancied Al? Maybe more than fancied . . . I don't care that Lewi's gay, why would I? But it still comes as a shock. Lewi wraps his arms round his knees and something twists in my stomach. I still can't believe wot I'm hearing about the catfish. I can't get my head round it.

'How, tho?' I say.

'I didn't think he'd fall for it,' Lewi says. 'I'd already made the fake profile for Sophie and that so I could talk to Al. Then we just used a different number. I knew all the things Al liked ... stars ... painting ... science stuff. Eli got his girlfriend, that Tara, to talk to him on the phone, send him voice notes and stuff. Al thought Sophie was real. That's when Eli started using Sophie to say these things about how horrible Al was, how ugly he was, and then them pictures ...' Lewi shakes his head. 'I wanted to stop, yeah? But I didn't know how to. And Eli ... Eli said Al deserved it.'

'Deserved it?' I say. 'How did Al deserve to be humiliated like that? *He was your best mate!*' I shout.

'I know,' Lewi says.

'Why did you pick up the phone when I called that time? Why did you switch Sophie's ... *your* phone back on?'

'I was reading through the messages when you called,' Lewi says. 'I missed him, and I just wanted to read through what we'd said. Then, when it didn't stop ringing, I just snapped and picked up without thinking.'

I shake my head, and I have to move away from him. It's all too much. I pull Al's drawing out my pocket and shove it in Lewi's face. He stares down at it, at all these people surrounding Al, with the words '*Help me!*' The symbol drawn over and over.

'Wot is this?' I ask him. 'Wot does that symbol stand for?'

Lewi pulls himself up off the ground. 'AAC,' he says.

I look at the drawing. I dunno why I'd never noticed before, but it ain't two mountains, or a swirl. It's two As stuck inside a C.

The C has been half joined up, so that it looks like a circle. But it still don't make no sense . . .

'Wot does AAC stand for?' I shout. 'Is it to do with some website?'

'I'm sorry, Nate,' Lewi says. 'I just can't . . .' Then he runs off. He's gone before I've even got a chance to grab him. I turn and I see Megan standing there. Her face is proper pale and I know by the way she's staring at me that she heard everything Lewi said.

'He did *what* to Al?' she says. 'Nathan,' she says. 'Is it true? Tara was in on it as well . . . ?'

But I don't answer. I just go.

I try to switch my phone on, but nothing happens. The empty battery sign just flashes up, no matter how many times I press down on the button at the top. I'm pissed that I didn't charge it before I left home. I walk past the funeral cars and the driver standing outside. All I feel is numb. Eli and Lewi had humiliated my brother just cause they thought that Al was better than them. And cause Lewi was weak and wanted to fit in with them all.

I start running. I just wanna be at home. My shoes pound the pavement and I run past the 105 bus that's heading into town. I pass more houses and that same upturned settee.

If Al found out that Sophie was really Lewi and the others messing about, then he would've been devastated. Properly upset. He'd never even had a girlfriend before and I could tell from his messages and drawings that he really liked her. Was that wot made him do it?

I run faster till I reach my house, then I shove the key in the door and nearly fall inside, running upstairs to my room. I grab my charger and plug my phone in. I try to switch my phone on right away, but the red symbol with a charging battery flashes up.

I go to my desk and throw some clothes on the floor, moving them off this really old laptop that Mum bought for me second hand last year. I take it over to my bed, pressing the button to start it up, but it seems to take ages to come on. I go back to my phone in case it's working again, but the screen's still the same. Finally, the laptop switches on and I open Google and type *ACC*, then I wait for the results to load.

There's websites about loads of organizations and that, some church things and medical stuff . . . I scroll down and see a link that looks a bit odd, with no details or nothin. I click on it and when the website loads I see the symbol in the corner. This time there are words underneath:

Anti Al Crew

For anyone who hates Al Bryant and thinks the world would be a better place without him.

I scroll down to the bottom of the page. There's all these pictures like the ones Al had drawn of himself in his notebook, but they're even worse. His lips have been made even bigger with Photoshop and that. His body is stretched out so he looks like some sort of giant, and they've made his skin even lighter.

Each picture has loads of comments:

He's so fucking ugly lol.

Look at his hair

Wot colour is he even supposed 2 b?

He looks like a monkey.

If I looked like that I'd kill myself.

look at his lips!!!

Al's the flower and I'm the bee, he'll get stung, and then we'll see.

If only he didn't look when he was crossing the road then at least a car would come and finish him LOL.

I bet he's a virgin – some1 that ugly has 2 be.

Urgh, look at him . . . I feel sick!

The comments are mostly anonymous or have weird nicknames – *Anon88, SeekNDestroy, IronMan57, KillSwitch, SnyperLife, Anonymous, Anonymous, Anonymous, The Defender* – that was Eli's nickname. That's why Eli had been acting so weird and trying to keep me away from Lewi. He'd done this.

Even tho I know it's only gonna make me feel worse, I read through more of the comments. I can't stop myself.

He thinks he's better than every1. I wonder if he knows how gay he is

The stupid fag!

Someone's taken a picture from Al's Facebook profile and copied it to a picture from a porn site, with a naked guy kissing another one.

He's so fucking stupid. Al thought some girl actually liked him. PMSL. Who says they luv some1 they haven't even met tho.

AAC – we should kill the fucker

Maybe we should give him some rope and let him do it himself.

Lol.

PMSL

That's so funny!!

If ur reading this, Al, do us a favour . . . at least then we won't have 2 look at ur ugly face!

Y does he act so white anyway??

I think we should find him and break his legs . . . or we shld slash his face and make him better looking!

I keep scrolling. There's more pictures of monsters, or Al's face being copied on to other pictures. People having sex from porn sites, Al's face copied on to a picture of someone giving a blow job with the comment:

Phone this number if you like men – you'd have to put a bag over his head.

Al's mobile number is on there and more comments:

This site is so funny

What did this guy ever do to you?

He existed

He wears the same coat to school every day and he smells

He's such a fucking weirdo.

I've seen him staring at me at lunchtime

He looks fit. I'd like to give him my number. Lol!

This has made my Friday – thanks 4 the entertainment!

Who thinks someone fancies them when they look like that?

Loll?

Here's his number if you want to tell him how much u hate him.

Someone has copied Al's number there again. I keep scrolling, past the pictures and comments and laughing faces, at the guest book that's been signed at the bottom, then I read the last two comments.

I poured bleach over one of his paintings in art class today.

You should've poured it over his face. At least then we wouldn't have to look at him.

Did Al see this website and all these comments? He must've . . . and, if there was one website, were there more? Wot about Facebook and Insta and Snapchat? Was that why Al would always say he'd lost his phone? I remember the way his face would go funny sometimes when he got a message. Was it cause of people sayin stuff like this? Why didn't he say nothin?

I open a new tab on my laptop, then go to Insta. I search *#AAC*. Loads of pictures come up, but hardly any of them are to do with Al. I click on the people tab instead, then an anonymous Insta account called AAC comes up. There's photos of people's arms with the symbol scribbled on it, with a laughing face or a fist underneath. Just like that first picture I'd seen on Facebook, with Eli and Lewi and Cole. I click on one of the posts. There's a comment from the girl on Facebook who told me about the website, the one who said, '*they should be ashamed of themselves*'. She's *liked* some of the posts, then put a laughing face with an emoji fist.

Then I see a screenshot of messages from Al to 'Sophie'. The post says:

When ur desperate and have no game!

I look down at the blue and grey messages under the picture:

> I told u I dn't even like u. Ur so ugly – as if any1 wuld!

> Please, I don't understand what I've done . . . I don't get it. I still really like you. Axx

> Well, no1 likes u . . . u shuld do every1 a favour and disappear.

> I don't understand what I've done. I know you're too good for me . . . Sophie, please. No one gets me like you . . . we have so much in common.

There's a space in the middle of the screenshot where Lewi's ignored the message, and Al's sent another one:

> Please, just tell me what I've done. I really like you, Sophie. You're not like anyone I've met. Please reply.

Then there's another one from 'Sophie':

> Beg and I might think about it.

Al messages back with:

> Please, please, please.

Then the last message says:

> It's still no. Even if u beg, u fucking ugly weirdo.

There's another post of Al staring up at the camera, bare chested, and one of him naked. This time it hasn't been taken off a website, it's actually him in bed. The post says:

Why you shouldn't send pics 2 ppl u don't know.

There's laughing faces and people commenting with the being-sick emoji or the one with a mask over its face.

I'm just about to click off, cause I can't take reading any more of those awful comments about Al, when I notice a video on the hashtag. I click on it. The camera shows someone weeing into an empty plastic bottle and a black bar comes up across the screen with laughing emojis in it. The camera moves and I see Al in the distance, trying to walk quickly away down one of the side roads beside the shops. The camera turns round and I see Cole's face, then he turns the camera back to Al and I hear Eli shout:

'Yo! I think you'd better run now!'

I hear the pounding of loads of feet, so I know it's a crowd of them after him. Then there's laughing and the sound of the wind against the camera. I see Al try to run away, but Eli grabs him by his Afro to this alleyway, round the back of the shops. There's a few other people standing by on their phones. Laughing, shouting, taking pictures or filming it. But no one does anything. No one tries to help Al.

'Please, just leave me alone,' Al says and I feel my heart slamming against my chest. The camera shakes sideways as Cole laughs. I see Lewi and that girl that Megan knows, Tara. Lewi had said she was in on the Sophie stuff and here she is, too. There's the sound of more feet running and people cheering. Eli punches Al in the stomach, and he falls to the floor. I want to look away, but I also wanna see wot they do to Al . . . wot they did to *my* brother. Eli holds a fluorescent bottle of bleach up to the camera and he unscrews the red cap.

'I should blind you with this,' he says. 'Or maybe I should do you a favour, yeah? Sort your face out . . .' Eli laughs again, like this is all some big joke.

I can see how scared Al is. How terrified he looks. Al shakes his head. He's crying and he holds his hand out in front of his face. He looks over at Lewi, like he's asking for help, but Lewi just stands there.

'Please,' Al says, but Lewi doesn't do anything.

Eli crouches down and holds the bottle of bleach in front of Al's face.

'How about we make you drink this? Heard you like the taste and that.'

Al shakes his head, Cole laughs, and I hear someone else sniggering in the background. I catch Lewi's face on the camera. For a minute, he looks sorry . . . Not just sorry, *afraid*. But then his face changes and he laughs along with everyone else. Al buries his face into the pavement. Hunched over just like in his drawing.

356

'*Please* don't. *Please* don't.' His voice comes out muffled.

Cole points the camera right in Al's face, even tho Al's tryna turn away from it.

'Beg,' Eli says. 'Then maybe we'll leave you alone. Tell everyone how ugly you are. What a fucking weirdo you are. That you make people sick.'

Al repeats the words and the crowd laughs.

'Don't think that's good enough, tho,' Eli says. He holds out the bottle that someone had pissed in at the beginning of the video and reaches down with his other hand to grab Al by the hair again and knees him in the face. A black bar comes up across the video, with the flexed-muscle emoji and the laughing face.

'Look at the camera, yeah?' Eli shouts. 'Right in it, and you tell everyone what your choice is. Bleach or piss? Which is it, eh?'

The camera moves away from Al, and Cole starts to do the Countdown theme tune. Eli raises his eyebrow to the camera and then another black bar comes up across the screen, with the words *Decision time!*

'Bleach or piss?' Eli says.

Al looks up at Eli. 'What did I ever do to you?' he says.

'You were born,' Eli says. 'Now you better tell me, or I'll do both.'

'Piss,' I hear Al mumble.

There's laughter, and cheering, and I hear people shout from the crowd:

'Nah, man, that's peak!'

'Shame he picked piss!'

'Yo, pass us your phone!'

Another bar comes up across the video: *He's made his choice!!!* With vomiting emojis.

Eli empties the bottle all over Al, splashing it in his face and in his hair. Someone else opens a bottle of Coke and pours it over Al, too. Eli kicks him and Al curls up on the ground as everyone laughs. Eli kicks him again, then someone else comes over, too. Al is on his side, like he's waiting for it all to finish, and I have to look away as I hear the crunching sound and Al whimper.

Cole carries on laughing as he holds the phone, and I see Lewi walk up to Al and boot him, too.

They move away, but Al stays curled up on his side, not moving. It almost looks like he could be dead. Eli picks up Al's rucksack and empties the bleach inside, covering all his books, schoolwork and other stuff. Eli puts the camera even closer to Al's face, so that it's zoomed in on him.

'If you grass,' he says, 'we'll get you even worse.'

He throws the empty bottle of bleach at Al, but Al doesn't move. He just stays in that alleyway, crumpled and alone. I hear more laughing and the camera shakes, a hand reaches over to cover the screen and everything goes blank.

Every part of me feels numb. I can't stop seeing Al curled up on the ground. Everyone laughing. Or standing there, watching. Even Lewi, who was supposed to be Al's *friend*. This is why he did it. Killed himself. *That* website, *this* video, the comments and shares and *likes* . . . Al went through all of

358

this on his own and didn't ask for help. He couldn't tell anyone wot had been happening. I look at all the shares the video has, hundreds and thousands. There's so many comments – laughing emojis with tears coming out their eyes, two hands held up, with lines either side of the fingers, so it looks like they're dancing. And, if it hadn't of been Al, if it would've been some other guy. I realize that maybe I would've looked at this video and found it funny, too. Maybe I would've sent it to Kyle. That's the worst thing. I know that I would've been like the people commenting on Al. Finding it funny that he was so hurt and upset cause he's just some random on Insta. Nothing to me.

I hear Al and Eli's voices over and over in my head: *'What did I ever do to you?' 'You were born.' 'What did I ever do to you?' 'You were born.' 'What did I ever ...'*

I pick up my laptop and throw it at the wall. The screen smashes, but I don't care. I go over and I stamp on it till I hear it crack. How could I have not known that Al was going through all this?

And this time Eli had just acted like it was nothing. He'd gone back to school, he was going to some girl's party, he'd just been able to get on with his life ...

I grab my phone off the charger and go downstairs. I've got loads of missed calls from my mum and Saul.

'Where've you been?' Saul says, coming in the front door. He's sweating and out of breath. 'I've been tryna call you and that—' He stops when he sees my face. 'What's happened?' he says. 'Are you all right?'

I shake my head. I don't even know where to start. How to explain about the website, or the hashtags, and that video. I know that Saul would wanna help get revenge on Eli and that, but this is summat I have to do on my own. Now I finally know the truth, I owe it to Al to make someone pay.

'I'm fine,' I lie.

Saul nods. 'The car taking us to the cemetery is outside. Come on, Mum's waiting.'

The car turns off the motorway and parks up outside the cemetery. I get out, and walk past all the different gravestones and I head towards the one near this mound of earth, at the back. I see my dad, and Ms Davis, and Mr Ballan. Kyle's there, too. He smiles at me from the other side of the burial ground, but I still feel so numb. The vicar stands there again, saying all this stuff about God, and love, and heaven.

Megan walks over to me and I watch as they lower Al's coffin into the ground. My mum picks up a fistful of dirt, and she goes towards the grave, then opens her fist. I watch as she closes her eyes, and then whispers summat, like she's saying her final goodbye. Saul gets up and does the same.

Megan pulls me to one side. 'Are you okay?' she asks. 'I can't believe Lewi would catfish Al like that. I thought they were supposed to be mates.'

I shake my head. 'You don't even know the worst of it,' I say. 'Wot they did to Al . . . This website . . . Eli destroyed Al's life. *All our lives.* And he just gets to carry on untouched.'

Megan stares at me. 'What are you talking about?' she says. 'What did they do?'

But I'm suddenly angry at Megan, too. That girl in the video was her mate. How could she not know wot they were doing?

'Ask your mate,' I say. 'The one who's going out with Eli. She knows all about it. You expect me to believe that you had no idea, when you hang around with her? AAC.'

Megan looks proper upset, but I just ignore her and walk over to Al's grave. I pick up some of the mud and scrunch it in my hand. I open my hand and watch the dirt fall.

'What was all that about?' Saul asks. 'With you and her. What's going on, Nate?'

'Nothing,' I say.

NATHAN

chapter forty-six

Sometimes I'd think that if I just ignored it then it would all stop. That the comments and messages and the pain would disappear. And that everything would go back to how it used to be. How it was before ...

I hear the noise of everyone downstairs – people who've come back to ours to eat sandwiches while Al lies in the ground alone. Megan was supposed to come, but, after the thing at Al's grave, she just went home. I felt bad straight away for snapping at her like that. But wot was I supposed to think? She's sent me a message saying: *OMG, I've just seen the video, and that website!* But I've ignored her. As soon as we got back, I went to my room and changed into some tracksuit bottoms and a hoodie, and now I'm sitting staring at the clock, just waiting.

Finally, I grab my phone and open Facebook. Lauren's already tagged me and Saul in the album *Al's Funeral*. Nice. She even *checked in* to the church and the cemetery. But I'm not worried about stupid Lauren right now. Instead, I search for the event invite for that party Eli's gonna be at. Megan's mate Tara's not even bothered to make it *private*. I take a screenshot of her address. She only lives on the other side of the estate.

I check to make sure that no one's in the hallway, then I push Saul's bedroom door open. If I'm gonna take on Eli, then I want him to suffer as much as Al did. I look under Saul's bed, moving all this junk about, then I pull out a thick metal bar. Saul's kept it under there ever since we've had break-ins. I shove it under my hoodie and go downstairs.

My mum's in the kitchen with some people from her church and others from the estate. Plates of food have been put out and Phoebe is pulling the crusts off a sandwich. Saul comes out the living room, a can of beer in his hand, and I pull up my hood.

'I'm just going round Kyle's, yeah?' I tell him.

Lauren comes over to Saul, slipping her arm through his, and resting her head on his shoulder.

'I'll walk you down,' Saul says.

'Nah,' I say. 'I'm *fine*. And anyway since when did you ever walk me anywhere?'

Saul shrugs. 'It's been a hard day,' he says.

'You don't need to worry,' I say. 'It ain't like I can change anything, is it?'

Saul nods. 'That's what I've been telling you, all this time.'

*

I keep the bar hidden inside my hoodie as I walk. It's dark outside and I go past all the houses with their lights on, down another road, past the boxing gym. I walk along the road that runs beside the motorway. I don't need to look at the screenshot on my phone to check the address cause I hear the music before I even get there. There's the heavy thud of bass and the front door is open.

Loads of kids my age and some older are standing outside or sitting on the wall. Most of them are drinking, or passing spliffs around. There's a girl without any shoes on having an argument with some boy. A couple of lads in hoods eye me up and down as I walk inside and I move the bar to make sure they can't see it. The house smells of damp, weed and sweat. The main lights have been switched off, and there's a few flashing colours from one of those crap disco machines. The music's proper loud, and the hallway is thin and narrow, with all these people lined up inside it. Smoking, drinking, laughing, or off their faces. Jeremiah runs up to me. He's drunk and holding a bottle of Jack Daniels.

'Eh, Nate,' he says. 'I'm sorry, yeah. I just wanted to let you know ... I was out of order, *innit*.'

'Not now,' I say. 'Have you seen Eli?'

Jeremiah points towards the living room, spilling alcohol down himself.

'He's in there,' he says. He tries to put his arm round me. 'I was thinking—' he says.

I shrug him off me. '*Move, man!*' I say and head into the living room.

There's even more people in there, and I start to feel all hot and sweaty. My hoodie sticks to me, and my palms are really clammy. Drink has been spilled on the carpet, and food has been crushed into the floor. I scan the living room: there's a few people dancing, some girls taking a selfie, some guy asleep on the settee and people posing next to him for selfies or filming him on their phones. I see Cole taking something, in the corner of the room, and then I spot Eli.

He's stretched out on one of the sofas with Tara sitting on his knee. Eli clocks me and scrunches up his face. I walk towards him.

'Eh,' I say. 'I need to talk to you.'

The music's so loud that the floor shakes, and the speakers vibrate around us. Eli looks at me, then he leans his head back, pretending he ain't heard me. More people come into the room and start dancing.

'I said, I need to *fucking* talk to you,' I say, moving closer to him.

Tara stops kissing Eli's neck and gives me a funny look. Then Eli says summat to her and she gets off his knee. Eli gestures towards the other end of the house, and I walk back along the hallway and out to the front garden. The air feels cool on my face and I pull the metal bar out from inside my hoodie. I grip tightly on to it to try and stop my hand from shaking, while keeping it mostly hidden from Eli.

He follows me down the garden path and on to the pavement outside. He lifts his cap up, to run a hand through his hair, and then he shrugs. His eyes are red, like he's been taking stuff, and his chain glints in the street light. I feel myself starting to get nervous. Eli looks down and clocks the metal bar. He laughs, making me even more angry. I can't stop seeing flashes of Eli's face from that video.

'Are you serious?' Eli says. He looks around to see if anyone else is watching. 'D'you really think you're gonna do summat with that?'

He moves forward and pushes me, and I stumble into the road.

I turn to face him, angry. 'Why'd you do it?' I shout. 'Why my brother? Why Al?'

Eli shakes his head. 'Dunno wot you're talking about,' he says. I see a few people look over at us from the garden. There's some laughing and a girl comes out the house, fanning her face with her hand.

'Yeah, you do,' I say. 'Everything you did to Al. That video. Them comments. *Sophie.* Lewi told me.'

Eli shakes his head. 'I knew he was a fucking grass. And anyway some people make it too easy. He was a right weirdo your brother, all that stuff he used to say . . . Thought he was proper clever, better than everyone else.' He laughs. 'It's like he weren't even from this planet. Not my fault he couldn't take it. They were just words. And that piss thing? We were all messing ab—'

But Eli doesn't get a chance to finish his sentence. I whack him across the face with the bar. The metal falls from my hand with the force and clatters to the ground, but I don't need it any more. I just punch Eli in the face instead. Someone screams behind us and then someone else shouts, '*Fight!*' Eli grabs hold of his face and staggers back.

'Just words?' I spit. '*Words* that killed my brother. That made him take his own life. Why? Cause he was different? Cause he weren't like you?'

'All right,' Eli says. His mouth and nose are bleeding, and we're both outta breath. He wipes some blood away with the back of his hand. 'It's not like I knew he was gonna do that,' he says. 'Maybe we went too far, but I didn't know he was gonna kill himself, did I?'

He looks at me, but doesn't even try to throw a punch. I thought that this would make me feel better, but it don't. I turn to walk away, but then I hear Eli mumble: 'You're fucking mental, just like your headcase brother.'

I see red then. I run towards him and tackle him to the floor. This time Eli does fight back and one of his punches connects with my jaw. I feel a shooting pain, but I don't care cause it ain't as painful as wot happened to Al. It ain't as painful as having no brother.

I'm on top of Eli now and I go to punch him again, but he moves out the way, and my knuckles crunch the pavement. I yell in pain, and then I hear someone shout: 'What are they doing? Get 'em out the road! Get 'em out the road!'

There's a crowd all along the pavement and more shouting. I can't tell if they're on Eli's side or mine. I hear someone say: 'Yo, wot you doing? Get your phone out, man.' And I think of the video again. Of how this is just like the way it all started . . .

Eli has more blood pouring down his T-shirt. I feel

something warm down the side of my face and I realize that I'm bleeding, too. But suddenly I'm proper tired. All I can think is, *Al's dead, Al's dead, Al's dead.* And, no matter wot I do, nothing will ever change that. I should be with Saul and Mum and Phoebe. I should be with my family.

I get off him and stagger into the road. Eli runs out the way as a flash of light comes towards us. And at first I think it's someone taking another picture ... and it takes me a minute to work out wot it is. Lights moving – two of them.

I hear the screech of brakes and I feel the impact of the car.

I think of looking up at the stars on that roof with Al.

Then everything goes dark.

Kyle leans back on the seat of the swing, holding on to the metal chains. He drags his feet along the ground and lights up a cig. He inhales, then passes it over to me.

Two girls from another school sit on the swing next to him. One of them is sitting on her friend's knee. Kyle gets his phone out and takes a video of them.

'Get off,' the girl says, pushing her mate away.

Kyle laughs and I laugh, too. I move forward on my swing, looking at the old town hall building and the statue of that Cromwell bloke. And I suddenly don't wanna go home. Al will be going on about some stupid fact and my mum will only look disappointed that I'm not as smart as Al. Or that I'm not cute like Phoebe or protective like Saul.

One of the girls gets up and walks over to me. 'Give us a smoke of that,' she says. I lean over and hand her the cig.

My phone vibrates in my pocket and I pull it out. Al's calling me. I don't wanna hear about some stupid painting or weird fact. I just wish that Al could be normal. That he could be like everyone else. The phone carries on ringing and Kyle looks over at me.

'Ain't you gonna answer that?' he says.

I think about ignoring it. Cancelling the call. Then I roll my eyes, and click on the answer button.

'Wot, man?' I say. 'I'm out with Kyle and that.'

There's silence for a minute, then Al speaks, but he sounds all weird. His voice is muffled. I can tell that summat's wrong . . . really wrong, even tho I can't hear him properly. He ain't making sense and it sounds like he's crying. One of the girls shrieks, and Kyle laughs. I stand up and press my hand over my ear so that I can hear better.

'Wot is it, Al?' I say. 'Wot's up?'

'Nate,' he says, sounding real faint still. 'I can't do it. I just can't. There's this video and this website . . . It won't stop.' His crying gets louder. 'I just wanted to let you know that I love you, bro.'

My stomach sinks and every part of me starts to shake cause I know. I know wot he's saying . . . I know wot he's gonna do.

'Just stay there, Al,' I say. 'Don't do nothing, yeah? I'll fix it. Just stay on the phone.' I turn to Kyle. 'I've gotta go,' I tell him.

My trainers hit the concrete and I run as fast as I can. I run faster than I ever have before, this stitch creeping into my side, my legs turning to mush, but I keep going cause Al needs me. I don't believe in God or nothing, but I pray. I pray that if there is some sort of God up there, if he really does exist, then Al will be okay. I turn on to my street and I run up the garden path, turning my key in the door. I throw my rucksack on to the floor and I head up the stairs.

'Al!' I shout. 'Al ... Al ... '

I keep going, I'm tired and my heart is pounding, but I don't stop. I reach his room and then I push open the door.

'Al!'

He's sitting on the floor beside his desk, crying. He holds his school tie in his hands and he looks up at me.

'I can't take it any more,' he says. 'Help me!'

His crying gets heavier and I stare down at him, his huge Afro sticking up everywhere. There's an open notebook beside his foot with the words Dear Nathan *at the top of a page smudged with tears.*

I kneel down beside him, and put my hands on top of his, prising the tie away. He breaks down and I wrap my arms round him, just like he's always done for me whenever things get bad. Just like he'd done when our dad walked out.

'I love you, yeah?' I say. 'It's gonna be all right. There's another way. There's always another way. We'll get through it together.'

MEGAN

chapter forty-seven

Some days I'd be in that art room with Megan, watching as she sat there with her earphones in. Humming along to a Beyoncé song and sketching something in her pad. And I'd think how amazing she was . . . to just carry on with life. To keep going, even after her dad. She'd look at me and say, 'What? Am I singing too loud?' But I'd just shake my head. Maybe she didn't know just how strong she really was.

When I got home from the funeral, I looked up AAC like Nathan had said and had seen the website and that video of Al. Every part of me went numb. I couldn't believe that someone would do that to him. And Tara had known all along. She'd been there when Al was attacked and just stood back. Watched and laughed the same as everyone else.

Something in me broke cos it hit me that maybe if Al hadn't been through any of this, if there wasn't a website or those comments, if Eli didn't plan that attack, then Al would still be here.

I couldn't believe Lewi, either. All those times he'd told me how much he missed Al. Loved him even. But he'd been involved, too. How could he do that to someone he was supposed to care about? I knew why he was proper cut up and guilty now. Too right.

I've felt sick about the whole thing all weekend and just stayed at home. I couldn't face seeing anyone. Especially as Nathan's mad at me, too. He was right, though. How could I not have known what Tara and Eli and that had done? How could she keep that from me?

Now it's Monday morning and I'm waiting outside my form room for our teacher. The corridor's packed and everyone's talking loudly. Like they're excited, like something's happened. I pull my phone out, trying to ignore all the noise. I'm still not sure if I should send Nathan a message or not.

Jeremiah comes up to me and puts his arm round my shoulder. 'Yo, Megan.'

'Get off,' I say, and I shrug him off.

'Was hoping you'd be at Tara's party,' he says.

I don't bother telling him that I wasn't invited.

'Shit went down,' Jeremiah continues. 'I'm telling you. It was like Jay-Z and Solange in that lift, mate.'

I pull a face. I'm really not in the mood for Jeremiah. 'What are you on about?' I say.

Jeremiah's eyes widen. 'Wot, you ain't heard? That Nathan came at Eli with a metal bar. Proper messed him up as well. They were fighting in the road, yeah? Then, the next minute, Nathan got hit by a car. It was better than any show on Netflix!'

I suddenly feel weak. I put a hand against the wall to steady myself. It brings it all back. The car crash, my dad. Now Nathan? I feel myself starting to shake.

'Is Nathan okay?' I ask, even though a part of me is dreading the answer. 'Is he all right?' I shout.

Jeremiah pulls a face. 'Okay, chill out,' he says. 'He's fine. The size of his head probably saved him!' he laughs.

Relief floods through me. I'm just glad that Nathan's still here, that I haven't lost another person I care about. Our form tutor arrives and unlocks the door. Going inside, I take a seat at one of the empty desks. I stare round the classroom, at people doing their homework last minute, talking loudly. Scrolling through their phones. It's hard to even look for too long cos I just keep thinking – who else knew? Who else stood there while Al was being attacked, then went and liked his memorial page?

Tara's late. She comes through the door, muttering a half-arsed sorry to the teacher as she sits down at a desk.

'You knew,' I say, getting up and walking over to her. I'm struggling to get the words out cos I can't believe that this is the person who used to be my best mate. 'You fucking knew about that video. What Eli had done. The website. You helped them play that trick on Al, sent him voice notes and that and you didn't say anything to me?'

Tara looks down. I wonder when exactly she changed so much? When she stopped being kind and fun and nice. What happened to her? What happened to us?

'Well?' I shout and slam my hands down on the desk. Tara jumps. 'You don't even have the decency to say anything?'

Our form tutor looks over at us. 'Megan!'

Tara still doesn't say anything. She pulls at this loose bit of thread that's hanging from her jumper. I don't know if she's embarrassed, or she just doesn't care.

'You know what?' I say. 'Fuck you.'

I storm off and pick up my school bag. I don't want to be in this classroom with these people who probably all had a part to play.

'Megan!' my form teacher says, coming over to me. 'Stop this now!'

But I slam out of the classroom, trying to hold back the tears. I hear footsteps behind me, and I think that it's probably going to be my form tutor coming to tell me off. But then I hear Tara's voice: 'Megs.'

I stop in my tracks. I turn and she walks towards me.

'I did know,' she says. *'All right?* But loads of people have stuff written about them online. It's just how it is. I knew you'd react like this – that's why I didn't tell you. That's why I kept it from you.' She pauses. 'Eli might have taken it too far, yeah? But it was Al's decision to do what—'

The words hit me hard. 'Because you all made his life a misery!'

'I was just there. I didn't *do* anything,' Tara says.

I shake my head. 'That's just as bad,' I say. 'In fact, it might be worse.' And I walk away.

I slide down on the floor, with my back against my locker. I don't even have enough strength to move. To pick myself up and go somewhere else. I look down the long stretch of corridor, and I think about that time I saw Eli picking on Al. How I didn't do anything, didn't stand up for him. '*I was just there*,' like Tara had said. Maybe I'm just as bad.

The bell for the end of form goes and I don't want everyone to just see me sitting here. So I pull myself up. I don't even want to be in school. I just want to go home. I walk towards the main entrance and hear the sound of chairs being pushed back, teachers reminding people about homework, mobiles *pinging*. Life going on. I pass the canteen and see Lewi. He's sitting alone in one of the blue plastic chairs. We stare at each other for a moment, then Lewi gets up and slowly walks towards me.

I'm not sure I even have the energy to be angry any more. I'm just hurt, broken. *Tired*.

'Megan,' he says.

'Maybe I could expect something like this from Tara,' I say. 'Definitely Eli. But *you*?'

He shakes his head. 'I know,' he says. 'I loved Al, *I did*. I . . . kissed him and that . . . When he didn't feel the same way, I got embarrassed!'

'And that makes it okay? Al wouldn't have cared if you were gay.'

'I know,' Lewi says. He shrugs. 'I wanna fix it, but I dunno *how*.'

I look at him. 'This can't ever be fixed,' I say. 'But, if you do want to do something, be more Al. Be brave and own up. Tell someone what you, Eli and Cole did. Cos, if you don't, you'll just have to live with it. Eli will carry on unless someone stops him.'

Lewi nods.

'You owe Al that,' I say.

Lewi's face crumples. 'Megan,' he starts.

'I don't want to know,' I say to him.

Then I walk away.

NATHAN

chapter forty-eight

Van Gogh said: 'The great things don't happen through impulse alone.' He was talking about his paintings, but I think it's the same as everything else in life. That everything is made up of a series of small things . . . small moments, small actions, small steps . . . that are all somehow brought together.

I open my eyes and it takes a minute for me to realize where I am. Saul, Mum and Phoebe are all standing round my bed. I feel a shooting pain in my ribs and the side of my face hurts. There's one of those drip things connected to my hand and my other arm is in a cast. I look at the table beside me. It's covered with *Get Well Soon* and *Thinking of You* cards. I try to sit up, but I feel that stabbing pain again and I let out a groan. My mum rushes over to my side and rearranges my pillow.

'Careful, love,' she says. She looks like she's been crying. 'You don't want to sit up too quickly.'

'Nate!' Phoebe says, and she comes over to the side of my bed. There's all these tubes everywhere and Phoebe hugs me gently.

'You all right?' I say, and I kiss the top of her head.

A nurse comes in and smiles at me, then places some notes in the pocket at the end of my bed.

My throat feels hoarse, dry. 'Wot happened?' I ask.

Saul and my mum share a look.

'There was an accident,' Saul says. 'At that party. There was a fight and you ended up . . . you ended up getting run over. The driver didn't stop, either. Police think they were over the limit.'

I try to move again, but I yell in pain, pressing the side of my ribs with my free hand.

'Wot happened to Eli?' I say. 'I know I had a fight with him.'

Saul nods. 'Yeah, and next time you wanna use my metal bar you should ask. All right?'

I try to smile, but even that hurts.

Saul shrugs. 'His face is pretty messed up, but he got off lightly. Considering.'

The nurse comes over to me and slips a band on my arm. 'I just need to check your blood pressure, Nathan,' she says. She presses down on something and I feel the band tighten round my arm, then release. She smiles, then undoes the band and writes something down on her pad. 'You're all good,' she says. 'I'll get someone to bring you a higher dose of painkillers now that you've woken up. You'll be in quite a bit of pain for a while. You've got a broken arm and a few fractured ribs.' She pauses. 'You're very lucky, you know. That car was really going at some speed. It could've been much worse. Someone's definitely watching over you.' She puts the notes back in the pocket at the end of the bed and then walks off.

The lights on the ward seem proper bright, and I squint, turning my head so I can bury my face in the pillow. My mum leans down, moving my hair out the way.

I realize that I dunno how long I've been in here. It could've been ages.

'Bet I need a trim,' I say.

'I'm telling ya,' Saul replies with a nod.

'Thank God you're okay,' Mum says. 'We were so worried, Nathan. I really thought ...' She shakes her head. 'The important thing is that you're *fine*. That's all that matters.'

I suddenly feel all hot. My face starts to sweat and my mouth is like sandpaper.

'You need to rest,' my mum tells me. 'Will you stop moving about!'

'I could do with a drink,' I say. 'And I'm a bit hungry and that, too.'

My mum nods, and holds out her hand for Phoebe to take. 'I'll see what I can do,' she says. 'I don't know, you get run over by a bleedin car and you still manage to have an appetite.'

I laugh as they leave the room, but it proper hurts, so I just lie back instead. I look up at the ceiling. Saul comes over and sits at the end of the bed.

'It all came out about the video and that website,' he says. 'The police were round and everything. It's gonna be used as evidence in the inquest into Al's death. Can't believe what those scrotes did to Al.'

'How did the police find out?' I ask.

'Lewi ended up going to the school, y'know? Told them everything they'd done, how Eli planned it all. Set it up. They've all been excluded.'

I feel my chest tighten. 'Is that it?' I say, sitting back up. 'They get time off school and wot did Al get? If it weren't for them, he'd still be here. Where's the justice in that? Can't we take 'em to court or summat? Get 'em sent down?'

'No,' Saul says. 'They can get done for what they did to Al in that video. For assault and that, and for some of the pictures. But the other stuff they did, it ain't illegal. There's no law and that.' He pauses. 'Mum's worried that, if it goes to court, they might press charges against you as well, tho. You know, for going after Eli. Someone took a picture of you hitting him with the metal bar and people recorded the fight.'

I'm so angry that part of me just wants to yell.

'I'd do it again,' I say. 'I wanted to let him know that wot he did wasn't all right. But wot you're saying is that people can just get away with stuff like this? They can make Al feel like being dead is better than living and nothing? Nothing happens to them?'

'I know,' Saul says. 'It makes me angry, too, trust me.'

We sit there in silence for a bit. Maybe there was no point in going after Eli if nothing was gonna change. If all this was just allowed to carry on. Cause next time it wouldn't be Al. It'd be someone else tagged in all those comments, or lying on their side in an alley. It would be someone else wanting it all to go away ... wanting it all to end.

I hear footsteps along the corridor, and I think that it's probably my mum, or maybe the nurse has come back. But then Megan walks towards me.

MEGAN

chapter forty-nine

I used to look at those paper cranes hanging from the museum ceiling. And I'd think that even in times of great trauma, of great tragedy and sadness, there is always still hope.

I stand to the side of the hospital cubicle thing and I feel proper awkward. I haven't seen Nathan since Al's funeral when he went off at me, so I don't even know if he'd want me here. He looks *really* battered and bruised, and he's got this drip sticking in his arm. His face lights up, though, and I'm just relieved that it seems like everything's okay between us again. There's a bit of bare chest showing through his hospital gown and he moves the blanket to cover himself. I feel myself going red.

'Hi,' I say.

'Hey,' he says.

His brother looks at me, and then at Nathan, and he raises an eyebrow.

'I'm gonna go and see where Mum's at, yeah?' he says, and then he disappears down the corridor.

I feel myself blush again and I sit at the end of Nathan's bed. There's so much I want to say to him.

'Nate,' I start.

'Megan, I'm so sorry,' he says before I can say any more. 'I can't believe I went off at you at Al's funeral. I know how much Al meant to you and that you never would've stayed quiet about anything like that if you'd have known.'

'Yeah,' I say. 'I confronted Tara as soon as I saw her in school. D'you know what she said? That she kept it away from me cos she knew I'd react "like this". That everyone gets comments online and Al shouldn't have been so sensitive.'

Nathan swallows hard.

'Tara isn't my real mate. Not any more. She hasn't been for ages really. I think now that Al was probably the only true friend I had.' I look at Nathan. 'You've probably not seen it, but it's been in the papers and stuff. They've written about Eli . . . called it a "campaign of hate".'

Nathan looks down at his hands. 'I thought that going after Eli would help. Make me feel better, but it didn't. I still feel like there's this hole inside me and I dunno how to fill it.'

I reach into my bag, and I pull out the paper crane that I'd found in the art room that Al had left folded up. I've been carrying it around ever since I found it. I give it to Nathan.

'Did Al ever talk to you about these?' I ask him. 'About how they were used as a symbol for hope?'

He nods with a smile. 'Yeah, all the flipping time. I saw them in the museum, too.'

I feel a bit embarrassed, but I keep going anyway. 'Well, I found this one in the art room and it almost felt like Al left it behind for a reason, y'know? Like he was saying that there can still be hope? And I know all this bad stuff happened to him, but his paintings were the same – full of hope. You should see his Burn Bright hashtag now. It's *proper* mad. People are posting about how amazing Al was, how great his paintings are. It's gone crazy with people from everywhere saying nice stuff.'

Nathan smiles. 'You made that happen,' he says. 'I just wish I could talk to Al, you know? Tell him all the stuff I couldn't say before.' He pauses. 'The day that Al killed himself he tried to phone me, but I disconnected his call. And, for ages, I felt like it was *my* fault ...' He swallows hard. 'If I'd have just picked up the phone, then Al would still be here. I was so desperate to find answers. To find someone else to blame.'

Nathan starts to cry and I reach my hand out to hold his. I know how he feels cos I'd blamed myself enough times for all the things I could've done better with Al.

'I've felt bad, too,' I admit. 'For not being a better friend, for not noticing that something was wrong, but it wasn't your fault. It wasn't mine, either.'

Nathan smiles and I wipe some of his tears away.

'I had this dream, after I got hit by that car,' he says. 'That I'd picked up the phone. That I'd gone back in time to . . . save Al. People like Eli just destroy lives, and get away with it.'

'What would Al want you to take away from all of this? He wouldn't want you to get revenge or to torture yourself going over what happened. Al would want you to remember him for how he lived – fearless. Kind, brave. Burning bright.' I pause. 'You can still tell him how you feel. I wrote my dad letters after he died and they helped me, I dunno, come to terms with it more.'

'Yeah, that's what my counsellor said.' Nathan looks really awkward for a minute, like he wishes he hadn't told me that.

'Oh, it's really not a big deal,' I say quickly. 'I'm glad you're getting help. Some things are just too hard to carry on your own.'

Nathan nods, and then he clears his throat. 'I know Al's not here and that, but I'm so glad we met through him. It's like the one good thing that's come out of all this.' He pauses. 'And I know I've looked better than I do right now and there's probably a load of other guys you'd rather go out with. But I've been working on a list of the reasons—'

But I don't let him finish cos I do what I should have done on that boxing-gym roof. I lean forward and I'm careful, cos he's obviously still got a cast and that, but I kiss him. Nathan doesn't do anything for a split second, maybe cos he's shocked, but then he moves his free hand to touch my hair and kisses me back.

NATHAN

chapter fifty

You know, for a star to be born, there's one thing that has to happen: a gaseous nebula must collapse. The star must compress in on itself ... the atoms must squeeze and react before they can create something new. So collapse ... crumble ... and remember ... this is not your destruction. This is your birth.

I carry on kissing Megan, moving my mouth with hers. My face is proper swollen and bruised so it hurts, but it's worth it. Megan pulls away and she looks a bit embarrassed.

'I had to do something to shut you up,' she says. 'You've become dead gobby since you got knocked down.'

'All right,' I say.

Megan pulls her phone out to check the time. 'I'd better go,' she says. 'My mum's going to want me home for tea soon. But I'll come back, yeah?'

'Yeah,' I say.

'Maybe you can tell me that list of reasons next time?' she says with a smile. Then she picks up her school bag and disappears out the door.

Mum, Saul and Phoebe come back, and my mum wheels this little table over to me. She puts some food on it, opening one of those sandwiches that you get from the vending machine.

'Your girlfriend gone then?' Saul says, messing up my hair. 'Must be love if she's into you, looking like that.'

'Shut up,' I say, but I can't help but smile.

Phoebe laughs and comes over to me. 'I didn't know you had a girlfriend,' she says.

My mum raises her eyebrows. 'Neither did I.'

I mouth, *'Thanks a lot, yeah?'* to Saul.

They all stay till the nurse comes to check my blood pressure again, and they're told that they have to go cause visiting hours are done.

When they leave, I just lie there and listen to the sound of machines beeping and beds being wheeled past in the dark. I turn on my side, but I can't sleep.

I open Insta on my phone and search #BurnBright. I stare at Al's paintings and scroll through the comments all talking about how talented and wonderful and special he was. I click on a photo of the painting he'd done of me and him on the boxing-gym roof. I stare down at the stars and the estate. At

387

Al's huge Afro and the smile on his face. Then I click off Insta and put my phone down next to the paper crane that Megan left me.

I think about wot Jo and Megan said, about writing a letter to tell Al how I feel. I look around the cubicle and I notice that there's a pen on the table with all the cards.

I pick it up, and then I unfold the crane, so it's just a crumpled piece of paper. Megan was right. It ain't about going over wot happened. It ain't about being mad, or tryna get revenge. Tryna find someone to blame. Al would want me to remember how he lived. He'd want me to focus on the future, on the light.

I start to write:

Dear Al,

I never thought I'd say this, but I get wot you were banging on about now - I really do ...

Author's Note

I was fifteen when I attempted suicide as a result of being bullied. School was one of the hardest times of my life, and, like Al, I found it difficult to see a way out. Just like Al's experience, I had a website made about me, and things became progressively worse. Even though social media then wasn't what it is today, this almost felt like the beginning. When I was told how lucky I was to be alive, I couldn't see it. I had lost all hope, and I had no idea how I would get that back. It wasn't until an old primary-school teacher, Mr Wright, gave me a small ceramic box that I realized I had a reason to live. With this box, he also gave me a card reminding me of the story of Pandora. That no matter how dark times may seem, there is always hope.

This novel was a chance for me to explore that, and a way to pass on hope, just like Megan did with Al's paper crane.

Suicide is the third leading cause of death among young people, resulting in approximately 4,400 deaths a year. Suicide kills three times as many British men as it does women. There is still a significant stigma surrounding mental health, and I hope that this book encourages people to seek help, to open up and start conversations. Especially with regards to suicide and bullying.

Please remember to always be kind, but, most importantly, know that you deserve to be here. It will get better, and it is never your fault, no matter how different you are. So speak up and seek help – there is no shame in admitting that you're hurting. On the following pages you'll find a list of organisations that provide information, confidential support & a listening ear when you need it most.

Like Al, you were born to live. You were born to shine. But, most of all, you were born to burn bright.

Suicide Prevention

PAPYRUS HOPELineUK – confidential help and advice
Call: 0800 068 41 41
Text: 0778 620 9697
Website: www.papyrus-uk.org

CALM (Campaign Against Living Miserably) – helpline
and support
Call: 0800 58 58 58
Website: www.thecalmzone.net

Samaritans – 24-hour helpline and advice
Call: 116 123
Email: jo@samaritans.org
Website: www.samaritans.org.uk

Bullying

Ditch The Label – international anti-bullying charity. There
is also an option to report online abuse and an online support
community.
Website: www.ditchthelabel.org

Bullying UK – helpline and support
Call: 0808 800 2222
Email: askus@familylives.org.uk
Website: www.bullying.co.uk

Survivors

Survivors of Bereavement by Suicide – support for young people over the age of 18

Call: 0300 111 5065

Email: email.support@uksobs.org.uk

Website: www.uksobs.org

Diagnosing Mental Health in Teens

The Association for Child and Adolescent Mental Health Services – information, help and support for adults and young people

Call: 0207 403 7458

Website: www.acamh.org

YoungMinds – helpline for parents

Call: 0808 802 5544

Website: www.youngminds.org.uk